Also by Tim Binding

IN THE KINGDOM OF AIR

TIM BINDING

A PERFECT
EXECUTION

DOUBLEDAY

NEW YORK   LONDON   TORONTO   SYDNEY   AUCKLAND

PUBLISHED BY DOUBLEDAY
a division of Bantam Doubleday Dell Publishing Group, Inc.
1540 Broadway, New York, New York 10036

DOUBLEDAY and the portrayal of an anchor with a dolphin
are trademarks of Doubleday, a division of
Bantam Doubleday Dell Publishing Group, Inc.

Library of Congress Cataloging-in-Publication Data

Binding, Tim.
A perfect execution : a novel / by Tim Binding. — 1st ed.
p.   cm.
1. Executions and executioners—England—History—
20th century—Fiction.   I. Title.
PR6052.I77294P37   1996
823′.914—dc20   95-45941
CIP

ISBN 0-385-48412-7
Copyright © 1996 by Tim Binding
All Rights Reserved
Printed in the United States of America
July 1996
First Edition
1   3   5   7   9   10   8   6   4   2

To Simon Gibbs for his friendship through the years

OBTAIN A ROPE FROM EXECUTION BOX B MAKING SURE THAT THE GUTTA-percha covering the splice at each end is uncracked by previous use

Find the required drop from the Official Table of Drops making allowances for age and physique

At the noose end of the rope measure thirteen inches (allowance for the neck) from the centre of the brass eye, mark this by tying round the rope a piece of packthread from Execution Box B

From this mark measure along the rope the exact drop required (this must be to the nearest quarter inch), mark again by a piece of packthread tied to the rope

Fasten the rope by pin and tackle to the chain suspended from the beams above, and, using the adjusting bracket above so adjust the rope that the mark showing the drop is exactly in accordance with the height of the condemned man

Take a piece of copper wire from Execution Box B, secure one end over the shackle on the end of the chain, and bend up the other end to coincide with the mark showing the drop

Put on the trap the sandbag with its head making sure it is fitted with sand of an equivalent weight to the condemned man

Put the noose round the neck of the sandbag and drop the bag in the presence of the governor

The bag is left hanging until the hour before the time of execution the next morning. At this time examine the mark on the rope and copper wire to see how much the rope has stretched. Any stretch must be made good by adjusting the drop

Lift the sandbag, pull up the trapdoor by means of chains and pulley blocks, set the operating lever and put in the three-quarter safety pin which goes through the lever brackets to prevent the lever being accidentally moved

Coil the rope ready and tie the coil with packthread leaving the noose suspended at the height of the condemned man

All is now ready

ONE

HE ALWAYS TRAVELLED TO WORK UNDER AN ASSUMED NAME, THOUGH TYPI-
cally it was one he never changed. In later years, when he retired and it
became public knowledge, there came a time when schoolchildren would
dance around concrete playgrounds singing of his fabled false identity and
the case which made him, as one newspaper tactlessly put it, "hang up his
hat." Within the service and throughout all branches of the judiciary, this
name was better known than that which the parish priest had intoned at
his christening, and though as a baby he was bathed in a copper bowl
with Jeremiah Bembo stamped upon it, and when he was old enough,
pulled a starched white napkin out of a silver ring with Jeremiah Bembo
burnt onto the patterned surface, and despite the fact that the only three
books he possessed until the age of fifteen, his Bible, his prayer book and
an illustrated history of England, all had Jeremiah Bembo decorated on
their title page in his father's ornate and religious hand, when at last he
chose his own profession he decided to discard it, not out of shame, or
through wilful disobedience, but rather out of a natural sense of propriety
and a practised eye to the future, for the sake of the sons and daughters he
had yet to spawn. Solomon Straw he elected to call himself, Solomon it
was said for the need in this world for unflagging authoritative wisdom,
and Straw in recognition of human frailty and the knowledge that under

certain conditions there was not a man nor woman in the country who could not end up in his hands. When called upon to make the journey to Leeds or Cardiff or any of the other fifteen designated sites in the British Isles, he would travel with *Solomon Straw* embossed upon his two pieces of luggage, *Solomon Straw* inscribed on the inside of his beige felt hat and *Solomon Straw* engraved on the inside lid of the mahogany box in which he kept his loaded revolver. He was one of the few men in Britain permitted by the Home Office to carry firearms under an assumed name, but in reality this was of little consequence. There was not a policeman in the land who did not know the name of Solomon Straw, and what he did for a living.

He lived in the West Country now, though he was brought up near to where the crime took place. As a boy he had ridden over every inch of that territory, even run races with his friends on the very lay-by where the man with the painted fingernails had first popped in the car. Knowing the area so well, he had followed the case with even more interest than usual. He could remember the lay-by perfectly as it looped off to the left of the dusty hill, exposing the soft flat green of the vale below. He could remember the broad sweep of gravel, the tall black and yellow AA box at the end with the pile of damp discoloured salt standing next to it, which the men from the council would come and dig into when the first frosts came. When the familiar brown envelope dropped through the door requesting his presence in three weeks' time, he had the feeling that there was a degree of complicity here that he did not fully understand, for it was there, or very near there, down in that valley where his grandfather's great row of greenhouses stood, where he had lost his eye. It would be the first time he had been to Oxford in over three years and even then he had only been there twice before in his official capacity, once in '52 to attend to Albert Fowler, who had shot the owner of a jeweller's, and four years later to dispatch Francis Wickert, the Oxford undergraduate who had poisoned three of the Oxford rowing crew in a vain attempt to be selected for the annual boat race (Oxford had lost that year). Wickert, though drawn to the crime by an unbridled vanity, had a point. He

5

should have been chosen. It was his class which let him down, not his ability, though after he was sentenced there were those who maintained that killing three of one's fellow oarsmen proved that the selection board had been right all along. He was not a team player. Wickert had a wonderful physique, the finest Solomon had ever seen. The very shape of him seemed to suggest that here was a life made for glory, a life to be picked out and held above the crowd. A dazzling creature with golden hair and golden looks, and yet there he was, to be broken on the morn. When it was over Solomon had stripped the boy down and watched while Alf his assistant hoisted the lad back up, Wickert's head lolling under the white cap, his limbs hanging loose. Once freed from the rope Alf lowered him warm and naked across Solomon's shoulders, to be carried through the cramped antechamber where the knife and the dank gutter waited. For the first time in his professional life Solomon felt close to losing control. He wanted to put his arms around Wickert and tell them, "No. This one you shall not break. This one you shall not rend asunder," but he did not, for what purpose would it serve? None, except his own irrevocable fall from grace. One mistake, one step out of line and that would be it. Finished. That was the rule. So he folded Wickert's body out onto the slab and climbed back up the drop, to pack away the chains and tackle, and while tidying up he could hear the crack of ribs as they opened him up to look at his heart, the rasp of the hacksaw as they cut through his skull to lift off the top of his cranium, even the heart-rending tear as they pulled back the skin from the back of his neck to make sure that he, Solomon Straw, had done his job properly.

"Very clean," the coroner had offered ten minutes later, still in his rubber gloves, standing in the doorway looking up through the crisscross of beams. "Vertebrae two and three. Fast too, wasn't it?"

"I've done quicker," Solomon Straw had replied quietly.

Alf, whose first time it was, was anxious to please.

"That's as maybe," he said, "but I bet you've never had to give the bugger a short back and sides before."

6

"It was what he needed, Alf," Solomon Straw explained. "I made it easy for him."

"Didn't come or nothing neither," Alf complained. "By the size of his tackle it should have been a bucket and mop job," and he broke out into a thin peal of laughter which echoed around the empty pit.

Solomon Straw spun on his dainty polished shoes and silenced him with a blistering look before walking out.

"Take a good look, son," the coroner told him, pulling off his gloves with a snap. "That's the last you'll see of Mr. Straw, or any place like this. He'll have you out as sure as my wife has headaches."

In any other circumstance he would have been right. A joke like that, a flippant remark, a crude aside, anything expressing levity would have ended Alf's career in an instant. He would never have been told why. He would simply have never been called upon again. There would be no more communication, no more letters of request, no more warrant cards through the post. Just, ironically enough, a silent and endless suspension. But this time Solomon Straw gave him another chance, not because he felt sorry for him or liked him (He did not like him. He thought him loud and uncouth and unworthy.), but because it was *he* who had lost control first, *he* who had loosed a momentary flicker of anxiety in the air, and, borne like an infection on the wind, it was easily enough caught. So he said nothing, made no reprimand and wrote no letters, simply collected his luggage and walked out. When he got home that night and took out his Execution Book, underneath the details of name, height, weight, length of drop, name of assistant and time taken, he added, "A young boy who lost his way, *as I very nearly did mine.*" Years later he told Jack Edge in a moment of rare confidence that when the letter came, telling him that his presence was requested once again in Oxford, he should have known better. Wickert was a portend of things to come. He should have refused. But of course he never refused. No one ever refused.

He travelled by train, in a first-class compartment which was reserved for him alone. He was not a snob but he would never allow his assistants to accompany him. They had to ride in another carriage, further down. The excuse given, and accepted, was the need for security, but in reality it was nothing to do with that, for at times an extra pair of hands would have come in useful. It was the singular peculiarity of his office and its determined isolation from the rest of life which demanded this. No one else in the land could do what he did, and he moved towards his destination as if encased in a cocoon of sanctified air. There was an area around him, a hallowed circumference of around two feet, into which few who knew of his trade would venture, and he could mark this space out in chalk, just as accurately as he marked out the spot on the trap where the prisoner's feet had to come to rest. A quick slap on the back and a smart step back was as much as he could expect, even from old friends like Peter Alcott or Fabian. So he grafted this enforced seclusion onto his demeanour and held himself apart, even when he would have been glad of the company. Besides, assistants came and went. None of them lasted. Some drank too much and stepped off the train with cheap whisky on their breath; some boasted about their work in bars and clubs; some crumbled at the crucial hour. Some, like Alf, he simply disliked for their cruel bravado, their lack of respect, their inability to accept the silent humility the job demanded. Usually they were never called again. But he had to be constant. It was his steadfastness which oiled the dread machinery, his unswerving sense of purpose which brought such calm to that bare stage. There was no one else. So the assistant travelled further down, in a second-class compartment, and only met up with him at the journey's end, by the ticket barrier, where he would be greeted by a curt nod of the hangman's head before Solomon walked off to the waiting car.

If it were a long journey, he would take with him the miniature ivory chess set given to him by his predecessor, Tom Beresford, on his retirement.

"Black and white," Beresford had told him. "That's all it must mean to you. He's been caught, tried and condemned. All avenues of escape, all ploys and gambits have been closed off. Now it's up to you to see the end is quick. Study chess, Solomon. Learn its patience and its skill but above all learn its capacity for sudden, swift, execution."

And that is what he would do. He would sit alone with his newspaper and his chess book, trying to discover how the masters could see so far ahead, how they prepared for every eventuality. That was the trouble, of course. Man's inability to look ahead, his craving for reckless impulse, his blatant disregard for the consequences of his actions, even when they were staring him full in the face. There were very few men he dealt with who had planned their crime, and even when they had, like Francis Wickert, none of them planned *not to get caught*. That was the great fallacy of detective fiction, for there the villains did nothing else. That's why he never read them. That and his friendship with the likes of Alcott. Who needed foolish stories when you could hobnob with the elite of Scotland Yard?

Beresford had retired early, broken by the demands of the military. Twenty-five in one day he had done, in an American army barracks down in Shepton Mallet. Twenty-five and not an inch out on any of them. If ever a man came back chastened by experience it was Tom Beresford, though it was also where Solomon's sole rival, Harry Firth, got a real taste for the work.

"Like a cattle market it was down there," Tom had told Solomon. "Meat on the hoof. Harry just couldn't get enough. They paid us for each man. Cash on the nose. In dollars would you believe. He said it was the money but it wasn't as simple as that. He liked it too much, grinning all the way back to London, jiggling those damned coins the while. Turned my stomach for good."

They had marched them out the cells one at a time, the sergeant-at-arms calling out each name as if he were at an auction. Once out every man had to stand to attention *on the drop mind* while their name, rank and crime were read out, a good few minutes that could take, with men praying to God and their mother and their families back home, two dirty great military policemen holding them up: men half-crazy, men with the bloody memories of war fresh on their bodies, men drugged, men fainting, men shaking with fright, soft shit tumbling down their trousers, one big buck nigger damning them all to hell, yelling, "I ain't done nothing, man, I ain't done nothing, just had me the Kraut's wife and daughter like everybody else. It weren't me that beat them to death. Ask the fucking captain. I wasn't even in the fucking room," a warehouse full of condemned men, sweating and kicking and sniffing at the scent of their own death.

"Couldn't even count, those bloody Yanks," Beresford had complained. "They even ran out of coffins. Put the last two in empty ammunition boxes! Stuffed them down as best they could, face down, arse up." Beresford threw in the towel soon after.

When the date was set, the authorities would write quickly, asking if he would be available, and as soon as he replied, and he always telegraphed back the same day, timetables would be consulted, warrant cards issued, and his assistant chosen. One week before his arrival, a handwritten letter would arrive from the governor himself, outlining the physical and mental demeanour of the prisoner, information which he would study with the utmost care. When he arrived and had settled in, he would spend a good part of the evening taking soundings from the guards who had been the condemned man's constant companions. These men, working in shifts, were always removed one or two days before the execution to prevent an unpleasant emotional attachment creeping in, for what Solomon Straw required was neither emotion nor compassion (and he brought the latter commodity himself) but unfettered, well-oiled cooperation. "If one is to take a man's life," he would explain, "it is only fitting that we should know something of him, not simply what he did wrong, but the whole of him, the why and the wherefore of him. His final moments have been entrusted to our hands and we must not throw them away carelessly without a thought to the poor creature who resides inside the body and who will fly up to heaven, or down to hell, as God wills it, the second we are done. Besides," he would add, his eyes shaking off this attempt at profundity, "there is a practical side too. The more we know, the better are we prepared should he kick up a fuss."

And unforeseen things did happen, as when they came for Wickert. He had been as good as gold all week, chatting with the warders, drawing portraits for their children, writing letters to his college, asking whether, under the circumstances, he might not be allowed to sit his finals early, but when the morning came and Solomon and Alf Wakenham walked through the door, Wickert jumped up as though jerked to life by a starting gun, pushing back the table with wild panic dancing in his pale blue eyes. Although Solomon had seen him through the Judas hole the day before, and later that evening, while he was testing the drop, had caught a glimpse of him walking round the yard, until he saw him close up he had not grasped how beautiful Wickert was. According to his friends on the force, half the jury had fallen in love with him, and if he had been judged on looks alone, and had he not been so flamboyantly arrogant, he would have got off scot-free. Although circumstantial evidence against him was high, there was no hard evidence that it was *his* anchovy paste that did for them, only the unfortunate coincidence that an hour after taking tea in his rooms, the entire team was taken short on the water and began clutching at their stomachs and vomiting heavily over the side of their new fibreglass racing eight. Indeed, on that first fatal occasion, the deaths of the two oarsmen were put down to accidental drowning rather than deliberate murder, for it was only when Tommy Mason, bent double with pain, tipped out and pulled the boat over with him, did he and his twin brother succumb. It was when Wickert was passed over *again* and insisted on being put in charge of the crew's refreshments that suspicions were aroused, and even then they might not have cottoned on had he not carved his victims' initials on each of the doctored oranges, ensuring that while all would be taken ill, only one would die, for as the prosecution so tellingly pointed out, to achieve his objective he still needed the rest of the crew *alive* and, if not kicking, certainly rowing. Standing by the river's edge, he had called out their names as they came in after practice, throwing the poisoned fruit out to them as they sat there recovering from their exertions. "Just like Remarque's bullet," he told them gaily. "Only one's got your name on it."

11

Once arrested Wickert showed no remorse and tried to put the blame on the Cambridge coach, who had been seen cycling up and down the towpath earlier that month, but a picture discovered in Wickert's rooms of the Oxford crew cruelly disfigured, with his own head superimposed upon every one of them, soon disproved this unlikely theory. Standing in the dock he was defiant and beautiful, contemptuous of the world and her petty squabbles.

"He knew what he was doing all right," the warder had told Solomon. "Tried to fix his way out by blowing them all kisses. And vain? Proper little Valentino. Forever combing his hair. Had a hand mirror in his pocket throughout the trial, would you believe, though we took it off him pretty damn quick I can tell you."

Now, as Wickert stood in front of him, with his fists clenched, ready for a fight, and his hair tumbling over his face, Solomon Straw knew what to do.

"Got to look your best, Francis," he said, and held out his own tortoiseshell comb. Wickert looked down, took it and ran it quickly through his thick, glossy mane, settling it back into its rightful place. On the second stroke Solomon took his hand, drew it gently down, and strapped his wrists behind his back. He turned and walked through the yellow double doors, into the execution chamber. Wickert followed in a daze, the two warders by his side, Alf a short distance behind. Three paces on, the warders peeled off. Two steps later and the three of them, Solomon Straw, Francis Wickert, and Alfred Wakenham, were on the drop. Solomon turned, held out his arms and stopped Wickert dead on the mark. He took a step closer while Alf bobbed down to strap the boy's ankles. Francis was staring hard, his breath coming in gasps. They had lied to him! He had asked his warders what those doors were for and they had told him that they were the doors to the store cupboard! They had played dominoes and cards with him and let him win, knowing all the time that it was all next door! Everything. The drop, the noose! Everything! Right next door! Every waking moment he had been right next to the execution chamber! A few feet away! He never thought it would be so close, that he would be there already! He wanted more time! More time! His eyes darted this way and that, as if he were trying to recognise something. Anything. The rope was level with his head.

"There, there," said Solomon Straw, brushing a loose hair out of the boy's eyes, "that's more like it," and before Wickert could reply, he whipped the cap out of his top pocket, drew the noose close, crouched down, tapped Alf on the shoulder, and in a blur, went for the lever. Wickert was gone.

As his fame grew Solomon Straw began to receive other treatment not previously accorded to men of his profession. Known as a fastidious eater, inquiries would be made as to what type of dinner he would require (he had an aversion to ham and cold meat in general, and woe betide the authority that gave him a plate of sandwiches) and whether he wanted breakfast before or after the event. (He always ate before, despite what Tom Beresford had witnessed down in Somerset. The Americans had laid on a midnight feast with barbecued steaks, fried chicken, mashed potatoes, and sweet corn, unheard-of food in wartime England, mountains of it laid out on trestle tables and surrounded by cans of beer. Everyone, except him, had got stuck in an hour before they were due to start, and by about eight in the morning, after they had been hanging men for seven hours solid, they all trooped off to the mess hall to have another crack at it.) On occasions Solomon would be asked if he would care to join the governor and his wife (and often the prison chaplain) for supper and though he always preferred not to, for he did not think of these times as social occasions, he felt it incumbent upon him to accept. They were not a success those meals, for no matter how gracious and charming the host, everyone present knew that there was only one topic of conversation on the menu, and that was a forbidden fruit, hanging in the air above them all. Only Solomon could have plucked it down and this he refused to do. He never discussed his calling with his own wife (nor indeed his own vicar) and he saw no reason why he should encourage others to behave differently.

There were other ways his journey was made easier. When the time came for him to travel, particularly in the later years, when opposition to executions was at its height, certain guards would be assigned to the appropriate train, guards who had been forewarned of his presence, who had come to know him down the years and who would see to it that he reached his destination undisturbed. There was one guard Solomon Straw favoured above all others, Jack Edge, for Jack Edge alone amongst his brethren could play chess. Jack Edge was a good player and a quiet man and though Solomon would sometimes catch him staring at his hands like everyone else he knew did, Jack Edge never once asked him to divulge stories and anecdotes he had long since locked away. Whenever he fancied a game Solomon Straw would stretch his legs and walk down to the guard's van where Jack would be sitting on his swivel chair, filling out his logbook or reading the paper. If he was not too busy, he would beckon Solomon in, slide the door shut, and hand over the folding canvas seat. They didn't meet up often, perhaps three or four times a year, but Solomon was always glad when there was work to do in the West Country, for he knew that when he arrived at Paddington Station, Jack Edge would be there, leaning out the window, waiting for him to show.

"Catch you later, Jack," Solomon would intone as he passed him by and Jack would tip his cap in reply. They were evenly matched.

There was one time however when Jack Edge came to appreciate Solomon's skill, his sense of purpose, his quick determination, better than any other layman, when to all intents and purposes, he saw Solomon Straw at work. It was February, and it had been a hard month for trains, wet and cold, and treacherously dark, with freezing rain and sudden wild flurries of blinding snow. It had been a busy time for Solomon too, eleven in three months, and each time he had followed the bad weather. He was tired of travelling, tired of the long delays and draughty corridors, tired of seeing the cold gloom of prison looming up at his journey's end. It was a Sunday and Solomon was on his way to Exeter, glad to be sitting in with Jack, snug in the guard's van, a pot of tea brewing on the stove while the train steamed its way west. All that night it had been raining hard, and by dawn half the country was covered in ice. Stopping at

14

Swindon, Solomon had looked out the window and caught sight of Jack, hammer in hand, chipping away at a frozen coupling, and some time later, just out of Temple Meads, both had caught the noise of wheels spinning out of control as they tried to bear down on the rails.

"It's at times like these," remarked the guard, watching translucent meadows rush by, "that I'm glad I never made the grade. They catch it on all sides up top, bollocks roasting like a couple of marshmallows and icicles hanging from their arses."

Solomon smiled. Only Jack Edge could use that word in front of him without guile. "Keep your eye on the game, Jack," Solomon warned, tapping the board. *"Something* of yours is catching it."

Suddenly he was pitched forward, diving over the pieces into Jack's upraised arms. They clung together, spinning round while Solomon's feet clattered after him like a dog chasing its own tail.

"Would you look at the state of my shoes," he said, when finally they came to rest. "What the bloody hell's going on?"

"Nothing good, that's for sure," Jack replied. "Karl jammed on the brakes good and proper that time. Best take a look."

Looking down along what would have been the platform side of the train they could see nothing, just the long line of carriages curving into a slight bend and the plumes of smoke coming towards them. Then, as the steam began to rise and dissipate, they made out the thin figure of the fireman standing by the engine, waving his arm above his head as if he were lobbing a ball over the tender.

"Move yourself, Mr. Straw," Jack told him. "Whatever it is is on the other side."

They moved out into the corridor, Solomon a respectful distance behind. On the adjacent track, some fifty feet behind, the rails disappeared into a mountain of rich, sodden soil. A slice of earth had slid from the top of a high cutting and sat, like a richly decorated cake, complete with grass and bare bushes, firmly on the track. Solomon was reminded of the day when he had buried his mum and dad in mounds of wet sand and had planted sandcastles and windmills all about their heads, patting the mounds down with the back of his metal spade. This was as smooth and as decorative as his creation, but nearly fourteen feet higher.

Jack Edge looked at his watch.

"That is where the up-train will be in about fifteen minutes' time. She'll smack straight into it if we don't look lively. Out the way, Mr. Straw. I've got work to do."

Jack Edge pushed past him and went back to his guard's van, pulling out from under his chair a long flat metal box with a large padlock swinging from the catch.

"Detonators," he explained, dragging it across the corridor. "If you could help me out with it. I've got to get far enough up the track and lay them down." He swung open the door and climbed out. Standing on the bottom rung he held out a hand.

"Gently does it, Mr. Straw. It weighs a ton."

Solomon Straw grasped the metal handrail on the side of the carriage and, hanging onto one of the end handles, eased the box out over the side. How many times had he stood underneath like that, his arms outstretched while someone had lowered a precious cargo to *him?* How many times had he stood, with upturned eyes, half expecting the whole caboodle to drop on top of him in a suffocating embrace?

"That's the ticket," Jack was telling him. "Bit further and she's all mine."

It was the ice that did for him, the ice and the cold wind and the slippery iron steps on which he stood. As he reached out to take the full weight in his arms, a stream of water from the roof of the carriage ran clean into his eye. Jack missed his footing, and fell back, pulling the box clean out of Solomon's grasp. It bounced down the steps, and as Jack fell back on the ground, landed squarely on his right hand. Jack screamed, as shrill and as clear a scream as any warning whistle, and tried to pull his hand from out under. By the time Solomon had jumped down and lifted the box away, the frost was already heavily stained with blood.

"The first-aid box," Solomon asked. "Where's your first-aid box?"

Jack danced about in pain, hugging his hand to his chest.

"We haven't got time for that. It's the effing train we have to worry about. The key's in my pocket. Open it up, for God's sake. I can't do it like this."

Solomon did as he was told. Squatting on his haunches he opened the lid. In the box lay two rows of flat metal disks, each one wrapped in greased paper. Jack stood over him holding his crushed hand aloft. Thick lines of blood were running down into his sleeve.

"OK, Mr. Straw. This is what you have to do. Take six of them in your pocket and run as fast as you can up the track. For God's sake don't fall over on them or we'll still be picking you out the trees next summer. We have to go down the track a good half mile, for she'll be travelling at some speed and by the time they've heard the bangs and put the brakes on they'll be right on top of it. I'd like to give a bit longer but we don't have time. Don't worry, I'll be with you. You place them down so and snap them in so that they hold in place. Try one now, see? See how it fits? Right. When we get there, when I give you the nod, get one down, then run another fifty yards, get another down, then another fifty yards and get another down. If we put them too close they won't hear them, or think they've run over a firework or some other kid's trick. If we've got any more time we'll run further up and put a couple more down but there's no telling how long it will take in this weather. Look lively now."

So Solomon Straw did as he was told. Picking up the detonators, and with Jack running behind him, he was reminded of those days when he had started out, how he had followed instructions then, when speed and agility and the need for urgency were impressed upon him. "Look lively," his instructor had said. "Look lively. They'll die of old age if you carry on like this. Come on, let's get some *speed* into it," and moving now against the wind, he ran to a rhythm he had not heard in years. Cap noose pin lever drop. Cap noose pin lever drop. Cap noose pin lever drop. He could have run for hours. Ten minutes later Jack Edge pulled him up.

"OK, Mr. Straw," he said. "Start now. Get that first one down and fly like buggery."

17

"And that's *exactly* what he did," Jack would say later. "Flew like buggery. Never seen anything like it. Half crouching, detonators in hand, and he ran along that line, slapping them down as if he had spent years at it. Bang, down they'd go and I'd be running my full best trying to keep up with him to see if he was doing it properly, but he was way ahead of me, like Zátopek with a baton in his hand, or one of them Cossacks on their blessed horses, everything in one motion and as smooth as glass."

It was the only tale Jack Edge ever told concerning his most notorious of passengers for while he regarded Solomon Straw's profession as entirely normal, in this instance he was amazed. The Day Solomon Straw Saved Lives. But Jack Edge had never seen Solomon Straw at work, and bending down, moving, his hands as quick as his brain, was his stock-in-trade.

As he helped Jack back up into the train and bound his hand with the roll of bandage rescued from the rusty first-aid box, Solomon wished someone else had been there instead. He regretted having to touch Jack Edge, to treat him tenderly, for he knew how sensitive people were coming into contact with him once they knew his calling. He felt the same way himself, particularly with those to whom he was closest. When he was down in the pit, with a freshly hanged body flopped over his back, his face pressed up against a warm and naked side, on those long journeys across the chamber with his assistant looking down upon the two of them, sometimes he could not tell which was his flesh, the living flesh, and which was the condemned flesh, the dead flesh. It was as if once alongside its deposed companion, his skin underwent a profound osmosis, inviting the dead cells to merge with his own. He would move his head slightly or tense the muscles in his neck, hoping that such a shift would be sufficient to make the delineation clear, but usually he would have to shake the body with his shoulder, raise its weight a couple of times, before he broke free—a dangerous manoeuvre, for it could wake the man out of his sleep and send a torrent of hot urine flooding down his back, but it was worth the price. Anything to establish which side of the grave he was on. His wife's breasts were the same. He would wake in the night and find his hand underneath her nightgown, holding onto one of them. Not moving, with its full weight resting in his palm, her chest rising and falling barely perceptibly, he found it hard to distinguish not simply which was his hand and which was her breast, but where the difference lay between this flesh lying in his hand, and the other, carried on his shoulder. She was as warm and tender as any executed soul might be, but she felt no different, no different at all. What was his wife's breast trying to tell him? That he was dead? That his wife was dead to him? That he was dead to her? She was pale, his wife, no doubt about that, pale and fleshy. She was not firm like him, and not firm like the men he had hanged. Not as firm as the women either. She had been firm once, firm and strong, but she had grown pale over the years, pale and soft like a corpse, and when he pressed her flesh with one of his fingers the indentation would remain for far longer than it should. It was hard to be close, hard enough at the best of times, but made harder for her by this roving eye he had for Death. It was as if he had a mistress, a bit on the side. Death winked at him, Death left messages for him, Death lifted her skirts and he went running. When he came back, despite his precautions, his vigorous washing, his immediate change of clothing, and his determinedly avuncular manner, his wife could still smell the perfume his lover had left on his neck, still trace the kisses she had bestowed upon his lips, still detect the pleasure her caresses had brought to his eager hands. Intimacy was out of the question. He was no better. After about a week, when the smell of the pit had left his nostrils, she would awake to find her nightgown bunched around her neck, with his hand digging her far-side breast from out under the feather mattress. Pulled out of her sleep, understanding what was required, she would turn over onto her front and wait. Neither spoke, for like his dinners with the prison governor, there was only one thing laid out on their dark table of love. He would climb on top of his wife and find the body of the hanged man already there, his soft, dead lips planted on her neck, his long, dead arms outstretched over hers, and the full dead weight of his body resting on her white and morbid buttocks. The hanged man would lie on top of her, and he would

19

have to lie on top of *him,* put his arms around *his* shoulders, place his lips upon *his* neck, lie hopelessly lost, within *him.* No wonder they lay so still. No wonder they dare not move. They would lie immobile, his hands beneath her, willing her breasts to move, waiting for life to seep out, uncalled for. Only then could they return to the living. Perhaps that was why it all came to an end. Because he had been too close to *life* that day, his life, her life. *Life* had come, and not seeped through, but gushed down the stairs, Judith propped up against the stair wall, her legs hanging down, all sorts of stuff that he had never heard about coming out. He had been in the kitchen pouring a last cup of tea before he left for the station. His bag was in the hall, his bag and his hat and the mahogany box that slipped into his inside pocket. The doctor had said she had a good week to go and he was only going to be away for a day. "Jem," she had called out, "Oh, Jem. I don't think I should have done all that weeding, it's coming for Christ's sake," and he had rushed out to find her halfway up the stairs clutching at herself. "It's a bit sudden, girl, isn't it? I thought you got plenty of warning. I'll go and get Dora," and she said, "No, don't leave me it's coming out now, Jem, I can feel it," and she had fallen back, her thick pale legs in the air, and this great swollen thing between her legs which he had never looked at before, staring him in the eye. "What do you want me to do, Judith, get some hot water?" and she said, "Bugger the hot water, get up here you great baby and catch it," and he had climbed the stairs and looked into her, her legs practically over his shoulders, buttocks bouncing up and down while she pressed her hands down on the stair carpet. "New last year," she complained and then out he popped in a great rush, their little Stanley, all black hair and black eyes, dived headfirst into his arms, slippery and bloody. How had he managed that, he wondered, how had he managed that, on his way to a hanging with the birth blood of his son on his hands? and as he stood there, wondering what to do, the other thing had arrived. He buried it in the garden, as his father had his, buried it in the back garden in unconsecrated ground, with a couple of large stones over it so that the next-door neighbour's dog wouldn't get at it. And as he stood there, looking

20

at it, he was struck by the fact that by the following morning there would be other flesh, dropped through the noose of life, to be cut down and wrapped in white sheeting, which would also find its final rest in unhallowed ground and that his hands would have sent it there. Hands that had held his son, his Stanley! Nothing had been the same after that day. He could see that now. That's what Stanley had done and though he hadn't realised it at the time, hadn't realised it until years later, that's why he loved him. Stanley had saved his life. Now, in the pub, his wife was not a corpse, not when they lay in bed, not ever. She was quite jolly these days, like he could be, what with the pub to run and Stanley to look after, and every now and again, after a busy lunchtime, and if Stanley was off with one of his friends, they would go upstairs for a bit of how's-your-father. Sometimes he would catch her looking at him afterwards, remembering how it had been. He did it himself. He would be downstairs pulling pints, his small delicate fingers holding the straight glasses steady, when, handing it over, he would wonder what his regulars would think if they knew what he had done, what he had seen. He wondered too whether they knew just how clearly he saw them, saw them all. As he poured their drinks and smiled at their jokes he would say to them, "I can see you. I can see you better than you can see me. I know your sort. I know all your sorts. I know what you do, what you scheme at night, what little tricks you have up your sleeve. When you come in with your pockets bulging with too much money, or your old woman turns up with her face all puffed up, or your fancy piece totters in on her high heels with her ankles suddenly thicker and her breasts unaccountably swollen, I know what you've been up to, and what you might be capable of. What all of us might be capable of. And I wonder with the right amount of beer inside you, the right amount of fear and desperation coursing through your veins, whether in years past you wouldn't have had to face me and my little pocket handkerchief one bright and early morning."

Until Jack Edge turned up in the village it had been over ten years since they had clapped eyes on each other. 1964. Jack had kept the train waiting ten minutes that day. If Judith hadn't given birth, if Solomon

21

hadn't missed his connection, there would have been no unsightly scenes, he wouldn't have had to hide in Jack's van on the way back and his name would not have been bandied about the papers like some common or garden clown at Billy Smart's Circus. He would have left the profession with his dignity intact. Strange that it had been the birth of his own son which was the cause of his downfall, while it was the birth of the twins which brought Danny Dancer to book. They had staked out the hospital where Danny's wife had been taken, so Alcott had told him later, police in the grounds, police on the ward, even police riding shotgun in the ambulance.

"She might have been in labour but it didn't stop her from swearing like a trooper. And her a vicar's daughter."

"Vicar's *sister*," Solomon corrected.

"Aye. Well I wonder what he made of it all then. With him in attendance."

In fact he made a great deal of it. Her brother was one of the leading lights in the campaign to stop the execution. It was he who had led the vigil outside Downing Street all that preceding week, who had appeared on television arguing for Danny's innocence, and he who, to this day, campaigned for the boy's posthumous pardon. Father Rooney was his name. He had been there at the execution, and when it was over, Solomon had met him by the prison gates. He had stood in front of Solomon and made the sign of the cross, had blessed him and his family, blessed little Stanley, while the screams of that poor demented mother could be heard coming from outside. Father Rooney had written to him too, some weeks later, a letter sent to the Home Office and forwarded in one of their official brown envelopes. He had felt uneasy about opening it, let alone reading the blessed thing. And then of course he could not forget.

I looked into my brother-in-law's eyes, as you must have
looked into them, not a moment later, and I saw an innocent
man. He smiled at you. Do you remember? He smiled and said

that phrase they claimed he said to her, the phrase that was his undoing. "No hard feelings," he said, and turning to me, added, "Remember that, Gerald. Remember to tell Mum and Eileen. No hard feelings," and with that he walked out of my life and into yours. Guilty men don't act that way, do they, Mr. Straw? They may be grim. They may be defiant, unrepentant. They may even be resigned, and maintain dignity. I have seen it myself and I am sure you have seen it many times. But they do not go serene and wise and full of grace. Eileen's Danny, thief though he was, went like that. You know it and I know it but you know it better than me. Join me in our struggle to clear our Danny's name. Redeem yourself.

He had not kept the letter. For a time it lay in his Execution Book, up against his last entry, text against text ("His word against mine," he called it), but when he banished his book, sent it away never to see it again, as he was wrapping it up, the letter fell out and dropped onto the floor, a single sheet of blue paper with faint lines upon it and that small insistent handwriting sloping slightly to the left. He felt guilty then, guilty that he never replied, guilty that he pretended to himself that he had never received it and he vowed then to use it as best he could. Later he threw it into the sea, for what could he have done, after all that happened? But though it was gone forever the words were not. And Father Rooney had blessed his child, blessed little Stanley who had been born barely twenty-four hours before. The priest had not known that. He knew nothing of Solomon Straw. He had simply made the sign of the cross and said, "I am praying for Danny and for Danny's wife and for Danny's children who will never see their father, only hear bad things about him. And I will pray for you and for your family, Mr. Straw, and hope that they will not grow up hearing bad things about you."

He had dealt with enough priests in his time, priests and vicars and other men of the cloth, most of whom disapproved of his work, but he never carried out his duties in the presence of a relative before. There had been much debate amongst the warders as to whether the governor had been right to accede to Danny's request, and allow his brother-in-law to be there at the execution, but reluctantly the Home Office had admitted that they could find no rule which stated that the priest in question could not be related to the condemned man. In the end that part could not have gone smoother.

"Sorry, Gerry, I have to go," Danny had said. "Can't keep the famous Solomon Straw waiting," and standing up and putting his hand behind his back, continued, "See? No hard feelings. Remember that, Gerald," he added, turning his head half round. "Remember that to Mother and Eileen. No hard feelings. Now stay with me and don't upset yourself. I'll see you in God's good time."

It was a quiet morning when Jack Edge strolled in. The door was open, the flagstones cool, the air dark. Judith was hanging up the tea towels on the line in the yard. Stanley was outside in the garden. He had only just opened. There was no one else. They didn't recognise each other at first and if it had been up to Jeremiah he would have served the man his drink and stepped out the back and let his wife take over until Jack had gone on his way. It was not to be, for Jack was no passing visitor. It was only after he took his first sip of his pint of mild and looked Solomon in his eye (his false eye as it happened) that he registered who his new landlord was.

"As I live and breathe. If it isn't Mr. Straw."

Jeremiah wiped the bar down and pointed to the small sign hanging above the hops.

"The name is Bembo. Jeremiah Bembo. I'd be grateful if you would remember that."

Jack Edge nodded.

"You and me are going to be neighbors, Mr. Straw. I retired not three months back. Bought a bungalow down the road. Near the old windmill. Needs a bit of work, but then don't we all. It'll give me something to do. Get me out from under the wife's feet. And how are you keeping? Given up your travels I hear."

Solomon Straw regarded the man with equanimity. It was bound to happen. A warder, a governor, a retired policeman. Better it was someone safe and trustworthy, someone decent and sensible like Jack Edge rather than some hothead assistant who still harboured a grudge.

"Forgive me if I appear churlish, Jack, but let's get one thing straight. My name is Jeremiah Bembo, the local landlord. That is all I am. That is all I want to be. The name to which you refer, and which you must never use again, not in this house at least, I know only from children's playgrounds and other common folklore. To my mind he has never existed, a phantom, a bogeyman. Like the Pied Piper. Nothing to do with the here and now. Nothing to do with *me*. Do you follow my drift?"

Jack Edge nodded. "You can trust Jack Edge," he said. "You could always trust Jack Edge." He held out his hand. Jeremiah stood for a moment, looking at this unwanted arrival, and then took the grasp firmly.

"Well then, well met, Jack Edge. It's good to see an old face again. A face I can trust. Neighbours, you say? Well then, maybe we should resurrect our games of chess. Maybe this time you'll win one or two. Let me get you another pint. On the house this time."

Over the following months Solomon Straw began to enjoy this link with the past, for he knew that when he was with Jack Edge he could let his guard down in a way he could with no one else. In the large taproom decked out with hops and wooden tables, Jack Edge would sit in the corner of the inglenook with just himself for company. When the two of them fancied a chat and there was no one else about they would huddle in the corner of the bar, talking low in the quiet of the morning, with the fire lit and the sun throwing shadows through the lazy door, though

25

should anyone else enter they would break off and Jack would take himself back to his seat. Jack the Badger the other regulars called him—he only came out when no one else was about. After closing time, when Solomon was all washed up and Judith had gone upstairs, he would pull out the ivory chess set from under the bar and they would sit down for an afternoon's game and when it was over, and weather permitting, they would walk round the village, to stretch their legs, Jack's terrier barking at their heels. One such Friday afternoon they were walking as usual back past the village school. It was break time and the children were running round the playground, shouting, fighting, and playing tag. A small group of girls was gathered in the corner of the wire fence. They were holding hands and standing in a circle. One girl stood in the middle, with her head hung down. She had a scarf tied round her neck, and held the loose end high above her head. As the two men grew closer, the circle started to move, and the girls began to sing.

> Solomon Straw went to work one day,
> Hanged young Danny for a grim day's pay,
> Polished up his eyepiece,
> Greased the trapdoor.
> Come and dance the quickstep for Solomon Straw.

> Ethel and her fancy man went out for a ride,
> Just got their knickers off when Danny peeped inside,
> Told them not to do it,
> To do it was a sin,
> Shame upon the two of you, I'll have to do you in.

> I wasn't there, said little Danny D,
> I'm not a killer, so don't look at me.
> I was up in Cardiff town
> Sleeping with a whore.
> Don't want to dance the quickstep on your greased trapdoor.

Solomon Straw weighed up the scales,
First you were in England, then you told us Wales,
Put on your dancing shoes
And try not to lie,
For I can see the truth through my cold glass eye.

So dance, little Danny, dance on the floor,
Dance for your mother on the greased trapdoor,
Dance for your children,
Dance for your wife,
For Solomon Straw is here to take your life.

"What do they know," Solomon Straw grumbled to his friend when they were finally out of earshot. "What does anyone know? How it all started. How it all ended. Nothing."

"Well, how *did* it start, then?" Jack Edge asked, and because they were walking along in the open air, because there was no conspiracy, no huddle to go into, because it was a simple question and nothing more, Solomon told him. Told him everything.

HE CAME FROM A SPRAWLING FAMILY, NOT BORN INTO A ROMANY OR GYPSY
tradition, but one which covered the Vale of Aylesbury and the hills and
towns which grew up around its edges. His father was one of three
brothers, and though they had all settled down and made homes for their
wives and children, there was a restless fire burning in every one of them.
It was an infectious family, a family which invaded other people's lives in
unexpected ways. When you sat at the table it was Bembo-grown toma-
toes which accompanied your fry-up, Bembo-grown potatoes that sat
round your boiled beef, and Bembo-grown peas you balanced on your
knife. At any tumbling town fete or wet gymkhana, it would be Bembo-
hired marquees which hid the summer dresses and frock coats from the
wind and rain, and Bembo-hired ropes which held those shelters fast.
And if you were a religious family, and few admitted otherwise, as often
as not it would be a Bembo-printed Bible which adorned your dresser
and a Bembo-printed prayer book which lay before you on your Sunday
pew.

Although he had heard much about him, before he stole up to
London for his interview at the prison, Jeremiah had never seen his
grandfather, but standing there before him, he knew, from that implacable expression on the dead man's face, that despite what everyone would

say, he was doing the right thing. The war was at an end, and it was time for him to make his move. The vegetable business lay in ruins, the plane had seen to that, that and his left eye. Although it had seemed like a good place in his grandfather's time, protected by the broad sweep of hills, when the war came the greenhouses could not have been in a more vulnerable place, for although Aylesbury didn't have anything to offer, over at Luton the Vauxhall car factory had been turned over to the production of tanks and by the time the German planes had ducked and weaved and opened their bomb doors, desperate to drop their load anywhere, they were poised right over the whole glittering shooting match. The planes came in relentless waves. Wilfred used to joke that they might as well float up a couple of barrage balloons with DROPPEN SIE BOMBEN HERE plastered all over them. Bits of Germany had been falling out of the sky all that year. Wilfred had a piece of a Messerschmitt 110 strapped across the bonnet of the van, while Will's father, out poaching one night, had stumbled over the spot where a German pilot had fallen to earth. Jem had been out with him setting traps, but it was his uncle who had fallen into the hole.

"In the perfect shape of a man it was and he lay at the bottom, as limp as a rag doll. Like he'd been put through a mangle," he told them, "not one solid bone in his body. We could have folded him up and sent him home in a Red Cross parcel."

"Wish I could send Mr. Punch off in a Red Cross parcel," Will grumbled. "I think this war has gone to his head. He ain't half giving me some stick these days."

They were of itinerant Italian stock, buskers and mountebanks and puppeteers, and Jem's father, Reuben, when in full flight, still spoke in the parley of his forefathers. Their grandfather, the Great Bembo, had been famed in Dickens' day. Cruikshank had drawn him, Mayhew had written him down, while the Prince of Wales had watched him with an indifferent and wandering eye at a private performance down in Brighton. He was a showman, a puppeteer, and even his eldest son, who now ran the religious bookshop up in London, and who despised the works of

29

his younger brothers, had to concede that amongst them all there was a need to proclaim themselves to the world, to stand before an audience and perform. It was the Great Bembo himself who sat, stuffed for posterity like his close contemporary, Jeremy Bentham, at the top of the bookshop stairs, frozen in an attitude of unforgiving exhortation, looking down on all who came through the door. He was still now, but in his time he had travelled the length and breadth of England, pushing his handcart before him, in which lay his trumpet, his swizzle, and the treacherous Mr. Punch. Mr. Darwin had changed him, Darwin with his lengthy Devil Tongue. Nothing Mr. Punch had done could ever compete with his wickedness. If Mr. Punch had got hold of Mr. Darwin he would have beaten him all over town and given Jack Ketch someone far more deserving to put through the noose but the truth was Mr. Punch was not best suited for defending religion. So his master drew up another travelling show, with magic lanterns and preachers and men of the old science, with seven live monkeys and three dwarves dancing in attendance and a sideshow of pickled babies, shrunken heads, and dried monkey feet, all heralded by a solitary snare drum which called the faithful to muster, ready to take the fight to the foe. But such constant battles need a regular supply of ammunition, and so the Great Bembo had extracts from the Bible printed which he handed out as the curious public flocked in, wrote pamphlets which his elder son sold to them during the interval, and had his wife sitting behind a striped stall from where she enjoined the crowds to buy her decorated crosses and embroidered prayer mats on their way out. He was part of a great crusade, defending an institution which in the past had done nothing but denounce him and which now was eternally grateful for the expertise he could bring. He revelled in the irony and drew strength from it. He was a man of God now, clutched to the Church's breast, but at heart still a traveller with an eye for turning a quick penny or two. There was money to be made as well as souls to save and as he needed a base from which to organise his troupe he found premises in one of the backstreets of Covent Garden and turned it into a shop and had his name painted above the awning. It was devoted to artefacts of God and the Church, and began by selling pamphlets and Bibles and beeswax candles. But he had a flair for publicity, and it was not long before Bembo's had become a landmark in London. It was Bembo's which burned copies of Darwin's book in a brazier outside the shop. Every man or woman who added to the conflagration was given a Bible to take home, with their name inscribed on the flyleaf in the proprietor's long and flourished hand. The fire burned for six months. It was the Great Bembo who you would see, walking the streets of London, handing out copies of his handiwork, the most popular of which was *Man and His Garden: Why Dogs Do Not Eat Vegetables.* That was his final legacy, for when he grew tired of travelling and wished to leave London, he started the small market garden a few years before the Great War, down in the Vale of Aylesbury. Memories of the home country he had never seen. Three sons he had by then, and in time the three became infected in different ways. The eldest cocked a snoot at the rest of them and returned to London, expanded the bookshop, and became a supplier to the Church for all its requirements. The other two stayed with their father. The youngest, Jeremiah's uncle, turned travelling into a stationary business, with tents and marquees out to hire, and resurrected his father's Punch and Judy and when he could took them travelling again. And Jeremiah's father, the middle of the three sons, kept on with the market garden, added to the number of greenhouses, and taught his son the glory of growing. Jeremiah liked the earth. He knew that everything he could want for was here all around him. There was no need to look further. But like his cousin, he had a restless streak in him, a slow current which would surface every now and again and demand more.

"We all have it," Will's father, Silas, would say, "even your Uncle Jonas. Once you become a man, Bembo biology takes over. The need to command space. Why do you think he had your grandfather stuffed and mounted if it weren't for a show? He may think he's a cut above the rest of us, but for all his airs and graces he ain't no better."

Jem lived with his father, and his uncle's family, in the large farmhouse that the old man had left them. The house had been divided in half so that the two families could live their separate lives but when he was four Jem's mother had died and he had spent most of his early years being looked after by Will's mother. She was taller than either of the grown men, and younger too, a child bride in a full woman's body, bedded and wedded not six months after her sixteenth birthday. In the early days, when they were small boys, she seemed to Jem more like a grown-up sister rather than Will's mother, always eager to join them in their childish games, swinging them about the parlour, chasing them in and out of the garden, leaping out with them on the rope over the brook before crashing into the water below. Only in the evening, when the men came back from work, would her spirits still, and then not for long. The two families would take supper together and then father and son would retire to their own part of the house, where Reuben would sit him down and have him read out long passages from the Bible. Through the stone wall he could hear Will's high-pitched voice singing old music hall songs and acting the fool, with his mother laughing in encouragement. Jem would stumble over the chosen verses, wishing that he could lighten his father's heart in such a way, but Reuben would look up, annoyed, as if he could not understand why his son should be faltering so, and with an impatient turn of his hand, bid him continue. Jem had no such gift and his father no stomach for it.

The two boys grew up together. They were much the same age, with Jem one year younger, though it was him who folk took to be the elder of the two. Their schooling was intermittent, particularly in the summer, when there was much work to do out in the fields and the family had no qualms about using their offspring as ready labour. Still they had time to do the things young boys did, to make friends and waylay enemies, to fight in the playground, and to ride their bikes around the countryside late into the summer night. At the weekends they were often accompanied by a gangling young man with an eager grin who worked during the week from dawn till dusk alongside Jem's father and the other men. Quite where he came from Jem never found out but

Loopy, for that is what they called Leonard, was as much a part of the family as the two ageing dogs and had been with them for as long as he could remember. He had been discarded by his parents, who had offered themselves for potato work one weekend and left after three days in the dead of night. Loopy did not live in the house but in the barn across the yard, though he always took his meals in the kitchen, with the rest of the family. They did not pay him a proper wage, but gave him handfuls of sweets and shiny new pennies which he kept all together in a jar by his bed amongst the straw bales. They all thought kindly of Loopy. When Jem had fallen into a bed of nettles it was Loopy Leonard who had picked him up and carried him home on his shoulders and when Will had cast his rod too eagerly and followed the line into the pond it was Loopy who had fished him out and wrapped him in his bottle-green jacket. He had taken care of them when they knew no better, played their games and grown up with them as best he could, and now that they were older, and knew what was what, they had to play his games and take care of him. He was safe and gentle and their very own.

In Jem's thirteenth year Will's mother ran off with one of the hired hands, a tall, muscular young man, only a couple of years older than she had been when she had first arrived. Though he only ever saw him the once, Jem remembered him well, for earlier that summer the young man had come across them all, swimming, and larking about in the river, and from her laughing invitation had stripped to his long johns and jumped in. Neither Will nor he had thought more of it, but it seemed that the sight of his bodily youth and his careless ways had quite turned her head. Within a month she was gone, leaving a note on the kitchen table for them to find where the supper should have been. They had all trooped into the kitchen that evening, not fully understanding the silence and the six empty places before them, and had stood behind their respective chairs while Silas read the letter in silence before handing it across to his brother. No supper was had that night, just a loaf and a knife and a pot of her homemade jam put before the two boys while the two men talked in the parlour. Later Reuben took his son back to their quarters and made him read the Bible for an extra half hour, while through the walls he could hear the sound of his cousin crying. He had never heard Will cry before, except for when he had fallen off his bicycle, and he wanted to join him and share his tears, but a look from his father told him that this was not possible. This was another sound he would not hear. The following morning, before they set off to work, Will's father went through the house removing every trace of her he could find, her clothes, her favourite chair, the mirror she would comb her hair in front of, even the pennants she had sewn for the double-ridged tent. For a year nothing was heard of her, and then news came that she was back, deserted by her young lover, and living in near destitution somewhere in town. Reuben went to see her once, but on his return the boys were called in, and with Will's father sitting silently at the back, were told that they must never try and see her, never try and write to her, and that if she ever tried to make contact with them, they were to tell him at once.

"I know it's hard," Reuben told them. "Will especially, but you got to remember, you ain't got no ma now. She's gone, good as dead, and that's that. Me and Silas are all you've got and we haven't done badly by you this past year. Besides, you'll be grown men soon enough, with sweethearts of your own. You won't be needing mothering."

"Will's already got an eye for the ladies, I can see that," Silas put in. "And Jem won't be far behind. But remember what happened to your old father, Will, and watch out for them. Don't give them nothing. Just take what you can get and leave the rest behind."

"I don't know about that," his brother admonished. "That don't seem to be fitting advice for a child on the threshold of manhood. Just remember it were Eve that bit into that apple, and that's what Will's mother done, just like the Bible said. They say there's good women in this world, and I daresay there are, but, leaving my own good wife aside, God rest her soul, they're plenty hard to find. My advice is to leave well alone, until you're sure. It isn't only beauty that be skin deep."

"What if we see her," Jem asked, "when we're in town on errands or up at the station, delivering?"

"Pass her by," Reuben told him sternly. "Tip your hat if she's close like and you're in company, for that's polite, and I don't want people tattling about how we don't know how to conduct ourselves, but that's all. She's a stranger now, not of this parish, and you must treat her as one."

"Will you do it, Will," Jem asked Will later, "like Father says?"

"Do what?"

"Pass her by. Pretend you haven't see her."

Will stood his ground. "Haven't seen who?"

"Your ma."

"You gone soft like Loopy? I ain't got a ma. Remember?"

So Jem, like the others, never talked about her, and in time found it hard to think that she had ever been there. Once in a while they would be reminded of her, for news of her would find its way back to the house, via a visiting tradesman or one of the porters up at the station. She had got a job at a draper's; she had taken up with a sailor; there had been a fight over her in a dance hall; she was up before the magistrate for stealing from her employer; but through these intermittent and sorry tales, the brothers never wavered. As each story was brought before them to be inspected and pronounced upon, it would be met with a curt nod of the head and nothing more. No comment, no questions, no expression of surprise or regret. Just silence and cold stares until the subject was changed. Faced with their studied indifference, in time, even these withered and died.

By the time the boys left school and were working their way into manhood, the five of them ran the whole place. Only at the height of the summer did they feel the need to take on outside labourers, and even then they did it out of reluctant necessity. They didn't want any more cuckoos in the nest. The marquee business took hold in the good-weather months, while Jem's father's business ran the whole year through. So Wilfred and Jeremiah and Loopy Leonard worked together; in the week trenching up the potatoes, pruning the fruit bushes and working in the long flight of greenhouses and at the weekend, travelling about the countryside in the back of the van, putting the tents up on a Friday and taking them down by Sunday evening, Will chatting up the girls who worked in the kitchens and stables, and Jem, ever the foil, happy to watch his cousin working his charm. Will could shin up those poles like a monkey and hang there, swaying from side to side and grinning from ear to ear.

"You know what you are, don't you, girl?" he would cry. "A thief."

"How do you mean?" they would ask.

"You've just taken my fancy," and as often as not he would slide down to their arms, which though they might not open for him then, would remember their admiration later in the evening. It was while the tents were up that Jem and Will and Loopy Leonard would go off for a Punch and Judy show. They would set up anywhere: on the green, outside the pub, in a market square. Jem would start drawing the crowd in, squeezing out tunes on his battered accordion, while Loopy and Will would set up the frame. Will would do the show and Loopy would be the bottler, passing round the hat at the end. They all had a part to play.

Wilfred was young for a Punch and Judy man, but he had the patter and outlook for it. He was seemingly easy Will, with dark wavy hair, and dark twinkling eyes. He was small like Jeremiah, neat in appearance like Jeremiah, but altogether looser in temperament. Both were quick but when Jeremiah was quick it was because he was concentrating hard, pushing himself to work well, while with Will it was because he felt such dexterity attractive and he wished the world to see his beguiling display. Jeremiah admired his cousin's theatrical skills, but if asked he could not answer truthfully that he liked Will's performance and the need to say honest, rounded words mattered to him. He had seen other Punch and Judy shows down on Weymouth front and Studland Bay, but they were more for children than for adults, while Will's was as his grandfather's had been, wild and bawdy and violent. They were all there, Mr. Punch, Judy, the Beadle, the Baby, the Crocodile, Scaramouch and Jack Ketch, though with Will, apart from the beginning, you never knew which of them he would use. That's what he had inherited from his grandfather, his unnerving sense of place and play. Though he could not see his audience, he always judged their mood correctly and would change his routine according to the company standing before him. There were the bloodthirsty audiences, revelling in Punch's savage beatings and murderous intent, there were the loud audiences, who guffawed at Punch's crude kissey-kissey and his saucy songs and there were the fearful audiences, who held their breath when the hangman came, and watched in awe as Punch fought with the very Devil himself.

"I don't need to look at them," Will would boast to his cousin, "I just got to hear them cough, hear them stir a bit when Mr. Punch first comes on, and I knows where I am see. Like dad says, it's a gift we've all got. You just don't know how to use yours yet. Any road I ain't got time for peeping. I'm too busy keeping an eye on Mr. Punch, making sure he don't try and hang *me.*"

Apart from Mr. Punch, who would sit dangling his legs over the side, Jack Ketch was the only puppet who had legs. Tricked into his own noose, he ended up swung out from the stage hanging from the gallows, with his concertina neck stretched to a grotesque length. ("I bet there's something of your old man's you wouldn't mind this long, missus," Mr. Punch would shout into the audience.) No matter how many times Jeremiah saw it, when it came to Jack Ketch's end he would turn his head away. There was something wrong in that reckless finale. Jack Ketch had come to do his solemn duty but Mr. Punch would make a fool of him, pull the rope tight and raise a huge cheer. A real crowd pleaser whatever their mood. It was as if they were seeing their own histories of private cruelty made good, praised in public and thrown wilfully into the air.

"Bravo!" Mr. Punch would shout at the close. "Satan is dead. We can all do as we like. Good-bye, ladies and gentlemen. Thank you for your patronage and I hope you'll come out handsome with your gold and silver," and Loopy would jump to his outsize feet and dance round with the hat. Loopy's ungainly cavort reminded Jem of one of the illustrations in his embroidered history book, a depiction of a medieval fair with a man and his dancing bear. The bear had a collar and chain around his neck and had his paws outstretched. Some in the crowd had sticks in their hands and were poking at it. Barking dogs snapped at its heels. From the expression on its face, the bear knew it was being taunted, but not why. It had been led to a place set up expressly for this purpose. It lunged and raged. All it wanted was to be left in peace. The people laughed to see such sport. The Punch and Judy crowd were much the same, sniggering at Loopy's antics, calling out names, making jokes, ridiculing his very appearance. Jem could see their eyes bright with vicious delight. They revelled in their indifferent cruelty, their mocking jibes. They had seen the show and now had a real creature to taunt. Mr. Punch drew the very worst out of a crowd.

"I hate to see them laugh at him," Jem would tell Will. "Like something dressed up in a zoo. It's not right."

"You worry too much," Will would reply. "He loves coming out with us. We're here to see him OK."

On a good day they could bring in three, four, even five pounds. Will would take the lion's share, Jem ten bob or so and Loopy a few pence. Though he wished to appear free and easy, Will was mean with his money and did not care to spend it, unless it was for a purpose, like chatting up some girl he fancied. Then he would turn his back on the two of them and wade in with the gin and black currant, with his all too plausible patter flowing effortlessly in her direction.

They had been fortunate to have use of the van for it meant they could cover a good deal of ground, even driving through the night to spend a couple of days at the seaside, but the war had put a stop to all that. At times Jem wished Will would be a little more serious, a little more grown-up, tone his language down a bit. It had been all right him playing the fool when they had been boys, but times had changed and even young men needed a sense of responsibility. Especially young men. The destiny of the world lay in their hands. It was a powerful time to be living and though he was exempt from the call-up on account of his father's market garden, he was determined to do his bit. So he joined the Home Guard and was given the job of fire watching. He tried to persuade Will to join with him, but his cousin would have none of it.

"Bugger the Home Guard," Will had told him. "It's ENSA for me. I want to get out there and do something that'll get me noticed. You get all sorts running those outfits you know, people in show business, people in the BBC. Could be my lucky break."

That's what Wilfred wanted to be, a comedian with a string of jokes and a couple of song-and-dance routines thrown in between, though his dad told him he was crazy, that the music hall was dying, if not dead already. Stick to what we know he would tell him. Stick to the business and Mr. Punch. But Wilfred was like his granddad. He wanted fame.

One bomb had nearly put paid to all his plans. It was high summer, and as usual Jeremiah had been working for his uncle that weekend. Though the war was in full swing, Uncle Silas had never been busier. They had been putting up one of his largest marquees, a four-poled affair with flying pennants and long striped awning decked out with fairy lights, set out for a big society wedding, with a hired orchestra coming down from London, and his uncle's finest raised parquet floor laid out on the covered turf. Jem and Will had polished that floor all afternoon. It was exhausting work.

"Good job I've had a lot of practice wanking," Wilfred had joked, "otherwise my arm would have dropped off by now." Jeremiah had told him to get on with it and not to be so crude.

Instead of going on a Punch and Judy run that weekend they decided to stay put and sleep in the grounds near the house. There was a girl working in the kitchens who Will had taken a shine to. She had come out earlier in the afternoon to look at the marquee and caught them on their hands and knees, with their shirts off and Wilfred laughing and joking as usual. Loopy was up top fixing the lights. They had heard a footfall and stopped work. She stood at the entrance still dressed in her apron. She was dark and watchful. Her hands were white with flour and she was slightly taller than both of them.

"Don't you come any closer," Wilfred had exclaimed, standing up and giving her the once-over. "More than our life's worth. Take you dancing on it though when the party's over."

The young woman dismissed the invitation.

"What do I need with your fag ends," she exclaimed. "And you busy with woman's work at that. Can't nobody find nothing better for you to do?"

Jeremiah got to his feet and regarded her solemnly. He was embarrassed to be half-undressed. Will had no such inhibitions, and stuck his thumbs into the belt of his trousers and stared at her, willing her to stare back.

"This is weekend work, same as yours," Jeremiah explained. "We got proper work waiting for us back home. Work the country needs. You'll probably be eating some of it before the day's through. If we're called up, we'll go well enough, isn't that right, Will?"

Will grinned.

"I'm in no hurry," he admitted. "The way things are going I'd rather be planting potatoes than pushing up daisies. Anyway if I go, who's going to look after all you lonely young women?"

"We don't need looking after," she said sharply.

Jeremiah nodded. "That's right. You tell him, miss," he said.

Wilfred blew on his cigarette. "Aye. Well," he said, "that's as maybe. But I think in the right company there's nothing you'd like better than a quick turn on the floor."

Loopy dropped to the ground with a thud. His boots were tied up with rags and as he landed he slipped and fell at her feet. She sprang back with a cry.

"Steamboat!" Loopy cried, jumping up. "Dance the Steamboat!"

"Give over, Loopy," said Will, walking over and pulling him away. "Frighten the poor girl to death."

"Don't mind him, miss," Jeremiah told her. "He's with us."

"Steamboat!" Loopy repeated. "Dance the Steamboat."

The girl looked at him for an explanation.

"It's the name of a country dance," Jem explained. "Me and him go down to our local hall every Thursday evening. Loopy knows all them dances off by heart. You might not think to look at him, but he's a real treat to watch. Like a swan on water. If I had half the feet he has, I'd have been married the twelvemonth. Ain't that right, Loopy?"

"If you had half his feet," Will smirked, "you'd have probably *had* to get married the twelvemonth. You know what they say about feet."

She smiled despite herself, then straightened her face. "I wouldn't be much use to him then," she said, looking at Jeremiah. "I only know the polka."

"Oh don't you worry 'bout that," Jem told her. "He'll dance to anything."

"My speciality, the polka," said Will. "One two three hop, right?"

She bent down and took off her shoes and walked towards the grinning man.

"Well, that settles it," she said defiantly. "I'll dance with him then."

"What about me?" Will called out. "I asked first."

"Well, go to the top of the class," she said, and catching his insolent, questioning face, added, "Maybe later," and spun round the room in Loopy's grateful arms.

That evening when he had washed and changed, Will brought her back and tried to get her to give a repeat performance on the grass. Jeremiah looked on.

"Get your box out, Jem, and give us a tune, can't you?" Will demanded. "I've got a real corker here." Jeremiah said nothing. For the first time he wanted no part in Will's intent.

"Come on," Will admonished. "We haven't got all night you

41

know. If you squeeze yours maybe someone will squeeze mine," and Jeremiah, blushing in the dark, noticed with regret that the girl laughed and told Will not to talk so.

"Don't blame me," Will pleaded. "It's in the air. I mean, no guesses what the lucky bride will be doing this time tomorrow."

"I can't think what you mean," she said. "Anyway you're wrong. It's *today*." Wilfred just pulled her a little closer.

"What?" he said, looking at her with mock indignation, "you mean they're at it already," and had carried her off into the night.

"Can you believe it," he told Jeremiah when he returned. "Her name is Judith. Guess what I told her?"

Will was in an expansive mood. They were bedded down under the stars, hidden from view by a bank of daffodils. They could see the big house through the silhouetted stalks, a long, gabled building with dark ivy climbing up the brick walls. The kitchen was busy with last-minute preparations. It was an age away. They lay on the grass, hands behind their heads, both thinking of their lives to come.

Jeremiah sighed. "Go on, then."

"I told her fate had brought us together, that she was destined to help me in my quest for fame and fortune. 'How come?' she says. 'Well,' I say, 'your name is Judy and I'm a Punch and Judy man, but new to the trade.' 'So?' she says. 'The thing is,' I tell her, wiggling my hand around, 'I need a bit of practice.' "

Jeremiah said nothing.

"Don't you get it, Jem?"

"Get what?"

"The joke! Think filthy!"

Jeremiah turned and looked away.

"I suppose she got it then."

Will poked him playfully in the ribs.

"Course she got it. And a lot more besides. Though thanks to this afternoon my arm was that stiff I hardly had enough strength to pull the frenchy on. Want to sniff my fingers?"

Jeremiah made a sound of disgust. That was no way to talk. What would she think if she heard them talking like that? She looked a good sort an' all.

Will dismissed his complaint. "No need to sound so high and mighty. I wasn't the first there and I won't be the last." He waved at the house with his cigarette. "In God's truth I don't get this marriage lark. What's he after, this captain or whatever, what's marrying her ladyship? I mean why's he bothering, eh? That's what I want to know. If he doesn't get his balls blown off on manoeuvres, this is no time for a man to be tying the knot. Everyone's at it. And who can blame them? Take them land girls. Why doesn't your pa get some of them down? Like cows at milking time they are. Classy bints too. Never known to fart. Do you think that's what the blushing bride is doing right now, holding her arse over the khazi, having a last blow before she shows her all tomorrow night?" He raised his buttocks and let rip. "Bums away," he shouted.

"Perhaps he loves her," Jeremiah argued, ignoring Will's sound effects. Wilfred sniffed contemptuously.

"Loves her! Have you seen her close up? Your dad's shire's got a better set of gnashers than that. Loves her old man's money more like."

They were interrupted by the uncertain drone of a solitary plane circling low overhead, flying slowly as if searching for something.

"What's he doing here?" Wilfred had asked. "There've been no raids this evening."

Jeremiah looked up.

"He's probably lost, poor bugger. He's up there with the whole world laid before him and his mates behind him and all he can see is his own end coming."

"Don't give me that," Will complained. "That's a fucking German up there, here to shove it up our jacksies." The plane turned and died away.

"That's right," Will shouted into the dark. "You just bugger off out of it." He turned over. "Come on, Jem. Let's get some shut-eye. I'm jiggered."

The next morning they woke to find a solitary bomb the size of a prize marrow lying smack in the middle of the main marquee. It had been caught in the quartered hollow of the canvas dip with the four poles leaning ominously inwards. It looked like a fish in a hammock, and oddly calm. And they hadn't heard a thing.

"What did I tell you," Will said. "The sneaky bastard. Lost and afraid, was he? Wishing he was tucked up in bed with his fräulein, was he? If ever I catch one of them dropping out the sky I'll put some of our rope to good use and string the cunt up myself. That'll get his end coming."

Everyone had run for cover and stayed there until the army bomb-disposal team from Hitchen came. With his uncle's block and tackle they secured a rope round it and hoisted it up into the air while they all watched from a safe distance. The awning was the colour of Will's puppet show frame, the bomb the colour of Jack Ketch's sombre uniform and when they swung it out, to be lowered into the waiting wheelbarrow, the audience oohed and aahed and inhaled its collective breath. After it was disarmed and the crew trundled it away, a great cheer went up.

"With a bit of luck, that's the nearest one of those fuckers will get to us," said Will over the noise.

"Shh," Jem warned. "Watch your language." Will turned to him, annoyed.

"What's my language, Jem? The same as bloody yours."

They heard a stifled laugh behind then and turned to find the girl looking at them both. Will winked at her and, jerking his thumb over his shoulder as if to indicate his presence was urgently required elsewhere, hurried off. Jeremiah blushed, blushed for the second time in her presence, partly for his cousin's ways and his own awkwardness, but mostly for what Will had claimed they had done the night before. This time she saw his discomfort.

"Don't you worry about me," she said, coming up to stand by his side, watching the men in khaki lifting their trophy into the back of their lorry. "He sings a lot of songs, does your friend, but not everyone dances to the tunes."

They looked after him, weaving his way back to the tents.

"He's my cousin," Jem said, ready to defend him. "He don't mean any harm. He's says he's going to be famous one day."

She put her hands into her apron pockets. "Yes, well it seems in these parts he's quite famous enough already."

Jem couldn't make out what she was trying to say. Had he treated her badly last night? It wouldn't be the first time.

"He's all right once you get to know him."

She turned and faced him. "I don't want to get to know him. If he thinks a couple of shorts is all it takes to get me on my back."

Jeremiah looked down at his feet and blushed for the third time. She studied him for a moment.

"You don't like that sort of talk, do you?" she asked.

Jeremiah shuffled uneasily and kept his eyes on his scuffed boots. She stopped his foot with one of her own.

"Nor really do I."

They were the only ones left on the veranda now. Both knew it was time for her to go back in.

"So what did he say about me then?" she asked. He looked up at her. She was too good to lie to, and yet, how could he tell her? He wasn't used to such delicate matters.

"Nothing much."

"Nothing much! A likely story! Do you believe everything he tells you?"

He forgot himself and laughed. "What, Will? Goodness no. If I believed everything . . ." He fell silent again.

"Yes, well then. Just because it's about us girls and that, don't mean to say he's telling you the truth, now does it?"

He could find no answer in his heart.

"Well then," and she stalked off.

When the wedding was over and the guests had gone, Jeremiah walked back to the house and waited. He could hear them clearing up now, washing plates and glasses, hear the half-formed jokes turn into laughter, see the waves of steam rising out of the iron ventilators set high up in the wall. He walked down the drive and waited. At about ten a sudden shaft of light flooded out as the women prepared to cycle back to the village. She was there, alongside a larger, older woman. Jeremiah stood back on the grass's edge as they came towards him. It was only when she cycled past that she recognised him. She came to a sudden stop, using her foot on the gravel as a brake.

"Still here?" she said.

"We pack up tomorrow," he explained.

"Nothing to catch any more bombs in then. You were dead lucky last night. Could have put paid to your accordion days."

Jeremiah nodded. "That's what I wanted to talk about," he said. "The thing is, I could have played some tunes for you yesterday evening but I didn't want to." She waited.

"I wanted to play them. But not for Will see, nor his fun and games. Just for you." He bent down and picked up the oddly shaped grey case standing by his side. She hadn't noticed it before. As he lifted it, the accordion inside moved and moaned a wheezing chord. "I could play them now if you like."

She looked at this young man standing against the dark sky. He looked serious and full of grave intent. She didn't know what he did, not really. She didn't know who he was, not really, nor what he would turn out to be, but do we ever, she thought. She got back on her bike.

"Not now," she replied. "I've had enough for tonight. Play them for me tomorrow, when you've done packing. I'll be down at my dad's pub in the morning."

Their Accordion Days, that's how they remembered them, of weekends spent in shirtsleeves and summer frocks, with ropes and pulleys and cries of encouragement from the older men, and the sight of her, her hand held against the sun, looking up in concealed admiration as he hammered and hauled and drove his skill into the hard green ground. The sky was the only way they apprehended the war then, the low rumble of the bombers, the pitch-tossed whine of the fighters, the distant dogfight they might claim to see, and with Jem and his cousin as near as humans on the ground could be, poking their heads up into the dangerous air, it was no surprise to anyone that Jem and Judith were married before the summer ended. The whole of the vale was in the throes of snatched romances, official or otherwise, but though there was a quickness to their courtship, it was not conducted in haste. Judith would have found a place for him by her side, at night or at other easier times of the day, but Jem felt no need to leave such a mark on the body of this young woman. That type of branding, that type of woman, was to Will's liking, and that would have been the conclusion his father and Will's father would have drawn, comparing her with their own wives, one dead, one wayward, sometimes seen in town but never acknowledged, never helped. So Judith was formally introduced to the household the following Sunday, in his father's half of the house, with the two elder men sitting at either end of the table while his cousin sat across, grinning at her while Jem served the meal. Though unaware that she was the first woman to have crossed either of the two thresholds in six years, she was apprehensive of being introduced so soon, but if she suspected that Jeremiah's interest in her might be governed by their household needs (often an overriding factor in such communities) the appearance of their dwelling quickly put her mind to rest, for like all men of travelling stock they took a pride in the neat polish of their surroundings. And as for their table! There lay the pick of vegetables, the freshest of fruit and thus, by means of blackmail and barter, a side of ham a whole regiment of ration books could not have captured. So she waited for her plate to be filled and answered their polite questions in an equally reserved manner, aware of their sense of pride, measuring, though not fully understanding, the depths of their ordered, masculine lives. For despite their ruddy arms and sturdy legs, their outdoor life, there was something fragile and guarded about the way they lived, with their silver napkins and polished cutlery

47

and white lace tablecloth, as if they had captured delicacy, tamed it and made it their pet, but were afraid that any day it might break out of its cage and run away.

After lunch, while Will and Jem washed the dishes (and she had the grace not to offer herself—she was their guest and they would have taken it ill had she been so forward) Jem's father took her out the back and showed her the neglected onion beds, complaining at the government restrictions that had reduced the number of hands he could hire. She rolled up her sleeves, took a hoe lying against a pile of wood, and cleared the lines for an hour or more, before it was time for tea and the ride home.

"I'll be asking her just as soon as she's ready to say yes," Jem told his father on his return. "In the meantime she's to become one of us, do you hear. I want to make it impossible for her to even think of another way of life."

At first, when Jeremiah put it to Will that he wanted Judith to accompany them on their Punch and Judy runs, Will was loath to comply. He was a superstitious man descended from a superstitious line, and though women had their place in travelling fairs, the secret world of his papier-mâché folk was not one of them. He feared the distractions she would bring, warning that her very presence might even make a milk pudding out of his hero.

"Punch and Judy is like the Navy," he complained. "No fit place for a woman."

In those early weeks, Jem still nervous in her company, Loopy lumbering about her feet, Will all but ignored her, driving the short distances petrol rationing allowed in silence, as if he were a pilot engaged in a fight to the death, forswearing the use of his eyes or any of his other senses for anything but the danger ahead. It was the weight of extra pennies in the hat that changed his mind, when he realised what a young woman's face rather than Loopy's grinning countenance could do to the takings. (Not that anyone ever told Loopy. No, they found him other work to do, tasks of greater import, wrapping old Mr. Punch up in his black velvet cloth, putting his stick and his length of sausages beside him, laying him out in his box, turning his head to one side, straightening his clothes and thus protected, taking him, and all his companions back to the safety of the van.) After that Will wanted her to accompany them as often as possible. He would draw up outside her father's pub and push open the passenger door.

"Hop in, girl," he would say, as if it were he who was courting her, not his cousin squatting in the back with Loopy, playing pat-a-cake and I Spy and other simple games the poor man enjoyed. She would lean over and give Jem a quick kiss, before examining the bag of fruit Will always brought, not simply the apples and pears that grew in abundance that year, but, thanks to their Covent Garden connections, unimaginable luxuries for wartime England, such as apricots and grapes and, most favoured of all, clusters of tangerines wrapped in translucent tissue paper and smelling of stolen evenings under distant lemon trees. Will had a passion for them and would eat the lot unless Judith intervened. He didn't see it as a selfish act. He was simply showing off his assertive appetite, making an entertainment, and thus a virtue, out of his greed. He would peel the fruit and, scraping the pith off with his little white teeth, would suck out the juice segment by segment, before spitting the discarded skins out onto the floor.

"You're a messy bugger and no mistake," Judith would tell him, "worse than a monkey in a cage. Why can't you eat them properly, like any normal man?"

"It's the juice," Will once replied. "That's all I want in life. The feel of the flesh and the suck of the juice. What's better than that, eh? Here, Jem, have you ever closed your eyes and stuck your face inside a melon? Lovely."

"Will," Judith warned.

"What? What have I said? Jem, tell me what I've said."

"I don't know," Jem answered. "What have you said?"

Will burst out laughing. "I haven't said nothing, have I, Judith?" He poked her in the ribs. "Tell you what though." He tossed an orange in the air. "I'll save one or two of these for every show and throw them out to the kiddies at the end."

Try as he might, Judith would not warm to these conversations, nor the frequent pats of her bare knee, nor the quick driving kisses he gave her on the way home, but if that's what it took for her and Jem to be together, so be it. But soon she became more than their quartermaster or the bottler, for she was a young woman amongst young men eager to impress, and as is always the case, they started to take their cue from her. Will did not notice. All he knew was how she had placed herself at the back of the crowd and watched his performance and how, on the way home, she started to talk him through it, telling him when Mr. Punch's timing had been just so and when it was not, warning him of an opportunity missed or a joke taken too far and though he was loath to admit that an outsider, and a woman at that, could ever make improvement on the traditions of Mr. Punch's parley, he loved his art and recognised well enough when another spoke the truth in his own language. Small wonder he patted her knee and snatched those kisses. So Will embraced her, introduced her to his puppets, and let her stroke Mr. Punch's hook nose and stick her fingers down the crocodile's throat. And while Loopy set up the frame and Jem played his accordion, she began to help him, laying the props and the puppets out in order, even offering to mend Mr. Punch's tattered clothing.

"Patch up Mr. Punch!" Will exclaimed. "Why, he'd rather have an internal examination from a coon-coloured horse doctor than have a strange woman interfere with his clothing. Now Judy is another matter. He'd hate to think Judy had been spending the housekeeping money on needless frippery instead of his beef and beer. Stitch her up some new clothes, why don't you, and let's have Mr. Punch's blood proper boiled."

One Saturday, out with the tents, while she was looking, as ever, to her Jem up above (and he seemed to have become as agile as Will that summer), Will brought his wooden hammer down upon his thumb instead of the stake it was meant to be holding, and as she held it under the garden tap and bound it with her own handkerchief, he asked himself whether he had done it deliberately, to bring her as close to him as he dare without declaring himself, for it was clear, with his thumb swelling to twice its size, that he would only have one hand fit to work his puppets that afternoon. So he drew Judith in and closed the awning behind them and showed her how she must squat on her haunches and to what height she must raise her arm, and, seeing how she was going to work her, how she should shriek and scream blue murder when Mr. Punch appeared. And an hour later, with her fiancé looking on, Judith manipulated her namesake, held her aloft while Mr. Punch beat her about the head and body and threw her dear baby out the window, and with that done, and with Will nodding in encouragement, she raised the crocodile out of the deep, measured the ponderous tread of the police-man and, at the very close, swung Jack Ketch's legs out over the stage and stretched his long and susceptible neck.

Loopy went around with the hat that afternoon, for Will was kneel-ing in the dark beside her, kissing her while the crowd cheered as Mr. Punch took his bow. It was the first friendly kiss he had ever given a woman, the first kiss where he had asked for nothing more, and as soon as it was done Judith pushed Judy aloft for her share of the applause. He saw the mud on her knees and the flush in her face, saw her laughing at the hot thrill of her first afternoon's triumph and he wanted to kiss her again, with the same feeling of friendship but with something else open-ing up at the end of it. It occurred to him that Jem's courtship had only succeeded because his had failed. Jem would not have had a look-in if he had played his cards right. It wasn't Jem she wanted. It was the other side of him! And he was there beside her now. All he had to do was to reach out and pull her close and turn her face towards him and away from his cousin outside.

"That's the way to do it, Judith," he heard Jem say, and the flap was pulled back and Jem's hand came down. Judith turned and looked back at him, suddenly aware of what Will had done, surprised that his lips could convey such feeling, shocked by what might have been had this happened before, thankful that it had not. She laid the puppet down at his feet and, rising into Jeremiah's arms, emerged blinking in the daylight.

"Here, I hope you didn't mind your intended pressed up against me in the dark," Will called up, hoping to embarrass her. Jeremiah held her and shook his head.

"Well, you bloody well ought to," Will retorted, angry that Jem should be so placid in his good fortune. "Mr. Punch has taken quite a shine to that young lady. If I thought he stood half a chance I'd tell him to go right ahead."

"Mr. Punch is married," Judith reminded him. "I don't allow things like that."

"Oh, that wouldn't stop Mr. Punch," Will told her. "He'd turn his wife into a string of sausages if he thought he could get his hands on you."

"Well, he can't," Judith told him sharply, feeling the edge in Will's voice. "Can he, Jem?"

Jem smiled, for he knew something about Mr. Punch which Will did not. Though he had murdered and caroused and drawn his ugly conclusions as of old, it seemed to him in the space of one afternoon that Mr. Punch had changed, not grown softer, as Will had feared, but more pitiable. Like a headstrong sailor who has rowed out too far, Mr. Punch lay in the heavy seas of his own conceit, afforded glimpses of the safe haven he had left behind, but helpless before the strength of his own weakness.

"No, he can't," Jem told him softly. "And I'll tell you for why. She's to be married too. Ain't that right, Judith?"

That evening Will, as always, asked them to go with him for a drink, but they declined. It was soon time for Judith to go home, but before she did Jem sat on the edge of the van with the back door open and played his accordion once more while she danced in her bare feet on the wet grass, with Loopy at first and later, after Jem had sent him off to bed, on her own, in front of this quiet man who never made a move

52

towards her except to mark out the territory of his respect. And when she had danced, they sat together and Jem kissed her like he always kissed her, with caution, before taking her home to her waiting father, to ask for his trusting, honest handshake.

Yes, their Accordion Days, that's how he remembered them, with Judith standing in their small back garden while he sat in the doorway playing polkas into the summer air. They could have stayed in the farmhouse, but Jem was adamant. "Room enough for us I no doubt," he had said, "but not our marriage."

They found a cottage to rent on the edge of their land. Two rooms downstairs and two rooms upstairs, room enough for three, four or even five of them. They didn't care. Despite the uncertainty, it was, in those early months of their marriage, a marvellous time to be alive, for like the keys on his accordion, everything was black and white. Their lives seemed to move to a compressed harmony. He would set off in the morning accompanied by the squeak-squeak-squeak of the front wheel against the battered mudguard. Before his marriage he had barely noticed the sound. It was simply the noise his bicycle made. Now as he pedalled to work it reminded him of the newly discovered motion he had left on his marriage bed. In the evening, his back aching, his arms heavy, the same noise would hasten him home. Three nights of the week he would leave the warmth of his home and cycle to Aylesbury, to lie out on the Town Hall roof upon a carpet of phosphorescent pigeons' droppings and watch for flames, his soul hovering over the blackened town. Every time he saw the telltale flicker he would leap up, run across to crank the stiff handle, hear that rhythm again while above him the siren soared. In the midst of it, he would think of the German pilot and how, unwittingly, that man had laid the egg of his own, sudden courtship out into the night. He remembered the black bomb lying on its striped sheeting, serene and swollen, and he wanted to come home one day and find Judith serene and swollen too, and leaking milk. Out of chaos, order. Out of order, chaos. That was where his heart lay! As England grew darker Jeremiah sparkled. He felt himself part of something huge, unfathomable, a minute speck in a huge tumbling life. He cycled down the roads with his hands held atop his head, his thoughts soaring, his eyes noting every detail. The rim painted round the bath coupled with the falling silent bomb; the inspection of the ration book in partnership with unnamed roads, without signs, leading God knows where. He knew that one day, on such a road, he would turn the corner to find a sign, bright and bold and pointing straight at him.

He wished he knew whether the German had made it home that night, whether he would return, whether he *had* returned. He imagined him flying back time after time, burdened with a lonely duty in which he took no pleasure. He saw him taking his plane ever deeper over this land, his solitary bomb growing ever heavier, the likelihood of him returning to his family ever more remote. One night, when Jem would be cycling home from fire duty, his plane would run out of fuel, he would bail out and Jeremiah would be waiting below, to catch him in his arms. All that late summer he worked in the open air, digging trenches, planting winter vegetables and early potatoes, waiting for him to fall out of the sky. Every time he heard a plane he would look up, half expecting to see the white flower of an open parachute trailing down.

"You know, Judith," he told his wife. "I keep thinking of that German up there, the one that dropped the bomb on us. It may sound daft but I feel I know him. He didn't want to kill us, kill you and me, but there he was flying here to bomb our factories, and do us down. He had learnt his principles and followed his instructions and now he was on a mission flying into enemy territory, dark and inhospitable, with Will and me standing below, shaking our fists at him, wishing him the very worst. And yet he had to stay calm, to look ahead, to see the burning world below him and keep his hand steady. Who knows? He might have had a wife just like you to go back to. And a little shiner. He had his mates to steer home too, and keep their families together. What a brave chap."

"You're talking like one of Mosley's boys," Judith retorted. "He was like that, you know, before the war, the old boy up at the house where we first met. He used to stand in the snug every Sunday after service, pull on his thumbs and brag about National Socialism. Made me want to spit in his beer."

"I'm not talking about Germans. I'm talking about, I don't know, about order, and chaos, that we're a funny mixture of it and in the midst of it all, you have to find your own place and be calm."

"Order sounds like Mosley to me. I wouldn't talk about order in front of my pa when we next see him. My uncle got done over by his mob about four years back. He's dead now. Went down in the North Sea. And where's Mosley now, eh? Safe as houses I shouldn't wonder, with his high and mighty friends keeping his nose clean. We should have topped him and bunged his body out over Berlin."

"You're talking like Will," Jem complained.

"Yes. Well, he can go with him as far as I'm concerned. The sooner you're shot of him the better."

Jeremiah let it pass. Since their wedding, he didn't go out with Will anymore. He couldn't forgive him for lying about Judith. If it had been a lie. When he heard her talk so vehemently against him, he wondered whether it wasn't all true, that Will must have done those things he had boasted about that night. It was not something he could ask him now, nor her, and yet whatever had happened, the two of them had shared an evening of unknown intimacy which held him in thrall. Will had done nothing to correct the impression he had given, not even when Jeremiah had asked him, much against Judith's wishes, to be best man.

"Who else can I ask?" he had said. "He'd never forgive me if I chose someone else. And he is my best pal, whatever you think."

"I'd rather have Loopy than him," Judith had told him. "At least he'd do it for our sakes, rather than his."

Their celebrations had been held in the very tent in which they had first met, erected at the back of the market garden, with the greenhouses forming a shining backdrop. The reflection of the marquee shimmered on their green panes, and from their still interiors had come the pale blooms which filled the tent with blushing colour and heavy scent. Judith had no folk to speak of, so the arrangements were left very much in the hands of Jem's family. His father had brought a band down from London, a group of four men who played a stream of Neapolitan love songs, *"Tuorna a Surriento," "Tu ca'nun chiange," "Catarí, Catarí"*; men, if not directly related to them, then from the greater family fold. It had been a large reception, with friends from the two villages. Only Will's mother remained uninvited.

Jem knew Will would put in a memorable performance. It was, he understood, the best man's prerogative to embarrass the groom and Will, fully charged with his responsibilities, would go to the task with relish. Before he had not minded. This was going to be his day, his and Judith's (he never called her Judy), and though he might not enjoy speeches and public celebrations, he had been prepared to let others have their fun, even if it meant them getting drunk and making fools of themselves. These things he would never do. He would be content to sit at the head of the table, quietly enjoying the quick happy looks from his bride.

It was a good speech and without the crudities that Jem had dreaded. Even Judith had raised her head in the air and smiled. But when everyone thought it had come to the end, and the talking started up again, Will rapped on his glass again and held his hands in the air.

"Before I wind this up," he said, "and we can get down to the serious business of dancing, I am going to demonstrate to you all what sort of a fella Judy has married." Turning on his cousin, Will left his place at the table and led him to the dance floor. He nodded in the direction of the band. They struck up. *"A canzone's Napule,"* Jem remembered. To the amusement of all, they proceeded to dance a long and graceful round. Will took the lead, Jem followed.

"See how docile he is, missus," Will called out, "how easily he is led. He's not the sort to come home at one o'clock in the morning ready to belt you round the ear, is he?"

"Nooo," they replied in chorus, as if a pantomime audience.

They turned again.

"See how quickly he learns, ladies," Will observed. "Like a dog he is, eager to please. *Better* than a dog. This one will polish the floor, carry the shopping, do no end of chores. He'll be doing the ironing in no time, won't he?"

"Yees," came the reply.

"That's two things every wife prays for. A man that's house-trained and does what he's told. Now who can tell me what's the third?" He paused.

"It's no joke. Am I not right, ladies? It's no good having a decent boiler if the stoker isn't up to the job. Now we all know Jem is not used to stoking. As a matter of fact, he's hardly used his shovel at all. To tell you the truth, I'm not even sure he knows where to put it. If you went down to his garden shed and asked him to let you take a good look at it, you'd discover that it was all clean and shiny, like he'd been polishing it all this time. Don't laugh, missus. This is serious. We don't want him digging the wrong hole for himself, do we? But as I always say, if you want to make sense of the layout, the best thing is follow someone who is familiar with the terrain. Now I had the good fortune to walk out with the young woman in question before she saw the light. That's right. In the dark. Only once mind, but I got a good memory. So here and now out of the goodness of my heart I am offering to accompany the happy couple on their honeymoon and at the appropriate moment give him a guided tour of the premises. And after that I guarantee that like the best of dogs, he'll always come when he's called."

Men banged their fists on the table, and women held their hands to their mouths. Will clapped his cousin on the back.

"Oh, Jem," he shouted over the noise. "You should see the look on your face. It was only a joke, sweetheart. You know my motto. Think Filthy!"

Jem brushed his hand away angrily. Judith sat gripping the table-cloth as if she were about to pull the wedding cake clean off the stand. All around him men and women were laughing, taking great mouthfuls of cider and beer. He looked at them in all their befuddled stupidity. He could never be a part of them. Never. He could only look at them with disgust and think himself, why not admit it, above them all. He grabbed Will by the shoulders.

"That's the trouble, Will. Everything's a joke to you, the war, this wedding, *my Judith*. Everything's there to be milked by your dirty comic hand. You never know when to stop. That's not a talent. That's a disease."

That night, their first night in their new home, he had hardly dared to touch her. Will's words had turned his hands into harbingers of thoughts he dare not admit to possessing. How could he demonstrate to her that though they would do the same things, move over her secret places, there was no similarity between them? She lay there burning with shame, afraid to move lest by some precipitate action she might confirm in his mind all that Will had implied. Only in the following weeks did they begin to feel at ease with each other, when the familiarity of their everyday surroundings wore those unwanted defences down. It was the little things that broke the barriers: passing each other on the narrow stairs; catching sight of each other in the mirror while washing in the china bowl on the bedside dresser; collecting wood for the downstairs fire in the nearby copse. Then, as quickly as they had been erected, the barriers fell, and with each breach came the marvellous revelation that their intense and sudden romance could become as healthy and natural as the food on their plate. And then the German came.

That morning he had stood half-dressed by the bedroom window and watched Judith walk back from the henhouse with five eggs in her hands. Her feet were bare, as were her arms, and her hair was as rumpled as last night's sheets. As she stooped to go inside she had looked up at him and waved. She was young and happy and still languid from last night's broken sleep. She had jumped out of bed the moment he had opened his eyes and had left him with only a fleeting brush of her breasts to wake him.

He had shaved slowly wishing they were back in bed. Below he could hear her putting a pan on the stove. When he had come down in his shirt and trousers and stocking feet and seen them bubbling away, he had told her he would take them just like that, two hard-boiled eggs, but she had said no, he needed more than that, and had cut him two thick slices of bread and plunged the eggs into a basin of cold water. He had taken his boots from the bench next to the stove and sitting on their one chair had pulled them on. On the table stood his breakfast, a plateful of fried mushrooms. He sat down and watched her in the yard working the mangle while he ate. There was a rhythm to her arms and to the swing of her hair and the noise of the handle came clear through the door. Squeak, squeak, squeak. When the eggs had cooled she came back and took them out and pressed them down on the cold marble top and eased the broken shells away with the back of a spoon. They emerged white and oval, and they rolled about soft and warm in the palm of her hands. He came up behind her and bit into one of her shoulders. They went into the front room and made love on the floor, still clothed, her hair smelling of white bread and her damp hands running up and down his back, caught underneath his shirt. They did not take long and after it was over she had kissed him once, pushed him off, and had gone back to work in the kitchen. He had heard her singing to herself. It was good when they both wanted to make love quickly, without any expectation. There was no time to make mistakes.

"You going to lie there all day?" she called out.

"I might," he had answered. "Best place for me."

"You won't get any dinner," she said, "or your money or anything else besides."

When he made to leave, her face was still flushed. He knew the rest of her would be too. He lingered at the back door. He would have liked to have taken her upstairs and spent the whole morning with her. It was at times like this, he thought, when they were both fresh with desire, when she would get pregnant.

"I could come back for lunch," he had said hopefully. "Who knows? You might be making supper with a little 'un inside."

"What do I need with a little 'un," she had laughed, handing him his lunch box and pushing him outside, "when I'm married to a great big baby like you? Just eat your dinner. Or you won't be no use to anyone."

He worked alone that day. His father had driven to the station at first light to load the boxes up on the morning freight train. He had taken Loopy with him to help him. By lunchtime they had not yet returned. Jem was not worried. The line was often blocked. Will was nowhere to be seen. He spent most of his time cadging rides up to London, attending auditions, hanging round bars, trying to break into the world of entertainment. If he wasn't careful, his father had warned him, he would get his exemption revoked. Jem ate his sandwiches alone out of his tin box. Judith had cut one in the rough shape of a heart. It lay on top, the last one she had made, the one after their time on the floor. He did not eat it but sat in the empty greenhouse thinking of her a few miles away. He could have spent the whole morning with her. No one would have known the difference. By late afternoon, his father still hadn't come back but another raid on Luton had begun. Out in the potato fields he could hear the muted crump of the falling bombs and the louder pounding from the guns, but the sky was too overcast for him to see anything. The attack hadn't lasted long, twenty minutes at the most, and then, after a lull, the gunfire started up again but this time there was no dull drone of enemy craft to accompany it. The sky was still overcast, with long, tapering threads of thunderous grey racing across a foaming sea of white, layer upon layer of muted colour, moving like shifting gauze upon a stage. Then, for the first time that day they parted to show the timeless blue beyond, calm and pure and full of peace. A shaft of light, as if cut by diamond, sliced across the earth, cutting through the far wood, and the outlying fields. Jem looked up. Flying through the gap came a German reconnaissance plane, spluttering and coughing and falling fast. It flew at right angles to him, nearly five miles out, and as he followed it, he saw a man jump and drop quickly into the trees below, his parachute opening only for the last few hundred feet of his fall. At that moment the plane quivered, caught it seemed by the glancing rays of the sun on the long line of glass. It turned and settled back, as if in recognition of its prey, and began to run in a straight descent. Jeremiah stood and watched. There was no noise to the engines now, only smoke, black and thick, pouring from the plane's lungs and streaming from its belly. It rushed towards him, creaking on the wind, silent in death. He could see the insignia painted on the wingtips, see the colours and the numbers, hear the wings shaking and shuddering. It did not seem of this world, it was too large, too quiet, and too close. Only when it neared the greenhouses, when it faced them head-on, when its propellers suddenly started up again, did it take on life. Jeremiah took a last look at the long line of glass before him, his father's life work and his inheritance. It was about to be demolished before his very eyes. There had been no need for Will's barrage balloons. No need for messy bombs or signs in German. One wounded pilotless plane was all it was going to take.

The plane struck the first greenhouse a few feet below roof level. There was a moment when Jeremiah could see it all inside, when it seemed almost to be captured, suspended like a great stuffed bird in a decorated cage, with a landscape and a view to keep it in perpetual motion. Then it burst through, chunks of glass churning in the air, smashing headlong into the second and the third, and the fourth, from greenhouse to greenhouse it flew, engines screaming. The air was broken into maddened fragments. Jeremiah put his hands to his head while bombs of light burst around him. His eyes were shut but he could see the bones in his hand and thin strips of luminous pink flesh. He stood alone, illuminated in a brilliant broken world. There was danger all around him and he let it swirl about. It was as if he were out on the rooftop again, complete and whole but made of endless whirling pieces. He felt as if he were about to be torn up and thrown in with them. It was here to envelop him. The engines died as suddenly as they had started. Jem took his hands away and looked. The plane hung high in the air. Below stood the last greenhouse. On the trestle table inside the tin box lay the sandwich which Judith had fashioned for his lunch. He had a crazy notion to run in and save it. Somehow he knew that Judith would never cut sandwiches for him again, not with their life pounding in her heart, the juice of him still swimming inside her. The plane coughed and then fell back like some aged bird of prey, thankful for its newfound bed. There was a crumpled sigh and the air grew still again. There was nothing left of the greenhouses except for one wooden door at the far end swinging open onto a carpet of smashed dreams. But he had no thoughts for that. His pilot had come! He would need his help! He looked over in the direction of the fall. The road before him was a dazzling trail of light. He shielded his face from the glare and began to run. A single sliver of glass, removed of its motive power, borne on the breeze, floated gently towards him and buried itself deep in the jelly of his left eye.

It became the secret talk in the pub for years to come. There had been nothing like it since the day they cornered the fox, smashed in its muzzle and threw it snarling into the threshing machine. They were never ashamed, not amongst themselves. When the shutters were drawn and everyone else had gone home, they would have a good laugh over it, how they set off in the van armed with a couple of jugs of scrumpy and the tools of their trade. Will had come back from London that lunchtime and the boys had spent a long afternoon session in the pub. They had all heard the plane come down. Then Barney had come tearing up in his van. He had seen where the man had bailed out, in the wood near where he lived.

"Let's go and get him," he urged them. "We don't want them boys over at Princes Risborough having all the fun." A deserted table, an unfinished game of dominoes and a half-open tin of tobacco, were testaments to their hurried departure.

They found Jeremiah an hour into their search. It was an eerie sight that met them, a glittering man walking in circles, a sodden handkerchief over his eye, as if he were holding an overripe plum to his face. Dark blood caked his features and the slivers of glass embedded in his clothes were luminescent in the half-light. He was near blind with pain.

"By heaven," one of them said, "that's some strange suit the bastard's wearing."

"That's no pilot, you daft ha'porth. That's our Jem. Look what the bastard's done to him. He's cut to ribbons. Get him in the back, boys."

"The pilot?" Jem asked. "Have you found the pilot?"

"Don't worry," someone shouted. "We'll see you home all right."

"I can't see," he cried out. "I can't see."

They laid him out in the back of the van on an oil-stained sheet of sacking. They were singing, as if on their way to work. Their interest in him was only that the sight of him propelled them further in their dark chase. The day had drawn to a sudden close, heavy clouds obscuring the light, as if the world had agreed to be their accomplice and drawn a veil over their intent. Out on the open road, the driver had kept his headlights masked, but once in the wood he ripped off the covers and switched the lights on to full beam. The van bounced and twisted and flung itself from side to side. Someone jumped out and guided it over the worst of the ruts. Jem lay there clutching his screaming head, the legs of men all around him.

"I can't see. I can't see," he called out again, and one of them leant in and whispered, "No, but you'll hear him right enough."

It was dark by the time they found their quarry, hanging over a narrow track by the straps of his parachute. His left arm had been torn off at the elbow and blood had gushed down the side of his tunic, but with his body acting as a weight, the tangled harness, wrapped around the upper forearm, had acted as an impromptu tourniquet. His legs were caught in the glare of the lamps. The men clambered out with whoops of joy. As they jumped out they picked up whatever was at hand: a gardening fork, a wooden mallet, a length of rope. The man called feebly to the men below, hoping that they would cut him down and bind his wound, a request, though understood, they resolutely ignored.

Jem, overcome with exhaustion, had fallen into an anguished sleep, a kind of peace. He thought he had been brought to safety, but though he lay as still as he could, there was no comfort in this rest, only the knowledge that should he wake, his torment would start up again. "The pilot," he wanted to say. "Have you found the pilot?" but he could not. The loss of blood and a sudden thirst would not let him. Then he was awake again. He could see nothing now, but listened to their voices as through a thick red mist. He heard every word. They came from the lips of men he knew, men with whom he worked and played. Though they used words he had heard many times before, though they laughed as he had heard them laugh before, cheered as he had heard them cheer before, lying on that cold metal floor he realised that he had listened to this language all his life without understanding its true meaning. It lay buried in everyone, ready to rise up and engulf the world. It lay within the German hanging from the tree. It lay within the men below. It lay, God forbid, within him too. He had imagined it, at worst, a cruel pastime, like the drunken cockfighting nights held in neighboring farms, when even the local magistrate would attend, and at best, an innocent pleasure found in the circus and travelling shows. Though he could see none of them, he knew them all. They were the same men that had laughed at his wedding, that had cheered for Mr. Punch and taunted dear old Loopy.

"Can't let the bobbies have this one."

"Them'll put him in camp and fatten him up."

"String the bastard up."

"He's already strung up. It's what we do now."

"Well, I'm not cutting that bastard down. Let him rot there, I say."

"Hang on, Fritz, Christmas is coming."

Laughter.

"How much Fritziness do you think he's got in him?"

"A mite too much I'll be bound. Here, Fritz. You hoping for a crack at our nurses, boy?"

"They go for anything, those nurses. It's all that dead meat they handle."

Someone clambered up on the bonnet.

"What you trying to hide, Fritz? The family jewels?"

More laughter.

"Look, he wet himself. Dirty bastard."

"Shit himself too by the smell of it. Get they trousers off of him."

"Bags I his boots."

"Game on!"

They took they trousers off of him.

"That ain't much to write home about there, Fritz."

"Pitiful."

"Slice his bollocks off. My dogs could do with a bit of extra meat."

"He don't half move about. Hold him still, can't you. Let's see what the cunt had for breakfast."

"He's bleeding a lot, by God."

"If I knew he was coming I'd have worn my apron."

"He's not coming. Just breathing heavy."

More laughter.

"My missus better watch out. I'm getting the horn on me."

"Don't I know it. This is better than badger baiting."

"Get you a spade and break his bloody back then."

It didn't mean that much to them, slicing open the man's belly with a great sweep of the hooked scythe, one man jumping up to catch his feet while others reached up and poked at him with hay forks and pruning shears, blood running down the handles. "That's right, have a good dance, Fritz," they cried, and Loopy, simple on his pint of beer, had lifted up his head at his favorite word and shouted, "Steamboat! Dance the Steamboat!" They watched the legs writhe frantically in the air.

"Get that petrol can out the back. Then we'll see some footwork."

Jem jumped out his bed of pain to a scream of mortal terror. The finger of glass pointed out from his eye. Dazzling light stabbed to the core of his brain. He wanted to reach in and tear the eyeball out. Holding his hand over his one good eye he peeked through the narrow aperture of his fingers. He could see the men standing in a circle, leaning on sticks and spades, their breath rising towards the feet of another, hanging in the air. There was a rope tied around those bare feet, and one man pulled upon them, to hold the struggling man still. Jeremiah stepped forward into the centre of the circle. There was a glint of a knife in someone's hands. He snatched it out their grasp.

"Cut him down," he commanded. "Cut him down and save your souls."

He took his hands away and looked up. It seemed for a moment he could see perfectly through the prism of the glass. The man hung there turning in his harness. But not just one man but a host of them, twisting in the colours of the rainbow. Then they slid together again. One man. His German. Still alive. His eyes were blinking. He had come from heaven.

"It's all over," Jeremiah called up. "You're safe now." He handed Loopy the knife.

"You just shin up there and cut him loose," he said. "Let him drop on my shoulders. OK?"

Loopy nodded, put the knife between his teeth and climbed the tall birch. Once stretched out on the high branches, he began to saw through the man's harness. As each strap was severed the man jerked like a dangling puppet on a set of broken strings. Below, the men began to stir again. They muttered and moved their spades along the ground. Someone said something, Jeremiah could not tell what, and they all laughed. He silenced them with a thunderous look. They could easily overpower him, but he knew they would not. They could not. He was in command. The German toppled onto Jeremiah's back. As he walked back to the van, with the body of the man over his shoulder and Loopy and the others trailing in silent attendance, he knew that this was the first of many such journeys. He had stepped into the path of chaos and brought it to a halt. He had imposed order. Order and chaos! Chaos and order! Though there was not a man amongst them who had not wished to prolong their enjoyment, in the presence of this small young man they had felt compelled to desist. He had found his stage.

By the time they got to the police station, the man was dead. Nothing they could have done about it, Will told them. He had ripped himself open coming down. Jem had it all wrong. They might not have behaved like Florence Nightingale, but they would have got him down in the end. Only Loopy knew better, but no one thought to ask him. Jeremiah sat on a chair in the corner waiting for the ambulance to come. Will had come up to him.

"What did you expect, Jem?" he said. "I couldn't let you drop us in the shit like that. He was only a German, for Christ's sake!"

Jem turned his head away. He rode with the body of his dead friend into Aylesbury, begging his forgiveness.

And then at last there was stillness. He was raised and lowered and carried with care and set down in a place of warmth and quiet and there he slept. When he awoke his head was swathed in bandages. He felt the white sheets and heard a stirring near him. Judith was by his side.

He spent many weeks in hospital. Complications set in. Blood poisoning, a high fever, an eye which blossomed and wept thick, glutinous tears. He took time in recovering, longer than was expected. He was languid and did not respond well to medication. It was as if his body did not want to heal, as if it were awaiting further punishment. The doctors were surprised to find such persistent lassitude in such a fit young man. Judith came every day and sat with him. Will appeared a couple of times at the start, standing at the foot of the bed telling him stiff jokes, but Jem was no company for such treatment. Will was awkward with him and Jem knew the reason. He would lose his eye. When the false eye came, a month later, wrapped in tissue paper in a small box, Jeremiah held it in his hand for a moment, looking at the pupil and the dull colour of the iris, before handing it back to the matron to slip in. She greased it and tipping Jeremiah's head back eased it in with her thumb. It popped in suddenly and pressed against his brain. It was cold, cold and hard, and for a moment Jeremiah could not see at all. All he was conscious of was the weight of it and its deep, dread temperature burning at its core like a frozen jewel. He blinked and waited all morning, sitting upright, for his wife to appear. When she arrived he had his hat pulled down over his brow. A pair of pyjamas and his old hat. Judith wanted to laugh but then remembered what she had to tell him.

"What do you think, Judith?"

She looked away.

"That bad, eh?"

"No. It's not that. There's something you must know."

She pulled the screen around them closer, sat on the bed, folded her hands and pursed her lips. Jeremiah's head fell, knowing what it was she had to tell him: that in these weeks of suspension Will had intervened and had won her over again. He could imagine how it happened—a chance meeting outside the hospital, driving over to see if she was all right. Perhaps he had persuaded her to help him once again, working alongside him under the hot canvas, mesmerised by his quick and eager hands. He lifted his head and blinked again.

"It's Will, isn't it? I wondered why he hadn't come to see me."

She put her hand out and stroked his head. "No, Jem, it's not Will. It's Loopy."

With Jem no longer on call and Judith reluctant to help there had been no one to keep an eye on their loose and amiable fool, just Will, and he was crouched down with his hands in the air. They'd done the usual wedding reception the Saturday following Jem's accident and Will had taken Loopy on to a small afternoon fete a mile outside Thame. Will had realised something had gone wrong when Loopy failed to pass round the hat. That and the distraught boy who was left looking for his errant elder sister after the show had finished. They found them both a couple of hours later, Loopy wandering around the wood crying, his hands all bloody, the young woman half a mile away, her head smashed in with one of the wooden mallets they used to drive in the pegs. She had left her brother with his friends half an hour before the show started while she went off and looked round the fair. No one ever found out what had happened, how such a man as Loopy had managed to entice this young woman into the wood, nor what had caused the attack. Loopy nodded to all that was put to him, but that was the nature of the man. You could say anything to Loopy and he would agree with you simply to please. As far as Jeremiah was concerned it was plain as a pikestaff that Loopy should be put away and looked after, but the law thought differently. By the time Jeremiah came out of hospital the trial was over (if you could call half a day of indifferent discussion as to his mental state a trial) and Loopy sat in the condemned cell with two clear Sundays laid out in front of him before the Monday of his execution. The family met soon after Jem's release to discuss Loopy's plight.

"It's a bit thick, don't you think?" Will commented. "Poor old Loopy waiting to meet his maker and all for following Mr. Punch."

"But Loopy!" Jem argued. "I'd never have thought he would do something like this. What got into him?"

"What got into her, more like," Will had said, revelling in a grim humour. "If you ask me, she must have tried something on. You know what people say about folk with simple minds. They make up for it in different areas. Probably thought he had a whopper and tried to get him to show himself or something. Loopy couldn't handle it, that's all."

Jeremiah's father dismissed such talk. As far as he was concerned Loopy had left their fold and that was that. He was adamant. There must be no contact with him.

"He finds himself in the wilderness, alone," he intoned. "It is where he belongs, for it is there, in that barren landscape, where he might discover salvation. It is not for us to come between him and the country of his maker."

Silas nodded. Loopy was to be the second member of the family to be banished. Outsiders all.

"You better behave," Will had muttered to Jem under his breath. "Otherwise you'll be next. Lucky I'm off out of it."

So Jeremiah's father invoked the Bible, and though no one dared breach his barrier, Jeremiah knew that this was not the sole reason. His father wanted to put as great a distance between Loopy and the family as possible, for everyone in the district knew that Loopy had been their responsibility and though no one had ever thought anything of it at the time, the manner in which he had been kept now looked deformed. It was not right to keep a grown man like a pig, in a stall with clean straw and fresh water. It was not right that he should work for nothing more than a stick of sherbet and a few bright coins in his pocket. It had been slavery of the worst kind, taking advantage over a poor trusting simpleton. The family did not defend themselves or ask their accusers, What else would have happened to him? Locked up in an institution? At least with them he had had friends and company, was fed and cared for, and yes, treated like a well-loved family dog, with its place and its ritual and their sense of obligation, not abandoned and discarded, thrown to the indifferent mercy of the State. And yet that is what they did now. Frightened for the first time in their collective life, the family betrayed their principles and enacted the precise cruelty they had attempted to avoid. The faithful dog had turned mad. Time to put him down. In those two weeks before Loopy's execution Jeremiah would spend his waking hours thinking how alone his childhood companion must be, shut away amongst strangers, cold and bewildered, not fully understanding the reason for his plight, but aware, like any frightened animal, that something bad was going to take place. And no friend in sight. When he'd first met Tom Beresford he had asked if he had attended to his old friend, and Tom had said yes he had.

"What was he like?" Jem asked, dreading the reply.

"Just lost and lonely and eager to please," Beresford told him. "He wanted to shake my hand so I let him. I tied his hands very gently, so gently he hardly noticed. 'Why you tying us then?' he asked, and I said it was just to keep his hands still while we went for a walk. The governor had told him what was going to happen, he has to, but I don't think it meant anything to him."

Solomon shook his head. "No, he would have known. He might have been slow, but he wasn't stupid. I bet his leg was shaking. He always jiggled his leg when he was upset."

Tom Beresford admitted as much. "I didn't notice it in the cell but once out on the drop it echoed round the chamber. They could hear it way down the corridor. A ghastly chatter it was, like a death spasm come early. It was a blessed silence when he went down."

Solomon nodded.

"That man was the main reason I signed up," he told him.

"And what was the other?" Tom had asked and Solomon had not told him, only touched the side of his cheek with his finger, which Tom took to be a sign of keeping stum. Only later, when he knew Tom could be trusted, did he reveal that he had been pointing upwards—to the cold glass monarch which now ruled his soul.

Yes, he had blinked. He blinked and he saw. Previously he had two eyes but could only see half the world, the world on show. Now he had one moving eye, warm and weeping and watching, and one still, unflinching, unfeeling, unable to look away from the hidden half of men's hearts and through it he could see the direction he was going to take. He saw more clearly than ever before, as if the blinding light of the crash had drained all confusing shades of light and dark from his vision. He had a new perspective on the world. He had to atone for his murdered German and his forgotten Loopy. He had to take residence in the place where revenge reigned supreme, where men and women faced themselves in the most final of circumstance, and where he could come to their aid. He would make this most unpalatable of dwellings his home, a testament not only to the German's life, and Loopy's life, but to life itself. Precious life would fall broken into his hands, and he would receive it, touched by a grace that had eluded all his predecessors. And if this course of action caused him grief, hatred and jealousy from those already engaged in this work, anger and alienation at home, then so be it. He would not complain.

He wrote to the Home Office two months later. His glass eye watched every word. He told no one of this letter. Why should he? Until he had been chosen there was no need for anyone to know. He waited patiently for the reply. He rose in the morning, worked in his father's fields and went home to his wife. It was strange. Previously he had thought of her as Judith, but now she was his wife. His glass eye saw to that. It was his wife, not Judith, who sat with him in the evening, hoping that the man she married would return. He knew he never could. He was alone now, entering into a world of his own choosing. She had no place within it. He could tell her nothing, bring her nothing, share nothing with her. He must close his very being to everyone and learn to shoulder his responsibilities alone. Judith sat opposite him not knowing what it was he could not tell her. She imagined his silence to be the result of his injuries. She supposed that they affected him more than he cared to admit, that he was worried that she found his disfigurement distasteful, or simply that they hurt him more than he would say. She would try and compensate for all these imagined feelings but at every turn he would look upon her and feel the cold chill of lonely death upon him. He could not tell her what was to come. She would find out soon enough.

His interview at Wandsworth Prison came six months later. It went well, as he knew it would. The only hurdle that worried him was the matter of the medical examination, for though he had recovered fully, he sensed that if the authorities found out about it, his glass eye would destroy his chances altogether. He did not try to hide its discovery, for he had no intention of basing his calling upon a falsehood, but nor did he volunteer the information freely. He would let the glass eye guide him, as it had done the moment it was placed inside his head. It told him to look straight ahead, to fear nothing, and he obeyed. The doctor tested his heart, his reflexes, took his blood pressure, listened to his lungs, asked faithfully about fainting fits and epilepsy and finally, after examining his fingernails for reasons he could not fathom, pointed to the card stuck up on the opposite wall. He didn't require him, as an optician might, to read from one eye and then the other, but simply requested him to recite what he saw out loud. He managed every line save the last. He heard nothing for six weeks. Then one Saturday in early January Judith brought an envelope to him while he was still lying in bed. The government's OHMS frank was smudged on the front.

"What's all this about?" she said, jumping back under the blankets, hitching up her nightdress and putting her cold feet on his. "You done something I shouldn't know about?" and had snuggled up to him while handing it over. Reserved though he was, she still made an effort to draw him close. He folded the letter out and read it quickly.

"Well come on then, what does it say?" she asked, and seeing the heading HM Prison, Pentonville, added, in a surprised tone, "You applied for a job in the prison service?"

He shook his head. He could no longer hide what he had done. "Not exactly."

She lifted her legs away from his and sat up. "Well what, for giddy's sake?"

"See for yourself," he said.

She read it once to herself, and then again, out loud, in a tone of growing incredulity.

"You have been selected to attend the course of instruction for assistant executioner. I should be glad if you would kindly let me know if it is your intention to attend the course."

It made no sense to her. There was no link between this letter and the life they had been leading. Her face, though puzzled, still wore an expression of lightness, of trust, of faith in the future. It was probably the last time he saw it for twenty years.

"What's all this about, then?" she asked. "Is this another of Will's jokes?"

The course lasted three days. He stayed in a hostel in the Euston Road and walked every morning to the prison, where the instructor waited. There were two other apprentices, Harry Firth, who he would work with over the years, and another man who disappeared after the first day.

"As often as not, they don't even last the morning," the instructor had told them. "Many think they can do the job, but once here, it's a

73

different story. And this is just the beginning. Wait 'til you see a live one. That's the real test."

There was much to learn in those three days. First came the examination of the long execution boxes, in which was stored all the necessary equipment. In Box A lay two lengths of heavy chains, some two foot six inches long, two shackles and the two cotter pins for the lever. In Execution Box B he found a folding wooden ruler, a coil of packthread, a length of copper wire, a set of pulley and blocks, two arm straps, two leg straps, two linen bags, two ropes of best Indian hemp with a brass eye at each end, and two sticks of white chalk.

In many ways it was a surprisingly simple operation, escorting the prisoner to the execution chamber, tying his feet, placing the hood and the noose over his head and pushing the lever. Even the formula for working the length of the drop was, for the most part, a matter of simple mathematics. It was skill and speed that counted, and a steady nerve.

"You've got three days to get it right," the instructor told them. "You can make as many mistakes as you like on day one and you can make half as many on day two. But by the end of day three you've got to be ruddy perfect. Otherwise no show. And remember, once you've been selected you never get a second chance. One false move and you're out."

"That is how it should be," Jeremiah told him gravely. The instructor winked at Harry.

"We've got a right one here," he said.

To begin with Harry showed more aptitude than Jeremiah. Harry worked for the Tote and he behaved as if he were still on the race course, enjoying the rush of it all. He was more at ease with the implements, quicker with his sums. He impressed the warders with his bright and cheerful manner. He gave them handy racing tips. He was a card, and they liked him for it. Jeremiah was slower, quieter. He handled the tools carefully, turning them over in his hands, feeling their weight. He did not speak much. He would spend his spare time in the condemned cell, looking at the walls and the bare bed and the door which led into the other chamber. He would climb down and stand in the pit, looking up at the bare beams above and the hooks where the chains would hang. Standing there he knew that at long last he had found his true home. There were matters to consider. He had a duty not simply to learn how it was done, but to absorb the whole process, to become the execution, to experience every nuance of it and to see how the path might be made smoother. Already he could see ways of making his mark. The leather wrist straps, for instance. They were thin and hard. When the instructor had placed them around his wrists they had dug into his flesh. He had said nothing at the time, but made a mental note. It wasn't right. It caused unnecessary discomfort. When he became an executioner he would have straps made specially for him. They would be wide and fashioned from soft calf leather. The condemned man would hardly notice him putting one on.

They took it in turns, he and Harry, to be the executioner (Number One) and the assistant (Number Two), while their instructor played the part of the condemned man. They learnt how to walk into the cell without a sound, how to surround the man, how to have his hands bound and have him following the Number One before he knew what was happening. They practised again and again. Later they were introduced to the bag of sand. Old Bill, he was called. With it, they hanged short men and tall men, overweight men and men made of skin and bones. They hanged men in a hurry and men who fought every inch of the way. They did it in two minutes, three minutes. Their worst performance took six. By the end of the second day they had it down to fifty-five seconds.

"Come on. Come on. Get some speed into it," snapped the instructor. "What do you want him to do, die of old age? Get that rhythm going. Get him trotting onto that drop like he's just won first prize in the county show. Smithfield Market here we come. You've got to get him moving to your rhythm. He doesn't know where he is, see, or what he's doing. You might think that strange but as like as not he's been up all night without a wink of sleep. His nerves are shot to pieces, he's just been singing hymns with the padre and the poor fucker's had no idea that the drop has been no more than fourteen feet away from the moment he stepped into the CC three weeks ago. Suddenly you come in, the door to the 'cupboard' opens and he can see the bloody noose over Number One's shoulder. What? It's your job to get him on that drop before it registers. It's only a dozen steps away. Only you've got to get him there without any fuss. You've got to tie his hands calm and quick. As Number One turns and leads off, Number Two gives him a little push, not hard, but just enough to get him following in Number One's wake. There you are, all three of you trotting along like you was all on Rotten Row taking the morning air. Good morning, Vicar. Nice day for a topping, what? Now you've got him there. You're moving well. Over you go, turn, that's right, Number One, turn, turn and face him and bring him to a stop. Put your hands up to his shoulders and bring him to a halt. Don't grab him; you're not doing the Highland fling at the Hunt Ball. He'll do as he's told. He's never been here before, remember? And unless you cock it up, he'll not be here again. He's not quite sure what he should do. He's terrified, more terrified than he has ever been in his life. He will obey you even though he knows you're going to kill him. He's breathing hard now, staring at that rope. God, he never thought it would be like this. He thought there would be prayers and a long walk. He thought it would be a drawn-out affair, not a quick in-and-out and all over the bedroom slippers. Number Two should have dropped to his knees by now, busy binding his legs together. Not too tight, Number Two. We don't want him to panic, especially now that he can't see anything. Number One has the bag over his head and is already slipping the noose over. Secured that strap, Number Two? Good, 'cause Number One is tightening the noose, adjusting that brass eye under the left jawbone. He won't tighten it to the right, will he, Number Two, because if he did the neck would be thrown forward instead of backwards and the poor bleeder would strangle himself to death and Bertrand Russell would get to hear about it and write a vigorous letter of complaint to the editor of *The Times*. No, we don't want to hear that nasty rattling sound. We want Number One to draw that noose tight under the left chin and then go for

76

the lever, knock that cotter pin out and push it right over. Bang! Down
he goes. Neck broken. Feet together, body still. Still with us, Number
Two? Got off the trap in time did we, as soon as Number One tapped
you on the shoulder? Better look sharpish, Number Two, or you'll be
down there too, hanging onto his legs for bloody life. You ain't got long.
Cap noose pin lever drop. Cap noose pin lever drop. Say it by your bed
before you say your prayers at night. Say it in your sleep. Say it while
you're seeing to the wife in the morning. Cap noose pin lever drop. Cap
noose pin lever drop.''

But bags of sand were only bags of sand. There came the time for
his final test. To witness a real hanging. To stand alongside the governor
and the chaplain and the undersheriff and see if he had it in him to be a
hangman of England. He had travelled up the previous day in his father's
vegetable lorry, his only suit hidden in brown paper between sacks of
unwashed potatoes. He changed in one of the stalls in the men's lavatories near the market. He was halfway through undressing when he realised he could hear someone masturbating in the cubicle next to him. Like
all newcomers he had asked the instructor whether the stories he had
heard about hanging and ejaculations were correct, for from Harry's
demeanour he knew what sort of men he was likely to find engaged in
this work and he wanted it clear in his mind what he might expect. Much
to Harry's evident disappointment, their instructor had told them that
contrary to popular belief, although many prisoners gained an erection at
the moment of death (due to the sudden whiplash severance of the spinal
cord), ejaculation did not usually occur.

"Aren't they ever messy down there?" Jem had asked, and the instructor replied wearily, for it was a question he had been asked many
times, that no, usually they weren't, and told him the reason: knowing
that he is to die at nine o'clock, the condemned man usually loses control
of his bodily functions in the early hours of the morning.

"By the time they're on the drop," he said, sipping his mug of tea,
"they're pretty well empty."

Harry had laughed at the idea of grown men pissing themselves, and warming to the theme, wondered idly whether the women did the same, and being thus embarrassed, bothered to wear any knickers at all.

"I wonder," he said, "if anyone's ever, you know, had one just after they've been topped. Be warm enough to make no difference. And with that muscular spasm you were talking about could be just like the real thing. Better than some most likely. It's a pity they don't take them down right away like. Leaving them on the rope for an hour seems like a waste."

Jeremiah had turned away in disgust. Was he destined to work with men like this all his life? Did they laugh together afterwards, making jokes about death and spunk and the size of a man's parts? He would have none of it. The man in the stall began to talk to himself, urging himself on. He could hear the man's arm beating against his leg, hear the wooden seat shaking against the enamel bowl, hear his feet kicking against the concrete. The pace quickened. The man was in the rushing throes of it and Jeremiah too found himself caught up. This is how it was for him now. This is how it was for all men. Solitary and urgent and without remorse. This is what led many of them to the gallows. Anger and rage and isolation. Jeremiah felt the need to listen to the end. He stood still and heard the man gasp, heard him sigh and shudder and gasp again, heard him stroke himself still, long after he had come, heard him stand up and pull on the bog roll, heard the rustle of paper as he wiped himself down, heard the man screw up the paper and throw it in the bowl, heard him pull up his trousers and buckle his belt, heard the chain pull and the lavatory flush and the man unlock the door and walk out the stall whistling. It was over. Back to normal. He presented himself at the prison gate an hour later.

"In many ways," the warder warned him that night, "what you have to go through tomorrow, watching an execution and not taking any part in it, is the worst thing you'll ever experience. When you're on the job, you won't have time to think about it. But tomorrow, well, there's nothing else to do."

That was not true, Jeremiah concluded, but then it was only a warder speaking, whiling away the hours in the section house, trying to impress upon him, a newcomer, the awfulness of the occasion. The man was wrong. There was a great deal he was going to do. He would watch Tom Beresford. Not the prisoner on the chalk mark, but the executioner. Jeremiah would examine his approach, learn the unseen intricacies of his craft. He would watch Tom Beresford like a hawk. He did not bother to contradict the warder, for holding one's counsel, taking stock, was how Jeremiah intended to make his mark. There was no percentage in shooting your mouth off in this game.

By the time Jeremiah entered the execution chamber, the governor and the undersheriff were already there. The door leading to the connecting corridor was open. Only the other door, which opened into the prison cell, remained closed. It was two minutes to nine. Tom Beresford would be standing outside the cell door by now, waiting for the stroke of nine. The governor looked at his watch, sweating. Up above the huge beam lay across, and from it the chain and the length of rope. The rope hung at head height, coiled round and bound up with packthread. It was cool and quiet, with the morning light shining in from the high window, not as quiet as when he had first seen it, gazing up through the great trapdoors, with the two planks laid across the gap, where the warders would stand if they thought there might be trouble. There were no planks today, though he knew where they would be, down in the pit, alongside the bag of sand, the stepladder, and the plain wooden coffin. By the shortness of the chain he assumed the prisoner would be a big man, though he hadn't seen his neck. The state of the neck made all the difference. A young strong neck needed a longer drop than an older, fatter one, even if the weight was equal. A woman's neck usually needed less than a man's. "How would you feel about that," the examiner had asked him. "Executing a woman?" I would treat her with the dignity I would any fellow human being," he had replied, though he knew that hanging a woman would be different. It was a man's world. There were no women present in an execution chamber, only men. At least when a man died he did it amongst his own. A woman went to her death alone,

79

with the knowledge that an hour later, she would be stripped by those men too.

The sheriff was trying not to show it, but his left leg was trembling violently. He was staring at the noose, with its soft leather wash where the neck would go. For Jeremiah, although the noose hung in the centre of the room and was in all respects the dominant feature, the most potent object was the lever, standing quietly to the side. While the noose transported the prisoner to his death, it was the lever that directed him there. It stood up at an angle, shaped like the lever in a signalman's box. Indeed its intention was much the same, to direct the passenger to his intended destination. That lever, Jeremiah thought, marks the end of the line, and I the signalman, the engineer and the guard all rolled into one. It will be my duty to put the passenger onboard, to take him to his appointed stop, and see that he reaches his journey's end, safe, and free from harm. And I will not harm them. I will make their journey as peaceful as possible. Into my hands they will be received, and I will treat them gently, and without fear or favour.

They could hear voices now, and Jeremiah looked around the room. It was always smaller than he remembered, even though he had learnt and practised in such a room and knew its dimensions. When he imagined it at home, when he closed his eyes and saw himself the master of that room, he always saw it as huge and almost boundless, while in reality it was no bigger than the condemned man's cell. The same size, in fact. Why did this room so grow in size when he was not there and yet shrink when he walked into it once more? The trap was the shape of a rectangle. The length of it, over seven foot, seemed to fill the very room. They were raised up now, marked with a neat chalk line where Tom would bring the prisoner's feet to rest. He had to stand his prisoner spot on that mark, otherwise the man would fall crooked, banging against the sides.

When Tom came through the door the sheriff gave a jerk, as if he had been electrocuted. His hands flattened out against the wall. Though Jeremiah was watching Tom, this reaction registered, and the thought ran through his mind that the other participants, the governor and the sheriff, also contributed to the proceedings, and that theirs was likely to be almost wholly negative. The room that Jeremiah had been trained in, with its long hollow noises and its cool atmosphere, was no more. In its place was a bare cell furnished with tension. It would take a man of extraordinary temperament to smother that charge and institute his own calming influence.

The prisoner followed, walking to a death which he now knew to be only seconds away. Tom was well dressed. He wore a dark suit and a dark red tie and neatly arranged in his top pocket was the white hood that in a few seconds he would put over the man's head, but which for all the world looked like a pocket handkerchief. Deception of course was part of the game. Deception in the door that the prisoner had looked upon for three weeks, deception in the time it took to walk to the drop, deception even in the dapper handkerchief. Like a magician with a rabbit in his hat. An illusionist. Tom's face said nothing. He was looking at the rope, and then Jeremiah saw his eyes take in the room, very quickly, the governor and the sheriff and him at the far corner. He glanced swiftly at the lever and then turned. The prisoner was following directly behind. He was wearing his only suit, the one he had been married in ten years ago, or worn as best man at his friend's wedding. It no longer fitted him well. He was a big man, with strong shoulders. He looked as if he had been a boxer in his time. If he had wanted he could have caused a lot of bother. But that would be unusual. Though they never drugged them, never got them drunk, nearly all went to their death without fuss.

Tom had his back to Jeremiah now. All Jeremiah could see was the prisoner's head, his eyes on the rope. Tom put his arms out and stopped him dead on the mark. It was almost as if he were taking a picture of him, and though he did not step back to see whether the man was standing in the right frame, the way he held his shoulders, adjusted him, he knew he was making certain that he was in the exact position. Tom pulled out the linen bag and placed it over the man's head. The noose followed. He drew it close, tightening the loop with the leather washer above the loop. Behind him his assistant was busy with the leg strap. The air was filled

81

with urgent breath. Everyone was breathing hard. You could see the breath coming out of the condemned man's mouth, see the bag fill out and then sucked in, see the shape of his wet lips through the cloth. The governor's breath was uneven. He was trying to keep it under control, but Jeremiah could see how deeply he drew his breath in, as if he knew that unless he filled his lungs with as much oxygen as possible he would faint. As for the undersheriff, he was panting so hard he had his tongue hanging out. Jeremiah was reminded of a dog he had taken into the yard to be destroyed, how the dog had shook while his father had loaded his gun. He could hear them both, their breaths more rapid, more urgent, almost as if they were with their wives or lovers, performing an act of love. They could not take their eyes off the condemned man. He held them fast, as if he were disrobing before them, tantalising them with his bonded display. He kept so still, his head so erect, his body so straight. Just the linen bag going in and out, in and out and his breath in time with theirs. Tom, bending low, tapped his assistant on the shoulder, and half running, half diving, dashed to the lever. Then the whole floor seemed to collapse, to disappear, not in a puff of smoke, but like that, pulled by an invisible source. And the noise! It seemed to shake the very walls. The condemned man must have heard it while falling, dying with that great boom ringing in his ears. Did he fly to the afterlife with that sound reverberating in his ears? Did he carry it with him for the rest of eternity? Boom! The man disappeared. One moment he was standing there, the next the rope stretched taut, perfectly still. Only the packthread, which had held its deadly coils, moved, spiralling down through the dust-speckled sunlight into the cavernous deep. Tom Beresford looked up at the governor, who nodded back with satisfaction.

"Eighteen seconds," the man called out. "Very creditable, Mr. Beresford." He looked across to where Jeremiah stood. "And Mr. Bembo. Any problems?"

Jeremiah shook his head and watched while the Number Two lifted up the trapdoor by the wall and climbed down into the chamber. Tom Beresford turned and smiled at him. He had passed. The governor was right. It was a creditable performance, but even though he had never seen an execution before, Jeremiah had already seen a way of improving the procedure. The cotter pin was slotted in at the base of the lever, so that the lever could not be pushed accidentally. Tom Beresford had to knock the pin out hard before he could push the lever. It hadn't taken him long, but it had slowed the operation down, and the manner in which he had to remove the pin, under such intense conditions, invited mistakes. The trick would be to insert the cotter pin so that only a quarter of its length was in place, still enough to hold the lever safely in check, but making it much easier to knock the pin out. It could be done as one fluid movement. It would speed things up. He wouldn't suggest this to Tom Beresford, nor to anyone else. He would wait until he became a Number One himself. And then, at his first hanging, he would put this and other refinements into practice. It would be . . . like magic.

When he had learnt what Jeremiah was up to Will had come down to demand that he put a stop to it. Will was on the radio now and beginning to make a name for himself. He was living up in London, though Uncle Jonas would have nothing to do with him.

"What do think you're trying to do?" he had shouted later, standing in their tiny kitchen, brandishing a loaf of bread he had picked up in anger. "End my frigging career before it's started?"

Jeremiah had stood there with nothing to say and looked at his boots. It was a trait which had endeared him to Judith once. She found no pleasure in it now. For once she was on Will's side.

"I mean who's going to hire me for a summer season when they know I'm related to a bleeding executioner?" Will spluttered. "I'm on my way, damn you." He turned to Judith. "Can't you make him see sense, Judy? I mean a hangman, for Christ's sake. Bet you wish you'd stuck with me now, eh, girl? I may put it about a bit, but at least I don't go around the country topping people."

Jeremiah raised his hand. "I'm going to change my name. Not just for you but for the whole family. For our children's sake."

Judith snorted as of old. "Whose children might these be then? Yours? Mine?"

Will had stormed out and let Judith start up again. But Jeremiah would not budge. It was what he was here for. Couldn't she understand that? He would keep the market garden on, restore the greenhouses if she liked. They could even move to Tring and help her father out with the pub if she wanted, but this he had to do.

And for twenty years this is what he did, unflinchingly, without fail. It was his motor in life. Nothing disturbed his equilibrium. Until Stanley came.

"It was all Stanley's fault," he told Jack, smiling at the thought of his only son. "Stanley and Danny Dancer did for me, thank the Lord."

"You were proper shaken the day after, I can tell," Jack Edge admitted. "Never seen you in such a state. I could tell something was up the moment I clapped eyes on you."

"I should have known better, Jack. As soon as I read about it in the papers. I should have known even before they caught him that he was not for me."

"Yes. What was all that about? Were you a relative or something?"

Jeremiah shook his head.

"No, not that. But for the first time in my life I felt uneasy as to the part I might have to play."

"How so, Solomon?" and though Jeremiah heard Jack's inexcusable lapse, he affected not to notice. He was too busy thinking of the crime.

TWO

THEY HAD NOT MOVED AWAY FROM THE OLD LAND, EVEN THOUGH REMINDERS of that sightless day could be found to serve their memories—the abandoned greenhouses still visible along the long stretch of road, their twisted frames now choked by brambles, the shards of glass still poking up in fields a mile away. Jeremiah had kept on the market garden business, selling fruit and vegetables like his father, but there were no more lorry rides to Covent Garden or weekend Punch and Judy shows with his cousin, just him and Judith serving the local area as best they could. The business had not expanded, rather it had folded in upon itself and the subsequent years had been counted out the hard way, in weeks of drought and days of sudden frost, of unseen pestilence settling on spring shoots and early rain rotting the summer fruit. Each day he returned from the fields with limbs which ached not simply from the depth of his labour but with the knowledge that there was no respite from this, no other recompense except that which a lonely night's sleep might bring. He took no pleasure in his work nor the land which sustained them. It was there to be fought. Only on those few occasions when he gained the upper hand did he feel anything close to kinship, and then it was only the momentary empathy the victor feels for the vanquished. He knew all too well that his triumph would most likely be overturned in the next uneven round.

He must have seen them all, Danny, Maureen, Ethel, even Colin, though he could remember only one of them. He went to town regularly, but moved about its precincts as an interloper might, not of a different race exactly but drawn in a different colour, with different shades of grey swirling all around him. He felt estranged from normal folk and was fearful lest his other identity might seep through his clothing. He imagined he must appear to them as some hatted figure in a black-and-white western, walking at the head of a procession with the ghosts of the hanged men of England following in his wake, while the shopkeepers and lawyers and barbers watched nervously through their frosted windows.

He knew many of the people of this town. He had lived near there all his life, but while in his younger days he was regarded as a reserved young man from an eccentric, if moderately powerful, family, now he was seen to have slipped into a charmless backwater. While his neighbours would nod to his raised hat and return his formal greeting when he had passed they would turn to each and mouth that the land had seeped into Jeremiah's bones and turned his soul into a place as dark and as still as the overgrown ditches he neglected to clear on his land. He knew what they were thinking and did not care. No one knew him. The barber who cut his hair and whose parlour was littered with crime-strewn newspapers, the dentist who stared at him with baleful eye and breathed law and order into his cavities, even the doctor for whom he dropped his trousers or bared his chest and whose own hands, he once admitted, itched for the return of the birch and the cat and every other device known to the prisonyard, none of them were vouchsafed his appointed task in life, even though, like him, they were professionals, harbouring professional secrets of their own, and would have understood the need for public, if not private, reticence in such matters. They were permitted to talk only to half the man. The other half was his and his alone.

To that degree he shared company with the poisoner and the strangler, the killers who burnt and buried their victims or sent them to one of the Great Eastern Railway Company's left-luggage offices. The taking of a life was not such a very difficult thing, nor for the most part did it appear a momentous occasion. At times it was almost an inconvenience, though the hunger for the task still remained. At times when no letters of request came, no travel warrants issued, when those black caps remained folded in their judicial velvet bags, he would become agitated, restless, scouring the newspapers for likely crimes which would in due course bring him the sustenance he needed. Perhaps that explained the prisoners' unnerving acceptance of him, recognising in his demeanour what they knew to lie within themselves.

There were some in the town who were aware of his other profession. There was Alcott, whom he had seen rise through the police ranks to become chief inspector at the early age of thirty-six, a handsome and ambitious man driven by a ruthless class-ridden morality, a less-famous version of Scotland Yard's Fabian. They would meet from time to time in the pub behind the square, near the market. Jeremiah could always rely on Alcott to give him useful background information, even in those cases the policeman had had no dealings with, but where Jeremiah might be called upon to perform his final official function. He would learn from him the true nature of the crime and the circumstances of the man's private life, how he had stood up under interrogation and how he was likely to behave when the time came for Jeremiah to assume his other name, and Alcott in return expected Jeremiah to indicate how the man in question had borne up to this ultimate test of manhood. Jeremiah would rarely go into details, but would make brief statements similar to Foreign Office communiqués. "He was a brave chap," he might say, or "The warders earned their pay that night," bare pronouncements whose meanings only the initiate could fully appreciate.

Most of the policemen of that town knew him and his work, as did the local magistrate, in whose house he had first met Judith. So too did Cecil Hardwick, the solicitor who had acted for him when he bought out Will's share of the business. To that extent, when the murder was committed he realised that he must have spoken to Ethel Whitley. She was the pretty, quiet young woman with old-fashioned hairstyle who had sat at the back taking notes. When he read her name he was tempted to pull out the buff-coloured file from his deed box, to see if any of Hardwick's letter had been signed in her hand. Those negotiations had been a messy affair and had matured the bad blood that had started to ferment between Jem and his cousin at the close of the war. All Jeremiah had wanted was to pay a fair price for Will's inherited share, but Will, or rather Will's lawyers and Will's accountant, had disputed the valuation. Just like Will to be parsimonious in his success, to look for jealousy where none was felt and to accuse his cousin of expecting charity when none was being asked. At the height of the impasse Jeremiah had driven into town at Hardwick's request. Cecil Hardwick, known in the public houses as Queen Victoria on account of the roundness of his physique and the gloom of his demeanour, sat him down and waved a letter from Will's solicitors in the air. It informed them that if he, Jeremiah, ceased to undertake "those penal functions of the State which my client believes to be detrimental to the furtherance of his career," then Will would sign over his share of the market garden for the nominal sum of one hundred pounds.

Hardwick sniffed at the document. "It is couched in language which, if you will forgive me, is most imprecise," he had observed. "Not at all what I would expect from a City firm. What exactly is this function they speak of?"

Jeremiah had said nothing, but picked up a sheet of headed notepaper, unscrewed his fountain pen and written one word before placing it in Hardwick's pink hand. Though only consisting of seven letters Hardwick had stared at it for a good minute before looking up, first to the young woman looking inquisitively up at him and then back to his client.

"And our answer?" he enquired.

Jeremiah shook his head slowly from side to side and rescued the note from Hardwick's grasp.

"For your eyes only," Jeremiah invoked him, stuffing it into his pocket. "Do the best you can," he added and without further ado walked out into the fresh air.

Will exacted his revenge. The bank loan Jeremiah had been forced to take out took him years to repay and had put a burden on the business that neither his father nor his grandfather had ever had to carry. There was no easy answer to making it more profitable, only longer hours and harder work. Judith started running a stall in the town centre on market day and Saturdays, though in faith she was pleased to spend the day amongst shoppers, taking their money, learning their gossip, seeing how others led their lives. When business demanded he would drive over with her and help out, marvelling at her transformation. Calling out prices, wielding the large knife while cutting cabbage stalks and cauliflower heads, the years seemed to fall off her and she became the woman he had seen standing on the parquet floor wiping her floured hands on her flanks, quick-witted, self-possessed, and kind. She seemed to delight in an unaffordable generosity, and, recognising hardship herself, would weigh the peas and the beans with such a flourish that the brass pound and two-pound weights carried no meaning at all. And all the while he hung back, shuffling amongst the boxes, unwrapping the produce, tipping whatever she had sold into gaping shopping bags while she moved on. It disturbed him to see her temporary happiness so cleanly on display. He preferred to stay at home, to tramp the lonely fields and ponder on the nature of his strange duty, what isolated peace it brought him, and how, for Judith's sake, he wished he had never married.

There was little said between them now. The rivers of love, the streams of hope, the gentle springs of sympathy, had all but dried up. On those afternoons when he could or would not work, when the weather or his sense of isolation prevented him, he took himself to the cinema. Sitting there alone in the balcony, his feet firmly on the floor, he would sit, a solitary man, with a solitary view ahead of him. Only two types of people went to the cinema in the afternoon, he reflected. Those who were alone and miserable and those who were with another and in love.

If he could he would sit close to such a pair, a few seats in front. It gave him a grim satisfaction to hear their rustlings, the promises of love, the pleas of lust, the squeals and guffaws that came from those darker, carefree quarters, and when he turned and asked them to be quiet, as he always did, he was rewarded with a brief glimpse of legs entwined in slovenly familiarity over the back of the next seat. For a moment he could remember how it felt to while away the hours with your lover in the dark when all the people with cares in the world were working in broad daylight not fifty feet away. Perhaps he had sat in front of Ethel Whitley and Colin Tarrant. Perhaps he had asked them to pipe down. Perhaps they had told him, like so many others had, to get lost. But no, they wouldn't have done that. For all their unexpected immorality, Ethel and Colin were not the sort of couple to raise trouble. Ethel and Colin. Ethel and Colin. Such a quiet, unobtrusive pair.

All that winter they had met in the local cinema. It was too cold for anything else. When Colin arrived, his hands still smelling of printer's ink, Ethel was usually already there, huddled in the freezing foyer, smoking a cigarette or leafing through the fan magazine she had bought at the kiosk. They didn't hang about, for there was no telling who might see them, though it was unlikely that anyone who knew his wife would be going to the Rex Cinema at five-thirty on a cold Thursday afternoon. The old and the indolent, that's who they were forced to mingle with, and they would sit and hold hands while loutish couples made uncouth remarks behind their backs. The things they heard. At least the dark spared her blushes. Ethel did not like meeting Colin there, but it was better than staring at him over a cup of stewed tea in the mock-Tudor café out on the bypass and until he took the plunge, that was as close to him as she was likely to get. She was no better. Twenty-three and still living with her mother! So their Thursdays followed the same routine. She was usually finished before five, and he would meet her half an hour later and they would sit through what was left of the main feature before he took her home.

"Why can't we ever see a film straight through, from beginning to end?" she would ask, staring out the car window on the bend before her mother's road.

"You know why, pet," he would answer, and lean over to open the door. "Better not be too late."

But now it was spring, and they abandoned the third row from the back for a drive out to the Beacon, which despite its beauty was quite deserted, thanks to an incident last summer when a teenager had had his left hand blown off by an unexploded shell. During the war the grassy slopes had been used for gunnery practice, something that Colin himself knew all about, having spent much of his call-up time down on the gunnery range at Lulworth Cove in Dorset. There were plenty of unexploded mines there. There were, he thought, plenty of unexploded mines everywhere. They would park the car and go for a brisk walk up the steep chalk path that led to the top. On a good day they could sit down and look out over the roll of the vale all around them. Alone with him, on that high hill, Ethel was reminded of the previous summer, and she often had the urge to kick off her shoes, lift up her skirt and run down the grassy slope. Colin wouldn't have any of it.

"Keep to the path, Ethel," he once said. "I don't want to have to take you home in a carrier bag," and he kissed her and pressed his beard on her skin. "Though there are bits of you," he added, "that I wouldn't mind keeping for myself."

So they sat with their arms around each other looking out, and after a while returned to the car, turned on the heater, and stayed there while it grew dark. Later they went to the nearby roadside pub for an hour before he drove her back to where her mother waited, ready to disapprove.

"There's no future in it, Ethel," she would say, "either for you or him. He's married. Same as you should be," and Ethel would tell her mother to mind her own business and run upstairs to wash off the smell of him, lying in the bath, remembering what it was like when he lay in the bath with her, her feet under his armpits. She had stood up in the bath that first morning and let him wash her. She had never had a man's hands soap her body before (she had never had anybody soap her body before), and she watched fascinated, as if it was happening to someone else, looking down at his slippery fingers sliding over her breasts. Round and round his hands went, all over her, *everywhere,* but always returning to her front. She could hardly wait for summer to come again, for despite all that had happened, they hoped to go away again, as they had done the year before. It had been a wonderful few days, walking in the Lake District. They had spent every daylight hour drinking in the summer air, talking of the future, *their* future, and in the evening had gone upstairs brazenly early and lain in bed listening to the folk in the bar below. It had given her a proper taste of Colin that week, and afterwards her working hours were filled with memories she played over and over again, sitting on drystone walls eating cheese and pickle sandwiches, holding the Ordnance Survey map trying to find a lost path, leaning back on her elbows while making love by a sunlit waterfall, giggling drunk in bed. They had fitted so perfectly. The more they were together, the more she wanted all of him. Her mother had thought she had gone camping with a girlfriend of hers.

"Get you," she had said, looking her daughter up and down as Ethel walked through the front door. "Done you the world of good, away from him," and it was true. She felt fantastic. Her skin was ripe, her legs were strong, and inside, she simply glowed.

"All that beer," she joked and indeed, that was the third part of the equation, the walking, the sex and the beer. She had never liked beer before, but that summer she developed a real taste for it which was to remain with her all her life. It had started that week when they had gone down to the bar on the second night and had got talking to the young man sitting alone up at the bar. He was unlike the rest of the customers, for while they wore pullovers and jeans, and were at ease with the outdoor life, he wore a dark, dirty black suit, and looked more like a waiter than a happy wanderer. He seemed lonely too, and Ethel, full of good spirits, gave him a broad smile and a good evening as they stood up at the bar waiting to be served. She ordered her usual.

"Can't drink rum and Coke," he had told her, only partly in jest. "That's a tart's drink. You're not a tart, are you?" and waving her protests aside had bought her a pint of beer. Not a half, but a whole pint.

"Get that down you," he said as she looked at it with horror. "That'll put hairs on your chest," and much to the amusement of both of them, she had drunk it there and then, without so much as a blink of an eye. Drinking beer was a much easier business than she had imagined. She didn't know what the fuss was all about and now, when she put her mind to it, she could drink a pint faster than anyone. She simply opened her throat and poured it down.

"What's she got under that jumper of hers?" the young man had asked Colin, "two camel's humps?" and they all laughed, even though Ethel didn't tolerate that kind of talk, especially from strangers.

Danny was his name, not that she could remember everything about him, because most of the time, when they met up with him, she was under the influence, if not drink, then from a long walk and a hot bath and Colin on top of her not ten minutes beforehand. "Fresh-faced," she told them later, "with a sly grin on his face." But it was his eyes she remembered most strongly, quick eyes, watchful eyes, eyes that didn't miss a trick. He was in charge of a group of boys, the Nettle Boys he called them, boys with plenty of sting to them, boys between twelve and sixteen, dumpling boys with down on their faces, weasel boys with un-easy laughter, boxing boys with the stares of men. He had brought them on an outward-bound course up from Luton (a coincidence they could have done without, for Colin's wife had relations over there, a brother and his wife, and her family was the last thing they wanted to be re-minded of), but as far as Ethel could see, the older boys spent most of their time drinking in the pub or sleeping it off in their tents down by the river. As long as they didn't cause him any bother, Danny seemed quite content to let them drink themselves into oblivion, though if any of them got out of hand it was a different matter. They had seen that the last evening when one of them had tried to pick a fight up at the bar. Danny had walked over and without warning had punched the boy hard in the throat, then once again for good measure in the pit of his stomach before leading him outside to be sick.

"Don't look so shocked," he had said on his return. "It's not the Girl Guides I've got under my wing."

Later that night as they lay in bed listening to them singing their way back to the campsite, Colin remarked that it was quite wrong for someone like Danny to be in charge of such an impressionable group, for he seemed to be pretty much a Nettle Boy himself. He'd admitted as much earlier that evening, after he'd made that pass at Ethel when she was making her way back from the toilets. He was going to the gents and had to squeeze past her in the narrow corridor. They were both tipsy. He had stood aside as she came up and as she turned sideways he suddenly pressed up against her and put his wet lips to her face.

"You could do a lot better for yourself than that," he said, a little too loudly, jerking his head back to the saloon. "He's got no spunk, Ethel. Not like you, I can tell. You've enough for two. Just like me. If we got together we could swim in the stuff," and he came up again unsteadily, and kissed her on the mouth, losing his balance slightly as he did. She pushed him away and he backed off, grinning.

"Bit out of line that," he said, "what with me not married a year, and you spoken for. It's the drink. Always affects me like that. It don't mean nothing," and he had stood there rocking on his heels as she made her way back to their table.

Despite the apology, she knew he hadn't meant it. If it had been anyone else she would have slapped his face or given him a good earful, for she hated that sort of thing, men whistling at you, touching you up in bus queues, making a nuisance of themselves while you were standing in line for half a pound of mince. But that week had released something in her, something she wouldn't be putting away in a hurry, and when he had leant up against the wall, looking at her with those gleaming brown eyes of his, daring her to do something about it, she had nearly pulled him in and kissed him back, just for the hell of it. She didn't tell Colin, for there was no harm done, just a young man with too much beer inside him, but when she and Colin got to bed that night she could hardly stop to catch her breath.

"What's got into you?" Colin had said, but he knew. It was the last night of their holiday. Danny's too.

"You know," Danny had said, as a great roar went up in the games room, "it may seem funny to you, me being in charge of that lot in there, but I was one myself, see. A real tearaway. Housebreaking, car thieving, bag snatching. I did the lot."

"What stopped you?" Ethel had asked. Danny smiled and waved his arm over the two of them.

"A lovely young girl from over the water. Twenty-one and never been kissed. So we go courting, see, and before I know it I'm engaged. And what do I find out then? Only that she's the sister of the local dog-collar merchant. So here I am the proud owner of a lovely wife, a babby on the way, doing my bit for the Holy Catholic Church, and, if I plays my cards right, a permanent stall in the local flea market. That is if I can get His Holiness to loan me their poxy van."

"What do you sell?" Colin asked.

"Whatever the old dears want. A bit of this, a bit of that."

"Not to mention," Colin added, trying to ingratiate himself, "a bit of the other."

Danny looked at him hard.

"No. I don't hold with that. Not as those who are married. Not decent girls. Tarts is different. You can do what you like with tarts. Rubbish in this world and rubbish in the next. They don't count. If I ever caught Eileen playing me for a fool I'd swing for her. And the babby too."

"You don't mean that," Ethel said.

Danny was insistent. "That way she'd never leave me. That way we'd be holding hands in hell."

96

All the rest of the evening he had looked at Ethel's fingers resting on the table. The cheap ring she had bought at Woolworth's hadn't fooled him for a moment and despite his stream of good-natured jokes and friendly inquiries, Ethel had the impression that he didn't approve of them at all. He was more inquisitive than was necessary, wanting to know where they lived and what they did and how long they had been married. Ethel had left all the false trails up to Colin, who talked about their two-up, two-down and their little garden out the back as if they'd lived there all their lives. Listening to all these stories seemed to her to point out the emptiness of their real life together, but Colin seemed to enjoy telling them. To cap it all, he wove a ridiculous story about his first wife being *dead*.

"I'm sorry to hear that," Danny had said. "Unexpected, was it?" and Ethel nearly jumped in with, "Well, it took *me* by surprise, I can tell you. Remind me, Colin. How *did* the old bat pop her clogs?" Colin mumbled something about not wanting to talk about it. If he hadn't wanted to talk about it why did he mention her in the first place? Why couldn't he have pretended that they had been married quite recently? He didn't need a dead wife to excuse their age difference. He wasn't that much older. As a matter of fact, why did he have to mention marriage at all? This was 1963, for Christ's sake, not Victorian England. And what bloody business was it of anybody else's anyway?

"What was all that about?" she had asked him when they got back to their room. "Why did you have to bring Maureen into it? I mean, the one time we get away from it all and up she pops, the matrimonial corpse." She was angry and flung her jersey clear across the room. Colin came up to her and kissed her on a reluctant cheek.

"He was getting too nosy," he explained. "It was the best way to shut him up. A death always stops these buggers in their tracks." His hands moved down as he pulled her closer. "I wish she *were* dead sometimes. Wish I could be with you like this every night," and he kissed her again and she forgot about Danny and his bad boys and Colin's yet-to-be-dead wife. Forgot until the next morning, when they had to pack up and head for home. They had a late breakfast, one last walk across the fields, a cry back in their room finished off with a final, tender lovemaking, quiet and sad, before coming down just before twelve for a farewell drink with Danny, foolishly promised the night before. He was waiting for them at the bar, while his boys held one more rowdy darts match with as much illegal beer as they could drink.

"Hark at that lot," he had said. "They're in no hurry to get back. Me, I can't wait. I expect you'll be glad to get home too, what with the garden and that. Who knows, if I get the van, I might drive over one evening and give you both a surprise. Easy to find is it, your place?"

"There's not much point in giving you our address," said Colin rapidly. "We're moving shortly."

"Oh yes?" said Danny, half smiling, and not believing a word. "Don't want a bad penny like me turning up in front of your new neighbours, do you?"

Ethel stepped in quickly. "It's not that," she said, "but our plans are a little uncertain. But we often spend our evenings out at a pub near the Beacon. It's lovely up there. The Dog and something, I think it's called, isn't it, Colin?" Colin nodded with a surly expression on his face.

"The Dog and Something," Danny had repeated. "I'll remember that," and they had all walked out together and stood, side by side on the asphalt car park while one of the Nettle Boys took pictures of them all, Danny in his scruffy suit, leaning against the bonnet, Colin and Ethel with their arms around each other, and the boys kneeling all around. After it was taken and Colin was walking back to collect their luggage, Danny had caught hold of her arm.

"No hard feelings, girl," he had said, squeezing her hard. "But you shouldn't be here," and with that remark, which travelled with her all the way home, he climbed in, started the engine and threw the van into gear.

"Mind he keeps his eyes on the road," he called out. "And keep a look out for us while you're at it. I wouldn't trust this heap to last the distance even if it had been blessed by the Pope himself."

Colin had dropped her off back at Crewe and driven the rest of the way home by himself. She wasn't going to see him for a while, for no sooner did he get home than he and Maureen were off for their annual week's holiday down in Dorset.

"I can't pretend I'm not jealous," she had admitted, while they waited for her train to pull in.

Colin put his arms round her. "Don't you worry, pet," he said. "This time next year everything will be different."

Eleven years Colin and Maureen had been going there. Eleven years since he had first met up with Maureen's brother, Frank, while doing his National Service. The way he told the story of that sorry romance Ethel didn't know whether to laugh or cry.

Colin and Frank Tapp had been in the same platoon, and though Colin had never cared for him, for Frank was fly and quick to temper, it didn't do to make enemies in that isolated world of disgruntled young men. At loose ends one weekend he had taken up Frank's offer and gone home with him to Aylesbury. Frank had a wife there, Avril, and a nine-month-old son, Ivor, but what he missed most of all were his dogs. He kept them for hare coursing. When they got there on the Saturday afternoon, Avril was nowhere to be seen. An empty pram stood in the hall. Frank dropped his kit bag at the foot of the stairs.

"Avril?" he had called up.

"I'm upstairs, washing me hair."

"How they been then?"

"What?"

"How they been? Dodger and Bosun? Is Nigger still off his food?"

"Can't hear a bloody word. Come up here or you'll wake the baby."

"Nah. They know I'm back. I can hear them whining. I'll just go and say hello. Make sure you're decent when you come down. I've got someone with me."

"You what?"

Frank took him out the back, to a long bare garden surrounded by high fencing where three bent and hollow dogs roamed about looking for something to do. For all his talk they didn't seem to care for Frank much, though with their thin faces and faraway stares it was doubtful they could care for anybody.

"Not allowed to keep dogs on this estate," Frank had said. "Had some bastard from the council round once, threatening me with an eviction order. Stupid cunt." Frank laughed.

"What happened?" Colin asked.

"I let Avril loose on him for half an hour, then came back and found him, trousers round his ankles and his pecker in her hand. Told him he'd been a naughty boy and if I ever caught him around here again the old man would get him sacked and I'd kick his bollocks in." Colin was incredulous.

"Didn't she mind?" he asked. Frank shook his head.

"Avril does as she's told. Otherwise she gets a good hiding. Anyhow she probably enjoyed it."

"But for a dog!"

"I'd do anything for them dogs. Part of the family they are, and that's all that should count, family." He looked up to a frosted window covered in condensation. "Oi. Avril," he shouted, "get your arse out that bath and come and make yourself useful. We're starving down here."

They uncapped a couple of bottles of beer and drank them by the open door. The dogs stood in a moth-eaten line and stared at them mournfully. There was a cramped emptiness to the place which made Colin think of prison. He wished he hadn't come. Avril came down a quarter of an hour later. At fifteen she had ruled the school yard. Now, despite the fluffy angora jumper and the eyeliner she looked nineteen going on thirty. Pale and pasty and desperate to get out.

"At last," Frank said, smiling. "Come here." He put his hands round her waist and looked her up and down.

"You put on weight?" he asked.

"You got any fags?" she replied. She pushed past Colin to the gas cooker.

"How's Ivor?"

She sniffed.

"Now he asks. Pain in the arse if you must know. Your mum called round yesterday. We're going round there for dinner tomorrow."

"That'll be nice."

"That'll be the first time I've been there since you were last here. Ignores me for three months and then as soon as she knows you're back—" She leant against the stove and blew smoke into the room. "And who's this then?"

"Colin. A mate of mine. One weekend pass and nowhere to go."

"So you thought you'd show him Moorefield Housing Estate. He must be desperate." Frank crossed over and took the cigarette from her lips.

"Now don't take on so. We'll all go out tonight," he said, giving her a placatory kiss. "Fix us up some tea and then go and put on something that'll get you into trouble."

The three of them had gone out, leaving Little Ivor to fend for himself. Colin had offered to stay behind and baby-sit.

"Nah. It's all right," Frank said, as they walked out the front door. "We done this loads of times. Avril adds a drop of cider to his feed. That puts the little bastard out all right. You need a night out, don't you, sweetheart?" His voice dropped. "That's not all she needs either," he said, and together they watched her tight bottom waltz down the street. "Good job I dropped in on the barber's last week and got some weekend passes," he called out. Avril looked back and winked. She was no longer married, alone every day with an unwanted baby to look after. She was a young woman again, out for the night. Radiant.

"I thought you were Catholic," Colin said.

"I am, but don't tell the Pope."

They had taken a bus to a pub in the centre of town where they bumped into his sister, Maureen. She was annoyed that Frank had turned up with his tarted-up wife. Not that it stopped her date looking at her tits all night, Colin noticed. He wasn't the only one. It was difficult to avoid them. She laid them on the table the way he was meant to spread the contents of his kit bag out every morning back at camp—ready for inspection. Frank sank back and bathed in their hypnotic glory.

"Don't get many of those to the pound, eh?" he declared whenever Avril leant forward to light her cigarette. After the fifth such observation, Maureen, dressed in a no-nonsense jumper and plain skirt, could stand it no longer.

"Pity Little Ivor's missing out," she remarked. "He must be the only male in Aylesbury who couldn't draw me a map of that cleavage." Avril breathed in deeply and tucked her wayward bra strap away.

"Wait till you've got ten pounds swinging from one to the other like bloody Tarzan," she advised, smoothing her front down. "Then we'll see how you like it. Anyhow, breast-feeding isn't hygienic. They can harbour germs."

"Depends where they've been," Maureen observed.

"Me and Maureen are getting engaged after the Budget," her companion offered by way of conciliation. Maureen pulled another face.

"Don't spread it about, Oswald," she snapped back. "We don't want to be giving the Chancellor of the Exchequer any ideas." Colin sat back in awe.

The next day they had trooped round to his parents' house for lunch. Little Ivor came too, beating his fists against his tiny hungover head. They were a well-off family, wealthier than Colin's mum and dad anyway, with a mahogany radiogram that dominated the front room. Frank's parents were not pleased to see their son. Duty had prompted this invitation, not affection. Frank had let them down. Luckily they still had Maureen. Maureen was classier than her brother, classier than Colin, and older than both of them. From the way she bustled about, Colin could tell that like her father, Maureen aspired. Last night, sitting next to the petulant and wriggling Avril, she had looked staid and matronly, but here she possessed a fevered domestic sexuality, overwhelming in its intensity.

It was she who ran the home, not her parents. They sat back and did as they were told. It was she who poured out the sweet sherry, not her father; she who fussed over the cushions and antimacassars, not her mother. When it was time to eat, she herded them all into the dining room and told them where to sit. It came as no surprise to Colin when she rolled up her sleeves and flashed the carving knife triumphantly in the air.

She sliced the boiled beef with brutal efficiency. Two and one-half cuts apiece. She sat down, tucked her napkin into the top of her brooch-fastened blouse and proceeded to dominate the conversation. She had opinions on everything. Red China. Lady Docker. *The Goon Show.* As Colin was the only guest she devoted all her merciless attention to him. Where did he come from? What did he think of the A-bomb? What did he intend to do with his life? Colin was amazed. She was flirting with him and the whole table knew it. He found her irresistible.

After lunch the four young people played table tennis in the garage. Maureen surprised him by beating Avril without dropping a single point. Colin won his match after he discovered that Frank had no backhand. The losers left to take the dogs for a walk. She picked up the bat and threw him the ball.

"What a carry-on," Maureen said, watching Avril totter after her brother in her awkward high-heel boots. "Mum says he'll rue the day he ever set eyes on her. Did you see what she was wearing last night?"

Colin wanted to bury his head in her staunch breasts and feel the full fury of her wrath.

Like the rapid succession of questions she had subjected him to at lunchtime, Colin returned her quick-fire service with unruffled composure. He knew he could not win, for she was stronger, faster and more accurate than he, but he could give a steady response to her fierce ability. She drove him relentlessly from one side to another, had him lunging for the net and scuttling helplessly to the back wall. She waited patiently while he stopped to get his breath back. After a while it became clear that while retaining the desire to win, she would often choose to prolong a point and see him dance to her tune before finishing him off with a final smash. He was happy to oblige and she admired his steadfast reliability. They played game after game. When they changed ends they could smell the nervous excitement on each other.

"If you don't mind," he told Frank on the train back to camp, "I think I'm going to make a move on her."

"Just remember," Frank had said. "She's my sister. Nearly as important as one of my dogs."

After that Colin saw her whenever he could. His rival dropped away without a murmur. When her parents left them alone for the afternoon they would dance to her collection of Victor Sylvester records in the confines of the front room. He would hold her, kiss her perfumed neck and feel her broad and rigid body arch with what he took to be desire. Before they got too hot and flustered he would break off and suggest another round in the garage. His game was improving. Though the configuration of her body, and more particularly the strong undergarments that surrounded it, were a source of much conjecture on his part, there was no sex to speak of, not until the night of their Christmas treat, when they came back from London after seeing a West End pantomime. Colin had no idea the show would be so rude. Maureen had spent half the evening with her hand in front of her mouth, her body rocking with suppressed laughter.

"That comedian was worse than Max Miller," she told him coming back on the train. "I'm surprised they allow him to get away with it."

"I'm surprised you understood half of it."

Maureen leant over and smeared his lips with her own. "Just because I don't tart myself up like Avril doesn't mean I'm a complete prude. You don't have to be afraid of, you know, being a man."

It was as if a spring had been released. It was all over before either realised exactly what they had done. She came down a month later and told Frank the inevitable news. He marched her over to where Colin was waiting.

"You stupid pair of pillocks," he told them. "After Avril and me I thought you two would be more careful. This could kill the old man. You better sort yourselves out before he catches on." He poked Colin in the chest. "And if this one here puts up any resistance send him over to the Naffi. I'll be waiting."

They honeymooned in the Castle Inn, the best hotel in Lulworth. Her father paid. It was there that the patting of the sofa first occurred, in the empty lounge reserved for residents only. It was all very well, she said as he sat down beside her, carrying on like two lovebirds *here,* but he better understand that when they got back, *fun and games* were over. She had let her parents down getting into the same sort of fix as Avril. If Colin hadn't taken advantage of her, none of this would have happened. Anyway, once this one was born there wouldn't be time for another, not by a long chalk. They had money to earn and money to save. They couldn't live on her parents' handouts for the rest of their lives. So after this no more. And seeing she meant to keep to her religion, there was no chance of very much . . . you know. It wasn't worth the risk. So he better get it off his chest while they were here. With that settled she patted the sofa again. "We could go upstairs now if you like. Before dinner?"

He performed his duties as quickly as he knew how, then fled to the bar while she made herself ready. At the meal he watched her sawing away at her steak, snapping at her chips in long, carnivorous starved intervals, oblivious to the turbulent waters she had cast them upon. Had he misunderstood what she had said? His face would question her. She would smile back at him and reach over to pat his hand.

The honeymoon turned into a polite formality, breached only by demonstrations of Maureen's relentless determination. She became impatient whenever she caught him lingering, whether it was over a meal, a kiss, or an early evening bath, detecting signs of an incipient indolence that she was determined to stamp out. In her book nothing should last more than the time it took to do it as efficiently as possible. He spent the days sitting on the shore looking out over the dull water and the tiny waves lapping aimlessly at his feet. Describing an almost perfect circle, for all its outward beauty, he came to regard the cove as a lifeless entity, a stagnant pond, still and acquiescent and without hope. Like his marriage, an implacable barrier sat across the entrance. No matter what power the sea possessed outside, once it slipped over the long finger of rock which stretched, half-submerged, across the cove's open mouth, and found itself trapped by those high, crumbling chalk cliffs, its will was quickly suppressed. By the time it arrived onto the shore it was feeble and without strength, fit only for rubber-ringed children and pale hairless creatures in woollen bathing trunks.

Since then they had gone there every year, and every year the cliffs seemed higher and Maureen's mouth ever-more treacherous. How oppressive it must be for Colin, Ethel felt. Yes, he was right. Next year would be different. Next year Maureen would be going to Dorset and that chalk prison all by herself. But knowing that Colin had to go there with her now made Ethel uneasy.

Four days later the letter came. They had been found out, and considering his wife's condition, he was putting a stop to it before things got out of hand. "Don't bother to reply," Colin had finished. "For I will not even open the envelope." Ethel couldn't believe it. How could he do this to her, after all they had said to each other? And what was he talking about, her condition? What condition?

How Maureen had found out about them they never knew, but Ethel thought she might have had Colin followed. There was a debt-collection agent in town who doubled as a private investigator. Ethel knew him quite well. His name was Lawrence Wheatcroft, an ex-policeman like all his breed, who had left the force under a cloud. A keen cross-country rally driver, he had let his enthusiasm for positive motoring get the better of him and had wrecked two of Aylesbury's three new Panda cars within the space of a week. He had been dismissed before he could get near the third. Lawrence did a lot of work for the firm Ethel worked for, serving court orders, identifying corespondents, tracing the odd runaway daughter, and had gone through a messy divorce himself. He had spent an illicit weekend with the dentist's assistant who worked across the hall from his office, a bosomy lass with buckteeth, and had been caught out by a rival based over in Stevenage. Ethel's firm had handled his papers. She remembered him coming in that morning in his rumpled suit and his shirttail hanging out the back. It was the indignity of being snared by another agency that had riled him.

"You would have thought," he had remarked to Mr. Hardwick, holding his wife's divorce citation in his hand, "vis-à-vis professional etiquette, that the bugger would have had the decency to slip me the nod. Mark of the brotherhood and all that. It's not as if it would have cost him anything. But no. Followed me down to Swanage without so much as a whisper. Two days he spent there. Seafront room. Balcony. Private bathroom. I've got the bill back home to prove it. Wife maintains that I should pay for half of it. Says it comes under the household expenses. That can't be right. Dearer rates than me too, the cheeky sod."

His pending divorce seemed a minor inconvenience. He made no apology over his behaviour, simply shrugged his shoulders and said, "As I told the wife at the time, it's one way of getting your fillings checked."

After the divorce was through he had asked Ethel out a couple of times. Not out for a drink, or to the cinema, but odd events far afield: a bell-ringing contest in Salisbury Cathedral, a riding display given by the Dorset mounted police (with free drinks in the VIP tent afterwards), and most brazen of all, a wine-making weekend down in Bournemouth. All involved a lot of driving. Each time he had seemed genuinely surprised when she declined, and then dismissed the rejection with a shrug of his shoulders, and wandered off with the air of an aggrieved ticket tout to offer them elsewhere. How many women took him up? she wondered. Was that all it took, an invitation to an event plucked from *What's On in the West Country?* And how did he pick his victims? Did he simply rely on the law of averages? How else did he get his discoloured fingernails on the effervescent Miss Mutton, who looked like the South African television star Michaela Dennis but without the exotic pets? A strong-minded girl, smart and conscientious but not the most discreet when it came to her employer. Ethel had come across her when she'd gone in for her very first checkup. She was proud of her teeth. Twenty-three and not a cavity in sight. It was four o'clock in the afternoon. Dr. Nash was in an adjoining room, gargling. Miss Mutton had sat her down in the chair by the huge bay window, tied the bib round her neck and asked her to open wide. She was a little younger than Ethel, new in town, and, by the look of her, single. A minute later she stood back and looked at Ethel with admiration.

"You've got a lovely set in there," she told her in a soft, Lowland accent." If you've ever got the time I'd like to make a cast of them. Perfect they are, just perfect. Just you keep brushing them properly. You don't want to let Mortimer Wheeler loose on that lot if you can help it."

She looked back in the direction of the outer room. The gargling if anything seemed to be getting louder. She leant forward conspiratorially, and put her hand on Ethel's shoulder.

"Look, I shouldn't be saying this, but next time you have to come in, for God's sake make sure it's a morning appointment. There're five pubs in the High Street and during his lunch hour he visits each one in turn. "Just a swift one," he says. Back here he's like a man with five thumbs. It's all I can do to get him to focus on the right hole."

She put her manicured fingers into Ethel's mouth once again and sighed with admiration. Ethel regarded her with alarm. She might mean well but Ethel didn't approve of this sort of talk. There were some things about Mr. Hardwick that she didn't care for, but she would never dream of telling one of his clients. She sat up in her chair.

"That's not a very nice thing to say about your employer," she said, half whispering. "I don't think he'd be too pleased if I repeated what you just said."

"You haven't seen him at work," Miss Mutton said. "The Middle Ages, that's where he belongs, him and his collection of wrenches. Thank the Lord he's not getting one of these newfangled water drills in, the speed they go. A salesman came round only last week to give him a demonstration. He didn't like it. Too precise, he said. He's not interested in fillings. What he loves is extractions. That's what he's got up on his wall in his office. *When in Doubt, Pull Them Out."* She straightened up. "Ah, Dr. Nash. This is Miss Whitley."

A large man loomed over her. He had ferocious eyebrows and an enormous nose out of which sprouted a fine mixture of hair. He smelt strongly of disinfectant.

"And how are we this afternoon, Miss Whitley?" he sang. "Arthur G-Nash at your service." He put his face closer. "Have you ever wondered, Miss Whitley, why so many words to do with teeth have a G in them? G-nash, G-naw, G-narl. All fierce, biting words. The G is not silent, rather it has been surgically removed. If I had my way I would extract the letter G from the alphabet completely. No more Grins, no more Grinding, and no more Gristle. I can't abide Gristle. Gristle makes me Grimace." He threw back his head and laughed horribly. The only dentist in town. Ethel closed her eyes and squeezed Miss Mutton's wrist.

She had not returned to have the cast made but when Lawrence Wheatcroft's divorce proceedings began and Miss Mutton was named as the third party, Ethel got to know her well and grew to like her. She lived with her sister who was training to be an air hostess. This was her first job since graduating from dental school. They had gone out together regularly, meeting for a drink after work, or joining up later for a quick Chinese. If it hadn't been for her, she would never have met Colin in the first place. Jill had taken her one night to the civic centre, where a radio show was being recorded, Billy Baxter's travelling quiz programme with bells and hooters and local amateur turns for light relief. A pound for every right answer with the two highest scorers playing for the week's big prize, on this occasion a romantic weekend for two in London. Though Jill was the more flamboyantly dressed of the two, the compere had picked her out of the audience straightaway and led her up onto the stage before she had time to object. The questions were easy enough, even the trick ones. She and Colin had been the finalists. She had stood on one side of the microphone and he on the other. The best out of three. She had won two in a row. After the clapping had died down the host had asked her who she was going to take.

"My mum, I suppose."

"Your mum!" the compere had exclaimed to the audience. "Is that the best you can do? Don't tell me you haven't got someone ready for your bottom drawers," and while the audience was cheering and the man was joking about young girls and fancy men, using one of his catch-phrases—"I'm a fancy man I am"—Ethel realised that the very idea of getting her mother on a coach up to London to spend a weekend on the town was too ludicrous for words. What sort of weekend would that be? Looking across at her rival, he had such a disappointed look about him that after the show was over she went over and offered him the prize.

"The thing is my mother is more or less housebound these days. I could take a girlfriend, but it doesn't seem quite right. You're married. Why don't you have it? It would be more fun for a proper couple."

Perhaps it was the braying laughter that had gone before, or the fact that he had stood in front of an audience and heard himself lay down falsehoods about his own life, but when he looked at her she thought she had never seen such a forlorn history behind his smile. An expression of endless regret tinged by secret longing.

"It would be nice to think that, but I don't think we're quite cut out for it. Having fun in London is not what our life is about."

Ethel didn't know what to say to this bewildered man. It was as if he were lost and afraid to ask the way. He caught her puzzled look.

"I don't know why I'm telling you this. It's none of your business. I mean," he said, flustered by his awkward use of language, "it's nothing you want to hear."

The compere interrupted them. He put an arm around her shoulder, and pushed his hand under her arm. Though the hand never strayed she could tell that his whole body was concentrating on the swell of her breast, gauging its size.

"A private word with the lucky lady," he said and drew her off into a corner. "Do you know, you're the best little winner I've had on the show for months. I couldn't help overhearing what you said to old misery guts over there. Bloody sporting of you." He lowered his voice. "I've got to go back tonight but you don't have to go to London with another party, you know," he said. "You could come on your own. I could fix it for you to get a bit of extra spending cash. Say twenty-five pounds? If you must bring a friend, bring a lady friend," he emphasised. "I'm sure I can find someone who could take her off our hands." He smiled and pulled out a cigarette case, with his name written on the top. "A present from Val Parnell, this case," he said. "Solid silver. Great bloke. Here. Have one."

Ethel shook her head. He took one out and lit it himself. She had seen his picture in the *Radio Times* hundreds of times. He was smaller than she had expected, and his hair was thinner than his photograph had suggested, but he was still handsome, in a tasteless sort of way.

"How about it?" he coaxed her. "We could take in any show you like. Best seats in the house. Go backstage afterwards and meet the stars. What do you say? You don't get a chance like this every day of the week." He squeezed her slightly.

Ethel looked at him. He was no different than the printer's representatives that descended on the town. Different patter, same wares.

"No, I don't," she said, "but I bet you do. What do you think I am? And get your hands off me." She walked back to Colin.

"Come on," she said, pulling his arm. "I'm going to buy us all a bloody good drink," and they had gone across the road with Jill and spent part of their winnings on vodka and Britvic orange.

She had learnt a lot about him that evening, most of which he didn't tell her. Behind the timid beard and the awkwardness in being in the company of strangers, female strangers at that, there was another man, one who had been hidden away for years. Whenever the sound of laughter erupted he would look around the room, disconcerted by the sound of people openly enjoying themselves, nervous of what he did not understand. He was a man of quiet habits, he admitted. He didn't get out much, except to the chess club. He liked walking.

Usually it was Jill who set the tone of the evening, and Ethel who followed her lead, but for once Ethel found herself responding to someone else. As they settled into quiet conversation Jill found herself frozen out. Neither of them wanted to listen to her jokes or be interrupted by her insistent laughter. In the end it was her friend who left and Ethel who stayed. Although she had always envied Jill for her outspoken attitude and her confident good looks, what Jill lacked, or refused to acknowledge, were the quiet pools and eddies in her soul that had never been explored. Somehow this man sitting opposite was slowly wading into hers. She could feel the ripples washing over her as he strode through, dragging unknown undercurrents to the surface. It was the best night out she had had for months and when the evening had reached its end and he said good-bye, there was real regret in his voice, as if he expected never to see her again. It was Ethel who made him promise that he would let her take him out for an Indian meal, as recompense for losing. He hesitated.

"You don't have to worry," she said. "I'm not like Jill. You'll be quite safe with me."

She had shared her prize, inevitably, with her friend. They had to share the hotel room, but they didn't mind. Jill was just the sort of person to take to London. She knew exactly what to do, where to go, and what to see. Sight-seeing, shopping, nightlife, the weekend was a great success. It wasn't until the final evening, coming back late at night from a hot and sweaty dance club that Jill's sister knew, that Billy Baxter turned up, not ten minutes after they arrived, as if he had been alerted to their return. They were sitting, at Jill's insistence, in the bar of the hotel having one last drink before bed and the morning coach home. Jill was bemoaning the scarcity of decent dancers that night. Ethel was thankful to be off her feet. It was about eleven-thirty and she was feeling tired. He came in, waving his hat in the air, as if he were making a stage entrance. He was dressed in an overcoat with fur round the collar and as he came towards them he executed a perfect little fox-trot.

"I've come to take you girls out, like I promised," he said. "I've got the car out the back."

From the way she swung her body around on the stool it was clear that this was the moment Jill had been waiting for.

"You go on your own if you want to," Ethel had told her. "I don't fancy another late night."

"You can't do that," he had said. "You're the guest of honour. No funny business. Scout's honour."

She agreed to go, to please Jill primarily. He took them to a drinking club and later on to a nightclub, in Soho, he said, though it could have been anywhere. They were led downstairs to a small room smelling of damp, with little tables served by girls with long tassels on their bosoms. There was another man waiting, who he introduced as Larry. They drank pink champagne, which made Ethel feel sick. They hadn't been sitting down twenty minutes before the light went down and a young woman came out from a curtain at the front. A Negress. Ethel had never seen one close to before. She was broad and fleshy, dressed in what looked like a loosely laced buckskin dress. She started to dance to the beat of a drum. All the talking had stopped and the men in the room were leaning forward, studying the dancer intently. Ethel looked across to her weekend companion. Even Jill seemed mesmerised. The woman arched her back over so that her hands touched the floor. She began to pulsate to the stark rhythm. The split in her skirt fell open and the thongs holding the dress together tightened. Ethel could see a long length of flesh revealed, stretching from her groin to her bare, veined neck. It was deep and dark and trembling under the strain. She could hear the woman breathing through her hanging mouth, see her pink tongue. The reverberation of the drum seemed to accentuate the rawness in front of her. Another woman, white this time, appeared. She was naked from the waist up. She straddled the Negress around the head and bending down started to pull at the black woman's straps with her teeth. Men began to shout. Ethel could not bear to watch. Catching Jill's attention, she nodded fiercely in the direction of the exit sign. Jill shook her head quickly as if not wanting to be noticed. She was clearly irritated by Ethel's suggestion.

"I'm off," Ethel mouthed. Jill turned her hands upwards. Ethel grabbed her coat and before anyone knew what was happening, ran out the door. She took a taxi for the first time in her life, oblivious to the expense, thankful to have escaped. It was approaching dawn before Jill returned. Ethel was fast asleep. For all Jill's bravado Ethel could tell that it had not been the great night out she had hoped for.

"It's nearly five," Ethel said, trying to look wide awake. "What you been doing all this time?" Jill gave her a funny look.

"Trying to fight off four hands with two, that's what. Want to see the bruises?"

"I told you I was leaving. I couldn't watch that sort of thing."

"It wasn't that bad. Not after we got shot of Larry what's-his-name."

"How romantic."

"If you must know, he spent half the time talking about you. Wanted to know why you had run off."

"Well, I hope you told him. What's he like? They say that comics can be real bad-tempered so-and-so's."

"He was all right. Talk about loaded. He's just moved into a big house outside the town, he told me. Tennis court, croquet lawn, everything. Bought it a couple of months back. Said we could go round there whenever we liked."

"I'm not coming all the way up to London to see some randy comedian. No matter how famous he is."

She watched Jill get undressed. She had a lovely body. Creamy was the word to describe it. You could see why the men went for her. Jill piled her clothes hurriedly in the corner of the room. Before she managed to pull her nightdress over her head Ethel couldn't help noticing. The marks were all over her.

"For heaven's sake, Jill, you weren't joking. Are you all right?"

Jill was close to tears. She wrapped her arms around herself, holding the pain in. "He had these bloody riding boots on. All the time. When I asked him to take them off, he turned quite nasty. They didn't half hurt."

Ethel got out of bed and came up to her. She wiped the hair from Jill's troubled face and hugged her. She had had two hours' sleep and had never felt stronger in her life.

114

"Come on, old thing," she said. "Let's get you to bed. You'll feel better in the morning. Sleep in as long as you like. Stuff the coach. We'll have a late breakfast and then go and find you the smartest outfit in town. What do you say?"

Ethel sat with her while Jill fell asleep. She thought about the condemned black woman walking like a caged spider across the floor and the white girl with her imprisoned breasts hanging down and the free men leaning forward, spit on their lips. She looked at Jill and remembered how she had hugged her, how her body had felt against her own. How warm and secure they had been for that short moment. Poor Jill. She would never learn. Not tonight, not tomorrow night, not ever. She and Lawrence hadn't lasted long.

"Don't you regret splitting up?" Ethel had asked her on the journey back. "All that notoriety and the unpleasantness. All for nothing?"

Jill had shrugged her shoulders. "Seemed all right at the time. He was always asking me out—would I like to see this, would I like to do that? Took me to see the Farnborough Air Show once. Then a Burns' Night over at Aston Clinton with bagpipes and real haggis. Then he waves these tickets to a dinner-dance do at Swanage. Some fancy car club he belongs to. And I thought, a weekend by the sea, away from bloody Aylesbury and my sister champing at the bit, wanting the flat to herself. We hadn't done much before, but to be absolutely honest," she lowered her voice, "I chucked the last boyfriend six months back and I fancied a decent bit of you-know-what and not in some bloody frozen Cortina parked out on Gallows Hill." She paused. "Not that you could do anything in that sardine can of his. Not even enough room to take your knickers off." They both giggled.

Yes, Maureen had Colin followed. That's how she found out. Like his next-door neighbour, Lawrence Wheatcroft was the only example of his profession Aylesbury had to offer. If Maureen had wanted her husband watched, Lawrence Wheatcroft would have been the man to do it. And what would he have thought when he found out who Colin was seeing? Was that why he had started asking her out again? That he thought her easy game? No, that had come before. That had been Jill's doing. Ethel had met her quite by accident at the chemist's.

"Hello, stranger," Jill had said, eyeing her up and down. "Haven't seen you in a while. Still single?" and Ethel had felt flustered and caught out on the wrong foot. Colin took up all her spare time now, even when she wasn't with him. All she thought about was this man, when she was going to see him again, what they would do, what he would say to her, what she would say to him. Standing there, Ethel realised that she hadn't talked to anyone properly for weeks. Everything she thought and felt was held in secret, filtered through Colin and Colin's life. She hadn't been Ethel for months. And here was someone who thought of her, well, as *her*. How could she have forgotten about their friendship and their late night confidences? More than anything she wanted to open up her heart again.

"Tell you what," she said. "If you're free next week I'll come over and you can make that cast you kept harping on about. I've lots to tell you."

"You're on," said Jill. "Come when it's quiet, when Sir Mortimer is off on his High Street gargle."

Ethel kept her promise. She sat in the swivel chair and bit into the soft plaster. After it was over she lay back and closed her eyes. She could hear Jill moving around, sterilising implements, preparing records, hear the swish of her coat, feel its breeze, feel the glare of the summer sun on her face while the words poured out of her mouth. She felt happier than she had done for weeks, lighter, freer, as if she were under the gas and having an abscess lanced. She talked and talked and talked. Every now and again an unseen hand would fall on her head or brush her shoulder, and when she had finished she thought she felt a light kiss on her lips. She looked up. Jill stood over her, holding the cast she had made up to the light.

"If only one of them, just one of them, could be as reliable as this set of yours. I've not had one yet who comes even close. There's always something. Start poking about and you uncover some bloody great festering hole. He's unhappily married, is he? Find me one that isn't. Just don't believe everything he says about her. Not yet. You've only his word for it."

"It's not like that," Ethel said, willing Jill to believe her. "Colin's serious. I just know he is."

Jill helped her out of the chair.

"At least he hasn't got children," she said.

"They had a baby. Long time ago. It died in childbirth."

"If he had children I'd tell you to forget it and come out with me some night. That's probably what I should be saying anyway. But you're right. If you want him, you bloody well have him and sod the lot of us."

Ethel was visibly cheered. She had been told what she had come to hear. Now it was time to leave. Out of politeness rather than any real interest, she asked, "And what about yourself? Been anywhere exciting?"

"You'll never guess," she said. "I went to that party that bloke invited us to."

Ethel was amazed. "Up in London?"

"It wasn't in London. He lives nearby. I told you, remember?"

"But after what he did to you! You must be desperate."

"I thought there'd be safety in numbers."

"And was there?"

"In a manner of speaking. Full of showbiz types. Met his brother or cousin. Couldn't quite work it out. Not a bit like him. Quiet. Bit sad. Jealous, I suppose. Wife works over in the market."

They were surprised to get an invitation at all. Jeremiah had not wanted to go. It was only when Judith realised that the house Will had bought was the one where she and Jem had first met that he agreed. They hadn't seen Will for over ten years, though like everyone else, it was hard to get away from him—what with his half-hour comedy on BBC television, his travelling radio quiz show on Wednesday mornings and his Thursday evening programme on the Home Service, *At the Foot of Our Stairs*.

On the face of it the house had changed hardly at all. The ivy on the walls was a little thicker, the gravel on the drive a little deeper, and a bright brick garage stood at one side to accommodate Will's new car. Lights were strung out along the veranda. Jeremiah parked his eight-year-old Morris Oxford round the side. Will was at the front door. He was dressed in a bright pink suit and a dark blue silk shirt. He had his arm around a young woman and his white shoes were covered in tassels. He drew Judith in and kissed her warmly.

"The first time I did that was round the back, out by the kitchens, remember? This is—"

"Jill." The girl shuffled uncomfortably. Will squeezed her waist.

"Jill's just arrived like yourselves. And she's been a very naughty girl. Didn't do like I asked her, did she? Still, we shan't hold that against her, shall we? I'm sure I can find something much nicer to do that." The girl twisted out of his grasp as he turned to his cousin and held out his hand.

"Jem," he said. "It's been far too long. My fault mostly."

"Mine too," Jem replied, and stepped in and looked around. The hall was high and bright with curved white walls and gold paint and white Persian rugs scattered on the floor. Chandeliers hung from the ceiling and a long, curved staircase led up to the first floor.

"No marquee tonight, then," Jem observed.

Will laughed. "Can't find the workmen these days. Besides, this is not an outdoor party, not in the winter." He took Jem's coat and whispered, "You'll be wishing you hadn't brought the wife later on. Some of the crumpet here tonight . . ."

Across the hall a couple came out of a room and chased one another down the corridor.

"Here. You can't go down there," Will called out. "That's where the housekeeper lives."

"Housekeeper!" exclaimed Judith. "And what does she make of all this?"

"She's broad-minded," Will told her, "like her employer."

He took them through into a huge room of bay windows and wide-cushioned sofas. It was full of young women and older men, where dinner jackets and gaudy suits swam amongst a sea of bare shoulders. Most of the women seemed little better than tarts, girls who called themselves models but who worked in gaming clubs and escort agencies, hoping to strike it rich. They behaved like overexcited children kept up for a late night party, dressed in flouncy clothes and feather boas, shrieking and squealing and running through the rooms. Will came up and offered to show Judith around the house. Jeremiah stood without moving for half an hour. Though smaller than most of the men, he stood out. No one talked to him. Some of the men were famous. He recognised their faces, but their bodies seemed too small for their heads. They looked like exhibits at a circus freak show, with the same smell of greasepaint and the same dazzling smiles. He had been close to many men in his time, men of violence and danger, men without remorse, and had grown up with the sound of travelling shows ringing in his ears, but here he seemed to be standing amongst creatures who came from a different species altogether, men with thick cigars and tortoiseshell cigarette holders who pawed the air and the passing flesh and revelled in the lewd wealth on display. There was no honest enjoyment in sight. He wished Alcott were here. Alcott would have taken out his notebook and started taking names. Alcott would have closed this place down in fifteen minutes. A man in a green silk shirt started to kiss another man on the mouth right in front of him. He could hear the clash of bristles on their skin. Though he did not want to, he looked down to where their bodies rubbed against each other. He pushed his way back outside. In the hall a group of girls stood at the top of the landing and one by one slid down the banisters to where a man wearing a blindfold stood with his arms outstretched. He watched as the girls came hurtling down, shrieking and whooping before knocking the man to the floor. The man caught the fourth girl and kept his balance. As he carried her off upstairs, legs kicking, another one leant over the balustrade and called down, "Hoi, shorty. You next for blindman's fuck?"

Jem hurried across into the opposite room and walked over to the French windows. He stood looking out into the dark, over to the croquet lawn and the bank of daffodils where he and Will had once lain, amongst empty cider bottles, dreaming of their future.

"Don't bother," a voice said. "The answer's no."

He turned. The girl he had met at the door was sitting alone on a swing couch. "I was looking for my wife," he said. "You haven't seen her by any chance, have you? She was the woman I came in with."

The girl laughed.

"That's a new one," she said. "As a matter of fact, I think I did. Just now. Went off arm in arm with our host."

"Will?" he said.

"Will?" she answered. "I thought his name was Billy. Billy Baxter."

"That's his stage name," he said. "Will's his real name. Wilfred Bembo. I'm his cousin."

She looked at him. "Never have guessed it."

Jeremiah looked at his boots. "No. Well, we've gone our separate ways."

"And he's gone off with your missus."

"Well, he always wanted to."

"You're taking it very well, I must say. Isn't that them in the car?"

Jem turned and ran out onto the grass, trying to wave them down. The car glided past.

"They've gone," he said stupidly.

"They'll be back," she said. She patted the sofa. "Now sit down and protect me from these Tin Pan Alley hyenas."

Will waved a half-empty wine bottle in the air. "Six grand this beauty cost me," he boasted. "Here, have a drink."

"You should have stopped," Judith replied, looking in the mirror to where Jeremiah stood. She took the bottle hesitantly, then put it to her lips.

"What for?" Will asked, taking the bottle from her. "I stopped for him once in my life and regretted it ever since. It's you I want to talk to. How you been then?"

Judith looked down at her hands resting on her pale dress. They were old, older than her years. "I've been OK," she said.

"Well, you don't look it and that's a fact."

"That's nice."

"You know what I mean, girl. You had something when I first met you. Where's it all gone now?"

"Run to ground," she said. "Through my hands and feet and onto the bloody ground."

"And what about you and Jem? He been treating you right?"

"We don't have time for each other much, what with him out in the fields all day and me at the market or over at Father's. Too tired to argue."

"He still alive then, your old man?"

"Arthritis plays him up some. Jem goes over most weekends to help him with the barrels."

Will took another swig out the bottle. "Jem! Should have left him years ago."

"For what?" she asked.

"For me, for a start."

Judith sighed. "Will. You'd have left me as soon as the veins started to show. Left me or kept me. Same difference. Jem may not have turned out to be the man I thought I was getting but he's still there, underneath it all. It's buried, that's all. Been buried a long time."

"Dig it up then. Make him look at himself. Does he . . . you know, very often?"

"What?" For a moment Judith thought he was talking about sex and turned away in exasperation. Then she realised what he meant and drew her hand over her face. As far as her marriage with Jem was concerned, it usually meant the same thing.

"The other business," Will was explaining. "You know, in prison."

She turned and faced the front. "Not often. Once or twice a month. Sometimes more. I try not to think about it. I suspect he thinks about little else."

Will patted her knee and leant over to kiss her on the cheek.

"I don't know if I should be alone with you," she said, pushing him off gently.

"You're not," he said. "Look in the back."

Judith turned round and gave a little scream.

"Don't worry. They're dummies. Part of my new act. I've been working on them for months. I'm going to have any number of them, lifelike size, all out onstage. There'll be an Auntie Rose and an Uncle Harry and a mum and a dad and a sister with big you-know-whats and a toffee-nosed brother, and I'm going to have them all sitting there in this front parlour, while I kick the stuffing out of them. I've been thinking about it for years, ever since I saw our grandfather sitting with his skin stretched tighter than a monkey's bunghole. Like it's carrying on his tradition, but in a modern way, see."

"And this is for pantomime, right?" Judith said.

"Nah! Sick of fucking panto. This is serious funny, not just slapstick. A one-man show maybe, if we can get the backing. I want to do something new. I'm tired of glad-handing it up and down the country." He took a hand off the wheel. "Here. I got a bone to pick with you. That time I came down here with the show. You and Jem might have showed up."

Judith patted his leg. "We would have done if you'd asked us. We were waiting for a proper invite. Jem was hurt when you didn't get in touch. He didn't say anything but I could tell. He's always thought highly of you, always defended you, even when you misbehaved."

Will threw up his hands. "When did I ever misbehave?" He put a finger to her lips. "No, don't tell me. He never really forgave me for my wedding speech, did he?"

Judith sank back into the depths of the leather seat. *"I never forgave you for that wedding speech, stirring it up like that."*

Will pushed the hair from his face. "It was jealousy, plain and simple."

"Will," Judith warned.

"It's the truth. That's all I've ever really wanted, a woman like you. But your sort never want me. You can see right through me. Woolworth girls is all I'm good for. Cheap and flashy. Sometimes I think I got it all wrong." He drew up on the side of the road and turned off the engine.

"I won't be here long, you know," he said.

Judith turned to him quickly. "Why, what do you mean? You're not ill, are you?"

"No, nothing like that. Just a feeling I have. I've got everything going for me at the moment, TV, radio, summer season up in Blackpool, pantomime in the West End. They're even asking me to do adverts for these new premium bonds. But it's all changing. I can feel it. It's not, how can I put it, musical hall anymore. The nudge-nudge, wink-wink is going." He jerked his head back to the house. "They don't know it yet, but pretty soon I shall be left out in the fucking cold. By this time next year I'll be lucky to get the guest spot on *Crackerjack.*" He stopped Judith's protest. "You're right, it probably won't be that bad, but it won't be good. Something is coming up behind me but I haven't got a clue what it is. And do you know why? 'Cause I'm out of touch, Judith, can you believe it? Billy Baxter, out of touch. My manager, Larry, he knows it. He's been signing up young hopefuls behind my back, la-di-da clever bastards from university who despise people like me. Says it's just to keep his hand in, but a year ago if he'd so much as looked at another act, even if it had been Spotty the Talking Dog, I'd have fucking fired him. I don't know, I might have to go away, somewhere where the climate for comedy hasn't yet changed. Australia, perhaps. South Africa."

He drained the bottle and threw it out into the night. "Oh, Judith," he said, grabbing hold of her hand. "I know I'm a bastard, but tonight I'm a lonely one. Come here, for old times' sake."

When they returned Jem was sitting on the swing seat alone. Will drew up and came hurrying across.

"Jem. The very fellow. We were just living old memories. Have you brought any booze out with you by any chance?"

Jeremiah shook his head and looked at his wife, hanging back.

"It's time we left," he said.

Will grabbed his arm and pulled him to his feet.

"You don't want to go yet. The party's hardly got going."

Jem shook his head. "Sorry. I've an early start tomorrow."

Will put his arm around him and tried to steer him back into the house. "Well, give the cabbages a miss. Have some fun for a change." He brushed down Jem's lapels. "Not that you're really dressed for a proper party. Why not pop upstairs and help yourself to something out of my wardrobe. Who knows, you might get lucky!"

Jem brushed him off. "So that's it. The moment you opened the door you looked at me as if expecting to find mud on my bloody trousers."

Judith clicked her tongue in anger.

"Jem!"

"Well at least I'm not dressed up like a nancy boy."

Will pushed him back. "And at least I don't go around with dead man's spunk on my boots. This is the uniform you wear to attend them, isn't it?"

Jem did not reply.

"It is, isn't it? Jesus fucking Christ."

Will stalked off. Judith and Jem stood side by side on the veranda. They looked after him, stumbling back.

"I don't know who I feel more sorry for, you or him," she said.

"Thanks."

"He doesn't have much."

"Just a house in Blackpool, this brothel and a brand-new car. Nice ride?"

"This is all a game and he knows it."

"I never thought I'd hear you defending Will Bembo."

"I never thought it would all end up like this."

"None of us can see into the future, Judith."

"When I think of me standing here all those years ago. If I knew then what I know now. Down there, where the car's parked, is where you tried to play the accordion to me that night."

"I know."

"You were a lovely player, Jem. Why did you stop? I haven't heard you play in years."

No one noticed them leaving. Halfway down the drive they came across the girl, walking home. Though she said it wasn't necessary, Jeremiah drove her into town. When they got home themselves, Jeremiah went upstairs and pulled the accordion from out under the bed in the spare room, and played it softly while she moved about below. As his fingers grew more confident, the tunes grew stronger. She came up the stairs with tears on her face. Pressed against her in the dark he did not need to tell her that the salt she tasted was from him too.

When she came down three weeks later and announced that she was late, Jeremiah had no inkling as to what she might be referring, thinking that she had missed the post or that she was expected over at her father's that morning.

"Should have got up earlier," he had said ungraciously, continuing to smear anchovy paste onto his sandwiches. She reached out and cuffed him, the first spontaneous physical intimacy since that night and said, "Should have blocked my ears up. I'm pregnant, Jem, damn it. Pregnant after all these years," and she began to cry again.

It was a paralysing statement. He could think of nothing good that might come of it. He was used to seeing the inevitable solitude of life's end. He could not imagine the harmony of life's beginning. He wrapped his sandwiches up in a paper bag and sat down by the stove.

"Well?" she said. "Haven't you got anything to say?"

He could not look at her. "By God, Judith," he said, pulling on his boots, "I'd have thought you'd have learnt to look after yourself by now," and had stumped off.

Ethel watched Jill as she pulled out the records for Mr. Nash's first patient of the afternoon. She couldn't imagine herself going to a place like that alone. Or in company for that matter.

"Never spoke a word to her the whole journey," Jill said. "He was that cross. I was embarrassed for her, but glad to get away all the same. Lucky to get out alive. They're all the same. As soon as they realise I've just changed out of a nurse's uniform they think I'm some sort of nymphomaniac. I don't go out anymore. My sister's never home and all I do is sit at home and stare at the box."

Ethel felt guilty. She had neglected Jill quite wilfully.

"Perhaps you should join the tennis club," she suggested. "Or the Young Farmers." Jill had hooted with derision.

"Perhaps I should get back with old Lawrence. At least he could make me laugh the morning after."

Ethel felt her cheeks flare. "Well, why don't you?" she stammered, hoping that her friend would not notice her rapid change in colour. "I'm sure he's just waiting for the chance." Jill shook her head.

"He started to go to seed," she said. "As soon as his wife pushed him out the door, personal hygiene went out the window. Never cleaned his fingernails, feet always filthy, stale beer on his breath. And as for his underpants, well best not mentioned. I couldn't stand it."

Ethel had left her, promising to meet up the following week, and had walked into Lawrence's rear end coming out of his office, his translucent flesh showing as he bent down to turn the key in the lock. White his skin was, and covered in light fluffy hair. She imagined it going all the way down to his bottom. Jill was right. He looked like the sort of man who wouldn't be able to wipe himself properly.

"Ah, the elusive Miss Whitley," he said, turning round, trying hard not to look down her front. "Having your molars attended to? Nothing painful, I hope."

He stood there breathing heavily. He had put on weight.

"Nothing that regular brushing won't cure, Mr. Wheatcroft," she said pointedly and waited until he had unblocked the corridor.

"Well, this is a pleasant coincidence," he announced. "I have an appointment with your learned employer. Perhaps I can escort you back to work."

She was forced to get into his car and drive the six hundred yards to her office. Quite unnecessary, but Lawrence Wheatcroft had wanted to show off his new secondhand Daimler.

"Bought it before the settlement went through," he explained. "The ex-w. can't drive." He smiled to himself before returning to the subject in hand. "Real craftsmanship here, you know," he had said. "Belonged to a judge. Chauffeur driven. You can tell by the way the upholstery has been kept. Feel it. Real leather that is."

Ethel did as she was told. Jill wouldn't have minded parking up on Gallows Hill with this to lie back on. No gear stick up the backside on this seat. In fact, no gear stick at all. For some reason the gear stick was on the steering wheel, not on the floor.

"Never seen that before," she said, foolishly.

"What's that?" asked Lawrence, looking hurriedly down at his lap.

"The gear stick. On the steering wheel."

Lawrence, relieved, nodded his head with eager anticipation. "Marvellous that, isn't it?" he breezed. "It's the way of the future you know, vis-à-vis gear sticks. Has to be. Frees the left hand."

He held his hand in the air and wiggled it about. Frees it for what?

127

Ethel wondered, but was wise enough not to ask. Lawrence was ready with an example of his own. He leant over and pulled open the catch on the walnut veneer dashboard. A woollen monkey fell out.

"Mascot," he explained. "Mother knitted it for Father during the war."

He pushed it back in and pulled out a paper bag.

"Liquorice All-sorts," he indicated. "Very useful in my line of work. With the hours I spend stuck in the car, never knowing when the next meal is coming, you need something decent to su—to chew on. Help yourself."

Ethel opened the bag up. It was filled with round purple sweets.

"They must have seen you coming," she said. "There's not much All-sort in here."

Lawrence took the bag and glanced inside.

"Wrong bag," he explained. "Can't stand those purple ones. Should be a fresh bag somewhere." He leant over again and rummaged around, changing gear with a flick of his fingers, as he slowed down.

"See what I mean?" he declared. "Much safer. Less distraction. Which is just as well. With pretty girls like you in the passenger seat, there are distractions enough." He turned, and leering at her, handed over a bag which must have weighed a good two pounds. No wonder his underpants were in such a state.

"Marvellous engine," he went on. "Done sixty thousand and sparks like new. Of course, being a six-cylinder job, she's a bit thirsty on the petrol. Twelve miles to the gallon. Not exactly the machine you want for chasing round the highways and byways," and he peered anxiously at the fuel gauge. "Still, got the old MG for that. Nothing better than the MG vis-à-vis a spot of poking in and out."

There was a fierce silence as they both realised what he had said. Not according to Miss Mutton it isn't, Ethel thought.

"It is very quiet," she admitted. The nodding started up again.

"It is quiet, isn't it? *Very* quiet. Do you know you could put a sleeping baby on this bonnet and it wouldn't wake him?"

Ethel digested this unusual piece of motoring information. She had never seen a baby on a bonnet. It would be an odd sight. Perhaps it was the way of the future, vis-à-vis family motoring. Lawrence was still thinking of his engine.

"You should take a look under that bonnet," he urged. "Some surprises there, I can tell you."

"Not of the infant type, I hope," Ethel returned. They were nearly there now.

"Infant?" Lawrence looked nonplussed, as if he hadn't a clue what she was talking about. He turned into the small parking space at the back of the building and pulled ostentatiously on the hand brake. Ethel lurched forward, hitting her head on the windscreen.

"If you like I'll take you out for a run sometime," Lawrence offered, oblivious to her discomfort. "We could go up to the old greenhouse road and have a bit of a spin along the flat. And maybe have a drink afterwards."

"Can't drive," she said. She could have killed herself. An excuse like that wouldn't last five seconds with a man of Lawrence's calibre. He seized upon it the moment it was out of her mouth.

"I could teach you. Piece of cake in this beauty. You'd pass first go. What do you say? It's nice up there this time of year."

It certainly was. She and Colin often decided to drive along that road on their way back from the Beacon, when he would let her lean over and take the wheel. It was a way of making physical contact while pretending to concentrate on something else. She would look out to the road, and follow his instructions, but all she was conscious of was his hands covering hers and his very life blowing on the back of her neck. Back in her bed the memory of his breath could keep her awake until dawn, for it seemed to be their most intimate of acts, at once spiritual and physical. It spoke of a life to which they both aspired, when they would always be close, he guiding her, she eager to discover, both of them looking forward to the road ahead. Those brief moments spent over the wheel were far more rewarding than the furious manoeuvres that went on up at the lay-by, when Colin hoiked her bra up under her chin and squeezed his fingers down into her underwear, exhausting exercises both, which at their uncertain conclusion left them more forlorn than when they started. But there was a devoted quality to this tuition which held all arguments of propriety and uncertainties of the future at bay. It was a simple act of unseated love, one which held boundless promise. In moments of optimistic reflection the memory of them would bring her smiles of hope, but when courage failed her, when it seemed plain that those treasured moments would be as close to Colin as she would ever get, her eyes would brim with grief. Now Lawrence Wheatcroft wanted to breathe all over her. Six months ago she had regarded his advances with an amused indifference, but now they made her angry. She got out the car briskly and waited as he came up over the other side.

"I really don't have any free time at all," she said quickly, and stalked off to the back door.

"Not to worry," he called out after her. "I'm quite prepared to make a nuisance of myself."

Yes, Lawrence had been hired by Maureen and had followed Colin that Thursday morning as he set off up north. The more she thought about it, the more unbearable it became. He could have watched them doing it down by the waterfall or when she had straddled Colin on top of that flat rock, her blouse unbuttoned to the waist. He could have taken pictures! She remembered what he had said in the office about his own entrapment. The same applied to them, didn't it? If he'd felt any sense of loyalty to the firm which gave him employment, he would have taken her aside and warned her what was going on. But no. He went right ahead and got on with his job. And Jill had told her he was a good sort!

Those three months away from Colin had been the worst months of her life, and she had wandered through them as if in a hall of mirrors. She would take a look at herself and barely recognise the face she saw. Her features would stare back at her, a stranger looking upon a stranger, whether in the bathroom at home, the washroom at work or above the basin in the ladies' toilet in the pub across the road, where she ended up after work, drinking too much. She used to wonder how Danny was faring, working in his market stall, mesmerising the ladies with his bright chatter and laboursaving devices, fixing up that van of his. Perhaps he been arrested by now, for what was his market stall for if not to pass off stolen goods? Even she could see that. Whatever he was doing, it didn't seem likely that he would go straight for very long. What would have happened that night if she had pulled him back, opened up her mouth and let his tongue in? He would have taken advantage of her, despite what he said about the little woman at home. And what was wrong with that, if that's what she wanted as well? Why shouldn't she go out and find someone like him, someone with a bit of spunk in them, instead of staying in with her mother, mourning over the loss of spineless Colin. Once or twice, when the regulars had left for home, she allowed herself to be picked up. Heartless bastards they were, with wives of their own, typical cheap by jowl salesmen, with their mock-leather sophistication, their two-tone jokes and four-corner fumblings, who took her up to their rooms and turned her this way and that as if she was stuck on a spit. She began to count the number of times. One, two, three, as if each one represented another step in the descent of her self-esteem. The fourth had been a lean man with the tongue of a dog. After the first drink he had moved his stool over next to hers. After the third their heads hung low and close. When she had downed the fourth he had pulled out a plastic doll from his suitcase and ordering up another, made it pee vodka and tonic into her glass.

"Bet yours never tastes as sweet," he laughed and led her upstairs. Only when he pushed her into his room did she realise that she had been afraid of him all along, and that the thin face which now broke the silence of his room with his dog's laugh, shrill and barking, had been looking at her with canine malevolence all evening. She recalled how, anxious to appear in control, she had interpreted his insults to her morality as testaments to her independence. He shoved her against a wall and started to pull at her clothes, not tearing them but simply plucking at them in a deliberate expression of contempt.

"You've got a nice handful," he said, squeezing her breasts hard. "No wonder men like you."

"Men?" she had said.

"Yes, men," he said. "You know, those creatures with cocks for brains." He pushed himself against her. "Come on. Kissy-kissy," and kissed her so fiercely she could scarcely breathe.

"I feel sick," she had said, and he had locked her head in the crook of his arm and had marched her into the bathroom.

"There," he said, holding her head down. "Now throw up in that fucking bowl, rinse your fucking mouth out and come out smelling sweet as a baby's fart. Or you'll feel the back of my hand and no mistake."

When she returned he was lying propped up against the headboard, drinking from a hip flask.

"Ah, Miss Ethel returns," and from the way he elongated her name, and the little leer that accompanied it, she came to the uncomfortable conclusion that he had met her before.

"Do we know each other?" she asked, stupidly, and he had thrown back his head and laughed. "Know each other? Why, Ethel, you're famous," and he toppled over sideways, giggling.

She gave up after that, if not the barroom drinking then the activity which they hoped would follow. Not that it mattered either way. Nothing mattered. How she held on to her job she had no idea. She must have made hundreds of mistakes. And then one evening, coming out of the office, waiting for Cecil Hardwick to lock up and walk her up the road, she looked across the road and saw Colin standing by his car. She waited until Mr. Hardwick had done his duty and left her at the bus stop, then ran back.

"I met one of our main buyers this morning," he told her. "He was full of this place. Couldn't wait to come back. Last time he was here, he met this bit of stuff almost as soon as he checked in, picked her up 'easy as winking,' he said. Bought her a few vodkas and took her back to his room. Talk about a goer. Not on the game, you understand, not anything like that. Quite open she was, told him what she did, how she lived with her mother, what her bloody name was." He banged his hands on the steering wheel. "He'll be there now, waiting to see if you turn up again tonight. I felt so bad at what I had done to you. I couldn't bear the thought of you going through all that again."

Ethel was unimpressed. "It's a bit late, isn't it, riding to my rescue? Not even a sorry or a good-bye, or a you'll-get-over-me. Instead I get something my boss might have written."

"You don't understand, Ethel. You wouldn't believe what I've been through."

Ethel found his self-pity hard to take. "What you've been through! I'm the one that got let down."

They had got into the car and driven out to the downs. He began to tell her a truly creepy tale. When he had got home that night, Maureen had greeted him at the front door, all smiles and unnecessary cups of tea, asking him how the conference had been. He had made up a very plausible story about Far Eastern printing methods.

"They might even send me over there next year," he had told her, thinking that when he and Ethel did run off, a fictitious trip to Hong Kong could give them a couple of days' start.

"Hong Kong!" Maureen had exclaimed. "I wonder whether they'd allow me to come along too."

The following weekend they had driven down to Lulworth Cove. Maureen had been in an extraordinarily happy mood, singing snatches from *The King and I* and other musicals, grinning at him as if she wanted him to join in.

"We are Siamese if you please, We are Siamese if you don't please," she had chanted. It was one of his least favourite songs, nearly as bad as "Mountain Greenery, Where God Made the Scenery, Just Two Crazy People Together"—another of her specialities. As the journey progressed the interior of the car had taken on an unpleasant intimacy which became as oppressive as the sickly smell of baby talcum powder which she shook over herself every morning. She had put on some orange lipstick and kept fluffing her hair in the mirror in her sun visor. If he hadn't known any better he would have sworn that she was deliberately shifting her legs about. The noise from her nylon stockings was unbearable. It was times like these that he wished the car had a radio.

They checked into the Castle Inn later that afternoon and were shown up to their room overlooking the steep vegetable garden. Maureen had looked out on bedraggled rows as if the Hanging Gardens of Babylon were dangling before her.

"Just think, Colin. Eleven years we've been coming here. Eleven years since our honeymoon. Only in those days, we had a double bed." She patted the narrow blue counterpane. "You take this one," she said. "There's a nasty draught coming from this window."

The dinner had passed amicably enough. To his surprise, Maureen drank a whole bottle of wine and elected to have an Irish coffee as well as pudding. Colin had neither. After the meal he decided to stay at the bar to have a couple of pints and though she did not try to persuade him otherwise, she was threateningly skittish about going up to bed alone. By the time he came into their room it was well after closing time. He was relieved to see that she lay fast asleep in the bed wedged up against the thin bathroom partition wall. Full of beer and fearful lest his frequent visits would wake her, he eased open his bedside window, and throughout the night relieved himself by kneeling on his mattress and spraying his urine out in controlled and silent arcs onto the lettuces below.

The next morning, while he was getting dressed, she said, "Why don't you walk down to the Cove before breakfast? Work up an appetite. I'll stay here and finish my book. You could do with some fresh air."

He was glad to get out. It did not take him long to reach the sea, past the village hall and the bakery, along the raised pavement which ran past the hidden field where the pigs grazed, down to the shallow pond where the ducks sat in clear green water. The Cove never changed. The beach was lined with banks of large round grey pebbles which made it difficult to walk upon. To the left, pulled up to the cliff's edge, rested the mobile gangplank with its huge iron wheels, which would be pushed out into the water when the paddle steamer from Weymouth came. To the right stood the creosoted boathouse with its wooden veranda hung with broken lobster pots and tarred rope. As he stumbled by he noticed a man sitting on the veranda above him, feet up, eyes closed, the morning newspaper on his lap. He was dressed in a pair of yellow-ochre cord trousers and a pale cream cardigan. The soles of his leather slip-ons were made for a polished ballroom floor rather than a pebble beach. Maureen's brother, Frank. He hadn't seen him in nine years.

"I don't believe it. Frank!" he cried. "What on earth are you doing here?"

Maureen's brother got up, all smiles, folding his newspaper in four. He was still the same as when he'd first met him in the army induction hut. Thin and undernourished, like the dogs he had kept. Frank leant over and tapped Colin playfully on the cheek with the flat of his hand. He was starting to go bald.

"Colin," he said. "Colin, me old son. You look terrific. The old man keeping you well?"

"I hardly ever see him these days," Colin answered. "Your father's more or less retired now. He doesn't have much to do with the firm. I think the local council takes up most of his time."

Frank grinned. "That's the old man." There was a pause.

"I still can't believe it," Colin repeated, "seeing you like this. It's so unexpected. You must come back with me. It will give Maureen such a surprise. Is Avril with you?"

Frank ignored the question. "You still come here regular?" he said looking out to the line of small jagged rocks, shaped like a set of pointed teeth, that poked out of the receding water.

"Every year, rain or shine," Colin told him. "Visiting the scene of the crime you might say."

Frank punched his arm playfully. "We had some times up here. Wool, Bovington, chasing all that skirt up at Durdle Door. You still like it here, then?"

"It hasn't changed much."

Frank nodded. "It's just that I've heard you've been enjoying other parts lately. Like the Lake District for instance."

"What?" said Ethel. "He said what?"

"What do you mean, Frank?" Colin asked.

"The Waders' Arms. Near Ambleside. Room five," he said. "Isn't that the main attraction these days?"

"Dear God," said Ethel. "But how?"

"Frank," Colin said.

Frank stopped him. "Don't try and deny it," he said. "It don't suit you. Me, I've been lying all my life. But you. It's as plain as the nose on your face. Edith Whitley, am I right?"

"Ethel," Colin corrected.

"Ah yes. My mistake. Ethel. Got a nice pair of tits, has she? Stand up all by themselves do they?"

"Frank. It isn't what you think."

"I don't blame you in a way. Can't be much fun having to poke my sister for a living. That's what they're there for, these working girls. I don't mind that. We've all done it. But it's all this other malarkey that gets me. Going on holiday. Holding hands. Dinner by candlelight. That's very nearly insulting."

"I don't know what to say, Frank. How did you find out?"

"Never you mind. That's not important. What is important is what she told me when I rang her up."

Colin was horrified. "You rang her?"

"Just in case it was a case of mistaken identity. I wanted to find out if you'd been home that week. I rang while you were at work. She was really pleased to hear from me. Said she'd been thinking about me and Avril only the other day and how we should all see more of each other."

"Maureen said that?"

"Yes. I thought it a bit weird too. Then she dropped the bombshell. 'Guess what?' she said. 'I think I might be pregnant.'"

"She's what?" said Ethel.

"She can't be," Colin said. "We hardly ever . . ."

"No 'can't be' about it," said Frank. "Think back, old son. If it's that rare you'll remember the occasion all right. A couple of weeks late, she said." Colin groaned.

"Naturally enough I didn't think it was quite the time to go questioning her about your whereabouts. Really happy she sounded, happier than I'd heard her for years. She had this plan worked out about when to tell you. Broke my heart just to listen to it."

"You slept with her?" said Ethel. "All the time you were seeing me? I always thought—"

"The thing is," Frank continued, "she doesn't want you to know right away. Doesn't want the child to come into the world in an atmosphere of recrimination. A reconciliation is what she's looking for. Love and affection."

"I don't believe this."

"I'm only repeating what she told me. She wants this holiday to be the place where you both start again, so that when she does give you the good news, it'll look like it happened here. Typical woman's fancy, but you have to give her credit for wanting it to start working again. The trouble was you'd been so lovey-dovey up north I thought you might be planning to spoil it all by telling her something else entirely. So I thought I'd pop down and straighten you out about one or two things, old pal, old chum."

"So she doesn't know you're here?" Colin asked him.

Frank shook his head. "I don't rightly know *what* she knows."

"You didn't tell her about me, then."

"Not yet." He sounded doubtful.

Colin stared out to sea. "What timing. After all these years. She would get pregnant now. She bloody would."

Frank jumped down and started to throw stones at the rocks poking above the water.

"Funny, isn't it," he said. "There you all were thinking me and Avril would never last, Maureen looking down her nose at her, Mum and

Dad treating her like she was something the cat brought in. Fighting and fucking, that's all you thought we were good for, and not always with each other neither. Well, look at us now. We ain't done too badly. We're still together. Ivor's a bit of a tearaway, but what lad isn't at his age? I only hope that when he brings someone home I won't treat her the way my mum did Avril. Never forgive them for how they treated her." A sudden thought struck him. He turned to face his brother-in-law.

"This Ethel tart. She ain't up the spout, is she?" he asked, his voice hardening.

Colin shook his head. Frank relaxed.

"Wouldn't be the end of the world, even if she was," he admitted. "You could always get rid of it. When I lived over there, that dentist used to do them for fifty quid. Half the shop floor went to him at one time or another. Only way they could keep their heads abovewater. I went with a girl who had to go there once. Nearly rinsed half her insides out. Now don't start getting any ideas. Maureen would kill you for just suggesting it."

"No," said Colin. "It never crossed my mind."

"Just as well." Frank handed him a collection of stones. "Now you just stay here for half an hour and sort yourself out. Nobody knows nothing, remember? You're not meant to know about the baby, just as she's not meant to know about Ethel Whitley and room number five. Just as I'm not meant to be here. Just as you're on a simple walk. Just as she's lying in bed reading her magazines." He came up close.

"One more thing."

"What?"

Frank kneed him hard in the groin. Colin fell to the ground. He kicked him once in the stomach, walked around and did the same to the small of his back.

"Look at that," he said. "Scuffed my best pumps."

He picked Colin up and sat him on the wall.

"No hard feelings, Colin, but shag that tart once more and I'll set

138

the fucking dogs on the pair of you." He took a last look at the Cove. "I'm off for some breakfast. This sea air don't half give you an appetite."

Ethel thought his tale was over.

"You could have waited until you got back. Had the decency to tell me in person."

"You don't understand, Ethel. It was the pregnancy that threw me. We came back from holiday and I waited and waited. Every morning I would wake up and look for signs. Every day I would come back from work and sit in the living room, waiting for her to break the news. Six weeks this went on. Not a single word. You don't know the turmoil I was in. I couldn't think straight. Frank rang up once or twice to see how it was going. Asked me had I written to you, if I'd seen you. Then one day I came home and found her crying. Told me that she had thought she might have been pregnant the other week but that it was a false alarm. And then she clung to me and said that seeing as how we were getting on so well, she was determined to keep on trying." He turned to face her. His hands were shaking. "I've been so afraid, Ethel. Like a death sentence hanging over me. I'm terrified that I *will* make her pregnant."

"So you're still sleeping with her?"

"Of course I am. What else can I do?"

"We must get out," Ethel said. "As soon as we can. We've got one thing going for us. She didn't count on you coming back to me. She thought she might get pregnant before that. You mustn't make her pregnant. Mustn't."

"But she knew everything, Ethel. Who could have told her?"

"I know who told her," she said. "And I'll bloody crucify him when I see him."

When Lawrence next came in, as he prepared to leave without so much as a nod in her direction, she called out, "If you please Mr. Wheatcroft. I'd like a word."

"Miss Whitley?"

"Outside, if you don't mind."

She followed him out to his car. The MG.

"No Daimler today," she observed. Lawrence rubbed his hands in anticipation.

"If it's about those lessons," he said, "my mother has just picked up a hand-stitched pair of calf-leather driving gloves in one of her bring-and-buy sales. Superb condition. When she showed them to me I thought to myself, 'These should get Miss Whitley going.' "

Ethel shook her head. "It's nothing like that, Mr. Wheatcroft. I don't quite know how to say this, but I have to ask you. Have you ever," she said, dropping her voice, "have you ever taken a *professional* interest in me?"

"A professional interest, Miss Whitley? How do you mean?"

"In your line of work, Mr. Wheatcroft. Have you ever had cause to make note of my presence?"

He looked at her with some amusement.

"I have always noted your presence, Miss Whitley. You may not believe it but I have always held you in the highest regard."

Ethel waved his answer away. Was he being deliberately obtuse?

"I don't mean it like that." She took a deep breath. "What I'm trying to get at is, have you ever had cause to follow me?"

Lawrence looked pained. "What, without your knowing, you mean?"

Ethel nodded. Though when had he followed her with her knowledge?

"Miss Whitley! As if I would." He caught her worried expression. "Why? Are you in trouble of any sort?"

Ethel shook her head. No, she wasn't in trouble, just a young woman out of her depth.

They had it all planned. They would start seeing each other again, but this time they would be much more cautious. They would meet on

Thursdays, which was his night at the chess club, and occasionally, when he could, on Sunday, when she went to church. They would have to keep their eyes open, and tell no one, and in the meantime, they would work towards their future. They couldn't stay here. That was out of the question. Bedford, Colin suggested. Bedford! They should emigrate, Ethel said. They could save up enough money and book a passage across to Canada or Australia. They needed printers there, same as anyone else. She would make inquiries. Sometimes you could get assisted passage. If needs be she could assume Maureen's identity. She didn't have a passport. All she would have to do would be to send off for one in Maureen's name. A brand-new life. Away from everything.

And so she felt as if they were moving forward again. Colin would pick her up on the corner of Bateman Street and as often as not she'd have a couple more pamphlets in her handbag for them to look at. Vancouver, Montreal, Sidney, Melbourne. She fancied Canada more than Australia. Australia seemed too pushy. Usually they turned left directly underneath the Beacon and, climbing up around its skirts, motored up to the National Trust parking area at the far end of the ridge. It was more secluded there, with better opportunities to lose yourself, whether by discreet parking under one of the clumps of trees or by getting out and wandering down the grassy slopes to find a secluded hollow. They could have gone to other places, to the zoo at Wipsnade or south towards Thame and the villages which lay underneath the hem of the Chilterns and, if they had the time, on their way back they would have turned off the main road like they used to, and taken the circular route, through World's End and Monks Risborough where Colin had allowed her to take the wheel, but since their exposure, neither of them felt safe out there anymore. The Beacon was their haven. Standing on the low pedestal built on its summit they could look out to a land they would soon be leaving. Northeast lay Toddington Church; northwest, Leighton Buzzard and the village of Milton Keynes beyond; eleven miles to the southwest, Pulpit Hill, which overlooked the foundations of the smashed greenhouses on one side and on the other, the secluded but open parkland of the Prime Minister's country residence, Chequers. Beneath them, a long way below, to the northwest, lay their homeland, the Vale of Aylesbury. Old-road country, from top to bottom. Bronze Age and Celtic cattleways, Roman roads, the region was a maze of tracks and lanes, dominated by the matriarch, the Icknield Way on its long journey from Norfolk to Wiltshire, creeping along the ankles of these hills like a long worm threading its way through the soil. Packhorses, sheep and cattle, soldiers and merchants, pedlars and pilgrims had all passed along those paths. But though they stood in the heart of the chalk country, the land they looked out on was blue clay land, not chalk, and when warmed by the summer sun a faint layer of smoky blue would hang, like a low morning mist, on the fringes of the vale's heavy blooms. Now, with the young year's warmth fresh upon it, the colour had started to seep up into the growing grass. Life was returning to the trees and the hedges and the haphazard clumps of juniper bushes which studded the hillside.

"I'm going to miss all this," Ethel told him. "I know Canada will have other things, things I can't even dream of, but I shall miss England."

"There'll be compensations," Colin replied. He thought for a moment and then stated, "There's more room in Canada."

When it got too crowded they would double back and then turn right, up towards Gallows Hill and the junction with the A4146. The Hemel Hemstead, Leighton Buzzard Road. Three hundred yards away was a lay-by, with a steep chalk path up to the Beacon. It was more exposed than the car park up on the top, with a dirty loop of white tire tracks made deep by skylarking cars and heavy lorries, but though weekend trippers would use it as a base for a quick climb in the daytime, it was not a spot much used by courting couples. It had a barren, wild look to it, inhospitable to the needs of romance, and usually by the evening it was completely deserted. Sitting there one evening, underneath the Beacon's slope, they looked out to where, thirteen miles away, near Bletchley, a brand-new town was going to be built. Though not a brick had been laid, Colin was greatly in favour of the idea.

"That's where we should be making our stand," he told Ethel, putting his hand inside her blouse. "A new town for a new couple. Sometimes I wonder if we aren't putting too much faith in Canada."

Ethel said nothing. The town was a haze in the distance, a mirage. Perhaps that's why Colin liked it here, looking for something that was not there. She preferred it up at the top, even if there were other cars around. There was a noise outside. A face loomed up at the driver's window. She screamed. Colin jerked his head up.

"What's up?"

"There's someone there!" Ethel cried, pulling her blouse together.

Colin peered.

"I can't see anything."

"There was, I tell you. Look!"

Up at the top, they could see a figure scurrying up the path. In a moment he was lost amongst the gorse bushes. Ethel turned to face the windscreen and began to button up her blouse.

"That's just what I didn't want to happen." She burst into tears. "Fancy being caught like some common little tart out on a Saturday night. I'm sick and tired of this, I really am."

He started the car and drove down to the pub. It was only when they had pulled up in the forecourt and got out, did Ethel realise who they had parked alongside. She looked up and saw him standing in the doorway.

"Get rid of him," Colin hissed. Ethel ran over and kissed him on the cheek.

"Danny! Fancy seeing you here."

He held her at arm's length, embarrassed by her display of affection. He smiled gently, then raised his hand in greeting to Colin, still standing by the car.

"Nothing fancy about it," he said. "Took me hours to find this place. I had a feeling you'd be here."

"What a shame. We can't stop. Colin's expected home."

She broke off, conscious of how strange that remark must sound. "He's expecting a call," she added. "From Canada."

"Long way to come out," Danny agreed, "if you're expecting a call from Canada. Relatives out there, has he?"

"Ethel," Colin called.

"Look, I've got to run. We just popped in to get a packet of crisps."

"They're on me," Danny said, and led her into the bar.

"So what are you doing here?" Ethel asked. "And what about your baby? A boy or a girl?"

"A boy *and* a girl, probably. Twins anyway. Not due for another three months. Her family is stiff with them. They never warned me once."

"But that's marvellous. You should be home looking after her, Danny, not gallivanting around the country."

"Expanding, that's what I'm doing. Have to with two more mouths to feed. Saturday, it's Luton market, Wednesdays are in Dunstable and now Thursdays I'm over in Aylesbury. Good day today. Thought I'd drive out here and see if I could buy my old holiday chums a pint on the proceeds. Still on the beer, are you? Or have you gone back to your old bad ways?"

"Still on the beer, thanks to you."

"I never met a girl who could drink a pint like you. A treat for a man's eyes, you were. Sure you can't stay for a quick one?"

Ethel blushed. "Go on then. Fifteen seconds' worth."

"That's the spirit." Danny ordered her a pint. They stood in silence as the barman pulled on the pumps. Foam slipped down the edge of the glass. Ethel could feel her gut turning. She knew she should run away but her legs wouldn't let her. Danny handed her the glass. It was wet and slippery. Her hand shook as she took it. Beer ran over his fingers onto hers. She raised the glass to her lips, then paused. She hadn't done this since last summer.

"Go on then," he said.

144

She tilted her head back and poured it down. It was warm and flat, just how she liked it. Her throat opened wide, gaping, her stomach swelling as the beer flooded in. She could feel every part of her breathing huge and hungry. Suddenly she wanted to carry on all night, to drink with her throat open to the world, to inhale the smoke of twenty cigarettes, to talk to Danny and bump into him on the way back from the ladies. She looked at him in his dark crumpled suit and white shirt. He held his hands together in mock prayer. He had lovely hands, small with long delicate fingers.

"Praise be to heaven for sending such a woman to live among drinking men," he said. "You best get back to your fella though. I don't think he's too pleased to see me."

She walked over and looked out the window. Colin sat in the driving seat, fingering his beard. He scowled at her and beckoned furiously. She stepped back to the bar.

"I think I could handle another of those."

"I thought you were in a hurry."

"I am. Why don't you buy me another one."

They watched in silence as the barman poured her another pint. It was a slow process, adding weight to their unspoken conspiracy. Danny paid for it and slid the glass over on the polished wood. As she took it up she looked towards the window and said, "Colin's very private. He doesn't find it easy to talk."

"Not to me, he doesn't."

"Not to anyone. Things haven't been going well for us lately."

Danny had to stop himself from smiling. "I'm sorry to hear that," he said.

"Don't be. I'm fed up with people being sorry." She turned to face him. "This is no accident, is it? I mean, how many times have you been coming here? Come, on, straight out with it."

Danny sighed in admission. "Two or three months," he said.

"Why, for pity's sake?"

"You know why."

"What. To see this?" She threw back her head and drank the second pint down. She wiped her lips with the back of her hand.

He said nothing, but stared at her, waiting. She felt she had to say something.

"Colin's all right. But you know how it is."

"I do. You can talk to me though. Anytime you want."

Ethel gave him a scornful look. "That's what you call it, is it?"

Danny held his hands up in protest. "As God is my witness. I could talk to you and you could talk to me? Wouldn't you like that?"

She studied him for a moment. His eyes were dancing up and down the length of her lips. She decided quickly.

"All right."

"You mean that?"

Ethel was firm. "If you want to," she said.

"Of course I want."

"Really?"

"Really."

"Cross your heart and hope to die?"

Danny held his hand to his breast. "Cross my heart and hope to die."

Ethel drained the few drops left in her glass. "Well, that's settled then," she said, and moved to go. Danny followed.

"I'm finished by one o'clock on Thursdays," he told her. "The market's dead by then. I usually have a pie and a pint across the road. Do you see what I'm getting at?"

"Yes."

"And while I'm eating I could watch that throat working again."

Ethel laughed. "Not too many times you can't. I've got work to do in the afternoon."

"And I've got to drive home. Two pints at the most then. That's a good half minute accounted for at least."

They walked out to the car park.

"Mark it in your calendar," Danny advised her. "Thursdays."

"I'll remember. Busy day for me, Thursdays." She walked over to where Colin sat staring out through the windscreen. Danny called her back.

"Ethel," he said. "Haven't you forgotten something?"

"What?"

"You never bought those crisps."

"He doesn't like them," she replied. "Neither do I."

She met him the very next week, a little after one o'clock. She couldn't see him at first. She pushed her way past a bevy of farmers and cattlemen out for the day, through to the saloon bar where the local businessmen were having their lunchtime drink. She was conscious of her singular presence, and felt the need to excuse herself, as if she were trespassing on their private domain. She was wearing a tight polo-neck sweater and a plain wool skirt with a good clean shape to it, one of her smartest outfits, but every time she sidled past another unbending male throng she wished she had chosen something a little less demonstrative. She was aware of conversations coming to an abrupt halt as she squeezed past, of eyes dropping automatically to her accentuated bust, of heads turning, following her progress as she eased her way through. Standing in the centre of the room, trying to see over their heads, she felt as if all the eyes of the pub were on her. Then she saw him, half-hidden, sitting alone by the window and dressed in the same tatty suit he had worn that first evening up in the Lake District. He looked as out of place here as he had done there. Two untouched pints of still beer stood before him on the warped surface of the small table.

"Are those both for me?" she asked. Danny half raised himself out of his seat, a difficult manoeuvre under such cramped conditions. She hadn't expected him to show such old-fashioned manners. Now that she was here, she didn't know what to say.

"And how's your wife?" she said brightly. "No complications?"

"My mother's looking after her," Danny replied quietly.

"That must be a help. My mother couldn't look after anything. It's all I can do to get her into the garden. Ever since that shell exploded she's terrified lest there's one lurking underneath her leeks."

"Lives nearby, does she?"

"Mum and I"—she stopped herself just in time—"see each other quite often. We live not far from her." Eager to deflect attention away from her domestic arrangements she added, "Though not for long, perhaps."

"Oh?"

Ethel was pleased to add a sense of urgency to their meeting. "We're thinking of emigrating," she stated simply. "Colin believes he could find better prospects abroad."

She could sense Danny's confusion. "I didn't know," he said.

She took him into her false confidence. "Neither did we until recently," she told him, adding for no reason at all, except to demonstrate to herself her invincibility, "I haven't told her yet."

"Her?"

"My mother."

Danny held his glass in the air, examining its composition. "If ever I decided to emigrate I couldn't tell my mother, that's for sure. She'd lock me up and throw away the key. A fierce woman, my mother. She wouldn't approve of you for a start."

"Oh, and why not?"

"Coming here on your own, without telling your husband. Meeting someone you hardly know, in a bar full of men."

"You noticed, then."

"Noticed what?"

"That I seem to be the only woman here."

"Do you want to go somewhere else then?"

"Don't talk foolish. I've only just got here. Had a good day?"

Danny took his first sip. "This isn't my sort of crowd really. This is more a professional fair. People come here with a purpose. Mine's more the odds-and-sods variety. Still, you never know. If you never take risks you never get anywhere. Don't you think some of these men look deadly dull?" He leant forward and looked at her while taking a long draught.

Her pulse began to race before he had finished speaking. *If you never take risks.* It was the sort of language that she longed to hear Colin use. *If you never take risks.* Colin and she had taken risks to begin with, meeting in the cinema and then their holiday up north. They were taking risks now, seeing each other every week, making love in the front seat of his car, but the real risks, where life changes, weren't being taken at all. Unless something happened soon they would never get to Canada. They would be stuck in Aylesbury for the rest of their lives, looking at the increasingly barren promise of an uncertain future alleviated only by Thursday evenings. Only there wouldn't be any future for them. Colin would be forced to give her up again, this time for good. Maureen would see to that. She might meet someone else, but not someone who wanted to emigrate and now that Canada had been conjured up before her, that mysterious expanse of land waiting across an ocean for her arrival, Canada was her destiny. That was why she felt empty and consumed with hunger. With disturbing clarity she saw herself recalling this moment as an older woman, in Montreal or Vancouver, or somewhere she had never heard of, in a white clapboard house with snow outside and the car in the drive and the family looking on as she told them of this hour in a crowded English pub, when first she heard her calling. "That's Mom all right," her children would say, begging her to pull out her scrapbook and show them yet again the boat on which she crossed, every rise and fall taking her further away from all she had ever known. She would recall the cheap rooms they had taken, the struggle they had faced, the children being born, the friends they made. All through her will. And if she lost Colin, if he fell by the wayside or wanted to come back, well, it made no difference, she could cope with that too. How things had changed! Before he left her she had looked up to Colin, waited on his every word, but since his return it seemed obvious to her that she was the stronger of the two. Was that the reason they never drove along the disused greenhouses anymore, that the days of taking lessons from him were over? Not that Colin had ever taught her anything. Colin had only pretended to teach her, just as she had only pretended to learn. It had summed up their relationship perfectly, driving along that straight road going nowhere. For the first time in their affair, Ethel could see what Maureen had to put up with. It wasn't that she didn't love him anymore. But she realised that Colin was no longer all that mattered. Love's torch had been held close but now, raising it above her head, the softer light revealed cracks in his once perfect form she had never seen before, while on a similar examination, her own body revealed a discovered strength and beauty previously unacknowledged. She was a neglected masterpiece. Maybe she should have taken up Lawrence's offer after all. She would need to drive when she got to Canada. Everyone drove there.

She looked across at Danny. He was still talking, telling jokes, impressing her with his quick wit, twinkling his eyes at her like some teenage fairground idol. She knew now why she was here. She had supposed that she agreed to meet him because she fancied him. She had done what Jill would have done, put on her best bib and tucker to see if he could charm her knickers off. But she didn't want Danny, Danny was merely the means by which she proved her own radiant ability.

She let him buy her another drink. And then another. She was getting quietly squiffy and enjoying every minute. If she made a few mistakes that afternoon, who cared? Not that she would. She would be in control. It amused her to watch Danny. The drink had gone to his head too. He had put it away in uneven gulps, trying to impress upon her the depth of his own drinking prowess, but within the space of three pints, his tone had changed from one of cocky assurance to that old chestnut, the soul-bearing confessional. Danny was telling her his troubles and hardly knew it. There was his wife with her swollen ankles, and then there was his mother, as strong as a stick, who meant well but who got in the way. Nowadays he seemed to be too busy to talk to her (his wife not his mother), and when he did get home, she (his mother not his wife) was too fond of sticking her nose in. By the time they got her (his mother) to bed, they were too tired even to argue. And now there was the problem of his brother-in-law, the priest. He was getting on Danny's nerves too.

"Feel like a prize rabbit I do, a bloody exhibit, always on show. Sometimes I feel like breaking out and doing something really wicked, just to set him right. Don't you feel that sometimes? That you just want to get out there and lose control."

Ethel smiled to herself. That's what this meeting was all about. Losing control. That's what Danny thought she wanted him to say. He thought he only had to twinkle his eyes, loosen her up with a few drinks and she would be writhing about half-naked in the back of his van. If not today, then next week or the week after.

"I don't mean robbing a post office or kicking in a phone box," he was saying, "but something that would live in my heart, tell me that I was alive. Give these fat farmers something to talk about."

"There're plenty of gossips in this town," she said. "That's why Colin and me have to go further afield. Otherwise it would get back to her in no time."

There was a game on television which she watched with her mother, where the contestants had to stand next to the compere for sixty seconds and answer a series of rapidly fired questions without using the words *Yes* or *No*. Not a particularly difficult ordeal, one would have thought, given the fact they knew the rules in advance, but hardly anybody lasted the full minute. Ethel heard the gong the moment she finished her last sentence. Ah, the beer had loosened her tongue more than she had thought. She stopped. Danny put his glass down and poked at a table mat.

"I don't understand," he said with his mouth full. "Get back to who?"

She took a deep breath. "Don't you know, Danny? Can't you guess?"

"Guess what?"

"Colin. He's not my husband."

"No?" If Danny was surprised, he was good at hiding it.

"No. He's already married."

"But on holiday you said—"

"I know what we said on holiday. It was our first time away together." She drained her glass. "And if things don't look up, it'll probably be our last."

"Leading you on like, is he?"

"Not exactly." She found herself telling him the whole story. About Maureen. About Frank. About Thursdays. Every time Colin's name was mentioned Danny nodded sympathetically, as if Colin's wayward behaviour was all he ever expected from such a man. "The point is," she concluded, anxious to defend Colin against Danny's looks, "he's not quite as spineless as you think. He just needs a bit of a push. Sometimes I wish that brother of hers would come back and put the fear of God into him again. Then I might see some action."

Danny was determined to exploit Colin's weaknesses. "Or he might run away again, only this time for good." Ethel was forced to acknowledge the truth in what Danny said.

"One way or the other, at least I'd know where I stand," she admitted.

Danny leant forward, lowering his voice. "Why don't you arrange for his brother-in-law to find out again? Plan it so that he *does* put another little rocket under Colin."

"Don't talk daft. There's no telling what he might do."

"Well then, get someone else to do it. Someone you can trust."

"I don't follow."

"Get someone else to put the frighteners on him."

Ethel laughed at the very idea. "I'll put an advert in the paper, shall I? Wanted, Discreet Gentleman to Put Wind up Married Man." They laughed. "Still," she agreed, "I need to get him on that bloody boat somehow. Once out of her clutches he'll be fine. Remember how he was up in the Lake District? Full of beans."

Danny was tired of talking about Colin. It was time to get to the matter in hand. "He was full of something, I'll give you that," he said. "Had a smile on his face you could wipe a blackboard with. What had you been doing to him, you wicked woman?"

Ethel recognised the signs as well. It was time to leave. She looked at her watch. "Got to go now, Danny. Duty calls and all that."

Danny was clearly disappointed. "So soon. We've only just started."

She stood up.

"What about next week?" he pleaded. "Somewhere quieter. Away from prying eyes."

Ethel shook her head. "I don't think so, Danny."

"What's this then?" He sounded annoyed. She was slipping through his fingers and he hadn't a clue why. Ethel tried to explain.

"We met on holiday and that was fine. I enjoyed talking to you. Let's leave it like that. I hope everything works out for you."

"I don't understand. I thought this was going to be a regular thing."

"I know what you thought, Danny, and it won't work."

"What won't?" he asked with an air of injured innocence.

"You know exactly what, Danny. But no."

Danny opened his hands in protest. "You've got this all wrong," he said.

"I've got it exactly right, Danny, and we both know it. It's just not my way of doing things."

Danny threw one last shot. "Not even to make that man of yours a wee bit jealous? That might speed him up."

Ethel smiled. "I'll just have to think of another way."

"We'd make a terrific go of it, you and I," Danny said, grabbing her hand. "I just know it."

Ethel released herself from his grip as gently as possible. "I'm sure we would under different circumstances," she said. "But not like this."

Danny admitted defeat. "No hard feelings, then."

She bent down and kissed him on the cheek. "No hard feelings, Danny. None at all."

She threaded her way back through the crowded room. Behind the bar the barmaid was standing on a chair trying to reach a bottle of twenty-year-old malt. A man with large trousers and a loose bottom was leaning over the counter to get a better look at her legs.

"Better make that a double," he was saying, nodding his head back to his equally oiled companion. "He's got a lot on his plate this afternoon. Or should I say palate." She recognised both the voice and the skin. He turned round all too quickly.

"Ah, Miss Whitley. Thought I spotted you as you came in. Care to join us in a quick snifter?"

Lawrence Wheatcroft and Dr. Nash were well into what looked like their third hour. Their lips had that soaked-overnight look.

"I tried to give you the nod when you came in," Lawrence continued, "but you only had eyes for"—he nodded in the direction of Danny—"your young man over there."

Ethel felt obliged to reassert the high standards she expected from her men. "He's not my young man," she said. "Just an acquaintance."

Lawrence nodded, one hand on the bar to keep his balance. "You know Arthur Nash, don't you? The Aylesbury Groper."

Dr. Nash swayed before her. Ethel held out her hand. "We've met once before. In a professional capacity."

Dr. Nash's smile defied gravity. "Your place or mine?" he asked inanely.

"Yours," she said. "Though if you had got it wrong, it would have been mine."

"Miss Whitley is a legal beagle, Arthur," Lawrence explained. "She is to Cecil Hardwick what Della Street is to Perry Mason."

"That accounts for the condemned-man look on her beau in the corner. Served his severance papers on him, eh? You must be one of those heartbreakers that Peter and Gordon sing about. 'A World Without Love.' A silken tongue and a heart of stone."

"I don't know what you mean, Mr. Nash."

154

Dr. Nash banged the bar. "It's not agreeable, Miss Whitley. It grates the heart. Us chaps are always getting led on. Looks like gin but turns out to be gripe water. Isn't that right, Lawrence?"

"That's the truth of it," Lawrence agreed. "Up the garden path we trot but when we get there the door's slammed in our face."

"I haven't slammed any doors in anyone's face," she lied, flirting with them both. "Not today at least."

Dr. Nash grunted in approval. "If you don't mind me saying so, that lad didn't look your type anyway." He clapped his drinking companion on the back. "Lawrence here would be a much better bet. More miles on his clock, but definitely firing on all cylinders, what?" He and Lawrence both laughed.

"Miss Whitley has spurned my every offer." Lawrence hung his head in mock despair.

"Your *every* offer?" Dr. Nash sounded surprised. "I find that a hard concept to grasp. What exactly was on the menu?"

Lawrence took hold of an imaginary steering wheel and negotiated a couple of dangerous bends at high speed.

"I'm not surprised she turned you down," Dr. Nash said, looking on at Lawrence's charade with scepticism. "An evening spent arm wrestling is not many girls' idea of a good night out." He thought for a moment. "A games captain might go for it, I suppose."

Lawrence raised his eyebrows in exasperation. *"Driving,* Arthur. Driving. Many is the time I have offered to teach this young woman the rudiments of the road, but she has turned me down flat."

Dr. Nash turned to her. "Is this right, Miss Whitley? Spurned the opportunity to glean from the goggles of Lawrence Wheatcroft, the Mike Hawthorne of Stoke Mandeville. Isn't that where you crashed the last one, Lawrence? Straight into their ornamental clock. Those daisies haven't told the right time since."

Ethel followed their tipsy double act with amusement. Had she been sober herself she would have found their suggestive bonhomie offensive, but after three and a half pints and Danny sulking still in the corner, she was determined to give as good as she got. She touched Dr. Nash playfully on the chest.

"The trouble is, Dr. Nash, Mr. Wheatcroft's got no stamina. What us girls are looking for is someone who will last the course. If he gets put off by a few false starts and wrong turns . . . ."

She walked away quickly. "Go on, after her, man," she heard Dr. Nash say, and then guffaw as Lawrence choked on his beer. Once outside she ran all the way back to the office, her face burning with fumes. When she got there she went straight to the washroom, pulled off her sweater and drank from the cold water tap for five minutes before returning to her desk. She spent the rest of the afternoon expecting the dread silhouette of Lawrence Wheatcroft's wayward bulk to come looming up on the engraved-glass door. It never appeared.

A WEEK LATER COLIN AND ETHEL PULLED INTO THE LAY-BY AT AROUND seven, a little later than usual. It had been raining for most of the day. There was no possibility of them getting out for a walk, for the ground lay thick with water and the path to the top was slick and greasy underfoot. Though a respite had come briefly from the west, where the sun had broken through the heavy cloud, the air was cold and chill, and the light was fading fast. Instead of turning off up to their usual parking spot, he drove straight down to the lay-by.

"Aren't we going to the top, then?" Ethel asked.

"Too risky," he told her. "I want to be able to see when anybody comes sneaking up on us. We've got to keep our eyes open."

Colin leant forward and switched on the small interior light. He brought out the transistor radio from the side pocket and balanced it on the dashboard. He always listened to the radio at this hour. His favourite programme was on.

Ethel turned and pressed her face to the restless dark outside. The past few days had filled her with an energy she found hard to contain. Danny was on her mind, Danny with his dark suit and his small hands, Danny who had lain in wait for her, nursing his desire. He had only kissed her once, but his intentions had touched her in a way she hadn't felt since she had stood in the bath with Colin. His presence had lit a restless ache within her and she could feel it smouldering still.

The show blathered on; brash voices and hard unforgiving laughter. She stared at the plastic radio buzzing behind the wheel, an appropriate enough device for such a cheap and tawdry programme, hoping that it might slip off the dashboard and break. Something had happened to her that morning which she couldn't get out of her mind. On impulse she had walked down to the market in her lunch hour just to see if she could catch a glimpse of Danny without him knowing. There had been plenty of stalls there, but she couldn't find Danny's anywhere. She had wandered about the pushing crowd feeling increasingly cheated. This was Thursday, wasn't it? He had said Thursdays, hadn't he? Of course he had. There was no other day *to* come, other than Saturdays. So why wasn't he here? A woman's voice had disturbed her.

"You're Mrs. Whitley's daughter," it had said. She looked around. It came from a woman standing behind a fruit and veg stall. She smiled at Ethel as if she knew her.

"That's right," Ethel had replied, taken aback. "How do you know?"

"I've seen you here with your mum," she said. "Never forget a face. How's your mother keeping? Haven't seen her for a while."

Ethel had answered her hurriedly. She was nervous, afraid that Danny might creep up behind her and catch her unawares. She glanced over her shoulder towards the stalls on the other side, half expecting to see him standing there in that familiar pose, hands deep in pockets, grinning at her embarrassment. How she wanted to see him! How she dreaded that tumbling moment of surprise!

"Can I get you anything?" the woman called out.

Ethel looked back, annoyed that the woman should persist in breaking in upon her private world.

"I'll have a bunch of bananas and six tangerines," she had said quickly.

A sudden blast of music had made them both look up. Across the way, the man behind the toy stall was holding up an enormous teddy bear and waving its arm at her. She had recognised him at once. The thin taste of vodka came swimming back.

"If it isn't Miss Ethel," he had called out. "Want to feel my cuddly toys?"

Trembling, she had turned her back on him, trying to fish the money from her purse. Her hands were shaking so much she had dropped her change down in between the boxes.

"Don't mind him," the woman had said. "He's like that to every woman. Shift that box along and we'll soon get your money out."

Ethel had started to comply but the man had moved out from behind his stall and called out, "Here, Judith. She don't need any conferences. She's got a lovely pair herself," and with his mocking bray running up the back of her legs she had grabbed the bag and fled.

The programme finished. Colin hadn't laughed much. Looking across she saw that he had fallen asleep. Ethel leant over and switched off the radio. It was dark and lonely and getting cold. She put her hands between her knees and shivered. Time they went to the pub.

There was a tap on Colin's window. Ethel looked up. Standing next to Colin's door she could see the shape of a man, dressed in a heavy coat. She could not see the head, only the torso and the gloved hand knocking gently on the glass. It was a hesitant knock, a lost knock, a knock asking the way. She reached across, waking Colin as she did.

"There's someone at the window," she said, and Colin, dragged out of his sleep, tried to kiss her hair. Ethel brushed him off and wound down the window. The damp air rolled in. A gloved hand appeared on the lip of the glass, curling in over the edge. Though it unnerved her, she did not act upon it. She was safe within Colin's car. Two miles away a warm fire waited and a welcome from the landlord. She leant over further, putting her arm around Colin's neck as she did so.

"Yes?" she said. "Can I help you?"

Had she not opened the window so far, had she been not so eager to appear relaxed, with nothing to hide, then the barrel of the gun would not have made such an intrusion, indeed he might never have poked it through at all. As it was, it loomed up out of nowhere and sat next to his masked hand. She had never seen a gun close to before, only in westerns at the cinema, where they lay in leather holsters with pearl handles sticking out, ready to be twirled and caressed by callused, suntanned hands. This one was small and insignificant, neither one colour nor another, with a dark little hole pointing maliciously at her head.

"Open up and be quick about it."

She couldn't understand at first, the voice sounded so strange.

"Open up and be quick about it." The voice made no sense.

"What do you want?"

"I just told you," it said, and poked the gun in further. "Come on. Hurry up. It's bloody freezing out here." He spoke as if he had been expecting them earlier. It was a complaint about their timekeeping rather than the state of the weather. The gun had not yet registered fully in her mind. She tried to restore things to normality by introducing events that usually happened on wet roads at night.

"What's the matter?" she asked. "Has there been an accident? Are you hurt?"

There was no reply, only stillness. A car went past. She could hear the swish of the tires and see the passing lights, and then, from the other direction, came the heavier noise of a lorry charging down the hill. As the beam of light fell on them she saw the hand that gripped the short stubby handle. Each fingernail was painted a different shade of red, from flaming orange to deep crimson. For the first time Ethel felt afraid. She looked over to Colin. His pale face stared at the muzzle inches away from him.

The close noise of the passing vehicles had agitated the man. Holding the gun steady, he banged hard on the roof.

"What's the matter with you? Are you deaf or something?"

He took a couple of paces back and aimed it directly at the windscreen.

"If you don't open up right now," he said, "I'll shoot through the effing window." He stood his ground, waiting for them to come to their senses.

"What does he want, Colin? What does he want?" she asked again, but Colin seemed unable to answer, transfixed by the sight of the gun. Bending down Ethel saw that the man wore a flat cap and had wound a scarf over his mouth. Colin came out of his daze.

"I don't know," he said, answering her question as calmly as he could. "Money probably." Colin rolled down the window further and called out, "If it's money you want—" He dug into his coat and pulled out his wallet. "Here," he said. "Take this."

The man waved the gun in the air.

"What do you think I am? A thief or something? Open the fucking door."

His voice buzzed strangely, like when she used to sing with a piece of lavatory paper against her mother's tortoiseshell comb. It gave the swear word a new slant to its obscenity, as if it were a child mouthing it.

"Go on, Colin," she said. "Do as he says, for God's sake."

Colin turned in his seat and unlocked the rear door. The man came up and opened the door.

"Face forward," he ordered, and scrambled in. He pulled the door shut and edged over so that he was sitting in the middle of the backseat.

"That's better. You can put that window up now."

Colin did as he was told and then made an attempt to adjust the rearview mirror.

"Keep your hands to yourself," the man told him sharply, "and don't none of you turn round neither."

"What do you want?" Ethel repeated.

Again he made no reply. They sat motionless while he made himself comfortable. There was a rug on the floor and Ethel could hear him taking it up and laying it across his knee.

"Well, isn't this cosy? Now that we're all here." He laughed, and his tinny throat wheezed like a whistle in a Christmas cracker.

"What do you want with us?" It was all she could think to say, though she was frightened to hear the answer.

"Nothing that you can give, and no mistake," he said quickly. He leant forward. "What's your names, then?"

"He's Colin," she said.

"Colin. Good. And what do they call you, then?"

"Ethel."

"Ethel," the man repeated. "I like that. An old-fashioned name. You can call me Albert." He put his face up close to the back of Ethel's neck. "Not that it's my real name of course."

"Why don't you tell us what you want?" She could feel herself trembling.

"What I want? What I want, Ethel, is for us all to go for a little drive and a chat. When it's all over you can drop me off at the station or the bus stop. How about that?"

"OK," said Colin.

The man placed his mouth directly in Colin's ear. "No one asked you, fish face," he said.

Ethel diverted his attention. "Sounds fair to me," she put in quickly.

"It is fair, very fair. I'm a fair man, I am."

Ethel tried to keep the conversation along as conventional lines as possible.

"Where do you want us to take you?" she asked. "Only my mother's expecting me back fairly soon," adding as lightly as she could, "She's a dreadful worrier."

"You've only one mother," he told her gravely. "What will she do if you don't come home in time? Call the police?"

She could stand it no longer. "You're not going to hurt us, are you?" She started to sob. The man leant forward.

"There, there," he said. "You're not frightened of me, are you?"

"Please don't hurt us," she pleaded again. "We haven't done anything to you."

He sat back. "How do you know what you've done?" he said. "How does anybody know? Every little action has its consequence, Ethel. Everything you do has an effect. You may think it goes unnoticed, but it doesn't. It has what they call repercussions. You piss in the water and someone else ends up drinking it. It's all right when no one sees you, then you're OK. But when you squat over them and aim it straight into their mouths, that's a different story. People sit up and take notice. They don't like it. From the moment I clapped eyes on you lot I said to myself, 'Those two are up to no good.' "

"No," Ethel protested. "You've got it all wrong. We're just here—"

"Don't tell me. To admire the view."

"We come here every week."

"I bet that's true." He placed his gloved hand on her shoulder. "Don't you worry. When this ride is over I'll know all about you and your little ways. And maybe you'll have learned something about me too."

"If that's what you want," said Ethel. "We can talk while Colin's driving."

"You'd like that, wouldn't you, you clever little minx. Get me to spill the beans so that you can shop me to the coppers when it's all over."

"No, nothing like that. There'll be no need for the police if all you've done is ask us to give you a lift. What's the harm in that?"

"That's right," he said. "What's the harm in that?"

"None at all," she said.

"None at all," he replied, and the laughter wheezed again. "An innocent little pleasure."

The man lapsed into silence. Colin made to speak but Ethel put her hand out to stop him.

"Where do you want to go then?" she asked again.

"Guess."

"Aylesbury? Dunstable? Hemel Hempstead?"

He snorted contemptuously. "I've done all them places till I was sick and bloody tired of them."

"Oh, when was that?" she asked.

"Never you mind. You just keep your eyes straight and your legs crossed."

"We could drive you to Oxford if you want."

"Oxford! Can't you think of anywhere better?" He started forward, struck by a sudden idea. "I know. We could all go for a nice drive up the A1. Stop at Scotch Corner, have a bite to eat, and then pop along up to Gretna Green! That's it. Why don't we drive up to bonny Scotland?"

Ethel's heart began to beat wildly. "Gretna Green? It's a bit far, isn't it?"

"How far do you usually go, then? All the way?"

She said nothing.

"You can get married there, you know. You're not married, Ethel, are you?"

"No."

"Thought not. Who'd be a married Ethel out in this weather if they had a proper home to go to? Do you want to?"

"What?"

"Get married."

"Someday."

"To droopy-drawers here?"

"That's the plan."

"Why not tonight, then? Don't matter about the ring. You can borrow one of mine. Though none of them are strictly wedding rings, you know, on the wedding finger. *Not like the one he's got.*" He began to sing "Love and Marriage."

At the end of the first verse, he broke off into peals of laughter. Ethel looked across at Colin. He was covered in perspiration and looked deadly white. She knew she would get no help from him. He seemed completely immobilised by the presence of this man. She put her hand on his knee to reassure him.

"None of that if you please," the man admonished. "No distractions for the man in the driving seat. Time to hit the road, Jack. I'm getting impatient."

He put his mouth up against Colin's ear again.

"No monkey business, banana-brain," it said. "No flashing lights or dodgy indicators. I've got a shooter, remember? Don't think I'm afraid to use it, 'cause I'm not."

This was how she remembered it, a night of dark elasticity, without punctuation. The journey had stretched and elongated at will—but always ready to snap her back to the present with a cruel flick of the wrist. Though he harked on about being driven to somewhere particular, after an hour it had become clear to both of them that he had no such plan in mind. At times, parked by the telephone kiosk, or across from the confectionery machine, there had been a ghostly serenity to the evening, as if they were becalmed on an unknown sea, unable to stir. Then their words had glued them to the very seats, hardly daring to stir for fear of disturbing their fragile equilibrium. When they were driving, as the dark slipped by, the subjects slid this way and thither, like labels skidding across wet glass. Whole hours turned into periods of suspended hallucination, in which she knew not of what she spoke, nor what she had heard. But always, through it, came that song.

"Do you know the words, Ethel? 'Love and Marriage'? You can sing along if you like. But we don't want Colin to sing, do we, Albert? Colin's got a bloody awful voice, I'll be bound, like a cow in labour. I daresay you'd rather set your farts to music than hear Colin sing, eh, Ethel? 'Love and marriage, love and marriage.'"

Round and round they drove, back and forth beneath the Beacon, sometimes turning off, travelling for a while in the direction of Luton or Dunstable or down the other side to Tring and Aylesbury, dipping into the dark world of closed hedgerows and steep banks, and she would hope that they might drive far enough along to emerge to where there were broader roads and streetlights, where ordinary humdrum existence might break upon him and bring him to his senses, but before long he would direct them back up onto the spine of the country, out onto the broad sweep of the downs, where normal life twinkled lonely light-years away.

"Albert's getting bored," he announced. "Wants to play a game. What do you suggest? Hangman? Flip the Kipper? I know. I Spy. You both know how to play, I suppose."

Ethel nodded.

"Well, bags I go first. I Spy with my little eye, something beginning with *c*."

Ethel could feel Colin tense beside him.

"Car," she said, the word sitting in the pit of her stomach.

"Car? What does the man behind the wheel think? Is it a car, Colin? No? No, Colin's pretty sure it's not, but a good try Ethel, good try. Colin, any ideas?"

Colin said nothing.

"Come on. This is for your benefit too, you know. What could it be, do you think?"

"Camel," Colin said suddenly.

"Camel! Well, he's got a sense of humour, I'll say that for him. Do you know I haven't seen a camel around these parts for a good fortnight. Camel! I see I'm going to have to give you all a clue." His breath ran down Ethel's bare neck.

"Four letters," he whispered. "Last one's a *t*."

Colin shifted uncomfortably in his seat and glanced across.

"What is it, Colin?" the man asked. "You sitting on the answer?"

Neither of them said a word.

"You think you know what it is, don't you, Colin?" the man persisted.

"We all know," Colin said quietly. It was the first remark he had addressed to the man since they had set off.

"Do we? Do we now? Aside from the fact that you've disobeyed rule number one, the most important rule, and opened your nasty little cake-hole before anybody asked you to, what makes you think you're so bloody brilliant? There must be hundreds of four-letter words beginning

166

with *c* and ending with *t*. Hundreds. You must be able to think of one, Ethel."

"Coat?"

"Coat! Sounds possible. I'm wearing a coat after all. But Colin's not. He's wearing a jacket. And you're not, Ethel. You're wearing a jumper. And seeing as it has to be something in front of me, otherwise I'd be cheating, it can't be a coat. Something else sitting on the front seat, perhaps. What do you think, Colin? Something sitting on a seat?"

Ethel was crying now.

"See what you've done, you thoughtless pillock," the man admonished. "You got her all upset. Just because you think you know the answer. Go on then, clever clogs. Tell us."

Colin gripped the wheel of the car and stared ahead. There was no life he would show now, no flesh, no blood.

"No wonder he brings you up here all on his ownsome, Ethel. Such a party pooper I never met. I'm disappointed in you too, Ethel. There's lots of *c*'s you could have had. I can think of one *c* that is warm and silky to touch and which flutters uncontrollably in a man's hand. But you don't see many chits this time of year. They've all gone to Africa with the camels. And what about that knobbly little thing under the skin that just longs to be rubbed. Cyst. No? No. You're quite right. It isn't that either. All right, I'll put you both out of your misery. It wasn't a Celt, or a Cart, but a C . . . C . . . Clot! Colin the Clot."

The country had never looked so enticing as that night, Ethel thought, and she was surprised that she should have been so conscious of its fleeting, radiant grace. When he was not talking, when there was silence, and the car roamed at will through the empty hours, it seemed as if they were travelling at the bottom of the swaying sea and travelling in some dimly illuminated submarine, with dark floating strands of green parting before their smooth and ageless progress. The colours were not of the night, the moonlight colours, the shades of evening through which she had sat and watched with Colin, but refracted through windows which magnified the intensity of a new life outside. It was as if she were travelling through a country she had never visited before, that he was leading them into an unknown land of dark and dangerous beauty. Every now and again they would turn upon a startled rabbit, or glimpse the tawny flash of a fox's tail, and she thought how her life was out in the wild too now, that she was now a part of it, chasing through the huge and roaming night in search of survival, conscious of every scent on the wind, aware of every sudden noise. Danger was running loose beside her, testing her strength, drawing on her spirit, and she would have to embrace it, run with it, feel its breath hot on her face, until the dawn came up and rest and home and safety.

"You know what that last line in the song, where Mother tells Dad? What's that mean, do you think?" he asked her once, while Colin was out buying chocolate from a dispensing machine. "You can't have none?"

"I think you know very well what it means."

"No, tell me, because I'm an ignorant arsehole."

"Well, I think it's a song about the sanctity of marriage, that someone is not going to give herself without being properly married, without having a wedding ring on their finger."

"Unlike you, you mean?"

Ethel tucked her hands under her legs. Together they watched Colin pulling awkwardly on the jammed metal drawer.

"I could do anything I like tonight, Ethel," he said. "Anything at all. Do you think fungus-face would stop me? He wouldn't lift a finger."

"He's not the reckless sort," Ethel said carefully.

"Not the protective sort either. What you have to remember, Ethel, is that in marriage a man's wife will soon become mother to his children. So he looks at his own mother and he says to himself, 'Will Ethel come up to scratch? Or is she just good for something else entirely?' Perhaps that's why he's not bothered about me. 'Cause he's not that bothered about you. Have you ever thought of that?" He leant forward. "I'm not blind, Ethel. I know what you and Colin are up to. Not that I want to pass judgement. I'm as broad-minded as the next man. But whatever he tells you, you've just got to look at the state of his fingers and your bare knuckles to know there's no future in it.

"Colin's kisses,
 Colin's kisses.
 There for Ethel's lips,
 But not his missus."

Ethel, anxious to change the direction of the conversation, asked, "Do you have a mother?"

"Don't be so bloody stupid. Course I have a bleeding mother."

"I mean, is she still alive?"

"I still talk to her, if that's what you mean. Always scolding me for my wicked ways. You must think I'm a bad person too, treating you like this. Not to worry. I haven't come here to—you know, though I must admit, given the green light, well, what man wouldn't, Ethel, lovely girl like you, lovely figure, not that I would want to make you do anything you didn't want to, I mean I'm not the one who drives you up to some godforsaken hole in the middle of nowhere to play havoc with your underwear, am I? Is this what you should be doing, Ethel, a woman of your years, no offence meant, but you're not a bloody schoolgirl fighting off some spotty teenager, are you? Sometimes it takes an outsider to point things out to you, things that you've known all along, that's all I'm saying. I mean let's face it, Ethel, you deserve better than this . . . this c—"

"Don't say it."

"What? That he's not a—"

"Yes. No. That word."

"Just a word, Ethel, like all the rest of them. You say it."

"No."

"Colin the C—"

"No."

"Tell me he's not one, then."

"He's not."

"Not what? See? You can't even deny it. *I* don't mind saying it. Colin the Cunt. Sounds like one of Muffin the Mule's friends. Here Comes Colin, Colin the Cunt. I don't like the man, Ethel. No use trying to hide it."

No. He did not try to hide it. And as the night drew into morning and she felt herself growing stronger, closer to the meaning of this encounter, for there was a purpose to it, greater than the one of his making, of that she felt sure, she began to find his dislike of Colin infectious. Like the time she had been forced to feed Colin the bananas out of the bag of fruit she had bought that morning. *Two* bananas, the man had joked, one for before and one after. Just playing with them he was but Colin rose to the bait that time, opened his mouth to remonstrate, and waving the gun in the air the man told her, "Peel back the banana," he said, "Nice and slow, that's it, don't worry about the skin, it's not the skin we're worried about," and she peeled it, dropping the skin to the floor, hearing the man telling Colin to turn and face her, sneer and laughter in his voice. "There it is," he had said, "all white in the night, waiting to be taken in the mouth, for that's where a good banana likes to go, isn't that right, Colin, down the mouth?" and without waiting for an answer for no one was going to give him an answer he told her to slip it in, just a small bit at a time, Colin staring ahead, his eyes not looking at her, nor her hand, nor her face frozen in the shadows of shallow interior light, "Open wide, Colin, that's it, just as if you were at the dentist's," and she could hear his foot shaking against the pedal, he could too, "Good job he's not driving at this moment, though I do hear tell that a certain class of people can drive along with their mouths full for several miles, without having to

170

pull into so much as a lay-by or one of these newfangled self-service stations, for who needs to service oneself when your nearest and dearest is feeding you such a long and slippery length, I wonder whether anyone has found out just how many bananas a person could get in their mouth at one time on such a journey," the man said, "There's one for the *Guinness Book of Records*," and she found herself coming to the conclusion that Colin deserved this evenhanded treatment, that it was right and proper for him to feel revulsion seizing every muscle in his rigid body, the number of times he had leapt upon her without consideration, "Not too far, that's it, you've got it, don't you bite on it, Colin, don't you dare," God, sometimes she had felt like that, bringing it all to a bloody halt, and as she looked at him again, this poor man of hers trembling while she pushed it in and out of his mouth, it was a form of torture, she knew and she an active participant, the man enjoying every minute chewing on the tangerines, "A bit further this time, Ethel, you can see he wants a bit more, mustn't be a tease, Ethel, a tease is just the worse thing for a man with banana on the brain, almost halfway in and no gagging. Isn't he doing well? You might almost think he's had extra tuition. Is that right, Colin? Have you been practising with someone else, while Ethel's back's been turned? Come on, Ethel, get that rhythm going, he's getting greedy, he wants it all, wants it all, well give it to him, give it to him, Go on! Go on!"

He grabbed her hand and mashed the fruit against Colin's face and leant back, exhausted.

"Let's see what else you got," he said.

By dawn they were parked in a field, not half a mile from where they had set off, twelve hours earlier. Colin was close to exhaustion. Within five minutes he had fallen asleep, leaving Ethel alone with him. For a moment the two of them sat in silence, listening to his gentle snoring.

"Why don't you come and sit next to me," he suggested. "We can talk better without waking him."

She got up out of the car and stretched her legs, the morning air cold upon her. Standing there, in the field at the back of the cement works, the tall chimneys growing paler as the rising sun bleached them grey, she suddenly felt wonderfully refreshed. It was all over. They had passed the night unscathed. Colin was resting; the man was quiet and pensive; a new day was breaking. Surely, now he would leave? Looking back at the car, with Colin fast asleep in the front, the man half-hidden in the back, she felt deeply alive. She was thankful, almost, that this night had taken place. It had given her (Yes! Her!) the physical and mental superiority she had been seeking. It was her life, her future. She would dictate the choices. Colin slept while she lived!

She opened the rear door and eased herself in.

"Don't be afraid," he said. "And look straight ahead. You might catch a glimpse of me and I don't want that. It would put you in danger. I could never leave you then, could I?"

Ethel shivering, said, "You can trust me. You know you can."

"I can for the moment, Ethel, but the trouble is as soon as I leave you you'll go to the police. You'll have to play by their rules, then, not mine."

"I won't tell them anything," she protested.

"Yes you will. You'll have to. Here I am on the loose with a shooter in my pocket, kidnapping young innocent couples at the drop of a hat. Who knows what I might do next time."

"Why should there be a next time?"

"This is the first gun I've ever owned, did you know? Never had one before, except shotguns, but then they don't count. Everyone who lives in the country has a shotgun. For the foxes. In the war we had them ready for the Germans. Do you remember the war, Ethel?"

"I remember my mum holding me up to watch the planes go by. Why do you keep that glove on?"

"Never you bloody mind," he said. "Nothing wrong with it, is there?"

"Nothing wrong," she said.

"I only wear it on special occasions. Like that western where the bloke always puts his on just before he shoots someone."

"*Shane,*" she said.

"That's the one."

"You like westerns, do you?" she asked.

"I've seen them all," he boasted. "Burt Lancaster, Gary Cooper, John Wayne. It was Jack Palance with the glove. Walter Jack Palance as he was then known. He only spoke twelve lines in the whole film. Did you know that? Alan Ladd and Jean Arthur were the stars. He never kissed her. Wanted to, of course. But he knew how to behave. Not like me. Why don't you give me a kiss? I'd like that. Go on."

He presented his face close to Ethel's lips.

Ethel's heart beat hard. "I'd rather I didn't," she replied.

"But you wouldn't mind," he persisted. "Before I go, like."

"I suppose not."

"Well then. Close your eyes. No peeking." He turned her head with his gloved hand and kissed her.

"There. That wasn't so bad, was it?"

"No."

"Quite nice really. I feel so close to you, you know, Ethel."

"No more, please."

"It's a wonderful time to be awake, Ethel, first thing in the morning, with nature stirring all around you and someone you admire next to you. I feel capable of almost anything at this hour, know what I mean? Something to do with the light. Stirs me up. I may look like a townie but I'm a country boy at heart. Always have been."

"Me too," said Ethel. "I'll miss it when I'm gone."

"When you're gone? What are you talking about?"

"Nothing."

"No, come on. What did you mean by it?"

"It's just Colin and me—we're thinking of emigrating." She put her hand in her skirt pocket and pulled out a couple of brochures. "See? We haven't decided where yet."

He leafed through them in the growing light.

"Leave the country! With him? After all this? And what about your mother?"

Colin woke up.

"What's going on?" he asked.

"You taking her from her fucking mother, that's what's going on."

Colin was confused. "What's he talking about?"

"He's not," Ethel protested. "We haven't planned it yet. Nothing is settled."

The man pushed her away. He started to shout. "You haven't told her, have you, you cunt? Your poor old mum what brought you into this world and looked after you. This how you repay her. Fucking off to Australia."

"Canada, actually," Ethel corrected.

"What difference does it bloody make," the man screamed, tearing at the pamphlets. "What does it matter, you piece of cheap shit."

"No, you don't understand."

"You cunt," he cried pushing her, and Ethel, without thinking, turned on him.

"Give me them back," she demanded. "It's got nothing to do with you. Why don't you sod off and leave us alone? I'm sick and tired of you and your bloody games."

"I beg your fucking pardon?"

"Go on. Piss off. You've outstayed your welcome."

"And you've turned round, you stupid cow. Didn't I tell you? Didn't I tell you? Might as well do it all now."

He tried to kiss her, grabbed hold of her hair and pulled her towards him. She felt her hands go up, striking him on the arms and chest. She wanted to struggle but in the struggle to lie still, to sleep. She wanted to scream and in that scream to hear its echo die away to perfect peace. She wanted to turn, to reach out and hit Colin, to pummel him awake, to tear and claw at this man, to wrench the gun from out of his hand and run with her trophy down the road. She wanted to be rid of them, and all the others in her life. His lips were on her face again, sucking at the flesh on her cheek. She bent her head this way and that, crying "No" through clenched teeth, trying to move her legs, to get a grip on the floor. She was as tall as him if not taller and perhaps at this juncture fitter. She had breathed the fresh morning air into her arms and legs while he was still poisoned by their stale breath and a night of cigarette smoke. The gun came up and smacked her on the side of her head. She had forgotten about the gun and it brought her to her senses. She paused in her attack, panting, thinking it was over, that they would all calm down.

"Have you learnt nothing tonight?" he was saying. "Do you want it printed in black and fucking white?" He banged the gun against her head again, while his other hand scrabbled about on her lap. She thought for a moment he was trying to put his hand up her legs and she brought them together hard, twisting away, but it was the brochures he was after, balling them up in his fist and hurling them into the air while Colin rose up out of his seat. He had sat quiet the whole night. Not a word of encouragement, not a word of defiance. There had been times when he could have acted. If she had been at the wheel she would have pitched the man forward by slamming on the brakes when he was off guard, leaning over the front seats, making her sing that dreadful song.

"You stupid bitch. You stupid bitch," he was saying. "You still don't get it, do you. What do I have to do to make you understand?"

Colin leapt up with a roar, trying to grab hold of not just the man or the gun or his hand but everything that had gone on that night, to reestablish his preeminence in his car, no doubt, like a caged beast at the zoo, breaking free.

"Love and marriage . . ."

"That's it," Colin was shouting, "it's all over. This has gone far enough. I—" He lurched forward, and she could see the flash of the man's fingernails, all the colours of red as he wheeled the gun back, dragging the metal across her face. At that moment the shot rang out,

175

filling the car with burning incense which made her nostrils flare and her lungs gasp and her ears pop. Colin's head spun on the axis of his neck, spun to face the front and the great arc of mess that fell like a sudden squall on the windscreen, his hands flaying out to the lost, falling world, his fingers smearing the patterns of wet blood before his body bounced against the door and toppled sideways onto her seat. She fought against the man while he held her close.

"Be quiet," he said. "It went off. I didn't mean it. I swear to God. I was only here . . . only here. It wasn't meant to end like this. I would have left you both. I promise."

He began shaking her.

"It was his fault, can't you see, turning round like that. Not that you'll tell them that, even though it's the gospel truth. I never meant to kill anyone. That was never the plan."

He held her still again.

"Kiss me, Ethel," he said. "Kiss me so I know you believe me," and suddenly she had nothing left, no energy, no room for sobs, no place for anger, no spirit, and no defence. She raised her head and felt his lips tremble against hers. Her jaw went slack. Her mouth opened. Colin lay dead in the front and now an unknown tongue began to creep over hers. It moved cautiously, like a young worm in a fresh corpse, working its way into the still, warm flesh. His hand moved under her jumper to her breast, burrowing beneath her brassiere until it covered her skin's hidden expanse. She felt him move the breast slowly, rolling it round the soft arc of its weight, his mouth complementing the rhythm, hand and tongue seeking to devour her quiet, untouchable secret. Outside she could see the distant chimneys of the cement factory rising up through the long grey grass of the meadow. A weak sun was coming through, revealing the glittering dew-rimmed spiders' webs that hung on the pale grass stalks. They swayed in obeisance to the light wind, so strong, so quickly torn apart. His hand fell to her waist, pulling her closer. A wider mouth was being asked for, a more compliant response. A hooter sounded, calling men to work. Breaking off, she turned to where Colin lay. He should be getting ready for work now. His hair needed combing.

"He was only Colin," she said. "Look at him now," and with that she felt her neck gripped hard and her face pushed down, pressed up against the back of the seat.

"No hard feelings," she heard him say, "No hard feelings . . ." and then, an explosion in her ear, as if she were bursting out of a tunnel into glorious light.

She told it to them first as she lay in hospital and weeks later, when it was safe to move her, back at home in the living room, which her mother had converted into a downstairs bedroom. Although her story had a beginning and an end, the events in between had no such prim timetable. They merged into one another, distorting the shape and progression of the night like sudden rain falling upon a fresh watercolour. Despite what she had promised the man, right at the outset she had told herself the importance of remembering everything about him which would help the authorities later. But lying in her hospital bed, wracked with thirst, alone and starved of life, when it came to filling in the man's outline with substance, a body and a character which would direct them to his lair, she realised with acute shame that she had failed in her duty. There ought to have been two Ethels at work that night, one putting the man at ease, the other committing his little mannerisms, his tricks of conversation, all to memory, but so anxious had she been about demonstrating the integrity of the former, she had quite neglected the needs of the latter. How tall was he? She was not sure. What colour were his eyes? Blue, but she could not be certain. She thought he had a good head of hair. Why? Did she see it?

Her image of him, at best confused, was tormented further by the fact that her powers of recollection had been damaged. Not by the

177

wounds to her head, which, apart from the loss of one ear had been miraculously slight, but by Colin's death. Part of her recollection of that night lay with Colin, just as part of his lay with her. With him gone a vital portion of her memory had been spirited away, and left in its place was the dead remnant of his own. She had no one to help her remember, no one to prompt or correct her, no one with whom she could collaborate. And yet, Colin was the key to the tragedy. Looking at his picture staring from her bedside table, remembering his last moments alive, the quick turn of his head, rubbing his confused eyes awake, remembering too how he had woken beside her on their precious holiday, wide awake and grinning, with only a few hours of snatched, sexual sleep behind them, she was left facing an unpalatable truth. It was not cruel accident that had led Colin's killer to the lay-by beneath Ivinghoe Beacon, nor blind fate that had directed him to lie in wait on a Thursday rather than any other day of the week. It was a planned and deliberate attack. The man was not waiting for any car, but his. "Colin," he had said, when she told him his name. "Good." This man had resented Colin. He was jealous of him. Who did she know who was envious of such an unenviable man? Who knew of their circumstances and the intricacies of their guarded arrangements? Who had tried to set them asunder? She knew the answer before she had finished asking the questions. "No hard feelings," he had said as he slid the van door shut. "No hard feelings," he had said as she rose in rejection from the pub table. Danny Dancer. She looked at Colin's picture and his eyes stared back in agreement. Danny Dancer. She said it out loud. The name filled the room. She said it again. It took form and stood before her. She raised her voice and summoned the police to her side.

THREE

JUDITH STARED AT THE NEWSPAPER, HOLDING HER HANDS OVER THE SWELL of her stomach. The child kicked against her, as if registering the shock that had coursed through her body. Danny's picture was spread out over the front page. The woman's too. Judith patted her apron pocket. The money lay undisturbed.

Apart from her, and the man who sold the pet food, most of the other stall holders lived on what Jeremiah's friend, Mr. Alcott, called the rim of the criminal's cup, always ready to sup deeper when the opportunity arose. Besides Frank and his tearaway son, there was a man who sold radio and TV sets, a balding furniture dealer, the thin leather-jacket boy, two bric-a-brac women enthroned on identical armchairs, the tattooed secondhand record stall holder, three or four clothes merchants, the budgie and tortoise man and Danny: a throng of leering misfits, with perspiring lips and cutout catchphrases, which they traded as eagerly amongst themselves as to the public on parade. Danny had turned up earlier that year and had set up his stall apart from the main body as if unsure as to whether he belonged in such disfigured company. She had noticed him right away, standing to one side of his display, his hands tucked into his trousers, waiting for the place to fill. He was what Frank disparagingly referred to as a "domestic," selling household goods, crockery and brushes, dusters and cutlery, saucepans and glass, all brought to life by a vaudeville show of cheap gadgets, guaranteed to work only when coaxed by his well-rehearsed hands. On that first morning, Judith recalled, it had been a Continental vegetable cutter which peeled potatoes, diced carrots, sliced runner beans and turned his hands raw in the damp morning air. He had spent the first half hour nailing it down onto a deformed orange box which skittered about his feet with every glancing blow. How right, she had thought, that this device, so bright, so cheap, with its untrustworthy promise of an easy life, should be harnessed to the fortune of this young man. He would have offered his own guileless wares to some unsuspecting bride by now, she did not doubt. After walking around his makeshift stage a couple of times, he had come over, his hands in his pockets, to ask if he could borrow a few vegetables. There was no question of money being offered, nor did the tone of his request give thought to the possibility that she might refuse. It was an acknowledgement that he was as new to the game as the bright aluminium pans which hung out along the length of his torn tarpaulin frame. She weighed out a pound of potatoes, gathered up a handful of carrots and watched as he balanced the bags in the crook of his arm.

"A beetroot would come in handy," he said without reserve. "They cut through beetroot better than a bacon slicer."

She had picked out three, still warm from the morning's cooking, and tossed them over. "Take something for yourself while you're at it," she added. "What about one of these nice Jaffas? You'll need something after your gabbing."

He shook his head. "Anything like that brings me out like the Michelin Man. Tell you what though. I'll take a couple of those apples," and he leant over and helped himself to two of last season's Cox before picking up the rest of his produce and ambling back, conscious of her following eye. Her customers received less attention than usual that morning, for when she wasn't banging cold weights down on the scales, or counting the wet change into outstretched hands, she was looking at him. He was like Will had been, dark and light on his feet, a man who looked upon women and dared them to read what mischief lived behind his eyes. He had a good voice too, clear and vibrant, with just the hint of a Celtic lilt. Judith saw how the crowd ebbed around him, bunching in noncommittal huddles while he ran his patter through, saw how he willed them beyond their better judgement to open up their closely felt purses with a simple shrug of their shoulders. He had the gift, marrying adult wit with boyish good looks. By the end of the morning there were only three left. As she was packing up, waiting for Jeremiah, he had returned bearing one in his arms.

"Here," he said. "Take it. They're all the rage."

She shook her head. "I'll stick to my kitchen knife if it's just the same to you."

He held it out. "Have it anyway," he said. "I can't be seen selling the same thing week after week. Bad for my image. I got this automatic cat feeder coming. The lid springs open on a clockwork timer. You can feed moggy when you've gone to the seaside for a weekend."

"Or knock him unconscious if he stands too close," she said laughing.

He looked around in mock fright. "Don't tell them that, for God's sake. I've got two dozen of the blighters to shift."

He watched her as she strained to stack the half-empty boxes.

"Here," he said. "You shouldn't be doing that. Sit down and read the instructions on the inside. There's recipes at the back. French."

She had shooed him away when she saw Jeremiah turning their van into the square, for he would have disapproved of her consorting with the likes of Danny, but in the following weeks they had taken to looking after each other, he the young man with the mild, flirtatious manner and her the older woman, capable, unsung, and pregnant. He arrived late, or if not late, then disorganised, with no thought for the food he might need for his stomach nor the change he might need for his till. She took to making an extra round of meat-paste sandwiches those Thursday mornings, which Jeremiah put down to the young one growing in her belly, remembering how she had once shaped them for him. At the close of the morning's business Danny would make her a presentation of the week's gadget before going off for a pint across the square, and though he would ask her to join him, she always refused, even on those days when she drove in herself. There was no telling who might be in that small, well-frequented pub—Chief Inspector Alcott, Cecil Hardwick, Arthur Nash, any number of people who would know her, mark the state of her physique and pass judgement over the company she kept. So she thanked him and shook her head and drove back to their house, with his new gift safe under a piece of sacking until next morning when she would hide it, along with the others, behind the row of blue enamel jars in the larder. The back shelf was full of such presents: a two-handled ice crusher, a loaf slicer (crust or no crust), a clockwork lemon squeeze, and, most cumbersome of them all, a device that would crack open as many as six eggs at one time; all made out of a variety of tin and all destined to fall apart in her hands. Like a child with a collection of mechanical toys who has learnt to preserve their fragile mechanisms by using them only rarely, once a month she would carry one of his offerings out onto the kitchen table and deliver herself into the gadget's unpredictable care, wondering how he arrived at his life and how she had arrived at hers. Standing there, watching a bleeding potato judder through the dim and treacherous blades, she could see him lurching on the latch late at night, hear the raging words thrown up and down the stairs, and feel the pulse of his young, feckless hands round her forgiving waist the next morning. Life with Danny!

Jeremiah tapped her on the shoulder.

"Time to go," he said.

She picked up the paper and followed him into the hall. There he stood, patting down his overcoat pocket, checking for his mahogany box and his rail warrant. A small black suitcase stood by the door.

"Come on, Judith," he scolded. "Don't stand there gawping. I've got a train to catch."

"And two men to hang," she thought, "waiting in an Edinburgh jail, counting the hours of their last weekend on earth."

They drove to the station in silence, the bag on his knee, her belly pushed up against the steering wheel. A charmed pregnancy, is what the doctor had told her, looking smugly upon Jeremiah as if it was him who was responsible for her rude health, but as yet, she had not come to terms with her baby. Only last week, in the tradesmen's hut where they brewed up their early morning cup of coffee, Frank had called out, "Never too late, eh, Judith?" while she stood tying her calico apron across her growing bulk. She had nearly burst into tears, for like Jeremiah, she feared the consequences of this child, how its unpredictable presence was destined to lay bare all the matters in their life which she had hidden away. She looked upon other babies tucked in their prams and saw in their wide-eyed regard what her own would bring, the hands that would point to unread signs, the eyes that would seek out hidden vistas, the mouth that one day would denounce them both, her for never having made a stand, him for who he was.

But there was a benign power here at work too. At night, when she closed her eyes and imagined the whooping yells which would excommunicate this high denomination of silence forever, she would open them to find Jeremiah looking down at her with such an expression of bewildered sadness that she half expected a solid tear to drop from his glass eye and bounce across her stretched skin like a marble dancing on a drum. He would place his hand on her and shake his head, unable to articulate either his feelings or his expectations, a captive in a prison of his own making. Whoever was changing and turning inside her was, in its slow uncurling way, changing and turning inside him too.

"I'll be back Monday evening," he now said as she drew up outside the station. He patted her shoulder. "Mind you don't overdo it. Get someone to unpack the boxes."

"Another month and I'll jack it in altogether," she told him, and he stood, half bending into the van, nodding in solemn approval.

"See you then," he said, and walked across into the station entrance. She did not wish him a safe journey. She had never done so. How could she when she knew the outcome of his visits?

She sat in the car park watching his train pull out, with him sitting there alone, with his revolver and his calculations and his long trip up north. Her husband had travelled the length and breadth of Britain. He had crossed the sea to Ireland and the Isle of Man. He had visited counties and cities she had only seen in postcards, and yet the view he brought back was always the same, of prison walls and prison bars, and the lit fear of the men's faces behind them. She had never been anywhere except Oxford and a fortnight by the sea in North Wales, when he had left her halfway through and travelled to Bristol to perform his duty there, meeting up with her the following afternoon, her in a bathing costume and he still in his suit and waistcoat, licking on an ice cream. She had stared out at the rolled trousers and the folds of fat sitting happily in striped deck chairs and vowed never to take another holiday with him ever again.

She drove on down to the market square. She was early. No one else had arrived to set up. As she climbed out, she looked across to the public lavatories, where a figure stood in the shadow of the scrawled doorway. She knew what she was going to do the moment she saw him.

"I didn't do it," he said, stepping out, and she said, "No," simply, as an agreement of acknowledged fact. It did not occur to her to press further, for she did not need an explanation or a defence. Let others inquire of his alibi, weigh the balance of his story against the geography of circumstance. He had not done it and that was all she needed to know.

"I didn't do it," he repeated, a little louder this time, and she nodded, looking about her, her eyes telling him what he knew already, that it was madness for him to be here, in the same town where his victims lived. No! Not his victims!

"No," she said, adding, "but you can't stay here."

He looked at her with that expression which admitted both guile and guilt, which had so bewitched her all spring, and stretched his hands out.

"No one knows about me and this place yet," he admitted. "I kept it to myself. Because of . . ." His voice trailed off.

"Because *she* lived here?" Judith asked.

He hung his head.

"You young fool," Judith said, remembering with a sudden flush the reckless power of desire. And all over such a mealymouthed-looking creature, she thought. She shivered, wanting to hold him in her arms. He looked so young.

"How long have you been here?"

"All night practically. I knew you'd come early."

"Me?"

He shrugged his shoulders and put his hands back in his pockets, like some pose he had learnt from the cinema. "I thought you might lend me a couple of quid. Or turn me in. Either way."

"You'll be picked up before the day's out, money or no," she snorted, and pulled the van door open. "Get in and stay down. We'll sort you out later," and pulling him by the sleeve of his jacket, bundled him into the back of the van and closed the doors.

All that morning, squatting on the cold metal floor, an old piece of sacking wrapped around his shoulders, aching with the damp chill that had settled on his very bones, he could hear her call out greetings, declining with heart-stopping regularity, the offers of help that were thrown her way. How did she do it? he wondered, keep such equilibrium with me shaking inside, and she, twisting the brown bags in the morning air, thought the same. And yet she knew the answer. She had only wanted Danny as a secret, had only found his presence attractive because it would have been forbidden, had only hidden his tarnished gifts so that she could take them out alone and let her guarded, guilty thoughts run loose through their machinations. Now, wrapped by her own hands, was the source of the secret itself, a living body which she could protect from those other hands which waited only to receive him when his spirit had floated up over the prison walls and out to the great roaming air above. She would save him. She would save him and no one would know, her eternal secret embedded in the wakening soul of her child. Her baby would turn and hear her secret murmuring. It would shift and squeeze its tiny hand, feeding on the goodness of it, listening to the pulse of it as it flowed from her through to its curled limbs.

During a lull in the morning's crowd she poked her head in and quickly handed him her sandwiches and the remains of her coffee, telling him fiercely that if he needed to go, not to be bashful but to do it in the flask. He had shaken his head, denying such a possibility, but almost as soon as he had drunk the lukewarm drink, his bladder filled to bursting. Pulling down his trousers he put the flask between his legs and began to fill it up. He was halfway through, feeling his liquid warmth on his hands, smelling its sour pungency, when the sirens came. The van reverberated to the beat of them and he pulled the sacks down to cover his nakedness, oblivious to the meagre protection they might afford. The murmur of the crowd subsided and then rose again as the men jumped out, a tall man striding in their wake, like an exultant conqueror.

"You'll not get much from them that way," Judith thought, and then the man turned and caught sight of her and raised his porkpie hat before striding over. Danny heard him greet her by her first name and heard her reply. She knew him! For one moment he thought that he had been trapped by the placid sympathy of a woman—a thing which had only happened to him once before, when he had wedded Eileen. He began to shake so hard he thought the van would start to rock on its ancient springs.

"Yes," Danny heard her say. "He came most Thursdays."

"What about last week?" the man had asked and she hesitated, wanting to tell him then and there how Ethel had run away. But she could not, not with Danny in the back.

"I don't think so," she said.

Frank came sauntering over.

"Mr. Alcott," he said with mock civility. "On cabbage patrol this morning are we?" and the detective, looking at Judith, as if reproving her for working alongside such a man, marched him to one side and spoke to him unpleasantly in the hook of his ear. Frank began to cringe like a dog expecting punishment, his head held low but upraised. Then his hands sprang to life, describing Danny's height and his dress, pointing to where Danny had kept his stall. Finally his fingers pointed back with conviction to Judith. Alcott returned with Frank trotting a respectful distance behind.

"Mr. Tapp says he thinks he was here," he told her in a tone that suggested he did not hold much store by what he had learnt from that quarter. "Jem's away at the moment, isn't he?" he added, the weight of the law resting on that fateful second word. "Glasgow, isn't it?"

"Edinburgh," she replied. It was an odd mistake for him to make. If anyone knew where the killers of a young policeman were to be executed, it would be a fellow officer. Suddenly she knew discovery was around the corner. In an hour's time the market would close and she would have to load the boxes back on the van. How could she refuse help? And even if she did, who would heed her protestations? The doors would be flung open and the capture of the innocent accomplished. Her armpits began to drip with sweat. She could smell herself. Alcott was looking at her intently.

"Are you all right?" he asked, beckoning to one of his men.

"I'm tired," she said. "Jem told me not to overdo it, but I thought I'd be all right. I was until you came. It was the sirens that did it. Made me feel all queer." She smiled weakly. A well-constructed lie was on offer now, one to which she knew he could subscribe.

"It's them vibrations," Frank put in. "They're designed to make people feel queer. You best be off home."

Judith nodded.

Alcott waved an arm. "What about all this?"

"Frank'll take care of it, won't you, Frank?"

Frank jerked his head in the direction of his stall. "Ivor's coming over in a minute. You get on home, love. We'll see you all right."

What would they have seen that morning, the careful citizens of her hometown? A woman, driven mad in middle age, mouthing inanities to herself, shouting above the noise of the traffic and the twenty-year-old engine. It was only after she had turned into the one-way system the wrong way and come up against the red face of the lorry driver glaring down at her, his bare arms thrown up in contempt, that she understood the meaning of her words and why Danny, crouched in the back, a thermos of leaking piss rolling round his feet, should be looking at her in the mirror with a degree of incomprehension that told her he would rather be taking his chances out in the High Street than locked away in her lunatic company. She had muttered the names low as they passed through the gates, acknowledging the reassuring wave of Alcott as she lurched off, louder as she picked up speed and turned, too fast, into the main body of traffic, and then, with the shopping crowd spilling out over the pavements, and the hooting horns and youths standing idly by, calling out to passing girls, they had come tumbling out, those forgotten names of her husband's dead, names she had never known, names buried in his black book beneath the floorboard, names that had seeped into her ear as he lay on top of her, her face pressed down against the sheet, his hands, his cold hands holding her flattened breasts still, touching a body that was not hers, pressing against a rump that was not hers, his mouth hovering near her heedless ear. Whose identities had she assumed all these years? What men had he brought into her bed, made love to behind her back? Was that why she had to be facing that way, the man's posture, so she could be a man to him? Parker, Wheeler, Schilling, Lewis, out they came, dropping through the trap of her mouth; Wells, Cartwright, Bingham, Longford; the one with the poet's name, Keats, who had cursed him to the end; the dwarf who needed over eight foot of hemp, Stolly;

189

the man who had sung music hall numbers to the very last, Ellis. How did she know these names? From whom did she learn their details? Russell, Walker, Mason; the multiple child killer MacCready, beaten religiously by warders and prisoners alike, who tried to speak to God through swollen lips which could not bear to touch; Littlewood, Glennister, Patterson, the one whose intestines fell out onto the floor, Fletcher; Norris, Roberts, Fleming, Wickert; he had been taken with Wickert, more than he cared to admit, she could tell from the way he had written the boy's name that same evening, staring down at bare details he set underneath, his weight, his height, the length of the drop, mouthing his Christian name and his surname over and over before adding a slow and deliberate sentence that became the boy's epitaph. What had he written? A question? An answer? An observation which invoked both? Adams, Everett, Isaacs, Osbourne, out they poured, witnesses to the one whom she would save from her husband's grasp; they did not come reluctantly, they stepped up in order, hooded and bound, no hope of reprieve. And it was she who pulled off their cowls, she who named them again. She was their resurrection!

"Concentrate on the bloody road, missus, not your knitting circle," the man had called out, and she had thrown the van into reverse, hardly looking in the mirror, mounting the pavement, knocking a metal rubbish pin from its lamppost mooring.

"Slow down," Danny shouted from the back. "You'll get us both nicked," but she could not, not until they had reached the outskirts of town and the turnoff and the straight run home. She knew what she had to do now. This afternoon she would fix him up with some new clothes. It was fortunate that he and Jem were of similar build. Tonight he could sleep on one of the chairs downstairs. By Sunday he would have to be gone. She had made enough money from the market that morning to get him a fair distance away, though travelling by train or by bus might be a problem. Perhaps she could drive him down to the coast, to Dover, or Folkestone. But Danny in France? Whatever, he must get away. To stay here was madness.

Five minutes later they pulled into the half-weeded drive. As they got out he stamped his feet on the packed dirt and looked around.

"Your bloke away long?" he asked and following his eyes she saw how he must see it, a small, bare brick house, with bare glass looking out onto a bare yard. There was no peace to these walls, no comfort at the window. It came to her how alone she was. He could kill her at his leisure if he so desired. This instant. An hour later. In her sleep tonight.

"Scotland," she said. "On business."

He patted his stomach. "I'm starving. You got anything to eat?"

He followed her as she walked into the kitchen and watched as she unhooked the blackened frying pan from the wall.

"So tell me," she said. "How did you get into this mess?"

He told her to the sound of bacon frying and the smell increased his appetite for the telling of his tale. The thieving had been the final wedge between him and his wife, so he started with that, hesitantly at first, moving around the kitchen picking up objects as he talked. She must have known what he was, she supposed, but as he unfolded his story of housebreaking and petty theft, Judith felt her faith momentarily drop away, as if he were a son or lover who had betrayed her trust. It had been the loan of the van that had done it, that and the willingness of the boys from Father Rooney's youth club: Charlie, Seb and Little Ivor. They had started in earnest during their holiday up in the Lake District, cruising around the town when they were supposed to be hiking across the hills with the others. They turned Kendal inside out that week. And when they got back they carried on.

"It was a kind of calling," he said, taking the plate from her. Judith nearly threw him out there and then. She had had enough of callings to last her a lifetime.

It became an established routine. He'd volunteer to take the lads off for a weekend camping: fresh air, long walks, a chance to see another side of life, that was how he sold it, all the tommyrot that Father Rooney could swallow. They were careful, mind. They didn't steal near where they were staying. They would drive thirty miles away, so no one would make the connection. Saturday afternoon would be spent looking for likely prospects. Saturday evening they would get drunk. Sunday was opening time, when all good families were busy in the House of God. Danny approved of that arrangement. It seemed a fair balance of need. Drainpipes, window frames, doors kicked off their hinges, there was no attempt to disguise their intent. Any cash was divided up equally and he'd slip the boys an extra ten or fifteen quid for the rest, depending on what they got. Afterwards he'd fence the lot. A weekend of B and B they used to call it. Beer and Burglary.

He wiped the egg yolk from the plate with a crust of bread and grinned. Food had restored his confidence. He was a sport again.

"When Eileen found out all hell broke loose. We had a terrible row that Wednesday night. Ended up with her throwing me out. I got in the van and drove down to Cardiff. I got there just after dawn and made my way down the docks. There's always one or two drinking clubs open, if you know your way around. Down there morning's no different from any other time of the day. I drank a lot that morning. Waiting for someone to come along."

"Someone?"

"Yes, you know. A woman."

"A friend, you mean?"

"No. You know. A woman."

A woman. Ah yes. Judith had heard of them.

"Jacqueline, she called herself. Well, she took pity on me see, took me back to her place. Fried me an egg. Made me a cup of tea. I must have passed out, 'cause I can't remember much else."

He remembered it well enough. Eileen and he hadn't been arguing about the thieving that night. It had been the other thing. He had stumbled home swaying with the heavy threat of sex. She was standing at the sink, washing up the day's dishes. Eleven o'clock in the evening and she hadn't finished the housework. Coming up behind her he had dipped his hands in the soapy water before clasping them to her bosom, a joke, but she pushed him off saying she had work to do. He tried to touch her again, remembering how she had loved it in the early days, when he would play with them, the only man that had ever played with them. Before the pregnancy he would have her stand on a chair so that he could pull her blouse up and suck them, and when they sat watching television he would ask her to sit naked from the waist up while he flicked at them with the ridge of his five outstretched fingers. It irritated her sometimes, he could tell, but he had been fascinated by them, how they could change texture and dimension, how they could collapse into themselves while at other times poke hard through her dress like brass thimbles on a thumb. His mother had caught them once, coming up the stairs in her bedroom slippers, popping her head round the half-open door without knocking, probably because it was eleven-thirty in the morning, and there he was sitting on a chair with his back to the door, sucking on them while stirring his tea. He hadn't noticed a thing but after she had ducked back out of sight and tiptoed back down Eileen had told him. "What must she think of us, halfway through the day and still at it," and laughing she had pulled his cock out and sat on him, the chair bouncing across the linoleum as she brought them off. That's what it used to be like. That was all he asked for. But now everything had changed and he did not understand why. Three days he had waited, three days with not so much as a murmur and that night, with a long evening's drink inside him, he needed attention. He had thrust his hands into the sink and pulling them out one by one, had thrown the plates to the floor, telling her that he didn't give a toss about the washing up, that it could stay in the fucking sink for a fortnight for all he cared, and again he lumbered up against her, trying to kiss her, hoping that her anger would turn into a different type of passion, but she began to strike out, complaining about the stink of his breath and his one-track desires, bringing her brother and his bloody van up again, and how he was going to get them all into trouble and Danny, pushing her across the room, had stormed out, her cries chasing him down the stairs. An hour went by before he realised he had decided on Cardiff, the van reeling along the road, coughing and spluttering, his arms wet and cold, his fists banging on the steering wheel in frustration. He had

193

thought of sex the whole journey, hoping that he might pick up a hitch-hiker, one that would show him a bit of leg and keep his mind occupied, but the road was empty and when he got there it was the drinking houses he craved, the pints of beer and whisky chasers, and it was not until well past ten o'clock and he found himself at a table in the middle of a near empty room, that he had looked across and seen, sitting up at the bar, a woman of about thirty, with two fresh scars running across the length of her cheeks, dividing her face into two halves with a bloodless no-man's-land in between. Above lay the eyes, dark and soft, touched with an old kindness; below the mouth stretched tight and painted cock-sucking thick. She must have been held down for that little operation, he thought. She was a half-caste, and her skin had that mesmerising glow which comes with such a mixture. She wore one of those string vests, the type that singer, Tom Jones, had made famous, and her dark gaudy breasts rolled visibly underneath.

"Pretty, eh?" she had said.

"Can't take my eyes off them," he said.

She used to be in cabaret, she said, until her accident. "Spit and polish is all I'm fit for now." It didn't take long, with her money paid up front, and she drinking white port and lemon as fast as he could buy them, for him to run out of cash, but not before they had established that they had lived once on the same street, when Danny's father had been around, and the recollection of those times dislodged his desire for a moment, remembering out loud his mother, and how his father left her, Danny not eighteen months old, the farewell note propped up inside his cot. "My little messenger of joy," his mother had called him, he told her, and she had kept it and its faltering punctuation in full view on the mantelpiece to serve as a warning to both of them as to the wayward tendency of the male race. So she had taken back her maiden name and given it to Danny, and the two of them had watched his father's feckless sap rise up through his bones.

Suddenly he had felt ashamed and with tears welling in his sentimental eyes, had moved to leave, but the woman had taken his hand

and placed it on her cheek, tracing the hard ridge of her scar on his fingers.

"It's not your mother you need now," she said. "Nor your wife, nor anyone else you know. Just remember to go back when the rage has left you. Meanwhile I'm still thirsty."

"I've run out of money," he admitted, still trying to evade the responsibilities of his purchase, but as if to impress upon him the casual depravity of her outlook she said she would make them enough to last them the afternoon, that is if he didn't mind the loan of his van for half an hour. So they drove around the backstreets, her head half out the window, calling out her wares. Three or four times they stopped, and each time, negotiations completed, he walked unsteadily up and down the street for ten minutes. When he came back she'd be sitting back in the passenger seat again counting out the crumpled pound notes. Pretty soon she had another fifteen quid, plenty for their needs, and Danny, in a woozy attempt at thanks rather than lust, made to kiss her but she turned her head away, saying "Not yet, not after what I've just done," and with that they went to the off-licence and thence to her room. It wasn't much of a drop, a bed and a gas ring and a sink behind a faded curtain. She stood by the window and tipped the bottle to her mouth, spitting the sweet liquid out into the basin, before pushing him onto the bed and freeing the lush bounty of her breasts into the drunken wet of his mouth.

It was midafternoon when they came to. A freighter load of Dutch sailors had come ashore. They could hear them singing streets away. Danny had wanted to stay but she wasn't having any of it. She shook him to his senses.

"You don't understand, chuck. If I'm not out there, they'll carve up the rest of me for a game of noughts and crosses. Now wash your cock and go home."

He was still drunk when she pushed him down the stairs, a couple of pounds in his back pocket for the petrol home. Somewhere outside Gloucester he must have passed out, for the next thing he remembered, it was dark and the van was pitched halfway up a grass bank. He reversed it back on the road and drove on until he found a proper lay-by for the night. It was dawn when he woke. He got home just in time for a bollocking before breakfast. He had too much of a hangover to go to market that day.

So no alibi did Danny have. Judith was relieved. It was as it should be, a fugitive from justice with every hand turned against him but her own. That evening they decided what to do. In the morning she would drive him to Cheltenham. From there he could get a train or bus back to Cardiff. He knew people there who could get him on a cargo ship, no questions asked. He might even try to slip across to Ireland.

She went to bed and drifted into troubled sleep, with Danny downstairs, wedged in Jem's armchair. She woke with a start. Danny was sitting beside her.

"What is it?" she asked. "What do you want?"

He buried his head in his hands. The curls of his matted hair rested on his dirty neck. She should have run him a bath. His voice was muffled.

"I can't sleep."

Judith sought to reassure him.

"There's nothing to worry about. No one will find you here, I promise."

Danny shook his head.

"It's not that. It's just . . ." He stood up and drew the curtain back. The moon was full and silver and shone through onto her bed.

"I can't go," he said. "Not yet."

"But you must. I thought we had it all planned."

"I know. But I can't. I have to wait. They'll not be long now."

Judith was wide awake now. "You mean your children."

Danny nodded. "I have a bad feeling about this, that I will never know them and that they will never know me. It's my only chance."

"You mustn't think like that," she said.

"But I do. They've got it in for me you know, her and the police. The law according to Ethel and Alcott."

He turned to face her. "What if I did do it?" he asked suddenly.

What if I did kill the man and shoot her. Would you have helped me then?"

She pulled herself upright, not caring how she looked or what he saw. "Yes," she said. "But you didn't do it, did you, Danny?"

He sank down beside her, saying nothing.

They sat there looking out to the cold bare sky. Though the air seemed still, they could hear the weathervane as it squeaked back and forth. And then it came to her, imagining the dull wet fields below, stretching to where they stood, those glass ghosts of her courtship. She would hide him in the one remaining greenhouse. The frame had stood firm these twenty years, the buckled girders now embedded in coils of grasping hawthorn, a thick canopy of wild blackberry and elder reaching out over the space above. Caught out in the freezing rain last winter, she had fought her way in there, marvelling at the dry shelter that lay hidden inside. He would be safe there. She took his hand.

"You're cold," she said. "Here, you great big baby." She pulled the eiderdown across and covered him, the shaft of memory at that phrase stabbing her hard. "And no snoring," she added, trying to mask the long hurt in her voice. "Or it's back downstairs with you."

They stayed like that, propped up against each other, half-asleep, until the light awoke their embarrassment.

"Get you down now," she admonished, pushing him off the bed as intimately as any lover, "and let me make myself decent. We've work to do."

If anything it was her, encumbered by her bulk, who worked the harder, and with greater purpose, marching around the yard, pulling the tarpaulin and the portable army bed from the stubborn holding of the old chicken coop, who gathered the buckled saucepan, the rusty Primus stove and the canvas stool in a small pile in the middle of the yard, thinking of the days ahead. It did not occur to her that she was breaking the law, that she could be sent to prison. It felt natural and right and strangely ordinary too. How could arranging these items to form a shelter be described as a criminal act?

They transported the stuff, not with the van, but in their arms, scurrying along the scraggy edges of the fields. Judith led the way, Danny looking over his shoulder, thirty feet behind. It took them an hour to reach it. Twice he ducked down out of sight on Judith's warning, only to discover that it was a pheasant she had disturbed. When they got there, he put his load down and scratched his head, unable to find the way in.

"Look," she said. "Through here."

She turned to face him and backed in, feeling the thorns tug at her coat and pull at her hair. Danny followed, catching the branches as they swung back in his face. Then they were in, standing under a wild canopy of latticed green.

"What did I tell you?" she said triumphantly, as if she had fashioned it with her own hands.

"It's better than a tent." He reached and touched the roof. "I could stay here for weeks."

"No one can see you from the road," she said. "Not that many come along here at the best of times."

"What about—"

"Never," she said emphatically. "Not since his accident."

Danny came up to her and put his arms around her.

"If you weren't expecting," he said, "I would lift you up to God and whirl you in my arms."

"Whirl me once," she said. "Then let's get you sorted."

Working with him she felt a contentment rising that had long lain dormant, recalling those days in her youth, standing alongside Will and Jem, working towards a common goal. There was a marriage of purpose here she had not felt for years, as they touched each other in easy familiarity. By the end of the afternoon they had made the hideout as secure as possible, with black tarpaulin stretched across the branches above, one side hanging down to form a protective wall for the camp bed. Beside it, on the flat ground, lay a transistor radio, a penknife and a torch. At right angles stood an orange box which held the cooking utensils, his knife, his fork and his spoon. In the space below were packed his provisions: tins of

198

soup, corned beef and creamed rice. A tin-opener hung from a protruding nail. They stood in the entrance, admiring their work. She had thought to leave him here this night, but now the time had come she could not. She wanted him back home with her.

"Come away now," she said, pulling at his arm. "You can stay one more night. But out at first light. I don't want any trace of you when he gets back."

There was no pretence that evening, no shuffle of intent or hesitant words. They went about the evening's business as if they had lived together all their lives. While she made the supper, a vegetable soup and egg custard tart, Danny sat by the open back door watching the long day vanish behind the ridge of hills. Afterwards he washed and dried the dishes and put them away in the cupboard on the wall. She dug out some old shirts and trousers she had found and these she held up against him to see if they'd fit before laying them out on the range to air.

"He'll not notice," she told him.

"Not unless he finds me in them," he said.

She put her hand to her mouth and laughed.

"He better not do that."

They went to bed early. She was thirty-five, with her husband's child inside her. She wore a nightdress and dressing gown. He wore his suit and socks. She held him all night.

At breakfast they were strangers again, unable to marry the intimacy of the night with the prosaic formality of what was to come. They skirted around the breakfast table, unable to touch, unwilling even to sit down together. There were no discussions now, no cursings, no commiserations, no hopeless prayers to the future. They had all gone before. Now was the time to accept the inevitable. There could be no postponement. Once he was fed she led him out into the yard, the morning frost still clinging to the air. She kissed him before he took his leave, kissed him as if they were man and wife and him on his way to join his regiment at war, kissed him as if she might never see him again, on the cheek and on the lips and on the cheeks and lips again, holding him close, brushing back his hair, holding him at arm's length before pulling him towards her again. Swallowing her tears she repeated the rules he must obey: to keep out of sight at all times, no matter what he heard; never to light a fire no matter how cold he grew. She would bring him dry clothes, fresh supplies of food and drink every day. If for some reason she did not appear, he was not to feel abandoned. She would never desert him. The only thing which could prevent her coming was the baby, and that, she added, patting her stomach, was not due for months. In any event she would always ensure he had three or four days' supply. If he needed her in an emergency he was to tie his scarf on the elder by the door. She would find out about when the babies were due. Perhaps, after they were born, and the hue and cry had died down, she could fix up a secret meeting. And after that, he must leave. Promise her that. Promise her that. She hugged him once more and pushed him away.

"Go now," she said. She stood there, watching him skirt nervously along the fields until he had turned out of sight.

She thought of no one else in those three weeks, not herself, her child, nor her husband, around whom she moved so strangely. It was almost as if she did not care, that she revelled in her wilful behaviour, her solitary walks, her sudden bouts of tears, her unfathomable need to stand out in the yard at all times of the day looking out over the bleak fields.

"What are you doing out there?" Jem would call out. "Don't know what's got into you these days. Spend more time outdoors than the cat." And she would stump back in, annoyed at how he had broken into her constant train of thought. Jeremiah was becoming infuriatingly unpredictable. When he was meant to be out on the fields he would appear suddenly at the door, checking to see if she needed help, just at the very time when she wanted to be left alone.

"Don't fuss so," she would tell him and after a cup of tea would lead him out the yard and back to his work, impatient at his intervention, hoping that Danny would not be too angry at her late arrival.

She went to him as soon as Jem was out working in the fields, calling his name softly as she pushed the branches aside to find him standing by his bed, his unshaven skin taking on a scabrous film of cold; she would have a hot drink and a change of clothes at hand, and watch him as he pulled the damp shirt from his shivering body, wishing she could take him home and let warm water run over her hands and onto his pale skin. It was not a belief in his innocence or a desire to keep him from the clutches of the law that made her so determined, but simply the need to have him for herself. Lying awake, imagining him curled up on the camp bed, listening to the hidden scuffles of the night, she could believe themselves succeeding, with Danny safe abroad with his young family and she a perpetual fairy godmother to whom they would always be grateful, but each time she pushed her way through and brushed the hair from her eyes she knew that this was not so. Every gesture, the manner in which he squatted on his haunches, the fugitive way he cupped his hands, the frozen hunching of his shoulders, even the way he stood and greeted her, always sensing betrayal and disappointment, was borne under the weight of his imminent capture.

"Any news?" he would ask, and she would reply, "Not yet," and each would busy themselves with some slight domestic chore, quiet in the knowledge that time was running out.

In that first week it was an adventure for them both, her outwitting Jeremiah, driving the van past his hiding place, knowing that he was safe inside, him watching the ordered world go by, oblivious to his presence—the two bicyclists on their way to work, the milkman, the postman on his scooter, the rider and his hunting horse, cocking a snoot at Alcott and his merry men hunting for him high and low. She would tell him stories too, as warm as any fuel, for Jem was a constant visitor to Alcott's lair and would sit in the snug listening to his languorous boasts. Alcott was in love with the woman, she told Danny, least that's what Jeremiah thought. Carried her picture around like a besotted suitor, forever bringing it out, smoothing it out on the table, gazing down on the crumpled features.

"Look at her," Alcott had urged, "poor slip of a girl, and that bastard in the back, like a monkey in a zoo, doing all sorts of unimaginable things in front of its audience," and Jeremiah had supped his beer in commiseration, thinking that whatever else she was, Ethel Whitley was not a poor slip of a girl. Physically, she possessed an almost sensual figure, but one which she hid under deliberately plain clothes, trying hard not to be noticed. An unusual attitude for a young woman these days.

"She lost an ear, you know," the detective added.

Jeremiah had known. He had known many times over.

"Fancy a girl of her age losing an ear," Alcott had muttered glumly. "She should have two."

"Her hair will hide it," Danny had said, when she had repeated the conversation, tired of Alcott's public house gallantry. "Her hair's thick enough," and Judith had nodded, conscious of how callous his remark sounded, and not caring.

"It's all right for her," Danny continued. "He believes anything she tells him. I called him once, when the word was out that he was looking for me, but he didn't want to know. Just wanted me to give myself up so that he could wrap the thing up, all neat and tidy. Well, he's not going to get me that easy."

"He's not going to get you at all, Danny," Judith told him. "Not if you're careful."

"I'll be careful Judith, never you fear. I'll see my babies and slip away under his lovesick nose."

But as the days turned into weeks, the opportunity she had seized, to become all things to him, mother, wife, friend, and lover, yes, she considered that once, were never fulfilled. She was his keeper and then, lo and behold, she became his jailer. A transition of hopelessness.

"Any news?" he asked a week later and, afraid to answer, she shook her head as he snatched the bag from her, examining what she had brought. There was no room for love now, the love she had felt swirling within her when she had lain against him, listening to the weathervane creaking with his breath washing over the back of her neck. He was an animal now, pitiable and selfish, unable to comprehend the risks she was taking, how in his struggle to be free, he might claw and wound her; and he, caged up in this prison of her making, would pace up and down all day, rehearsing his petty complaints in her absence so that when she arrived he could greet her fluently, in a full pent-up flood of recrimination; the shirt she had given him which had scratched his skin all night, the socks that were too big for his feet, and, most importantly, the news of his family she had promised to divine. One afternoon she arrived four hours late. Jem had been in the yard working on the tractor. When she got there he was pacing up and down, his face rigid with impotence and rage.

"Where have you been?" he demanded. "I've been waiting all day."

"I came as quick as I could. Here. I baked you a pie. It's still warm."

"What sort of pie?"

"Rabbit. Jem shot a couple the other day."

Danny turned up his nose. "Rabbit. That what the gypsies eat."

"It's what I eat." Judith put it down on the orange box. "If you have any sense, it's what you'll eat too."

Danny began to tear at it, half grumbling, half chewing.

"It's all right for you," he said, his mouth full. "You're not stuck here. The Primus keeps going out and I never have enough water. At least I'd be washed and fed in prison." He took another huge mouthful. "I went for a walk last night. Walked down the road a free man under the stars. Not a soul to be seen. I walked up to your house and back again. I stood looking up at darkened windows, thought of you lying up there, thought of my wife and my mother, thought of all the people safe and in their houses, and me, forced to live like a rat all on account of one woman. Then I turned on my heels, the nails on my boots ringing on the road as clear as a peal of bells. I wouldn't have jumped out the way for anyone. I was fired up, ready for anything. If a policeman had stopped me I would have killed him, smashed his head on the road, I was that mad. If somebody had stopped to give me a lift I would have taken it, or pulled them out and driven off to God knows where. To her, maybe. Ethel's house. To wake her up and ask her one good ear why in God's name she was doing this to me. Because I didn't have her? Because I left her alone like she asked me to? Or what? As it was no one came, so I walked back here again. But I nearly didn't stop."

Judith was aghast. "You mustn't go charging about like that, Danny. Not even at night. You must be more careful."

"Careful?" he said, his voice rising in discovered anguish. "Being careful won't get me out of this mess, Judith. They're out to get me, those two bastards," and he looked at her with such an expression of bitter incredulity she almost thought that he was beginning to blame her for his troubles.

"Didn't I get you out from under his nose once already?" she asked him. "How long do you think you'd last on your own?"

Relenting, he said, "I'm not trying to deny what you've done, Judith. But God knows you weren't careful that morning. You were crazy. I wish my wife would be crazy like you."

"She has more to lose than me," she said. "I have just you."

"Me? I'm lost already."

She sat down on the bed beside him. He leant down and laid his head on her lap (That was all she wanted! That was all she wanted!). She could feel his muscles sink into hers. Perhaps he would rest for ten minutes. His eyes closed. His breath came even. A car passed. Was it slowing down? He sat up quickly, his eyes darting on the imaginary horizon outside.

"It's time you went," he said, pushing himself off. "Anyone can see that van from the road. You should park it further down the road and walk back."

But though she could try and rescue him from his solitude and pour oil on the waters of his despair, the cold she could not keep out, no matter how many bundles of dry clothes and cups of hot drink she urged upon him; there was no fire to warm his chill bones, to steam away the clinging damp. By the third week it had invaded every pore, every fibre of his body. His brain was as cold as his heart. His charm as numb as his fingers. He moved slowly, he thought slowly. Every time he revealed his lonely whiteness it seemed softer and paler than before, as if she could peel his flesh away with the back of a penknife. His lips had become cracked, the stubble on his face was hard and uneven, like an ill-used scrubbing brush, smelling of old tobacco and soup. He could hardly grasp the tin-opener and had cut his hand on the jagged edge, drinking it cold from the tin. When he lit his cigarettes he would hold the match until it died, oblivious to the flames that licked at the swollen tips of his fingers.

On that last day he was lying curled up on his careless bed, his greatcoat draped over him, plumes of thin smoke filling the foul-smelling den. He didn't look up but stared straight at the ground. The smell of urine was unmistakable. A glance to a thick puddle by the bed told her the story.

"Danny," she said. "Get up."

"What for?" His voice was flat, but not without emotion. "For another tin of tomato soup? Last week's *Woman's Own* perhaps?"

"Danny. You mustn't give up. Mustn't." She pulled his hands out of his coat and began to kiss them. They smelt of unwashed private parts, long held.

"I can't take much more of this," he told her. "I need something to keep out the cold."

"I'll make some tea," she said, stroking his head. "You should look after yourself more."

He sat up. "I don't want tea," he urged. "I need a drink. I'm fucking freezing to death, woman."

She stood up. "We'll light a fire," she said briskly. "We'll take the risk and light a fire."

He grabbed hold of her and pulled her down again. She could not bend.

"I don't want a fucking fire," he said slowly. "I want a drink. A bottle of whisky. I haven't felt my toes for the last week and my fingers are that stiff I can hardly hold a thing. It's killing me, can't you see?"

Judith walked across the square and stepped up to the bar after work. The usual Saturday morning crowd was gathered round the bar. As she gave her order to the overworked barmaid the man next to her turned. He raised an imaginary hat and beamed.

"Goodness gracious, Mrs. Bembo," he said. "It's not often we see you in here. Do you know Lawrence Wheatcroft and my assistant, Jill? My *ex*-assistant, I should say."

The young woman nodded.

"We met once at a party," the girl said. "You probably don't remember."

"I don't go to many parties," Judith said.

"Last year. I talked to your husband, on the sofa. While you went for a drive. About six months ago." Her voice trailed away in embarrassment. Arthur Nash had no such inhibitions.

"Mrs. Bembo. Perhaps you better tell us who exactly this whisky is for."

"It's for my husband," was all she could think of saying, wondering as she pronounced the words how long it would take for this particular lie to get back to him. Arthur Nash would not forget this purchase in a hurry.

"To get him over the happy event, eh? Take it from me, he'll need a little more than that, poor chap. Buy him a whole bottle, madam."

Judith made no response but waited for the barmaid to return.

"We were talking about this dreadful business on Gallows Hill, Mrs. Bembo," Dr. Nash persisted. "Jill here is a close friend of the unfortunate woman."

"I'm sorry," said Judith.

"Still, there's one good thing that has come out of it," he continued. "These two reprobates are getting hitched. Met up again while visiting the poor girl in hospital." He drank deeply.

"Congratulations," she said.

"They're off on a motoring honeymoon. Can you credit it?"

"The Continent," the large man admitted. "I'm looking forward to putting the Daimler through her paces."

"I'd have thought you'd be more interested in putting Jill through hers, eh?"

Arthur Nash drained his glass and laughed. The girl kicked him in the shins. "Careful, Arthur. I don't work for you anymore. I'm a real person now, remember?"

Arthur Nash changed the subject back again.

"Do you know, Mrs. Bembo, Jill tells me they've had the nerve to put that man's wife in the same hospital as her. Different ward, of course, but still."

"What man?" she asked.

"The one they're after," he shouted at her. "They seek him here, they seek him there, they seek the blighter everywhere. Don't bloody find him, that's the trouble. Too busy faffing around with this bloody breathalyser nonsense."

"Not today, I hope," the young woman observed.

"Nothing to worry about there," the dentist confided. "Constable or magistrate, they all need fillings. It's amazing how understanding people can be when they are faced with the prospect of a drilling without anaesthetic." He lowered his voice and gathered them around. "As a matter of fact I have it on the very best of authorities they've put up massive security around the place. Just in case sonny-Jim shows up. Twins, would you believe. Two of the little blighters." He banged his empty glass down. "That's the trouble with today's world. Too many women having too many babies. We should all take a leaf out of Red China. One baby per family. Any more and it's off with your gooseberries."

She carried the news back like a precious parcel, fearful that it would break in her hands. She told it to him slowly as he gulped at the whisky, hoping that he would take the news calmly. He jumped up and began to tear at the walls.

"I can't go on like this," Danny said, kicking the bed over onto its side. "You should have brought me a razor."

207

"You're going now? But what about the police. I told you. They're everywhere."

"It has to be now, Judith, can't you see? Do you think I'll last much longer in this hovel?"

A hovel. That is how he saw this place they had made together. Not a refuge or a sanctuary, but a hovel. He stood close to her now, red in his eyes.

"A razor, dammit," he hissed. "I want to be off tonight."

Then they heard another voice. Nearby. "Everything all right?" it said.

Danny picked up the bottle, weighing it in his hand. Judith shook her head.

"Ahoy in there. You OK?"

Pushing her way through she looked up and saw Lawrence Wheatcroft's head hanging out of a large blue car. His fiancée was next to him.

"Saw your van off the road. Not broken down, I hope," he called out.

"No." She stood there wondering whether they had heard their voices.

"Lost something, then? I was always good at hunt-the-slipper."

"No." She laughed. "If you must know I got taken short. Happens to women in my condition all too often. That's something you've yet to find out."

"When you've got to go you've got to go," said Lawrence, patting Jill on the knee.

They stared at each other. She could hear Danny frozen inside.

"Quiet here, isn't it?" Lawrence observed. "Not much traffic about."

"Hardly any."

He nodded. "I was counting on it. Thought I'd practise driving on the wrong side of the road."

"I see."

208

"Don't see the point of it myself."

"What?"

"Driving on the other side of the road. Don't see the point. Still, when in Rome."

"I better look out then, when I drive home."

Lawrence looked down at the surface. "Trouble is, this road's pretty narrow. Not much difference which side you drive on."

"Why don't you try the old airfield over at Dad brook? They've got runways there."

"Of course! Runways. The very thing. We'll be off then."

"When you got to go," she said.

She watched them as they pulled away. Danny came through.

"Who was that?"

"Just someone I met this morning. Thought I might have broken down."

He was still angry with her.

"You let yourself be followed? Couldn't you have been more careful, you stupid woman."

She moved to touch him, to reassure him. "Danny."

"Get away from me."

He was shaking. That was when she wanted to lead him back into the hideout and feel him softly inside her. He would soon be gone and she would never see him again, never hear his voice speaking to her alone. He would vanish from her life.

She was back in half an hour. She followed him back through the hidden doorway and watched him as he lit the Primus and poured the heated water into the cup. He put the razor to his face, forgetting that he had to lather his beard. The blade trembled against his skin.

"Here," she said, "let me," and sitting him down she began to massage the thick stubble.

"Don't cut me now," he told her. "I don't want them to say the first time they saw their dad he had paper stuck all over his face."

"I won't cut you, Danny. I promise."

"I wonder what they'll be like, my two. Dark like me, I hope."

"I don't doubt it," Judith said.

"I'd like them to be dark. Like me. A boy and a girl."

This was the nearest she had ever got to caressing him, turning the cheeks this way and that, wiping the stinging wet from his eyes. Danny sat on the edge of the bed, composed now, his former self coming through as she scraped the scrabby stubble from his skin.

"Did you bring me a clean shirt?" he asked.

"A white one," she said.

"A white one. She always liked me in white. Made me look, I don't know . . ."

"Special. Makes you look special, Danny."

He smiled. "It sets off the eyes. Dark eyes and dark eyebrows."

"Like your babies."

His hands reached up to her face. "That's right. Like my own babies."

He pulled the towel down and rubbed his face dry.

"Better, eh?"

She bent down and felt in her bag.

"Here," she said. "Take a look." She pulled out a mirror and gave it to him. He held it out at arm's length.

"Perfect," he said. "Not a mark on me."

"The name of the maternity ward is St. Stephen's," she said. "Though what use it will be to you I don't know. They'll never let you near."

"I'll use another name," he said. "I'll find one from the birth columns in the local paper. Pretend to be a distant relative, a friend. I just want to see them, that's all. Not so hard to understand, is it?"

He pulled on the shirt. "You'll not be getting this one back," he said.

"No."

"That's all right, then?"

"You could have all the shirts in Shropshire for all I care," she said.

"Not a very good disguise though, is it?" he grinned.

"No disguise at all." She brushed his jacket down. "Don't go. Please."

He held her at arm's length. "I won't if I can't. Understand? If I can, I will. And then . . ."

"Then?" She could not forestall the note of foolish hope in her voice.

"The wide-open spaces, Judith. Far, far away."

"Will you drop me a line? A postcard? Use a different name. I know, sign it Jill." She pulled open her purse. "Here's twenty pounds I managed to save."

He counted out the notes and tucked them in his top pocket.

"Do you have any change?" he asked. "I might have to make some phone calls."

"Change?" She was flustered. Then she remembered. She dug her hands in. The money was still there, wrapped in her handkerchief.

"Here," she said. "This might help."

She had supposed all along that she knew he would be caught and his final brief wave gave her confirmation that she was witnessing the last moments of his freedom. He knew it too. It was not a wave of encouragement or thanks, or even a gesture of farewell, but one which admitted the passing of all hope. As he set off, the fading light sucking his form into the nothing of dim oblivion, she sank to the ground. It was as if the child within her had died.

Danny stood full square in front of the bonnet, refusing to move. He hadn't realised he was standing in the middle of the road until the lone car shuddered to a halt not a foot away from his crumpled, damp trousers.

His shoes were filthy too. He pulled his overcoat round him and wiped the hair from his eyes. For the first time in his forty-minute vigil he noticed that there was a light drizzle in the air. The driver rolled down his window and stuck his head out. The woman pulled the sun visor down and straightened her hair.

"What's the matter with you," the driver shouted. "Trying to get yourself killed?"

"I was hoping for a lift," he said, looking back down the empty road. "Only there's been no traffic."

The man waved his arm, as if he could brush him from the road like a discarded crisp packet. Danny stood there, feeling the car's heat and the man's anger.

"You're the first car I seen in twenty minutes," he said eventually. "I wanted to make sure you saw me."

"You should wear something white at night, didn't you know that?"

"I don't have anything white," said Danny, "except for the shirt." He walked round to the driver's side. "It's a bit cold to be walking around in shirtsleeves, don't you think?"

The man revved his engine. "Where you headed for, then?" he asked reluctantly.

"Just into town."

The driver put his head back in and spoke to his companion.

"Go on then. Hop in," he called out. "And keep your feet on the rubber matting."

He reached back and pushed the rear door open. Danny climbed in. The seat was long and soft and creaked under his weight. There was an embroidered cushion in the corner. He plumped it up and settled back in. He had never been so comfortable, so soft, so warm. He was more tired and more alone than he had ever felt in his life. He wanted them to take him somewhere where there would be no trouble, only the dull murmur of the sea outside and lowered voices in the room next door and the seductive comfort of a strange bed with Irish linen and feather pillows and a warm body ready to envelop him. He could feel the welcome weight of the sheet on him already.

"Pushing your luck, aren't you? After what happened."

"What?" Danny opened his eyes. For a moment he did not know where he was. The car was moving now.

"The shooting. Don't you read the papers?"

Danny studied the backs of their heads. They sat further apart than they normally would, for his benefit no doubt. The man's hair was cut short and his neck was broad and fleshy and flecked with red. She had hers piled up, blonde wisps trailing down to the white of her bare skin. He could smell her perfume, smell the warmth of her, hear the rustle of her skirt as she twisted in her seat, the clink of jewellery on her arm. From the movement of the man's shoulder and the way in which he stared straight ahead Danny could tell that the man was playing games with his free hand, touching her, teasing her, trying to make her laugh or lose her temper—it didn't matter which; a playground game for lovers, made all the better now there was a solitary witness to exclude. He eased back. A leather arm strap rocked against the side window. He threaded his hand through and looked around. There was a heavy quiet to the car, reassuring, safe. A powerful car too. This car would get him to Cardiff, no trouble, and in double-quick time. Get him across to Ireland if he chose, with the money that Judith had given him. It couldn't take much more than twenty pounds to get a car across to Ireland, and these two would have money as well, not to mention cheque-books and driving licences. Looked like she had a decent pair of earrings on as well. Engagement ring? He couldn't see.

He looked around to see if he could spot any other likely pickings. A pair of tights poked out from under the front passenger seat. They were black, one leg inside out, pushed there by accident rather than by design. He dragged them out quietly with his feet. It was too dark to tell whether the knickers inside were white or pink. How long had they been there? Half an hour? A week? He tried craning his head forward, to see if her legs were bare, but he dared not move too far. The couple were sitting suddenly still now, as if they both had silent thoughts to contend with. Danny wondered what was on her mind. Had a quick grope reminded her where she had left her underwear? He knew what was on his own.

"How much does she do to the gallon?" he asked.

"Depends," the man replied. "Fifteen in town. Twenty-five vis-à-vis the open road."

There was the tin-opener in his pocket. He didn't know why he had brought it along, but at the last moment he had slipped it into his pocket when Judith wasn't looking. He could wait until the man stopped for a traffic light and then jab it hard against his neck and get him to drive somewhere quiet. Perhaps he could take them to the same spot as Colin and Ethel went. That would put the fear of God in them. He probably wouldn't have to do anything, just threaten them. Put them in the boot and drive off. That would be safer. A car like this has a big boot. Big enough for him at least. That was it. Him in the boot and her beside him. With her bare arse trembling on the seat. And if it came to a showdown before that? A quick stab, slicing it across the vein good and hard before sticking it straight into the Adam's apple and then, while he was clutching at his throat, the tights for her. Perhaps everyone had been right all along. Perhaps that was what he was. A kidnapper. A murderer. That's what Ethel had said he was, what everyone who listened to her believed him to be. And here was the final opportunity, a courting couple, careless and foolhardy, with a stranger in the back of their car, not ten miles from where it happened.

The girl turned in her seat and pulled herself up to face him. She looked strong and reckless. He could smell brandy on her breath. She leant over, a little too friendly for someone completely sober. Danny smiled back. He could just picture her in the backseat, skirt around her waist, kicking her feet against the door. Too posh for his van, though. Like Ethel had been. He put his hand in his pocket. The blade was not as sharp as he had hoped. Smaller than he had imagined it too.

"Where've you come from?" she asked.

"Just up the road."

"Going in for a night out, eh?" she said, wriggling at her own joke. She was flirting with him. Any other time he would have flirted back, no matter who was in the front with her. An insurance policy for the future, he used to call it.

"The hospital," he said.

"The general?"

"My mum's in there."

She tried to look concerned. Looking concerned could be a come-on too. "Nothing serious, I hope."

"Appendix. She'll be out in a couple of days."

The girl turned to her companion. "We could drop him off up there, couldn't we, sweetheart? Wouldn't be much out of our way." She swivelled round again. "What ward's she in?"

"Can't remember," Danny said.

"St. Michael's probably," she said. "That's where they do the general stuff. How long's she been there?"

"Three weeks."

"Three weeks!"

It was a stupid answer. He knew it as he said it. He leant forward to reassure her. "There were complications," he explained. "She's all right now, though."

Suddenly the girl's attitude seemed to change. She dropped back into her seat. "I've had my appendix out," she announced loudly to no one in particular. "And my tonsils."

"Anything else missing that I should know about?" the man asked, flicking on the indicator, waiting to take the main road into town. "Not getting faulty goods, I hope."

"Well, I haven't heard you complaining so far," she giggled, poking him in the ribs. She leant across and whispered something into the man's ear. "What?" Danny heard him reply softly. She whispered again and the man inclined his head upwards, looking at him in the mirror.

The man rolled down the window and breathed in deeply, banging his chest ostentatiously with his fist. The girl put her hand to her mouth, laughing, and wound her window down too. The bitter air leapt onto Danny like a pack of maddened dogs. It tore at his ears. It bit his lips blue. It chased the girl's tights and had them dancing on the dark blue floor. The man threw back his head and howled. The girl pushed her body back against the seat, stretching out, her arm full out the window. He could see her legs now. They were long and bare. It would be so easy. He could have those tights of hers around her neck in no time. The car picked up speed, swerving and overtaking, flashing its lights at the vehicles ahead. Danny clung to the strap and closed his eyes. He felt sick and giddy, like a child at a fairground and one ride too many. He was flung from side to side, losing his balance, sprawling out over the length of the seat, but they took no interest in him now. There was the hum of their car and speed of their life, that was all. They burst into the lit-up area of Aylesbury.

"It's the next turning on the right," she shouted at the driver. The man tapped the brakes. The car skidded slightly on the wet surface and slowed down. Danny bent down and grabbing hold of the underwear wiped his boots clean before stuffing them back under the seat. Let her try putting them back on now. They drew up outside the entrance to the hospital car park. He scrambled out. They sped off even before he had time to thank them.

It was several minutes before he could walk again, bent over the wall, retching, though whether through sickness or fear he could not tell. He stood up and let the rain refresh him. It was steadier now. Whatever happened after his visit, he had a long night's rain ahead of him. He took a comb out of his back pocket and slicked his hair back. He walked to the glass front doors and followed a group of visitors in as they pushed them open. He looked around at the reception desk and the ugly plastic chairs half-full of people spread out with a lifetime of exhaustion in front of them. There was not a policeman in sight.

216

He walked across quickly, pausing only to buy a local paper and a bunch of flowers at the kiosk before following the painted arrows down the corridor. He held the flowers high in front of his face, but no one took any notice of him. It was a place of private purpose and he walked along a corridor filled with private thoughts. The footsteps that he heard, coming up behind him, walking towards him, were not following him nor seeking to prevent his. They belonged to nurses marching on their way out, their shift over; to orderlies wearily pushing wheelchairs on rubber wheels, their task never done; to the slow sleepwalk of pyjamaed patients, anxious to prove their mobility; to the resigned tread of visitors, trying hard to appear cheerful. As he walked further into the hospital's interior, these itinerants grew fewer, as if there might be an inner haven of peace, which only the initiate and the lucky outsider might penetrate. An antiseptic Shangri-la. And then he was alone. A solitary doctor hurried towards him, his white coat flapping. For a moment he hid the name Danny was seeking and then he too passed. To his right, through the porthole windows of the swing doors Danny could see a ward sister sitting at her desk, twenty feet away. Then a nurse, cap awry, pushed through on her way out. Danny bowed before her. He had hoped for a younger woman. She stood impatiently while he explained the delicacy of his mission.

"I don't want to disturb the mother," he whispered, as if she might be in earshot. "If I could just see the babies. Is there not a room where the babies are kept?" He paused, fumbling for words. The woman looked up at him, amused.

"This is not a battery farm. They're with their mothers most of the time."

Danny shook his head, as if by disagreeing he could change the circumstances in his favour. "I thought babies were kept in a room of their own," he persisted. "You know, with a glass partition to look through." He had seen them in films. All hospitals had them.

"I can see you're no father," the nurse pronounced, a note of condescension creeping into her voice. "At the moment they'll be with their mothers. It's quite safe to go in. Just give your name and ask at the desk." She walked off briskly.

Danny hesitated. He looked back. The man who had given him a lift stood against the far wall holding a large stick of chocolate.

"You wouldn't get within fifteen feet," the man said. "They'll have a policeman there just in case." He bit off a large triangular chunk and started to chew. Danny looked up and down. The corridor was empty. All that could be heard were the nurse's fading footsteps. He clenched his fists. The man shook his head.

"You don't look fit enough for any of that," he said, "and I don't believe you'd be dumb enough to use that gun again."

Danny sighed. "That's just a lot of rot. I've never had a gun. You know why I'm here?"

"I read the papers. Twins, isn't it?" He pointed to the door. "See what I mean?" A uniform had appeared by the desk.

Danny stepped back out of sight. "I got a better idea."

"Oh yes?"

"I'm going to walk out of here and into the grounds. With a bit of luck I'll be able to see them from there. You're right, of course. You are stronger than me, but I've been waiting a long time for this. I'll give you a hell of a fight if you try and stop me."

"And if I don't?"

"Happy men are docile men, easily led, Mr. . . ."

"Wheatcroft. Lawrence Wheatcroft."

Danny dropped the flowers and trod them to the floor. "Pleased to meet you, Mr. Wheatcroft," he said, holding out his hand. "Do we have a deal?"

Lawrence put the chocolate in his pocket and led the way. Danny followed.

"How'd you make me?" he asked.

Lawrence nodded in the direction of the car park.

"Personal hygiene," he said. "The girlfriend got a nose like a bloodhound. Said you smelt as if you hadn't washed for a week. Soon as we'd left you I thought, 'What sort of man goes to see his mum stinking like an alley cat?' One who hasn't been able to wash, that's who. One living rough perhaps. Or hiding out. And what mum? Three weeks and still don't know the name of the ward?"

"Three weeks was a bit silly," Danny admitted. "It just came into my head. It's how long I've—"

"I know what it is," said Lawrence. "The whole country knows how long it is."

They walked out through the doors. From the outside the hospital looked like a child's Lego which had been knocked over in a temper, straggling in disorder over the grass. A concrete path followed the irregular lines of the building. They began to walk. Through the windows they could see rows of beds with their charts and chairs and cupboards stuck with jugs and flowers.

"Look at the poor bastards," Danny said, "shuffling after their stolen souls. I don't know which is worse, prison or hospital."

"At least in prison you know when you're coming out," Lawrence offered.

Danny came to an abrupt halt. "There'll be no coming out for whoever catches this one," he said.

"Still," said Lawrence, "if you're innocent . . ."

Danny laughed bitterly. "What, with the tales that woman's been telling? Innocence doesn't come into it." He moved on.

"She wouldn't tell tales, Danny. Not knowingly."

Danny caught on. "You know her then?"

Lawrence looked confused.

"You do, don't you? My God. You know her. Tell her, for God's sake. Tell her it wasn't me. It wasn't me. Oh Christ. Would you look at that."

They were standing four feet away from a pair of French windows.

A line of beds stood opposite. Most had visitors crowded round, but in one, slightly apart from the others, lay a young woman on her own, with a pale face and dark hair and a squirming baby in the crook of each arm.

"Those are mine," Danny whispered. "Do you see that? Mine." He ran forwards and started to bang on the glass.

"Eileen," he cried. "It's me. It's me."

He hammered on the glass with his fists and feet, trying to smash his way through. There was nothing Lawrence could do for him now. He ran up behind Danny and threw him to the ground. He could hear shouts coming from round the corner and the heavy pounding of boots.

"What you do that for, you thick mick?" he bellowed, sitting on Danny's chest. "You could have stayed there for a good half hour if you'd held your peace."

HE HAD ALWAYS KNOWN IT WOULD BE HIM, ENGLAND'S NUMBER ONE EXECU-tioner placed before England's Number One Murderer, despite what Harry Firth might have said. "The word is they are looking for a younger man," Harry had opined, always on the lookout to disturb Solomon's equilibrium, but Solomon had held his peace at this churlish foolishness. Danny had committed an assassination against England and it would be up to England's highest representative in the field of retribution to perform his task. It was not the killing that had marked him, Jeremiah thought, nor oddly enough the shooting of Ethel Whitley. Rather, Danny had broken the sacred trust that people held in the English countryside. He had undermined its inviolability, its sense of calm. The soft green slopes of an English view were no longer the province of poets and painters, the highway no longer safe for the hayrick and the family motorcar, the paths no place for courting couples and English women alone with their dogs. Danny had shown them that thieves and adulterers stalked the land. It was that sent him to the gallows as much as Ethel's testimony.

She had been the star of the court, not Danny at all, Ethel with her bandaged head (pure cosmetic, Alcott had told him proudly) and her neat white-gloved hands.

"She wore a dark skirt," Alcott told him, in a fever of restrained excitement, though what he expected her to wear otherwise he could not tell, a hula hoop? "and held her hands over the witness box as if it were a pulpit. Such poise! Such grace! The way they hung onto her words she could have been preaching a sermon."

Jeremiah disapproved of the drawing of this parallel.

"A pulpit is a sacred place," he reminded him. "Not fashioned for a woman's body. It would be a blasphemy."

"I'd rather have a woman priest than a woman judge," Alcott argued. "Can you see a woman judge sentencing a man to death? You'd be out of a job and no mistake." Jeremiah closed his eyes.

"You're forgetting yourself, Peter," he warned him, and Alcott, suitably humbled, resumed his tale.

From his boastful manner and the way he praised her delivery, Jeremiah had the impression that Alcott and she had rehearsed much of her testimony in those weeks before Danny's arrest. The courts of British justice were nothing if not theatre, what with the wigs and robes and the obligatory soliloquies, the galleries packed with faces eager for the Black Cap waiting in the wings, and critics scribbling furiously on their knees. Alcott had held his own review of the proceedings in the snug almost every evening, and Jeremiah, uneasy with his wife, had availed himself more frequently than usual, telling himself he would hear more about Danny and his demeanour from this tame policeman than by subjecting himself to the tittle-tattle of newspapers.

It was strange for Ethel to be sitting in court, retelling it as if she had played a part in this drama, for in many ways she felt that all that had happened that night belonged to someone else, a distant relation or someone who had lived a long time ago. A ghost. Now that she had recovered she was almost grateful that events had turned the way they had. She had not wished for Colin's death, but the outcome of that chilling night had been what she had craved for ever since she had met him—her release. She had no excess baggage now to burden her departure, just herself. She had booked her passage. Cecil Hardwick had managed to get her a job as a typist in a firm of solicitors. She was not afraid, not of the dark nor of cars, and though she balked at the thought of kissing a man again, she supposed that inhibition might pass in good time. She could kiss a Canadian, a strong man who knew nothing about her past. She could kiss him and marry him and mark her new place in the world. Now she simply wanted to clear the decks and have Danny dead so that she would be free to steam across the water and this new life. Thus she felt no inhibitions in slanting her story to fit this mould. She fed her morsels to the court with great care, the way Alcott and she had rehearsed in her front room, her mouth clean and composed, her hands resting quietly in front of her. Danny at the Lake District, Danny at the Dog and something, Danny asking her to meet him alone. Coming to the night itself, with the man tapping on the door, she could see the overcoat looming out of the dark again, but it no longer hid a shapeless man beneath its folds. She had cut it to fit Danny, and it sat on his shoulders as if a Saville Row tailor were in attendance.

So now came the time that lay within him, that never died, that was always in the present, never receding, never moving into the safer past, never refashioned, only repeated in the exact order of his dread memory, refreshed, in the hours when his son and his wife were absent, by his compulsive need to lift the banished Execution Book from beneath its floorboard cell and to turn to that awesome page, which, for all its brevity, betrayed the whole story by the tenuous grip of its lettering. Like a husband who, when the house is empty, takes from out its hiding place his secret store of pornographic pictures, to stare and shudder at their creased allure, Jeremiah would lay the book on his knee, fingering the texture of the leather binding before daring to open the window on his concealed world. Here lay his secret bodies, his private thoughts, the gasps and groans at which his very body trembled. And when he lit upon that final page, he was no longer Jeremiah Bembo, landlord of the Cow and Calf, with a newborn son and a forgiving wife, but back on Bedford Station, running along platform one, two and a half hours late, his hat falling from his head, his bag in hand, charging alongside the carriage door, the woman inside not rising to help, but watching him from the far corner, book in hand, as he wrenches open the door and flings himself in. As he regains his balance he notices a look of alarm on the woman's face. For a frightening moment he imagines his revolver must have fallen out and now lies exposed on the floor. He feels his inside pocket cautiously. The box lies undisturbed. Perhaps he has stumbled into a carriage set aside for women only. If so, there is nothing he can do but apologise. There are no corridors on this train. He moves to reassure her.

"Excuse me if I've got into the wrong carriage," he says, catching his breath and brushing down his coat. "But I've already missed one connection. I'll get out in the next stop."

"You're all right," she replies. "I can look after myself."

He sits down next to the window.

"Going far?" he asks her.

"The end of the world," she replies.

She is a small woman with thick freckled skin, thinning hair and doorstep arms. A survivor brought up in a hard-fought world. Like him she is dressed inappropriately for the time of year. The book on her lap is large and heavy, and as she raises it up once more he sees the cross on the front and the familiar initial impressed upon the leather cover that was his grandfather's trademark. It is a Bembo Bible. Usually he would not countenance staying in this carriage a moment longer than necessary, but today he is glad of the company. He has something glorious to shout about.

"That Bible," he begins.

"What of it?"

"It's a Bembo Bible, is it not?"

"I don't know about that," she says. "It was my mother's. One day it will be my granddaughter's." She stares out the window, her face set hard.

"But it was made by the Great Bembo, see?" He points to the gold-embossed spine, and the five-letter name at the bottom. "He was my grandfather. What an extraordinary day." He sinks back, contemplating the symmetry of this encounter. He is pleased he has met this woman. He wishes to engage her interest. It is a thrilling mystery he is confronted with, to want to share his joy with another human being. Extraordinary times!

"Forgive me if I have unsettled you," he begins, a little too formally for his liking, but he is so unused to opening his heart, "but I've just become a father. Rather suddenly, as a matter of fact. At the top of our stairs."

He sits on the edge of his seat waiting for the woman to respond. All women are fascinated by babies. They cannot help themselves. It is a fact of life. He waits, but no reaction comes. This woman shows no interest in his revelation at all. Perhaps she is a little hard of hearing. Extraordinary times!

"At the foot of our stairs," he says again. "Can you imagine that!"

"I thought you said the top."

"I did! The top! Just shows you what sort of state my mind is in."

He jiggles his knee, perturbed that he had unwittingly brought his cousin into the proceedings. Judith had been waiting this summer, hoping for Will's radio show to start up again, but inexplicably it has not returned for its summer run. According to local gossip, except for the housekeeper his house has been empty for some months as well. The woman manages to register a flicker of interest.

"What was it? Boy or girl?" She speaks as if there were cold ashes in her mouth.

"A boy!" Jeremiah laughs. "A great big bouncing boy! And such a size! Pardon me, not wishing to sound crude, but I never knew babies could be so big. It didn't seem possible."

It was true. Even the midwife, who arrived on her bicycle an hour after Stanley was born, admitted to being taken aback. "Surprised he came out so easy," she said, "considering the mother's size. Where he get that from?" and Jeremiah had no answer. His family were of no great girth, except Will's father, who was taller than the rest. Judith's side was no better.

"We are going to call him Stanley," he says.

"Call him what you like. It won't make any difference," and she falls into silence. The train continues on its journey.

It is here, in the privacy of his carriage, with his pocket chess set and his book of well-trodden strategies, when he lifts the pieces aloft and slots them into their preordained holes, that he shifts from an ordinary man named Jeremiah Bembo into the fabled Solomon Straw. By the time he steps through the wicket gate and looks up to the stern prison square with its studded doors and barred windows, he knows the transformation to be complete: the measure of his tread is firmer; his face bears an impenetrable skein of gravitas; his voice rebounds in the crafted housing of his authority. There is nothing which can ruffle the feathers of Solomon Straw nor disturb the ballast of his solemnity, but today no such change takes place. All he can remember is his wife bucking and heaving with the carpet all scrunched up and his baby coming out and him running up the stairs, his hands outstretched, not knowing what the hell he was doing, not thinking, not planning, running up the stairs. The urgency of it! The cries from her, the cries from him. Cries for humanity! Extraordinary times!

He looks up. The train has stopped. He can hear the links rattle and the steam hiss, feel the carriage rocking on its heels. The heat, it seems, has brought another life to a standstill. It had been like this all through the last few weeks of Judith's confinement. The heat had affected her more than he thought possible, not simply her swollen ankles or her irregular breathing, but more worryingly, her state of mind. In her foolish womanly way she had become obsessed with Danny's trial, blaming herself for putting her unborn child at such unwitting risk, however slight their encounters at the marketplace must have been. Jeremiah would walk into the kitchen in the morning to find her standing over the table, kneading her breasts while she mouthed the words from the newspaper spread out before her. It was the savage shamelessness of the act which disturbed him, her nightdress pulled open, grasping her flesh so tightly it was as if she were trying to squeeze drops of blood out onto the errant page.

Jeremiah had tried to console her, but she would have nothing to do with him. Ever since he had come back from the double hanging she had insisted that he sleep downstairs. She would not let him touch her. She had taken a fierce delight in abandoning all domestic propriety, spending the daylight hours lying in the hammock, her dress rudely unbuttoned, hoping for whatever breeze there might be to lull her into a loose and fitful forgetfulness. A number of times he had found her wandering along the side of the fields dressed only in one of his old shirts, her huge belly and private parts bare to the world. He feared she was going mad and had sought discreet but sound advice. Most people, Arthur Nash included, had vouchsafed that strange things were the order of the day as far as pregnant women were concerned, that once the baby was born all would change. Jeremiah was not so sure. The day after Danny was sentenced he had come across her spread out on the grass with not a stitch on, wailing to the heavens.

"Whatever's the matter?" he had asked, hardly knowing where to look. "Are you in pain?"

She had shaken her head and, raising herself up, held out her arms.

"Oh, Jem," she had said, tears shaking her body. "Is it you they will call? Tell me it will be you?"

"Call?" he had repeated.

"For the boy," she cried, "for the poor boy!"

The question had thrown him off balance. She had never asked such a question before. He hardly knew how to answer.

"More than likely. Now get up for pity's sake and put some clothes on. You can't be lying like this."

She had risen up unsteadily and clung to him, he in his soiled working clothes, she warm and naked.

"Thank God," she had said, clutching at him. "I am so sorry."

"What's all this about, then?" he said. "Never heard you take on this way before."

"He is so young," she said, kissing his chest as if in a fever. "He'll be frightened."

She began to kiss him hard. "Help him," she whispered, passing the words into his mouth. "He'll need all the help he can get." There was something wrong in her pleading, something wrong the way her hands ran up and down when Danny Dancer's would hang so still, wrong how her mouth reached fervently to his neck while Danny Dancer's would flap against his coat with all the passion of a door banging in the wind, wrong in the movement of her brimming, writhing body imploring his arms, while Danny Dancer's would be folded and emptied, unable to respond to the most tender of his caresses.

"They all deserve that, Judith," he said, pushing her away. "That has been my guiding light over the years. I'd have thought you would have known that by now at least. Danny Dancer will get no more, no less."

He led her back into the hammock, embarrassed, and released himself from her grip.

He lurches back to the present. The train has not moved. Ten, fifteen minutes pass. Jeremiah looks at the woman's dark tweed suit, her thick woollen stockings, and her heavy black shoes and begins to perspire.

"Do you mind if we have the window open?" he asks. The woman shrugs her shoulders. He gets up and pulls the window down.

"I feel like shouting to the world," he calls back, poking his head out. "It's such a glorious day."

"Can't say I've noticed."

Solomon is irritated. Who couldn't notice? The sun is shining and his baby has been born. Without warning a train bursts past on the other track. Solomon jerks his head back as thick black smoke fills the carriage. He put his hands out to steady himself.

"Something the matter?" he hears her ask.

"I've got something in my eye. I can't see." His voice is unnaturally high, frightened. For a moment he feels as if he is standing under a wave of breaking glass again, light bursting around him. "I can't see," he cries again. "I can't see."

"All right. Keep your hair on." She sniffs triumphantly and then, sensing his distress, says, "Here, let me take a look. Put your head to the light."

She is smaller than he and he has to crouch down, his knees half-bent.

"Which one?" she demands.

"My right." He lifts his head. All he can see is streaming light and the shadow of her face. She pulls the skin down from his cheek as he rolls his eyeball around.

"Look up," she says. He obeys. Why should he not? Why should he not look up, to the loose mesh of the luggage rack and smudged outline of her suitcase?

"Look down," she says. He obeys. Why should he not look down, to her handbag and her Bible, with the frontispiece fluttering in the breeze?

"Hold still now," she tells him, "or I'll poke your eye out. You men are such babies. I think I can see it now." She holds his head firmly, and with the corner of her handkerchief picks out a large smut.

"Filthy things," she says. "The sooner we have diesels on this line the better."

Solomon blinks. He can see more clearly now. Swimming into focus is the title page of the Bible and the ornate *B*, and underneath, as was the custom, lies her family name. He blinks again and stares at the inscription.

"That better? Roll your eye round again." She watches him closely.

"That's fine," he tells her and straightens up. He will change carriages at the next stop. He must.

"When you did that," she says slowly, "your other eye didn't move at all."

"That's because it's made out of glass," he stammers. "I had an accident many years ago. I'm used to it now."

The train lurches forward. She collides into him and flings her arms about him as they try to maintain their balance. "Tomorrow," he thinks, "I will embrace the body of your son. I will carry it to the examination room and lay him on the slab and hear him being opened up. You will not be permitted to view his body, with his stretched neck, nor will you be allowed to witness his lonely burial which only the chaplain and the gravedigger will attend. You will be escorted into the office where you may collect his personal effects and from thence outside where you may resume your weeping and your public protestations. And I will wait until the coast is clear and once more travel anonymously back to my home. Only this time it will not be the same. I have seen the rope of life and my son wriggling on the end of it. And I am about to bring the close of your son's life at the end of mine."

They sit down.

"Never doubt him," she says out of the blue.

"What?"

"Your son. Stanley. Whatever others may say, never doubt him. Even in his blackest hour. Promise me that."

He promises. He promises her many things, things she cannot hear, things that he has never promised to anyone ever before; that this execution *will* be different; that Danny will know nothing of his death; that it will be the quickest, most perfect execution ever performed. Emotion has crept into his work and he is afraid.

Although it is well outside the appointed hour of four o'clock by the time he gets there, there is nothing to suggest that this will be anything out of the norm. The governor, though a stickler for the rules, has been made aware of his domestic circumstance and has no wish to call into question the probity of Solomon Straw. The prison has not had a hanging for many years, not since he was here last, and they are looking forward to making their judicial mark. This is a small prison, and such an illustrious inmate as Danny Dancer can only enhance its reputation.

He is shown to his quarters for the night. Harry Firth is already there, sitting on his bed and smoking his roll-ups, half wetting himself with the thought that Solomon might not turn up. He says nothing. The time to put Harry in his place will be later, when it is all over. Nothing matters now but the job in hand, and all his energy and concentration must be devoted to this one end. As soon as he parks his suitcase they walk across to take a look at their prisoner. The corridor leading to the condemned cell is laid with coconut matting. It is put down primarily for the following morning, so that Danny will not hear them approach, but it is good to have it down now, when he can inspect him undetected. Solomon walks quickly up to the Judas hole and peels back the oiled eyepiece. The room is, as always, neat and compact. A bed, a table and three chairs. Not much else. The bed lies up against the near-side wall to the right, blue blankets folded neatly, pyjamas on the pillow. There is a small bedside table, and on it are two pictures, one of a young woman, the other of an older woman. Solomon recognises her face immediately. High above he can see the window curved and barred and throwing light down onto the table where three men sit. Danny is sitting in profile. On either side of him, one with his back to the door, are the two warders. They are playing dominoes. Danny looks like his picture. Small and dark, with not quite as much muscle on him as he had imagined. As requested the warders have made sure that he is wearing a loose, open-neck collar so that Solomon can take a good look at his neck. It is strong but not thick. As Danny raises his hand Solomon notices that his right arm is bandaged. He stares at him hard, for this is unexpected. He touches the warder and walks him a few feet away. "What's all that about?" he asks, annoyed that he had not been told before. "A suicide attempt?" The warder shakes his head. "Happened the last visit," the man tells him, "Danny's wife and children. He put his fist through the glass, after they left, after they had said good-bye, put his fist through. They wouldn't let

231

him touch them, wouldn't let him hold them, not even after he had written to the governor, offering to be put in a straitjacket, just so he could kiss them good-bye like. He wouldn't even let him do that."

He had to stand with two warders by his side, on the other side of the glass, watching his poor wife break down in front of him, holding their babies in the air, trying to pass a touch through that cold, unyielding frame. In her agitation the babies woke, clawing at the air, looking for the warmth and security they had come to expect, and with the warders staring ahead, she unbuttoned herself and started to feed them one by one, milk running down their chins, and when they were done Eileen coaxed a last few drops from her leaking nipples and smeared three kisses on the glass, one from each of them. And then it was over, time was up, a man in uniform took her arm and turned her away. She could not resist, not with two babies to hold, all she could do was cry his name as the warder pulled her away and the door opened and she and his children were gone, never to be seen again, knowing nothing of them, who they might be, what races they might win, what troubles they might graze against, nothing but that they were his, and he raised his hand and made a fist and smashed the glass. "And when was that?" Solomon asks. "Yesterday," the warder replies. "His mother's waiting for him now."

Solomon stands, unable to speak. He imagines what he would have done if he had been prevented from reaching Judith, if he'd been forced to watch Judith through a reinforced glass window, bucking and heaving not one foot away, the carpet all scrunched up and little Stanley slipping out helpless, towards arms which could not catch him. "And he has been quite quiet since?" he asks eventually. The warder nods. "No fits? No faints?" The warder shakes his head. "Been playing dominoes and Monopoly," he tells him. "And guess what?" He is about to make a joke. Solomon can always tell when a joke is on the way and if he can he will always try and forestall them. This time is no exception. He lifts his finger to his mouth and shakes his head. "Don't say it," he says. "Take him for his walk now so that we can get on with the job. Don't come back for a good half hour, OK? Now, I believe you have something for me." He holds out his hand. The warder hands him a slip of paper and moves back to the condemned cell. They can hear the scraping of chairs and the mutter of voices and a man saying, "And about time too. Keeping me all cooped up on such a grand day. A good clear sunny day, isn't that something to be grateful for? Who'd want to be going for his last when it's pissing down?" and Solomon wants to tell him that many do, many have woken to a bleak sky and the endless drum of rain, have felt wet upon their lips in their last turn around the yard, or the keen bite of an unrelenting wind. Which is worse, which is better, when you have no choice?

They pass into the execution chamber and wait while they take Danny out. Solomon unfolds the sheet of paper. *Height, five foot six. Weight, nine stone exactly.* He pictures the young man he has just seen, the distribution of his flesh, the structure of his bones, the state of his neck. He will give Danny a drop of seven feet eleven inches. A long drop, but not excessive. Exact. By the trapdoor which leads to the pit below stand two oblong boxes, labelled A and B. He opens Box B first. There are two ropes inside, one he has used three times before, and a brand-new one, stiff to the touch. He picks up the older one. It is already a hangman's rope and Solomon respects its quality. It will loop more easily, drop more loosely, sit more comfortably under Danny's chin. He runs it through his hand, feeling it inch by inch, paying particular attention to the warp under the leather wash, where the friction from the moving metal eye can cause the rope to fray. There is nothing untoward here. This rope will not let him down. He passes it over. Harry repeats the examination. This is not necessary, but it is a courtesy of which he approves, indeed which he introduced. It marks patience and cooperation as tools of their trade and signals thoroughness as his most valuable of ideologies. With Harry's help he measures the drop length along the rope and marks it with a strand of packthread before climbing up and shackling the rope to the chain hanging from the beam. Harry hands him the copper wire, and securing one end over the shackle, he bends it so that it coincides with the mark on the rope. Harry drags the sandbag over so that it stands exactly over the centre of the drop. It weighs the same as Danny and will stand in for Danny now until the morning. Solomon returns to the floor and places the noose around the soft indentation which marks Danny's neck. He walks over to the lever. The cotter pin is stuck firmly in. He knocks it three-quarters of the way out and nods to the warder, waiting in the corner. Now is the time. "Fetch him down," he orders. The warder scurries off. Though the governor may be the captain of this vessel, Solomon Straw is its pilot.

Five minutes later the governor appears. "Ready?" he asks. "Ready," Solomon replies. The governor moves to his appointed position, to the side of the door through which the prisoner will come, facing the noose and the executioner. He is not the one to face the condemned man in those final seconds, neither he nor the doctor, nor anybody else, certainly not cocky little Harry Firth. Only Solomon Straw. Only he will know what look Danny gave the world when last he looked upon it. He strides across and pushes the lever. The trap falls, the bag plunges. The bag will hang there overnight, stretching the rope so that in the morning there will be no give, only the prescribed measurement which will fracture Danny's spinal cord causing his instantaneous unconsciousness and death. "No problems?" the governor asks, and he shakes his head. "No problems." The governor stalks off, back to his supper. Solomon is not invited this time. He takes his meal with the warders in their canteen. He is back in his billet by nine, with Harry boasting to the chief warder and his mate. He does not attempt to still Harry's cheer, rather he is grateful that Harry can act as his foil, dipping into his fund of off-colour jokes, talking nobbled racehorses and shady betting schemes. This way he does not have to offer them details of his son's birth. He could not have brought himself even to utter Stanley's name. It would be a blasphemy, to sully his innocence in such a place. He feels dirty.

He is woken with a cup of tea at half past seven. Another glorious day. Harry raises his arse and farts under his bedclothes, a deliberate expression of contempt towards the man facing his last hour on earth.

That is what brings so many people to this work, Solomon thinks. Shit and piss and men dying in a sea of it. After breakfast they walk down to remove the sandbag, and make their final preparations. There is complete silence in the prison now. Not a cough, not a clatter of plates, not even the clink of keys. No one is moving. No one is playing cards or banging on the door or sitting on the can. They are lying there, the prisoners, counting out the hour. They are lying there, the prisoners, straining for the slightest sound. They are lying there, the prisoners, waiting for the cannon noise which will burst through this arid home like a fire through the brush. They are lying there, the prisoners, thinking of Danny. Every prisoner knows there is a noose waiting for him. Danny's death brings every one of them closer to their own.

Harry takes the weight of the bag on his shoulders while Solomon lifts off the noose. He measures the rope against the copper wire mark. It has stretched three-quarters of an inch, so he adjusts the length accordingly. They work without a sound now, for they are very close. Solomon steps down into the pit. As he eases the trapdoors off their retaining springs so that Harry can haul them up before he resets the lever he hears the murmur of prayers. Two voices, three? He cannot tell. The trap closes. Darkness descends. Above he can hear Harry moving about. It is cool in here and hollow like a chapel. The voices are distant now but their reverberation cannot fail to reach him. He falls to his knees and lends his silent voice to their cause. He returns, swiftly coils the rope to the height of Danny's head and holds it while Harry ties it up with packthread. He resets the lever, tapping the cotter pin in gently. He stands and surveys. All is now ready.

Back at their billet, they wait for the call. Half eight. Twenty to nine. Nineteen minutes to nine. Solomon can hardly keep his hands still. He takes out the hood and folds it, tucking it back in his top pocket. Within a minute it is spread out on the table again. He refolds it, and returns it to its home. Fifteen minutes to. Ten. Eight. Seven. At five to they are called and walk down the corridor and wait outside the condemned cell door. The governor and the medical officer are there now and a man who refuses to look at them, an observer from the Home Office probably, they never introduce themselves, a florid man with bloodshot eyes, hoping no doubt that the governor will have the decency not just to offer them one drink after it's all over, but two. At the moment the clock begins to strike nine the governor nods and immediately Solomon walks through, Harry following behind. All he is aware of now is the clock striking in his mind, and at each stroke he must be further along the path, moving in machinery as it rolls forward to the next click of the universe. The warders are rising, Danny too, and while the chairs scrape back, one warder moves the table aside while the other turns to the yellow doors, the doors that have remained shut these three weeks, and pushes them outward to reveal what is waiting not fourteen foot away. Light pours into the cell, a new light, a fresh glow and a hum that comes from the empty solitude of the place, the sort of quiet that comes from a front room never used, "Good morning," Solomon says, and as he moves behind and brings Danny's left hand down, he can hear the clock strike again and feel the muscles in Danny's arms tense as his eyes open and he sees what is before him, how near it is, how near it is! "Good lad, Danny," he says, "good lad," and Danny turns his head to where the priest stands, rosary and Bible in hand, saying, "Got to go now, Gerry, mustn't keep the great Solomon Straw waiting," as Solomon draws the other hand round and wraps the strap around Danny's wrists, he used it when he was last here for Wickert, in this very same cell, with the boy's hair falling in his eyes, no longer able to brush his hair back, he did that for him just before the hood went over, brushed his hair back, should he have done that? wasted a tenth of a second perhaps, or did it help him, did he free him to see his entry clearly into the next world? and with a tug he fastens it together. Stepping in front of the prisoner Solomon begins to walk, on the third stroke now, as Harry nudges Danny forward. It is important to set the motion going, to walk firmly. Not too fast, for then panic sets in. He has heard about that happening to one of the others trying to emulate his speed, hurrying the man too fast, Number Two pushing him in the small of the back and the man beginning to resist, but not him. He walks at a determined pace which admits nothing but its own volition and Danny follows. Danny follows the executioner's back and the space above him and the soft noose hanging so perfectly in the pale blue light, all coiled up like a snake in a basket. It is getting closer each step, horribly close. It is hard for a man to register that they have let him live so close to the means of his destruction all the time, how could anyone do that, to keep the killing machine next to where he slept and breathed and made his final pleas? These are his last moments coming, they have allowed no time, his last moments, no final requests, no good-byes, no statement, nothing. It is all gone. Just this brisk march. It is not the hangman's fault, that is why he follows him, not even the fault of the two men who now walk beside him, for they have only been in his cell for an hour, but the others, the three pairs of warders who stayed with him, who played cards with him, who laughed at his jokes, who helped him write letters and told him of their own children, they are the ones who betrayed him. The clock strikes again, the fourth time, and they are on the drop, and Solomon turns, holds out his hands, looks Danny in the face and stops him, yes he looks like his mother, same skin, same build, same snub nose, but there is a light mischief to his eyes and mouth even now which she did not possess, and as he looks down to check that he is on the mark, to where Harry is now bent, strapping the legs together, he can see that his feet have a similar intent, he can imagine them on the dance floor leading the girls around and around, way past their fathers and mothers and the time they were expected home. His fingers are in his top pocket now. Danny sees the linen bag flower in his hands, his eyes follow it as it rises over him, opening like a parachute, floating down over his head, hardly touching his face, so voluminous, so eager to let him down safely. What was his last look? Solomon cannot remember. He wants to, but he cannot, nor can he lift the hood to find out what it was, for to lift the hood would be to reveal another expression on Danny's face, for his legs are trembling, Solomon can feel them running up through the boy's body, see him beginning to shake as the clock strikes the fifth time. It is now when fear takes hold, when Danny can no longer

237

see, alone with only his breath and his beating heart and his tumbled thoughts for company; there is no order to his thoughts, not his wife, not his children, the letter on the mantelpiece, the whore with the scar across her face, his mother. His beating heart is confusing him. They would break his beating heart, his beating heart! Solomon pulls the bag down quickly and for a moment, just for a moment, presses his hand down on Danny's head, like John the Baptist might have done, a ministration to God, a gesture of love, wishing he could be with him always, wishing that he might never be frightened, never alone, wishing that he could take the pain and the fright from him, wishing him all the best will in the world. He has never done this before. No one sees, not even the man for whom it is intended, but Danny has felt it. Danny will fly out of this world with his companionship and his understanding and all good wishes for the future. The clock strikes again and he reaches for the noose, no time to lose now, the noose swinging over, gaping in his hand. He slips it over, tightens it under the chin, and he has done it, the clock still striking, seven he thinks, seven strokes and two to go, it will be easily done, bending down and tapping Harry on the shoulder as he dives for the lever, not dives, but it feels like that, slipping into something which envelops you, which for a moment blocks your sight and sound, has everything rushing through you, as you fall into the hollow booming world of your blood and the lever goes over and the clock strikes and the whole world collapses, booming and rushing, there is nothing to hear, nothing to see, only a blur of what, Loopy's life? Danny's life? Stanley slipping out? Judith bucking and heaving, the carpet all scrunched up in her hand? Solomon emerges, breaking through, the echo of the deep resounding in his ears, while men stand like suits around a swimming pool, not knowing how near the edge they might safely stand, while he looks round to see if everything is as it should be, the last strike sounding. He has done something for Danny's mother, something which she will not thank him for, something which he did for her and her son, and, God forbid, his own.

It is over.

There is a stillness.

The prison shudders and rises from its bed of self-pity. Men stamp their feet, whistle and jeer and bang their tin cups against the coffin lids of their cell doors. This is how it should be. This is how they join him. But there is another sound, unfamiliar, yet horribly close. It comes from the hollow pit and the shrouded head which lies not a foot below. Solomon looks down. Danny's head is rolling round the thread of the rope, his body twisting, his feet jerking hard into the air as if he were in a gymnasium. Danny is jeering and whistling and stamping with his fellow felons. The man from the Home Office staggers back, turning to the governor for help. Solomon pushes past him and tears down the steps, the medical officer racing behind him. They drag the small ladder over. Solomon rips Danny's shirt open and jumps down while the doctor bangs his stethoscope against Danny's chest.

"It's still beating but . . ."

Solomon pulls him away.

"Get the ropes, Harry," he cries. "Throw us a rope for God's sake, and you, take the weight off his feet. He's still alive, I tell you."

"It's a spasm, I'm sure," the doctor tells him, but Solomon takes no notice, he was in the kitchen when he heard her, and he ran back up the stairs, arms outstretched, Oh, Jem, she said, I think it's coming now. I shouldn't have done all that weeding. It is like pulling a car out of a lake. Solomon can see Danny's life streaming out of every pore, leaking down the length of his trousers, cascading over his shoes, there was a funny smell in the air, and a flood of water down the stairs, only not exactly water, he didn't know they called it that. They hoist Danny back up, catching him as he falls to the floor, his strapped legs hanging over the edge, twitching like a bucket of eels, her falling on the landing, like a cow that's been shot, dazed, not knowing, his head still covered by the hood. Bit sudden girl, isn't it? he said as she hoisted up her skirt, a red wet bubbling out of Danny's mouth. The doctor bangs his stethoscope against Danny's chest once again.

"Can't hear it now," he says.

"He's alive, I tell you," Solomon insists and pushes him aside, trying to work the noose free. It will not yield. He doesn't understand. There is no knot, no obstruction on the rope. Putting his hand round he can feel a gap between Danny's neck and the rope which shouldn't be there. He looks closely. The hood has caught in the eye of the noose. Now he understands. He had patted Danny's head. Instead of checking that the hood was smoothed down flat around his neck he had patted Danny's head. He had patted his head and wished him well and went for the lever and as Danny fell and the rope tightened, the linen bag was drawn up and became wedged in the eye. Got to go now, Gerry, he said, can't keep the famous Solomon Straw waiting.

"Is he dead?" he hears the governor ask.

"I'm sure of it," the doctor replies.

They stand back while Solomon struggles to work the noose free. His fingers are jammed against Danny's neck. The doctor is wrong, he can feel a pulse. I can feel it coming, she said, bucking and heaving, the carpet all scrunched in her hands. Finally he works enough slack through to lift off the hood. Danny stares back up at him grinning, his lips drawn back and his white teeth clamped together. As he lifts the bag clear, his tongue falls out onto the floor. No hard feelings. Remember that. The man from the Home Office cries out and slides to the floor. Solomon kneels astride him and starts to bang on Danny's chest. The bloody mouth hangs open and from somewhere inside comes another rasp and rattle.

"For God's sake, man," the governor cries out, but Solomon takes no notice. He takes a deep breath and starts to blow into his mouth. He is still there, he is sure. He can taste the warmth of him, hear the distant cry of him. Danny is with him in the room. He must never leave him. I'll go and get Dora, he said, No don't leave me, it's coming now, Jem, I can feel it, Danny twitches, he cradles his head and blows again, he can see it coming out, falling into his hands, and with each gasp he can feel him fade away. He lays the baby on his mother's chest. The doctor pulls him aside.

"He's gone, old chap," the medical officer says. "Perhaps not out-right, but there's nothing there now. All this," he pokes at Danny's legs, "is automatic. You must have seen it before." He takes Solomon's hand away and feels the back of Danny's neck.

"Quite broken," he says, "though perhaps not as cleanly as one might have hoped for. We'll soon see after the autopsy."

Using the linen bag as a glove he picks up the tongue and places it in his pocket. They lower the body down again. The man from the Home Office is helped to his feet. The chamber empties rapidly. There are no quiet words of congratulations from the governor this time. Just a quick look at the bloody smear on the floor before a march to his office and a stiff whisky and a long censorious report.

Solomon is left alone. He walks back past Danny's cell. He steps in. The bed is crumpled now, not like when he last saw it. The pictures and photographs are still there. A tin mug stands on the table. He puts his hand to it. It is warm, half-full of Danny's tea. His last cup.

Back at the billet he waits alone. He buries his hands in his face and starts to weep from his immovable solitary eye, weeping for the German he never knew, for the men he never saved, for his son who lies helpless at home, for Danny who lies helpless on the floor, weeping in his hands until Harry returns.

"What was all that about?" Harry asks. "You trying to resurrect them as well? He were deader than a doornail."

"I know," says Solomon.

"What are you going to tell them?" he asks.

"That it was a botched job," Solomon replies. "That it was my fault and that you had nothing to do with it."

For the first time since he has known him, Harry is magnanimous.

"It was an accident," Harry says. "Could have happened to any-one."

They wait by the prison gates for the crowd to disperse. They are sitting in the little gatehouse when Father Rooney walks past on his way out. He beckons him in.

"It was a bad business, Father," Solomon tells him.

"Pray for him," he says. "Pray for him tonight and pray for his family. As I will pray for yours."

He makes the sign of the cross and leaves. Forty minutes later Solomon and Harry emerge from the wicket gate. It is no distance to the railway station and he feels like walking. The sun is up. The demonstration has gone. He is on his way home. How he wants to be home. They walk up the short drive leading to the main road. As they round the corner they see Father Rooney talking to a small group. In the centre stands Mrs. Dancer. She stares at Solomon for a second, unable to remember where she has seen him before, and then she remembers. She looks up at the prison wall and the path from which he has just emerged. She knows who he is now and he feels helpless before her. He stands there with his hands hanging down, unable to move.

JEREMIAH STOOD BEFORE JUDITH'S BED. HE WAS ALMOST UNRECOGNISABLE, with his scuffed coat and his bare head and the patch pulled down over his eye.

"What happened to you, then?" she demanded.

"I got in a fight. It wasn't my fault."

"I should hope not. A fight indeed."

He put down the bag and laid his overcoat over the end of the bed.

"How is he?" he asked.

She pulled back the cover. Stanley lay there curled up against his mother's side, his eyes closed, his mouth barely open, a dark unknown thing forever in their bed.

"Sleeping," she answered. He sat beside her and put his arm round her. She looked up to question him.

"How was—?" He put his hand up to silence her.

"You must never talk about that, Judith. It must vanish from our lives. Look what's happened to me." He pulled the eye patch up over his head. The socket hung pale and empty.

He told her how it had happened, how Mrs. Dancer had leapt upon him, how the two of them had rolled down the grassy bank, Father Rooney sliding down with them, his hairless legs wriggling helplessly in the air, his fleshy white flanks smeared with streaks of municipal mud. Nimble Harry Firth had skipped down after them, pulling Mrs. Dancer off while Jem lay on his back, his arms around his head. She had stood there pulling and panting in Harry's grip while Jeremiah had brushed himself down as best he could. Suddenly she had lunged forward again, but instead of attacking him again she bent down, and picked something bright and glittering from the flattened grass.

"See what this is?" she had cried, wiping it clean on her sleeve. "A glass eye. That's what justice sees through in this country. Blind coppers, blind judges, even a blind hangman. You have taken the light from Danny's eyes, Mr. Straw, but I promise you all that in God's good time you'll wish you had never heard of me and my Danny."

She had run off down the street, waving his eye in the air as if she'd found the Koh-i-Nor diamond. Riding home Jeremiah had been forced to hide in Jack Edge's guard's van, a spare cap wedged unconvincingly on his head. There were no games of chess played on that return journey.

"It's all over, Judith," Jeremiah told her. "Everything. My work at the prison. Our work here. Every last bit of it. We're getting out. You, me and Stanley. We'll sell this business up and buy a pub. Shropshire way."

In the meantime they needed money still. The farm still had to be run, the business kept alive. The following Thursday he went to work in the marketplace while Judith stayed at home. He was astonished on that first day how the other traders swarmed around him, eager to help, enquiring after Judith and the baby. There were gifts too, a silver spoon from the bric-a-brac queens, an album of nursery songs from the holder of the record stall (not that they had a record player), and an old baby's high chair left silently while his back was turned by the furniture dealer. Halfway through the morning Frank Tapp sauntered over with a giant teddy bear which he carried in front of him by one of its ears.

"These things aren't much use to the kiddie yet," Frank admitted, handing it over, "but it'll look nice in the room. Avril says she'd like to come round one day, to see your missus, if that's all right."

It was hard for Jeremiah to envisage a stranger coming into his home. He placed the gift on the front seat of the van.

"Don't forget," Frank called back. "Clunk click, every trip!"

That first morning he had to field a hundred enquiries, take a hundred congratulations, and mutter his thank-yous. He returned home exhausted, his head humming with messages.

"All that rushing about," he said. "All that talking. Never knew the like of it."

Judith looked at her husband with amusement. She had never seen him so disorientated, so obviously out of his depth. The difficulty he had with people! The following day he was out in the fields at the earliest opportunity and did not return until it grew dark. There was no pressing need for him to work those long hours, and it was hot, dry work, even as the sun went down, but he needed the time to restore his solitary equilibrium. But he went eagerly enough to the market the next Saturday, and the Thursday after that. As the weeks wore on, and Cecil Hardwick prepared the papers for a quick sale, Jeremiah began to look forward to his twice-weekly trips into town. He joked with the shoppers and passed the time of day with his fellow stall holders, answering their catcalls with ones of his own. In the morning he arrived early to sit in the small wooden hut, and spoke to them of blighted crops and the vagaries of Covent Garden, and in return learnt of finds plucked from the scrap heap or elusive treasures that had slipped through their unlucky fingers. And at the end of each day he would come back with a humour, not borne out of solitude and introspection, but tempered by the hum of a common sharing. Though he knew he would be leaving soon, this rubbing of shoulders was an apprenticeship for his life to come.

One Saturday, the fifth Saturday of his new office, he had just finished stacking up the empty boxes in the van, ready for the journey home, when he heard Frank call out.

"Fancy a pint?"

Jeremiah shoved the boxes back as far as they would go and straightened up.

"Better not. Judith's expecting me."

"You're storing up a lot of trouble for yourself if you go on be-having like that," Frank said, grinning. "You come on over with me. Besides, if you're going to be running a pub, you better get some first-hand experience. When did you actually last spend some serious time in one?"

It was true, Jeremiah reflected. The idea of running a public house was based on the premise that being a publican's daughter, Judith would know what was required. He had not envisaged himself behind the bar, listening and talking. He had seen himself as the man who would be where the *machine* would lie, amongst the unsung coils, keeping the pub running smoothly. How like him to think of the cogs and wheels of it and the cellar below the trapdoor, where he could move about silently, rolling the barrels over the cold flagstone, checking the pipes, the unseen hand. How foolish! What did he know of public houses and their breth-ren? Nothing! What did he know of this one, across the market square, or Judith's father's? Nothing! In these years, when he had gone into one at all, it had been to sit in a conspiracy of circumstance with Alcott and his chosen few, a precious gathering of exclusion and deference.

"Just a quick one, then," he said.

"That's what I always have," Frank promised him.

Jeremiah had told Judith to expect him home by two, but the mo-ment he stepped in and sniffed the atmosphere, he knew he would not be. It was not the drink that would keep him, though he knew that might come in time. It was the possibility of admittance into a world of smoke and a long Saturday afternoon ahead. There was a glitter of glasses on the bar and wet on the lips of the men who had sought their com-pany, glasses standing on the polished wood, glasses hanging in the air, or in the crook of leathered elbows, glasses half-drunk, glasses drained, glasses standing empty with the foam sliding down, a barmaid calling out an order for sandwiches, a darts match in the corner, the door behind him opening again, and a greeting given. A chair scraped back, a man waved his hand in the air, trying to gain attention; "Game on!" someone shouted, and Jeremiah shivered, remembering that call, and all the years in between when he had feared the company of men and their cruel, laughing talk. He was less sure of his ground now. He had missed companionship those years, and what had he replaced it with? Perhaps men need such company, he thought, need a room in which to voice these obligatory pleasantries, not simply as a release but as an acknowledgement of their enduring presence. Cruelty was too frequent a visitor to be excused as an unwanted and unexpected guest. It was a close relation, tied by blood, part of a man's family, though why it bred in such profusion he could not begin to surmise. He had seen boys drawing sustenance from that deep well of bitterness as if it was the spring of life itself; he had seen young men proud and rampant, raging in its lusty thrall, seen old men thirsting for a single drop. Cruelty would be lying here, suspended in the barrels, to be drawn up through the clear clean pipes, to be supped and savoured and drunk in, and yet looking upon this crowd he could not help but long for his own participation in their public pantomime. It was good to be here, good to be one of them. He followed Frank in as he pushed his way through to the bar. The barmaid looked him full in the face, recognising him and whom he had sat with in the past. She studied his eye patch and the fading bruise on his forehead, trying to work out whether these bleak decorations might be the cause of his unexpected admittance to this cavalier crew. Frank moved to order but Jeremiah silenced him with a gesture and a look. He still had the power to do that to a man.

"Two pints, if you please," adding as an afterthought, "of your best bitter."

He turned and looked over the seated throng, oblivious to him and his hangman's thoughts. He would no longer entertain them either. He would be an ordinary man for a change. It was such a novel experience, standing at the bar, hearing others breaking into people's conversations, moving from one topic to the next. Frank made him laugh despite what Judith had said about him. He could see that Frank was not a good or pleasant man but he was enjoying his company nevertheless, enjoying the chosen confidences given out, even the hints about how to shortchange customers. There was an underlying assumption that as men drinking in this pub, they shared a common set of beliefs. Quite what they might be no one bothered to explore, but they were here all the same. He had been allowed in. He was accepted. A father at home, and now a fellow trader with Frank. He bought another round. And another. Frank tried to get in on the act but Jeremiah insisted. It was his time for celebration after all.

"If you say so, me old son," Frank replied, tipping back the contents. "Mine's another pint. With a whisky chaser."

"Make that two whisky chasers," Jeremiah called out after her. He caught Frank's eye as they watched the barmaid stand on tiptoe, glass in hand. Frank nodded at her legs and grinned back at him. Jeremiah shared the pleasure. He felt warm to this man, warmer than he had done to any man. The bar was filling up again. Jeremiah motioned towards an empty table by the window. He wanted to end the day with a confession, an intimacy. Frank followed him over. It was quieter here, as if a curtain had been drawn across. Frank leant back and began to roll a cigarette. Jeremiah looked to the opaque window.

"That was very decent of you all, Frank, to give us a present like that. It's not as if we know you that well."

Frank licked his cigarette paper and put it in his mouth.

"We're not all bad, you know," he said, spitting out a stray strand of tobacco that had stuck to his lip. "Not through and through. Only half bad. Look at my son. He could be all bad, 'cause he's his mother's son as much as mine, but he's got some good in him along the line."

"Most of us have," Jem said. "But sometimes it's hard for the good to get out."

Frank nodded. "Most have I agree. But some haven't. Take that Ethel Whitley. Now there's someone who is all bad to my mind."

"Bad!" Jeremiah felt obliged to defend Hardwick's efficient secretary. "I wouldn't have ever described her as bad."

Frank raised his eyebrows. "You knew her then, did you?"

Jeremiah shook his head. "Only on business. She always seemed such a quiet, pleasant young woman to me."

Frank waved the barmaid over, pointing his stubby fingers at the two empty whisky glasses.

"She never *seemed* nothing to no one. That's the whole point. That's why she got all that good press despite all the damage she'd caused. But we knew all about her and Colin. I tried to warn him off."

"It was common knowledge, then?"

Frank shook his head. "They tried to keep it quiet but they came unstuck. They went up to the Lake District last summer for a dirty weekend. Thought no one would find them there. Unfortunately my boy was there with Danny and the youth club. Ivor hadn't seen his uncle for years, so he didn't recognise him, but when he came back we had his photos developed."

"And in them—"

"Was Colin and Ethel, arm in arm. As soon as I saw it I recognised him right away. So I rang up Maureen to see what was going on. He'd told her he'd been on a printers' conference. Well, family is family and no one is going to mess about with my sister, even if she is on the wrong side of forty. Thought the threat of a good punch on the nose would be enough. Colin was a weak man."

"But it didn't work."

"For a time it did. By that time Danny was after her. He told me all about her when we next met up at Luton market. So I said, why don't you get a pitch in Aylesbury? Try your luck down here. Right on her doorstep. Used to pull his leg about it. 'You got anywhere yet?' I'd ask and he'd smirk back, 'Not yet, Frank, but I will.' And then one Thursday night I'm in here, in the little bar round the back, when in she walks and starts knocking back the old vodka and tonic. Danny was right. She was a good-looking piece underneath that Little Miss Muffet outfit of hers. And by the way she's sitting there, hoiking her legs around the barstool, you can tell what she's after. So nothing ventured, nothing gained. I start chatting her up. Four vodkas later, bingo!

"Didn't think any more about it. Then weeks later, months later, that Thursday I see her again down in the market. Danny's not there by then. Danny's given her up. Says he's wasting his time. Never told me she'd already told him to piss off out of it. Just pretended he'd lost interest. So when I see her standing outside your wife's stall I call out to her." He spluttered with laughter. "Thought she'd wet herself when she saw me. I didn't know my brother-in-law was knocking her off again, otherwise I'd a done a lot more than shout at her, I'm telling you."

Jeremiah lifted his glass to his lips and drank. It was hard to imagine Ethel Whitley having sex with a married man or someone she picked up, hard to imagine her wild upstairs, above this very bar with Frank. Hard to imagine anybody wanting, needing to do that. No, that wasn't true. He could imagine Will. He could imagine Frank too. But Cecil Hardwick? Judith? He looked around the room wondering. How many others? How many men? How many women?

"Didn't your sister never suspect?" he asked.

Frank pulled on his cigarette.

"Not the second time around, no. He always went out on Thursdays. Had done for years."

"Oh?"

Frank looked at him. "I shouldn't be telling you this. They had a child. Long time ago. They told everyone it had died in childbirth, but it hadn't. There was something wrong with it, that was all. Maureen wouldn't have anything to do with it, but Colin would go and visit it. Him, I should say. He was farmed out for a year or two but then got put in a special home. Colin would drive out to see him most weeks if he could. Thursday evenings. When he started seeing Ethel he started to take time off in the afternoon instead. God knows what'll happen to the poor bastard now."

They fell into a silence. Jeremiah got up and walked over to the bar. He felt slow and light-headed. Looking across into the snug he could see a familiar brown felt hat hanging on its usual peg. Alcott would have heard by now, how Solomon Straw had lost his nerve, how he had to be led out of the chamber and up to his quarters where a warder had stood over him until it had been time to leave.

He swung the door open and hung unsteadily onto the handle. Alcott sat alone, nursing his beer.

"Strange company you're keeping these days, Jeremiah," he said, hardly raising his eyes.

Jeremiah looked back. Frank was beckoning to a vivid blonde who was standing on the threshold, balancing on her high heels. He closed the door and walked across, trying to discern what expression played upon the detective's hidden face. Sympathy? Contempt? He wanted to explain to him the real circumstance of Danny's death, but saw that in attempting to surmount the treacherous explanation he would stumble and fall to his explanatory death. He tried approaching the matter from the subject forever in Alcott's thoughts.

"We've just been talking about someone you know, Peter. Ethel Whitley."

Alcott held up his hand. "Don't say anymore," he said. "I don't want to hear another word on the subject of that particular little miss." He paused. His need to confide got the better of him.

"You'll never guess what she's doing."

"Emigrating, I hear."

Alcott nodded glumly.

"I admired that woman, Jeremiah, admired and cherished her. She'd talked of leaving even in hospital but I thought that after the trial, after she'd settled down . . . I had hopes, Jem. I understood her predicament. More than most men. I hoped one day she might make an accommodation with me."

"An accommodation?"

"Matrimony. I had quite set my heart on it. I went round last week to find her packing a trunk. Vancouver, it said. Via Liverpool, Queenstown, and Quebec. Vancouver! It's enough to make a man throw in his handcuffs."

Jeremiah had to stop himself laughing. The idea of Alcott marrying

Ethel Whitley was an absurdity that only a man of Alcott's blinkered temperament could contemplate. He was fifteen years her senior for a start and like an unwanted elder tree seemed to grow taller and more unruly by the year.

"Perhaps," he said foolishly, "if you went and asked her, she might change her mind."

"Perhaps you could arrange for us to become marooned on a desert island," Alcott sneered, irritated by the unwanted advice. "Perhaps your friend next door will forswear villainy and join the Salvation Army. Perhaps some of us have outlived our usefulness." He went back to staring at his pint.

"You heard, then."

"Heard?" Alcott answered, bland innocence giving shape to his voice. "Heard what?"

"About what happened."

Alcott looked up again, expectant triumph on his face.

"No," he said. "Why? What did happen?"

Jeremiah could tell Alcott was lying. He was no longer Alcott's confidant. As far as Alcott was concerned he had crossed over to the other side. That's why he could talk to Frank, not because he liked him, but because he was on his side, where life stained his clothing.

"Nothing happened," he said. "Nothing at all."

He stepped out into the sudden light and drew his hat down over his eyes. The town was clear and bright. It had already forgotten the murder and the execution. It was a Saturday afternoon, back to normal. Jeremiah took off his hat and fanned himself before starting to walk, seeing the town as others saw it, an everyday part of their lives. He had always marched through these streets, or through any built-up area, with his eyes fixed straight ahead, fearful lest his progress might be diverted, that he might be recognised, pointed at, or chased after. But now he took time to look, to loiter, to be seen, to push his way needlessly through the dwindling crowd. No one stood in imaginary doorways marking his progress, no black-skirted mother clutched her wide-eyed child, whispering warm words of horror, no worthy raised his hat or muttered to his neighbour, no costermonger villain called out an overeffusive greeting. His phantoms had left him. He was an ordinary pedestrian moving along the alleyways and pavements, a shopper jostling amongst his brethren, stepping off the pavement for a mother and her pram, smiling at the young shop assistant undressing an unwilling mannequin, leaning against the corner with the other idlers, contemplating the state of his shoes. He was no longer alone.

He drove home with a sudden urgency upon him. Judith would be waiting for him out in the garden, half-conscious of his absence, but delighting in Stanley's company. He had visions of leading her upstairs while Stanley slept, curled in the leafy shade below. He could do that now, lead her to where desire lay quietly spread out on their bed for them, kiss desire on the lips and see her yawn lightly with the smile of a woken promise. There were so many creatures to wake from their years of slumber, so many paths, thick with brambles, to cut free, so many rooms, lying musty and unused, waiting with shutters to be wrenched open. So much sunshine to pour in, so much rain! As he drove along the flat road, pools of dazzling liquid sun danced upon the road. He could see nothing but their shimmering glare as the waves of heat rose before him, ever shifting, while he held the van steady.

Suddenly, out of the blinding curtain, a car burst towards him, huge and blue with horn blaring and crazy passengers laughing inside, their heads thrown back, their arms thrust out the window. Jeremiah pulled on his wheel hard, stamping on the brakes as the van lurched to the left and careered over the rutted verge. The empty boxes came tumbling through, hitting him on the head and back, and he was thrown onto the wheel, breath knocked out of him as he crashed through the thick tangle of bushes. When he came to he saw that the van had broken into an airy hollow. He clambered out, catching his clothes on the wild brambles. A cloud of bluebottles swarmed angrily about his head. An old camp bed and a couple of orange boxes lay scattered on the ground. A blanket, half-rotten, lay at his feet. As he kicked it with his foot a grass snake slipped away into the undergrowth. A boy's den no doubt. He felt something wet trickle into his eye. He wiped it away with his hand. Blood. He heard a woman's voice.

"That's it," she was screaming, "It's two bicycles on the Isle of Wight and bugger the Continent."

He looked back. A large man stood by the door of his car. Over on the other side a young woman was banging her fist on the car roof.

"Are you all right in there?" the man called out.

"Bloody fool," Jeremiah shouted back. "Could have killed us all."

The man pushed his way through, clambering over the broken brambles and branches. He inspected the van and then walked round Jeremiah.

"Not much damage vis-à-vis the van," he said. "But you've a nasty cut above the eye."

"Bloody fool," Jeremiah repeated. "Driving at that speed."

He sat down suddenly. He felt weak and giddy.

"You should be more careful," the man replied. "I'm as fond of a drink as the next man, but you were all over the place."

He was? Jeremiah started to explain.

"I didn't see you," he offered. "The sun was in my eyes."

"You've had one too many," the man charged. "That's your trouble. It's bad enough with two eyes, let alone one. I've a good mind to call the police."

"Hark who's talking," the woman butted in. "You're as much to blame as him, driving on the wrong side of the road like that."

"Jill!"

"Well, I'm getting fed up with it. Either your precious car goes or I do." She ducked down and slammed the door.

"Hang up my gloves?" the man said in slow amazement. "She can't mean it. She'll be suffering from shock."

"She means it," Jeremiah offered. "Now help me push this heap back out of here. I'll be all right to drive back. I've not far to go."

Together they pushed the van back out onto the road. It started up easily enough. A broken headlight and a dented bumper were the only damage he had collected. It was the remains of the last greenhouse that had suffered. He looked back at it before driving off. It lay torn apart, its rusting frame dragged down, its shape gone.

"This marks the end of my tenure," he said out loud. "In a couple of years' time there'll be no sign left of you at all."

He drove the rest of the way home at walking pace, the blood drying on his face. Judith was in the garden, lying in the hammock half-undressed, with Stanley on her stomach. She gave a start and then saw the sway of his body and the afternoon's alcohol brimming in his face.

"You been drinking?" she accused.

He nodded.

"Crashed the van a mile back. By the greenhouses. It wasn't my fault, Judith, honest."

"I've heard that before," she said sharply. Stanley stirred. She stroked her son's dark head of hair.

"You'll not hear it again," he promised. "Ever." He leant down and gave Stanley a gift of beery kisses. "I thought we might go upstairs," he said to her carefully, placing his hand over her loose breast.

She brushed him away. "Did you now."

"While he's sleeping," he insisted. His lips moved from Stanley's head to the gap in her dress where her stomach lay bare. There were things he had to say, things he had never said before. He took her hand and placed it against his face.

"It is beginning, Judith, but you must help me. I have to lay siege to it, to drive out this dreadful solitude that lies within me, but its walls are tall, its bars are strong, its locks hard to pick. But I have begun. This morning and this afternoon and now with you. I have borne it all these years, Judith, without thanks, except from those who I had no wish to receive it from, those officials who thanked me for my speed and skill. Not from those poor creatures who I longed to hear." He pointed to the sky. "Not from them, for I had silenced them, silenced them at the very moment when I would give them voice." He sat down and hung his head. Though the ground spun, he managed to say, quite distinctly, "It was love for them that drove me forward."

"Love?"

He caught her questioning look.

"Love for the most despised, the most hated, the most reviled. Love for the German, love for the most filthy brute. To release love in that chamber where there was nothing on offer but revenge. That is why I could not share my life with you, Judith. I tried but could not, not while I had my duty to perform. Else others would have usurped me, taken my task away from me, others like Harry Firth, meanspirited men whose treatment would not be like mine. There is not much a man can do in those few seconds, with a poor boy trembling his way to defeat, but whatever there was that could be done, I did. Except for that day."

She became agitated. "You mean Danny?"

He lay a quietening hand upon her.

"You must forget him and forgive me, Judith. We have begun again and we must not falter now."

"Your hands are shaking," she said. She levered herself up and spat on the sleeve of her dress, wiping the blood away. She had never looked lovelier. He put his hard hand to her again.

"Not upstairs, then," she said. "There is no cause to make a journey of it."

But it was a journey they took as she rose up out of the hammock and led him down to where they could lie hidden, where the tall grass grew, Stanley not twenty feet away. He laid her down like he had promised he would, where desire was to be found, slumbering on the warm earth, and as they lay both looked up, past the hammock, to their house with all their windows open: it was as if they could see their past lives fleeing out the rooms, rising up into the wide air. They lay quiet, so that they would hear him if he woke, moving slowly, deliberately, without haste, no sound other than their steady breathing disturbing the still afternoon, no urgency, just the gentle wind high above stirring the tops of the trees, no one between them now, no solitary looks, no lifeless flesh poisoning their every touch, no unwanted names whispered in her ear, no backs turned in a dread parody of an embrace, just their ageing limbs with the breath of the world upon them, just Judith and Jeremiah with arms outstretched, just Judith and Jeremiah with lips apart, just Judith and Jeremiah seeing the years of sorrow fall away with each word spoken, the folly of his afternoon forgotten. And when the moment came, when she saw it flicker in his eye, when he saw it flush unexpectedly in her face, it was as if, watered with their tears, they flowered, rooted to the spot, Judith and Jeremiah, never moving, Judith and Jeremiah.

He pulled his trousers back on while she smoothed down the lower half of her dress. He rolled over and looked up. He saw the huge sky, how high and clear it was, how infinite the sky's patience, how deep its wrath and its huge capacity for surprise. The sky had witnessed them. The sky had forgiven him. He had to tell her one more thing.

"Danny was meant for us, Judith, can't you see? Meant for you and me. Just like the German and little Stanley over there. They all fell down like bolts out of the sky, picking us up from our self-appointed paths, setting us down on some other unexpected route. Why somewhere in there we have a couple of letters signed in Ethel Whitley's hand. It's all connected, Judith. Me missing the train, you knowing Danny, Frank calling out to Ethel that morning. Even those tangerines you sold her that ended up in Danny's mouth."

"Not the tangerines," Judith corrected. "He was allergic to them. Made his hands swell up."

Jeremiah sat upright, looking through the haze, not wanting to believe what he heard. It was the boom of drink ringing in his head that made him unable to comprehend what she was saying. He licked his lips carefully and steadied himself by holding onto an overhanging branch. Judith swayed before him.

"Swell up?" he asked. "How do you mean?"

"Danny," she said. "Any citrus, oranges and stuff, made him puff up. Could hardly breathe. First time he ever ate one, when he was a child, nearly bloody killed him, he said."

Judith buttoned herself up and made her way to the kitchen to make them a pot of tea. Jeremiah followed remembering all the details with which Alcott had regaled him, Colin trembling in the driver's seat, Ethel as calm as a sea of glass, every foul remark glancing off her clean and unsullied surface while the intruder sucked noisily on the tangerines, spitting the skins out onto the floor. "Just like a monkey in a zoo," Alcott had said, "doing all sorts of unimaginable things in front of its audience."

It was the recollection of that word *audience* that struck the first chord, and then, as he sank back in his armchair, hearing the rattle of the teaspoon in his mug, Judith quietly advising their sleeping child that his father was nothing but a great big baby, it was that, the phrase she had used so affectionately all those years before, which reminded him of the other. It slipped into his head with the clarity of a bugler's call. "You're a messy bugger and no mistake," she had said. "Worse than a monkey in a cage. Why can't you eat them properly like any normal man?" not quite identical to that spoken by his uniformed friend, but the image was the same, of the man sitting there, sucking rudely on the fruit.

A monkey in a cage. How many times had he heard Judith say it that summer as they rode along the roads, Loopy in the back, playing pat-a-cake and noughts-and-crosses with him, while she sat in the front, fending off those lewd remarks. In his heart he suddenly knew it to be true. He could see him now spitting out the skins, spluttering with greed, laughing at his own jokes and patting Judith's knee. He could hear the voice and the mocking torment that supplied every syllable. Surely it could not be possible? And yet. He had a house close by, didn't he? Was that how the killer had escaped, skipping over the fields to his house not two miles away?

"Never ate oranges?" he called out. "Never?"

Judith came through and banged his mug down in front of him. "None of it," she said. "Why, what does it matter what he ate?"

That evening he took out the Execution Book from under the floorboards and opened it for the last time. The book felt heavier than he had ever known, his past life weighed down with the cold meat of revenge. Against the last entry lay Father Rooney's letter. He did not read it but he remembered the contents well enough. Father Rooney had been right. Now he knew why Danny had used the words which had sent him to the gallows as his own, biting his tongue, spitting the phrase out before Jeremiah's feet. Too late, he was certain of a new and terrible truth.

He went into the town the next day. He was shown into Hardwick's office by a tall girl with buckteeth, too forward, too bright and breezy, altogether too modern a young woman for a man of his solicitor's temperament. She wouldn't last six months, he thought.

"Better now?" she asked, flashing her teeth at him. "Could have been nasty, that crash."

Recognising her, Jeremiah flushed with embarrassment.

"I don't usually . . ." he began. "I wasn't used to it."

She tugged briefly at her tight fluffy jersey, then lifted her arms and pushed back the sleeves.

"Don't apologise on my account. If it hadn't been for you I'd be spending my honeymoon bent double over a map. God help us from a man and his hobbies."

She showed him into Hardwick's office. The solicitor leapt up from behind his desk and hovered behind the waiting chair.

"Take a seat, Mr. Bembo, take a seat," he implored, squeezing Jeremiah's hand hard, before dancing back to his desk. "What can I get you? A glass of water? A cup of tea? A nice crisp digestive biscuit, perhaps?"

Jeremiah had grown used to Mr. Hardwick's frenzied display of normality over the years. Ever since he had told him of his other work the man broke out in a fever of anxiety the moment he walked through the door. It was as if he feared that any displeasure he caused would involve penalties far outweighing the cause. Jeremiah looked around, half expecting to see Ethel Whitley sitting quietly in the gloom at the back, her notebook on her lap. Hardwick caught his glance.

"Sad times, Mr. Bembo, sad times. Miss Whitley gone. You and your new family to leave. The town will not be the same."

"Miss Whitley is emigrating, I hear," Jeremiah offered. Hardwick looked at his watch. No doubt it told of the tides and the moon as well as the date.

"Sailing tomorrow as a matter of fact." He brushed his suit with pride. "I arranged it all myself. It was the least I could do, even though I could not condone the conduct which led to her tragedy."

He shifted nervously in his seat, waiting. He knew better than to enquire as to Jeremiah's involvement in the case, though from the way his eyes flicked back and forth over Jeremiah's hands, it was a confidence he longed to be granted.

"And how may I assist you this warm summer morning?" he intoned. Jeremiah brought the book from out under his jacket.

"I have brought you something to look after," he told him.

"Yes?"

"A book."

"A book?"

"Of my past times. A professional record, if you like. Dates, times, method, as well as my own observations. It must be kept in safekeeping for my son. He must read it in time, but not yet. When he is of age. Then he must decide about his father. Before that date it is not to be opened by anyone, understand? Not even yourself."

A flicker of disappointment passed over the solicitor's face but Jeremiah had no doubt in his mind. Hardwick would follow his strictures.

He turned the van around in the road and drove out towards the Beacon and the house that lay at the sloping foot of its long rise, the house where the bomb had fallen and the steam had billowed, where he had stood and watched Judith dancing across that handsome shining floor.

It was still and quiet when he drew up. Even the birds seemed to have deserted its precincts. It was not a house for the day. Without the cover of darkness, without the bright clothes and the high laughter, the house stood revealed tall and unforgiving. A house of manners, however twisted. He parked his van by the garage. The doors stood wide open, the space bare save for a broken tennis racket and a case of empty champagne bottles. He knocked on the door then bent down to the letter box.

"Hello," he shouted.

There was no reply. He walked round the back and hammered on the kitchen door before returning to the front. He bent down again.

"Hello? Is anyone there?"

A curtain twitched back. The housekeeper no doubt. He could hear the tread of her stifled footsteps. He stood back, expecting the door to open, but it did not.

"What do you want?" a voice asked. The inflection was familiar.

"I'm trying to reach Mr. Baxter," he called out.

"There's no one of that name living here," came the defensive reply.

"Mr. Bembo, then," Jeremiah shouted. "Will Bembo. He lives here, I know. I'm his cousin."

"Cousin?" The voice came nearer.

"Yes."

"Will's cousin?"

"Yes."

There was a pause.

"What's your name, then?"

"Bembo."

"Your other name."

"Jeremiah. You must have heard of us hereabouts."

The door was pulled back suddenly. A tall woman with a full dark head of hair tied back in a knot stared back at him. She looked as strong and quick as she had ever been. She was seventeen years older than he, if memory served him right. Fifty-five.

"Good God," he said.

"Hello, Jem," she said, a hard smile on her face. "Guess you never expected to find me here."

"That I didn't. I thought you'd gone away."

"You never thought of me at all," she admonished.

"It was a long time ago," Jem said, not knowing whether he should shake her hand or lean forward and kiss her. What fun she had been! How she had twirled him in her arms! Will's mother! She turned on her heel.

"You better come in."

He followed her into the hall, bare and empty now, save for a sad deflated balloon, caught in the chandelier. He looked up at the stairway and the dark shining balustrade with its long lingering curve. She caught his eye.

"Seen some parties, this place," she said. "You were at the last, Will said."

"You were here then?"

"Out the back. In my little flat." She pointed to the green baize door that Will had warned the couple against.

"How long have you been living here?" he asked her.

"Ever since he bought it."

"I never knew."

"You don't know a lot of things," she replied. "Will's been looking after me ever since I came back."

"I never knew," he repeated.

"You weren't supposed to," she said, sharply. "Came to see me regular in those days, no matter what foolishness I'd got up to."

"We weren't allowed to see you," he stammered. "Silas forbade it."

"Didn't stop Will. I was his mum and he was sticking by me. Every week he'd come by with some of the money he'd made." She stopped

262

abruptly. She had no desire to engage his confidence. "So what do you want with him?" she said sharply.

"I've just become a father," Jeremiah explained. "A boy. I wanted to tell him. He is family after all."

"Family." She spat the word. "Fat lot of family you showed me. Will never forgave you all for that, giving me the cold shoulder when I came back, down on my luck. You especially. Never mind, Mum, he'd say. Fuck the lot of them."

The sound of her swearing offended Jem's sensibilities. She saw him shrink and mocked him.

"Not right from a woman of my years, is it, Jem?" she crooned. "Will always said you were a thankless prude."

"I'm sorry. I never meant—"

She dismissed his apology.

"The time has passed to make amends," she told him. "Let Will be. You've left each other alone all these years. I wouldn't let such a little thing as your son get in the way. Anyway there's nothing you can do about it now. He's gone abroad."

"Gone abroad? I thought he was doing a summer season down on the coast."

"Something better came up. A month on one of those transatlantic liners. Starts this week as a matter of fact. From Liverpool."

The porter took her luggage down into the cabin and after she had unpacked, laid out her change of dress for the evening and her clothes for next morning, she decided to walk round the great ship. She had arrived early and the vessel lay wide and empty, its partly covered decks whistling with unlocked echoes and soft internal breezes. The ship was not due to sail until that evening. Most of the passengers were not expected until the boat train came in from London and until then she, and a few others, had the ship to themselves. Walking along its great length, climbing, climbing, forever climbing until she stood, two hundred feet aloft, a queen herself, staring out over the dropped harbour to the thin measureless expanse beyond: it was as if she was mistress of this ship. Its wheel and its prow and its great engine lay restless; the huge funnels rose burning for her command. She could feel the power of the ship, feel the tide pull at the steel cables that held her fast, imagine the foaming path she would cut across the great ocean, leading to new territories. In a week's time she would be standing on new soil, taking in new landscapes, hearing new tones of voice, learning the meaning of new expressions. She wished it would sail now, when it could all be hers, hers to roam wherever she chose, hers to sleep in whatever bed she desired, hers to sit alone in one vast dining room after another while clutches of waiters stood abroad listening to the echoes of her precise cutlery. She longed to feel the shudder and beat of the machine, to sense the swell of the sea, with the wind on her face and her body glowing proud over the endless mass of blue. This ship was going to take her to the land where her new power lay, not a glamorous power, not one learnt at the hearth or in the bedroom, but a cold and anonymous power where she would be no one but what she chose to be; and that would remain a mystery even unto herself. Colin had tried to know her and it had killed him. No one would ever know her again.

She sat out on the deck chair watching the passengers come slowly aboard, some with relatives tearful and cheerful, some alone. She did not want to meet any of them. She took pleasure solely in the sight of the crew, the starched white stewards who bowed at her requests, the darkly uniformed officers with their braid and gold wristwatches who nodded courteously while passing, even those sweating overalled creatures who belonged below, but were still visible and who looked the other way, fearful lest they might catch her eye.

A steward brought her a pot of tea and later a plate of scones. She ordered China tea, not because she liked it but because it was on offer. She was travelling in style, her savings spent. She could choose anything.

"Go careful on the clotted cream," a voice suggested. "Wait until you've found your sea legs."

She looked up. A small, dapper man stood against the sun.

"Remember me?" he said.

Ethel held her hand in front of her eyes, squinting into the sun. "No, I don't think I do."

He stepped into the shadow. "Come on now. You must. Best little trooper I had all that season."

Ethel looked at him properly. Of course she recognised him.

"You're that comedian. The one who wouldn't take no for an answer. Billy Baxter."

"Got it in one. You had me worried there for a minute. Do you mind?" He sat down beside her and popped a sugar lump into his mouth. "They told me you were going to be on here."

"They?"

"The officers. They're always warned if . . ." He lowered his voice. "Look. I know what happened."

Ethel started to protest. She had been allowed to book under a different name.

"No no. All I can say is, in some way I feel responsible. If I hadn't brought you and that man together."

Ethel stirred her tea. Colin Tarrant. Now if she thought of that night and what went before it at all, it was not of Danny she thought. The intruder, as she now remembered him, had sunk back, had become a shadow again, a dark outline hovering in the back. It was Colin she remembered, Colin staring ahead, the sweat falling from his faltering lip, his feet trembling against the pedals. Colin quiet and sullen, Colin hot and bothered, Colin in the Car. Always Colin. Always Colin in the Car. Colin reversing; Colin crashing the gears; Colin with the hand brake on, his hands all over her. She did not hold the intruder responsible. She blamed Colin. It was Colin who had violated her week after week with his petty passion, imprisoning her, pressing himself upon her, unwilling to set her free. Every time she thought of him she wanted to take a bath and scrub every vestige of him off her tormented skin, to hold her arms out and submerge, feel her breasts float free, drowning his cries of petulant passion that still echoed in her ears. She had told her mother that she intended to take his photograph and throw it to the sea, a gesture to eternity, of what he had meant to her, but as the time grew closer, Colin's picture stayed where it had always been. She could neither take it nor destroy it. She could not bear to touch it. In the final rush she had ignored it completely. It stood on the mantelpiece, in the drawing room in her mother's house, where she had placed it the week she came back from hospital. That was all he was now, a faded picture on a mantelpiece. Small. Insignificant. Forgotten. Gone. She wondered how long her mother would keep it. Forever probably.

"How do you know that?" she asked him.

Will looked confused. "She told me. Your friend. That night in London."

"Jill?"

"That's the one."

Ethel fell silent remembering Jill's bruised body and her shuddering tears.

"She came back very late that night."

Will nodded sympathetically. "I'm not surprised. Running off with my manager like that."

"Your manager?"

"My *ex*-manager. Larry Cohen."

"But she told me that you and she—"

Will looked indignant. "Me and her?" he cried, astonished that she could ever contemplate such a thing. "Never. Begging your pardon, but I only had eyes for you, Miss Whitley." He laughed. "Old Larry thought Christmas had come early that night. Terrible one for the girls he was, Miss Whitley. Terrible."

"You weren't so good yourself, I seem to remember."

Will appeared to look surprised, then remembered why.

"Oh that. You shouldn't have taken any notice of that. That was just the greasepaint talking. We're all like that when we're performing. Pains in the arse the lot of us, begging your pardon."

"You certainly didn't believe in wasting any time, that much was clear."

Will offered up his hands in apology. "To tell you the truth, Miss Whitley, it's very hard for someone in my profession to behave any other way. It's not as if we're around every day like any normal suitor you might meet. We can't stand outside your houses, bring you all flowers, take you to the pictures. We have to act quickly, cut corners. So when I do meet someone who takes my fancy, I tend to jump in with the old dazzle and glitter. That's all the time I've got."

She held out her cup. Will poured the tea and added the milk. He inclined his head to the sugar bowl. She declined. She held the bone-china cup in her hand, looking out over the railing. She would make this trip once a year, not back to Aylesbury but to London perhaps, just for the pleasure of the unknown voyage and a heart she might snare.

"I can understand it grating on you," Will was saying, "but believe me, it wasn't meant like that."

She turned her head and looked directly at him.

"What was it meant like, then?" she asked him.

The quiet simplicity of the question unsettled him. Ethel could see him wondering how direct he dare be. He took a deep breath.

"I've had plenty of girlfriends in my time, Miss Whitley, I can't deny it. Can't say I haven't enjoyed it. That's the sort of man I am. But it's not often in travels like mine that you meet someone who genuinely interests you. Trouble is when you do you don't have the time to show the respect they deserve. It's the curse of show business and I apologise for it. No . . ." He stopped.

He stood up. "There. I've made a proper fool of myself."

"Not completely," Ethel said. "But tell me, are you not on a show now?"

"For a couple of nights I am."

"So should one not beware of the dazzle and glitter taking its toll once again?"

Will looked around. "Not at all. We are here on equal terms, Miss Whitley. Both travellers after all. For me, this is like sleepwalking. You'll never find me so relaxed. And you? This a social trip? Visiting relatives? Taking time out to think things over?"

Ethel patted her lips with one of the liner's embroidered napkins. "A new life, Mr. Baxter. I'm leaving England. Setting up anew."

Will turned and looked inland. "I don't blame you. If you want my opinion," he added, stabbing a finger at the lines of hazy smoke that rose above the chimneys and cranes, "England's done for."

He pulled out the cigarette case and held it open before her. "Remember this? My lucky calling card I used to call it." He weighed it in his hand then let it drop. Ethel gasped. They could hear it clattering its way down the ship's side.

"I'm like you, Miss Whitley, looking for a new life," he said. "You're going to Canada. I'm not sure where I'll end up. South Africa, probably. More opportunity for a white man there, and it's kinder on the goolies, if you'll pardon my French."

Ethel smiled, lowering her eyes. "I haven't heard of Canadians having any particular problems in that area," she flirted. "Though it isn't something they would advertise in the brochures."

Will's eyes twinkled. How he loved this sort of talk.

"But have they a sense of humour?" he asked, stepping up to the table once more. "It's one thing keeping the lower regions warm. It's quite another having to thaw a joke out over a frozen audience."

"A challenge, Mr. Baxter. Are you not moved by challenges, by cold impervious fronts, new pastures? What about your audience here for instance?"

"This lot?" Will rubbed his hands. "Strictly donkey and carrot stuff. They'll go anywhere I lead them."

"And where will that be?"

He tapped his nose. "Not where the entertainment officer wants me to take them, that's for sure. Came round this morning to give me a long lecture on the importance of maintaining the company's image. Jumped-up little pillock."

Ethel inclined her head, questioning his stance. He hastened to reassure her.

"Not that I'll be doing anything untoward. But people are out here for a good time. They want to let their hair down." He sat down again. "Why don't you come along one night? Tonight if you've a mind to. I'll be sure to get you a good table, discreet like." He folded his hands, as if in prayer. "And I'd be very honoured, Miss Whitley, if you might join me for a dinner one evening. In the dining room, or somewhere more private if you would prefer."

"Perhaps. I am not happy with crowds yet," she admitted.

"Of course, Miss Whitley."

"The name's Ethel, Mr. Baxter." She rose. "I think I'll go and lie down for a bit. Before we sail."

Will nodded. "Don't worry if you oversleep. Cruise proper doesn't start until tomorrow. Nothing much will happen here tonight."

He drank heavily the rest of the afternoon after she had left him, and when the boy woke him at seven the ship was already at sea. He felt fuzzy and in need of another shot. Quickly instructed as to the requirements of half-conscious comedians, the boy returned with a glass of foaming liver salts and left a half-bottle of Bells in the cramped dressing room at the back of the stage. Will knew he should not drink any more but the sparkling water seemed to awaken his thirst and once installed in front of the mirror he began to drink deeply again. He was nervous. His new routine was still not completely ironed out. The crucial moment was a five-minute play with the courting couple on their way to lovers' lane. He had plans to do a whole show around these characters, a history of their life, their courtship, their married life, their old age, but for now he was content to try out their introduction. The dummies were already in place, sitting in their cardboard car, hidden behind a screen. As he applied his makeup, knocking back the smell of diesel oil that seemed to float up through the ventilator with the taste of warm whisky, he began to feel strong again, quick and alert. His hands were shaking but his eyes were bright and when he smiled and cocked his head to one side, he could see the charm still at work. And this was not even a proper audience, not a paying audience. This was an audience who was getting him for free. After dusting his face with powder, rubbing the rouge into his cheeks, he took the bottle, his crooked thumb bent round the neck, and walked over to the curtain where he peered through the spyhole at his waiting public. He was not the only cabaret act on offer that evening. He had looked in at the other main auditorium on his way down. A Latin American evening was in progress, hosted by a song-and-dance duo who called themselves the Avocado Pair. The room had been packed out with people dressed up, laughing and shouting and twirling to the music. He felt nothing but contempt for them. Here the place was half-empty, and though the entertainment officer had warned him that this was to be expected on the first night, it shocked him that so few of his countrymen had seized this opportunity to catch him in the flesh.

"Perhaps it's true," he said to the mirror back in his dressing room. "Perhaps those college boys have got something." He wondered if he should put his glove on, but decided against it. No one would get close enough to notice the slight deformity. The glove might have to go. Maybe for good.

She was not there either when he took a final peek. The table he had reserved for her at the side of the stage was empty, the half-bottle of champagne untouched, the bowl of flowers unadmired. He had counted on her coming this night. Now he was filled with a bitterness he found hard to gauge. He bounced onto the stage without a moment's hesitation.

"Welcome aboard this fine and famous vessel, ladies and gentlemen. Hope you've all found your sea legs, or any other legs that have taken your fancy. What? What'd I say? No good looking at me like that missus, you've got a reputation to live up to. The SS *Hanky Panky* this ship should be called. Everyone likes a bit of fun. And here, you've got five days and five nights to do it in. No nosy parkers, no neighbours, no one will ever know what you get up to. No but seriously, sometimes you've got to keep it quiet. Take my mother—somebody, please. No seriously— a kinder-hearted woman you couldn't hope to find. But like so many mothers she's possessive. Can't bear the thought of her little boy leaving home to the arms of a scheming woman. And there's some things you can't tell a mother. Some things you shouldn't tell a mother. Some things even if you did tell her she wouldn't understand. Recently I've been going out with this lovely young thing from the office. A passionate girl, hard worker, there's nothing she likes better than doing a spot of over-time. Anyway, one day the phone rings. It's late and she's busy taking down dictation—well she's taking something down. Well I pick up the phone and says, Yes, who is it? and it's Mother. Hello, dear, she says, I was wondering when you were coming home, and I say, Oh in about an hour or so, when I've finished filling in this report. Will you be long? she says. No, I say, a bit out of breath, not at the rate I'm going. Well, she says, I'm surprised you can do any work at all what with all that racket going on. Racket? I say, Yes, she says, all that howling. Oh that. Well, I tell her, that's the office cat, Mother, mewing. She loves her tail being rubbed. Here, pussy pussy. So an hour or two later I come back for my dinner. Who do all those blonde hairs on your coat belong to, dearest? she asks and I say, Oh that's the office cat, Mother, she's moulting. Every time she comes near me I get a face full of fur. Oh, she says, they're ever so soft. Longhaired variety, is she? I keep my mouth shut. Makes a change. Well later I'm upstairs washing myself, when Mother walks in, without knocking, like she's always done. Wants to have a look at my number twos. And I'm standing there in my silk pyjama bottoms—oh yes, I'm a fancy man I am—when she takes a look at my back and says, Good heavens, Wilfred, look at those scratches. Have you been fighting again, and I say, No, Mother, it's that office cat again. Every time I tickle her tummy she rakes my back up and down with her claws. Now we live in a semi, right, thin walls with a newly married couple next door, and

271

halfway through the night I'm woken up by my mother shaking me hard. What's up, Mother? I ask. Listen, she says, Can't you hear it? and I listen and from the other side of the wall I can hear the young wife giving it her all. Uh-oh, I think. Now I'm in for it. Go on then, she says. Let her in. In? I says. Yes, that office cat of yours. She must be devoted to you to follow you all the way home.

"Now don't laugh. She's a good woman. But I'm lucky really. Still single. Not like my cousin. He's married. Married young. Publican's daughter. He's a bit of a clodhopper to tell the truth. He's out all day, working in the fields, digging potatoes, doing whatever farmers do, and when he gets home of an evening all he wants to do is to put his feet up. Nothing else he wants to put up at all. I don't know. It's not as if he was a sheep farmer or anything. What? What'd I say? Anyway, he doesn't pay her the attention she deserves and she's a young woman, right? Anyway, one day she goes to a party and meets someone who she knew before, and one thing leads to another. So she starts seeing this gent regular like. And her husband's so busy he doesn't notice. She tells him whatever and he just nods, turns over and dreams of brussels sprouts and cabbage. Well in time it begins to get to her that he doesn't seem to be taking any notice of the time she's spending away from home. Any excuse seems to do. She's thinking, Any other man would be waiting at the foot of our stairs with a leather strap in his hand. (She should be so lucky.) Anyway, one Saturday afternoon he's settled in front of the telly, paper on his lap, ready for an afternoon's sport and she's standing in front of the mirror, checking her lipstick, dressed in a nice white blouse and a nice loose skirt looking forward to some physical exercise herself, 'cause she's promised to meet her fancy man. Go for a ride in his fancy car. Play a tune on his fancy horn. So she says to my cousin, I'm sorry dear, I've just got to pop out to buy you some cigarettes and he says, What do you think those are on the sideboard? Are those cigarettes? she says, So they are. Well I must go out and buy you some more socks. All yours have got holes in, and he says, But dearest don't you remember you spent all last evening sewing and mending and now my socks are as

272

good as new. Well, she says, now you mention it, your socks are perfectly all right but I've just remembered there was a lovely cow's stomach hanging in the butcher's window this morning and I thought I'd make your favourite dish this evening, cold tripe and marmalade, but I quite neglected to buy the meat. I'll just nip down to the shops now and he says, Well now that *is* a treat, but don't you remember, Dick the butcher was pushed into the mincing machine last Friday and they've closed the place down while the police question the sausages. Well by this time she's getting impatient see, because she knows her beau's an important man who doesn't like to be kept waiting, and she's pacing up and down wondering what other excuse she can dream up when suddenly he pipes up saying, You know, Judith, you're out such a lot these days, in your best togs on and all. If I didn't know any better I think there might be another man. Well that is it. She can't stand it any longer. She puts her hands on her hips and says, If you must know you stupid old fart I'm going out for a bit of how's-your-father. Very well, he says, but don't change the subject.

"She was only a publican's daughter,
    And her arms were all freckled and plump.
    And whenever she could
    She'd grab hold of the wood,
    And give a good pull on the pump.

    At night she'd go down to the cellar,
    And secretly pull out the bung,
    After taking a peak
    She'd let the spout leak,
    And lap it all up with her tongue.

    Now some like their beer poured all fizzy,
    And some like their beer served up flat.
    But Jude liked it best

When it spilt on her chest,
And I wiped it all off with my hat.

But sadly she took no precautions,
This beautiful publican's belle,
After one long night's pull
Her barrel got full
And her belly started to swell.

Now some like their beer to be bitter,
And some like their beer to be mild,
But I think you'll agree
It's better when free
And you don't have to pay for the child.

"Boom, boom. And this is how it all starts. The courtship. This is where it all goes wrong."

He pushed back the curtain and stepped behind his cardboard car, the dummies strapped in the front seats, him crouching behind. He was like a one-man band, only this time the pulleys and strings worked their arms and legs, not cymbals or drums. He made no pretence of hiding. It was part of the fun, exaggerating their movements and even as the three of them rolled in, the audience began to laugh. He wished he had not drunk so much, for it was a taxing business, pulling and tugging, making all the noises, the car engine, the gears, working the air for the balloons, and he was not in the best of shape. Every time the engine revved, her breasts would start to swell. The faster the dummy drove the bigger they grew, but every time he slowed down to grab hold of them, they began to deflate. When he stopped, there was nothing there at all. So he started up again and sure enough, up they rose, pulling through her blouse. The crowd rocked with laughter. Will called out over their shoulders.

"You might think this is all far-fetched, but you all know what's going on here. The old familiar story. Whatever it is you've set your heart on, when you have it right there in your hand, it's never as good as you expected. Ain't that the truth, lads? All that wrapping, all those little bows, those ribbons, those clasps at the back. Just wasn't worth it. Like this poor sod here. Spent all that energy and for what? Let's face it, none of us ever learn. Never.

"Take these two here. She'll succumb to his blandishments, and he'll believe her youth will last forever. Sooner or later, they'll get married, like most of us do, even when it is probably the stupidest, most ridiculous thing they could ever do. Remember that song Frank Sinatra used to sing? 'Love and Marriage'? Well it's a load of bollocks, isn't it? What? Now some comedians make jokes about the wife, but I don't, see. I never make fun of them not because I don't have one, but because I feel sorry for them. I do. I feel sorry for the husbands of course, 'cause they're married too, but it's the wives I feel for most and what they have become, 'cause they were once young girls and ladies you must remember this yourself, when you were young, out on the dance floor, kissing in the back row of the cinema, doing all those things on the Axminster carpet you shouldn't be, wasn't it wonderful, weren't you alive, and didn't you give as good as you got? And that's my point. Look at you all now. What have you got to show for it now? Skid marks on your old man's underwear that's what and five minutes on Sunday morning. Five minutes of love and marriage. And remember—

"Be sure to lubricate the undercarriage.
This I tell you, Father,
Was what you failed to do with Mother.

"You used to be a princess, now you're just a scullery maid and the whole world has closed its eyes and passed you by and it's your fault. You let it happen. You let some poxy man waltz you up the aisle and walk all over you, and there's the pity of it, for while half of me feels sorry for you, the other half despises you for what you've done. You've thrown it all away, all the things you could have done, all the things you dreamt of doing. Take a look at what you've ended up with. Is that what you want? Course it isn't. Love and marriage, yes, love and marriage.

"Smells as sweetly as a whore in Harwich.
  Dad found out from Mother,
  You can't have one,
  You can't have fun,
  You can't have none if not a lover.

"Now ain't that the truth, ladies? Does your old man know? Has he any idea? Did he ever have any idea? He never gave you time to find out, did he? Well stuff him, that's what I say. What you need is a bit of spice in your life, a bit of excitement, a bit of Housewives' Choice. Take these two here. I haven't given them names yet. I've been trying all morning but I can't seem to think of the correct ones. What should we call him, for instance, and that useless hangdog expression on his face? *A* for Algenon? *B* for Bertrand, *C* for what, Christopher? Colin? I don't know. Never thought about names before. Not being a father. I mean, imagine someone looking at a little baby and deciding to call her Ethel. Now I know nothing about babies. Had some near scrapes but . . . But I know one thing. These dummies could teach us a thing or two. For one thing, they don't wear any underwear. Honest! Did you know that? They don't. Nothing. Just skirt and trousers. Look. See that? No underwear!

"Skirt and trousers,
  Skirt and trousers,
  It's not the cloth that counts but what it houses.
  Ask your local vicars
  If life's not better without knickers.

"I think we can learn a lesson from them. I do. Underwear gets in the way. You don't need it. All it does is give you extra ironing.

"Try, try, try and disengage them,
    For easier movement.
    Try, try, try, and you will quickly feel
    A great improvement.

    Skirt and marriage,
    Skirt and marriage . . ."

He stopped. A young couple was making to sit down at Ethel's table. A steward was removing the ice bucket.

"Excuse me, Gunga Din," he called, stepping out from the spotlight. "You've made me fluff my rhyme. What do you think you're playing at?"

The couple looked round, uncertain if this was part of the routine. Will stepped up closer and picked up the small white card resting against the vase of flowers.

"Can't you read? Reserved. Go on. Hop it." He pulled the ice bucket from the steward's hand and banged it back down. The plates rattled in protest. The steward stood completely still. "What's the matter?" Will demanded, pushing him away. "You deaf or something?" He turned to the couple. "You too, Romeo. Go on, piss off out of it. Go and dance the rumba next door."

He turned to the audience, breathing into the microphone, a hand resting on the empty table, watching the couple scurry from the room.

"Don't rate her chances much," he joked. "His double looked decidedly passé." He straightened the knives and forks and replaced the card. "I had hoped someone would be here," he said, "but it seems she's giving me the cold shoulder." He laughed. "As long as I don't get a cold leg as well, what? Room 405, ladies, room 405. Hot and cold running sores. Still, I'm buggered if I'm going to pay for an empty table." He walked back to the stage and yanked the female dummy out by the arm and dragged her to the table. He settled her back in the seat.

277

"Don't worry about him," he told her, jerking his head back to the other, sitting alone. "He's dead. Car crash. Just a puddle on the floor."

The hall was quiet now, with the occasional embarrassed mutter. There was no laughter. He sat down opposite his dummy and dipped a napkin into the iced water, dabbing the damp cloth onto his forehead. He picked up the bottle, popped the cork and poured her a glass. The champagne fizzed and foamed over the top of the glass. The dummy did not move. Will sat there, watching.

"I've been waiting for her all my life and now she's here she won't talk to me. Come on, say something, Judy."

He fumbled in his pocket and brought out the swizzle stick. He stuck it in his mouth and sat down, out of breath. There was another ditty to come but he couldn't remember the intro. There was the ditty and a quarrel in the car and then a tap dance. The audience was watching him closely now. They could hear his breath and his swizzle stick wheezing into the microphone as he sat there, staring at her and the audience behind. They sat bloated and lifeless, as dumb as the one in front of him.

He leant over and prodded her. "See," he said in that harsh metallic voice. "She's no bloody use at all. Doesn't come when she's called."

Someone started to slow-handclap him. Another whistled. He sat there panting.

"Would you care to take a walk on top?" he asked her. "I am not sure we are fully appreciated here."

"Try the gangplank," someone shouted. Will got to his feet and tucked the dummy under his arm. He stood before them and bowed.

"As Mr. Punch would say, good-bye, ladies and gentlemen, and thank you for your patronage. Satan is dead. We can all do as we like."

Back in the dressing room he slumped down. He pulled at the bottle's neck and let the liquid slip down. If only she had appeared tonight. It would have been different. He wouldn't try and see her this evening. It would be too hurried. He would cruise the bars tonight. Someone would be there, draped over a glass, someone old and faded but with just enough juice left in her for the night. A firm knock came to the door. The entertainment officer put his head round. Will caught his face in the small mirror.

"Catch the act, did you?" Will asked. "Didn't quite go to plan."

The man closed the door behind him. From his expression it looked as if he had been raised on a diet of lemons. He held a sheaf of papers in his hand.

"This is to notify our cancellation of your services, Mr. Baxter. You will disembark when we reach Queenstown." He moved to the dummy propped up in the corner and pulled the blouse open, exposing her balloon breasts. "We'll be writing to your agent. You were hired strictly on the understanding that you were to do a version of your radio program."

Will started to shout. "Billy Baxter's Way. I'll show you Billy's fucking Way." He bent down and pulled his trousers down. "Kiss that, you pillock. Only mind you brush your teeth first." He did not bend up again until he heard the man open the door and his footsteps hurry down the corridor. He turned, pulling his trousers back up. Jeremiah stood in the doorway, a brown carrier bag in his hand.

"Jem? What the fuck are you doing here? You my replacement?" He jerked his neck at an angle. "They're not topping people for fun now, are they? I know times are hard but . . ."

Jeremiah shut the door and lifting the dummy from the chair in the corner sat down. He brought out a bottle of whisky and a large bag of fruit. Will looked at the bottle in surprise, took it and unscrewed the cap.

"What are we celebrating, then?" he asked him.

"A son, Will. I've become a father." Will rubbed his face with his hands. He was sweating hard, struggling with the heat and the smell of diesel.

"So I heard," he said. "What's his name, then?"

"Stanley."

"Stanley. Good enough, I suppose. An old-fashioned name, Stanley. He could go into show business with a name like that."

"He'll not go into show business."

279

Will snorted. "You don't know what he'll go into. I can tell you that for a fact."

"No show business and no Mr. Punch." Jeremiah was firm. "Anyway, I haven't travelled all this way on his behalf alone." He leant forward, serious. "I only learnt yesterday. Bit sudden, isn't it? Going abroad like this at the drop of a hat?" He opened the bag and held it out. Will pulled out a tangerine.

"I've left England," he admitted, tearing at the skin. "Or rather, England's left me."

The peel dropped to the floor. Jeremiah watched as his cousin started to put the fruit in his mouth, segment by segment.

"How do you mean?" Jeremiah asked. "I thought things were going so well for you."

"It's a fickle business, Jem. One minute you're topping the bill and the next you're as welcome as a whoopee cushion at a funeral. No one wants to know."

Jem nodded. He understood that complaint.

"Who told you, anyway?" Will asked after a moment's silence.

"Your housekeeper."

Will looked up at him. "You saw her, then?"

"I did." He poured Will another drink. "Why did you never tell me? I would have helped. Honest."

Will spat the skin out onto the floor and popped another segment in his mouth.

"Would you?" he sneered. He took a swig of the bottle. "She begged to be taken back, you know, got down on her fucking knees, and you turned your backs on her like she was nothing. Half of what I made went to her in those days. You thought I was a tight cunt, didn't you? Didn't you?"

Jeremiah nodded. "We all did."

"I was like the rest of you, first, hating her for running off, but when she came back I just wanted to be with her again. She was my mum, for Christ's sake."

"All those years. I never knew."

Will nodded, spitting onto the floor again. "When I struck lucky I started to take her with me. Made sure I ate proper, saw that my costumes were always clean, straightened the landladies out." He held out his hand. "Pass us another, cousin, I haven't half got a thirst on me."

Jeremiah obliged, then changed the subject.

"You shouldn't have used Judith's name like that," he admonished. "It's not right. She would have a fit if she knew."

Will caught Jem's enquiring eye. "Oh you saw that, then? My last performance. You'll be pleased to see the back of me, no doubt." He laughed, only half in jest, chewing fast. "Bet you wish you never come to see me off after all. I must say, Jem, I didn't expect it."

Jeremiah put his hands on his thighs. "Well, I haven't exactly," he confessed.

"Well, if it isn't you and it isn't me, what is it? And don't keep me guessing too long. If I don't get my skates on all the best talent will be taken."

"I thought you'd decided on which one already," Jem told him. "She is on board, I take it."

Will spat out another skin. "Who's that, then?"

"Ethel Whitley."

Will look surprised.

"What is all this? You out to steal every girl I get?"

"Is that what she is? Your girlfriend?"

"Don't talk daft. She was one of the contestants at a show I did last year. Spunky young thing. Of course, she wasn't famous then."

"Famous?"

"Yes, you know. Gallows Hill."

"Ah that," Jem said.

"Yeah. Nasty business."

Jem took out the letter.

"Read that," he said, handing it to him.

"What is it?"

"A letter. From someone I met once. Someone I had hoped never to meet again."

Will read. He read quickly, scanning it almost like a script, his eyes flicking back and forth over it, as if he was studying his lines, looking for the potential in them.

"Well, what of it?"

Jeremiah poured him a drink.

"He was right. It wasn't him."

"No?"

"No."

"Well, surely you don't think it's the first innocent man you've topped. Or do you believe all that guff about British justice?"

"That's why you're here though, isn't it, Will? Another try at her."

"Another try? Whatever do you mean?"

Jeremiah stirred the floor with his foot. "You're a messy bugger and no mistake. Worse than a monkey in a cage. You better be careful if you ever eat one of these in front of Ethel Whitley. Better not let her know that Danny never ate them. Couldn't eat them. Was allergic to them." He raised his head. "And no one knew. Except our Judith." He bent down and brushed them with his hand. "Better clear this lot up for a start if you're thinking of inviting her backstage."

There was nothing else he could say, nothing he could confront him with. He knew that if he attempted an interrogation like Alcott would have done it would be to no avail. They had already found their culprit and no one, Ethel Whitley included, would be in a mind to find another. Will stared stupidly at the floor, his hands clasped before him. Jeremiah took hold of the abandoned glove lying, half-folded, on the table and eased it over Will's hand, smoothed it down over his bent and bulbous thumb, working the leather over his chewed, trembling fingers. He leant over and, dipping his hand in, picked the swizzle stick from out of the glass and pressed it into his cousin's hand.

"Let's get some fresh air," he told him. "The air in here is dreadful."

He led him out, through the half-deserted corridors, away from the faint squeals of laughter, past the glittering dining rooms and the chrome bars, out onto the uppermost deck where they stood in the dark night air. Will was thoroughly drunk now, drunk and defiant, lurching with rebellion and bravado, ready to stand in the wind and defy the world. He tipped the bottle to his mouth.

"Is that the last of it, then?"

Jeremiah nodded.

"Pity. Drink makes a lion out of man. All the rages, all the fears and humiliations, can be erased, explained, justified. Men do not lie when they are drunk for they cannot. They can only tell the truth."

The bottle was nearly empty now, but he began to pull on it, hoping as if by some miracle it might fill itself on its own accord. Above, high and mighty, the funnels roared, lit up behind them. Below, the great prow of the ship forged ahead. Looking out at the dark below, the night seemed to release Will from his sullen defence. He could tell elements anything. He began to speak his thoughts.

"It was all a terrible accident," he began. "One night I was coming back from work. It was late. Bloody car broke down. Brand-new and it breaks down. Who should come along but Colin Tarrant in his fartmobile, offering me a tow. He recognised me of course, but I'd seen hundreds like him, but then, when he told me who he'd been with that night I remembered him right away. Ethel Whitley. I'd fancied her the moment I'd laid eyes on her, sitting there in the audience, quiet, unassuming, not like the blowsy friend next to her, dressed up to the nines. She was like Judith, Jem, a younger Judith, quiet, determined—good-looking too only didn't know it, not yet. There she sat, sort of uncomfortable, a bit out of place and suddenly I wanted her more than any other woman in the world. Don't ask me why, I don't know, but I wanted her. It was like I was young again, had another chance. And I tried. After the show but all I could fucking do was flash my fucking cigarette case at her and she turned her nose up at me and went off with this twerp, Colin Tarrant. Colin Tarrant. The bloke Ethel Whitley preferred to me. And now here he was with a rope in his hand. So he towed me home and civil-like I asked him in for a drink. He didn't want to come in, but curiosity got the better of him. I'd had a bloody bad day of it myself. Just learnt the show was to be axed. Commercials had dried up and all I was getting this summer was some flea pit down in Torquay. I had a phone call last month from Val Parnell saying he had a spot for me. Great, I thought, but you know what? Only wanted to put me on straight after the dancing girls. A bloody warm-up man. Me! Told him where he could shove that small offering. So I pour out a couple of slugs of brandy and sit him down. He's acting like a little schoolboy, all thumbs and bum wriggling, so to get him talking I say, Do you remember that woman you were with that night? Does he remember? Out it all comes, the whole story. And I was surprised what he told me, 'cause he looked such a feeble little squirt, how he'd been seeing her this past year and how it had got all out of control. Apparently she'd got it into her head that they were going to leave the country and set up a new life. He had no intention of doing any such thing. He was married. He just wanted it to carry on as normal, but she wanted more. He was in love with her all right, but it was beginning to get too much for him. Well, why not get shot of her? I asked. It wasn't as simple as that. His wife had a brother who had already threatened him and he was afraid if he chucked her, Ethel would make a fuss, might suspect that the wife was behind it, like she had been the first time around. First time around! I couldn't believe it. This little fart had had two cracks at her. Fair made my blood boil. He wanted *her* to leave *him,* but couldn't see how it was to be done. She was so fired up with this emigration lark that any sudden indifference on his part she was likely to go round and cause the whole thing to blow up in his face. And that was the last thing he wanted. Even if he wanted to leave his wife he couldn't emigrate. Just couldn't. He could never leave, he said. Never. So that's when I thought of it. I told him, what if I put the mockers on her, make you look like a proper wimp and leave her feeling that you were no good? If we arranged it cleverly, he could park somewhere we had agreed on and I could jump in and frighten her off. I didn't tell him I still fancied her myself. The idea excited me, see how far I could push it, see that stuck-up little minx sweat a bit. It would be a bit of a laugh, dangerous too. God, I could get caught! That's what I liked about the idea. I could dress up, do something that no one would ever know about, a wonderful dark secret that would keep me alive. I hadn't been alive for so long, Jem. I no longer had an audience worth performing to, one that would put me on my mettle. I wanted to see what I could make them do, make her do, make him do. So we arranged it, sort of. He was to park his car, this horrible little traveller thing, in the lay-by, a mile away from the house, park in there every Thursday and one night I'd pop in and scare the knickers off her. He fell in with it because it was me, Billy Baxter, the famous comedian, suggesting it. He didn't know how to say no. He was under my spell. Everything I said made perfect sense even though we both knew it made no sense at all. It was just the drink talking. Even before he left I could see that. That the whole idea was crazy. When he'd gone I laughed myself silly just thinking about it, how the poor bugger would be terrified lest I *should* pop in one evening. I thought no more about it. Then one night, coming back from London, I saw his car parked up on the lay-by. I pulled up a little distance away and walked back. It was them all right. I crept up. It was all muggy inside, so I couldn't see much, but it was obvious what was going on. Her blouse was undone and he had his hands all over her blubber, rummaging around like he was trying to find the prize in a lucky dip, but then she looked up and I thought, God, I'm not ready for this and I ran off back to my car and waited till they drove by. I followed them down to the pub. There was another man waiting for her in the car park. Stone me if she didn't run up, throw her arms around him and kiss him there and then while old fartface sat looking out his windscreen, poor sod. The way she treated him. I followed the two of them in and watched from the other bar. She stood before him like some sort of breathless goddess, working her throat up and down for him, and I thought then, I'll do it by Christ, I'll put the fear of God in you, you thankless little trollop. So a week later I'm waiting in the bushes. Bloody cold it was, and they were late, bloody late.

I had a scarf wrapped around my head and a cap pulled well down and one of the old swizzle sticks from Mr. Punch stuck in my mouth. I only brought the gun to frighten them. Wore a glove on my hand to mask my bad thumb. No chance of them recognising me. It was just a lark to begin with, me in the back, Colin not daring to move, her wondering what the fuck was coming next, but then I really began to enjoy myself, began to play the part. I was Mr. Punch again. I could do it all again, travelling in the dark, feeling the bitter jokes well up inside me. It was just like I was back there with you and Judith, with me in command, as if Ethel was Judith and Colin was you. I could have a second chance, see, get the girl of my dreams, the quiet one with class, not the brassy bobtail as common as a barber's char with her tits hanging out that I usually end up with. I was in the driving seat, not Colin. Every time I prodded him, he'd break out into a sweat, hold onto the steering wheel as if he were on a dodgy roller coaster. Never seen anybody so frightened, terrified I'd spill the beans. But there was nothing he could do about it now. He had to go along with it. As for her, she began to enjoy it too, seeing me humiliate her man. It was something she had wanted to do herself, but under the circumstances couldn't afford to. He was her ticket out of there. But as the hours grew longer and he grew more desperate, I could see all her contempt for him rising to the surface. It was a demonstration if you like of what would happen to him once she got him to herself. I almost felt sorry for the poor bastard.

"This was all very strange. Very powerful. I was only going to be there a couple of hours but by now I couldn't leave. She had become my accomplice. I wanted to stay until I could take her in my arms. I wanted to crush his will in front of her and have her turn herself over to me, unfold herself to me. By the end I was getting there. She wasn't going to go anywhere with him, I thought, not after what I'd put her through, not when she'd seen what he was really made of. She sat with me in the back, quiet like, but happy to be there, intimate. She was kissing me, for Christ's sake, Jem, I had my fucking tongue down her throat and my hands, well my hands were where a man's should be, nothing bad you understand, nothing forced. I was on the verge of asking her to skip out with me, leave that slumbering pillock to his own devices when she says, as if it's part of the fucking conversation, 'I'll miss it here, miss it when I've gone.' After all I'd said and done! Not a word about me, not a word about the night and what we had said, not a word about her family, about her mum who worried about her, just another fucking performance gone wrong, another fucking telephone unanswered. You fucking bitch, I thought, you coldhearted fucking bitch, and I started up at her and Colin woke up, sudden like, shouting at me, 'This has gone far enough,' he says, as if he was going to spill my name, turning the tables on me. Suddenly I realised that it was me that was in his power. Not the other way around. He could ruin me if he wanted. I had no fucking choice, Jem, I couldn't let that happen. 'I know—' he started to say and I swung up, not knowing quite what to do, and the gun went off. I was left with her. What could I do? I tried to go back, to where we were before it happened, but it was no use, I could tell. No hard feelings, I said, and I meant it. I'm glad she's alive, I really am. I never meant her any harm."

Will had closed his eyes. Now he opened them to see what expression played on his cousin's face.

"And now you're here again," Jeremiah stated softly. "Quite a feat, you seeing her again."

"Nothing to it," Will boasted. "Common gossip that she was emigrating. Didn't take me long to find out when. I pulled a few strings, that's all. Offered my services for a couple of runs in return for a trip to Durban later on. Company jumped at the chance. They do it all the time."

"Taking a bit of a risk, aren't you?"

"She's seen me, Jem. Talked to me, taken tea with me. Never even crossed her mind. Never will. There was Danny and there was Colin. Not me. Not Billy Baxter."

"You must come back, Will. Tell them the truth."

287

"What? You out your fucking mind?"

He jumped up, onto the railings. Jeremiah could feel the tremble of the ship and see Will's hair sweeping back in the wind.

"Come down off there," he said. "You'll fall in."

"Fall in? Billy Baxter fall in? I haven't forgotten how to walk a rope even if you have. I won't fall in, Jem. Watch."

He cartwheeled once along the broad railing and straightened up. The dark sea sounded below.

"Come down, Will," Jem called. "You've had too much to drink. The air will make you giddy."

Will laughed and leant into the wind. "See? I'm not going to fall, Jem. Not on this ship, and not through Ethel Whitley either. It's over, Jem. Don't you understand? It's just another tightrope act, that's all. I've got away with it. I get away with everything."

As he spoke the wind dropped and he lurched forward. He flapped his arms like a rearing cormorant, trying to regain his balance, and started to straighten up, but as he did his foot shot out and the balance of his body reversed. He tipped backwards jerked on a gravitational string. He fell out into the night, his arms whirling furiously. He tried to grab hold of the railing but as he bent down his other foot slipped off the polished rail and he began to fall, his hands clattering against the railings. But he was close and though drunk, instinct and training informed his final desperate throw. His right hand caught the bottom rail and as his body jerked against the side of the boat, his other hand came up. His grip was firm. He was hanging against the side, his feet scrabbling for the deck.

"For Christ's sake, Jem."

Jem swung over, hanging on the pivot of his body, and reached down.

"Don't struggle," he said. "Hang still. I've done this hundreds of times."

He put his hands under Will's arms and started to pull Will up by the sheer strength of his arms. Hangman's lore stated that a dead body weighed more than a live one, that the presence of a living will provides an unseen rope up which the body hoists itself, but Jem did not find this to be the case now. He could feel life hanging heavy in this body, out of control, helpless, worthless. He could smell its tarnished odour as he buried his face into his cousin's neck as he kissed the perfume and the greasepaint and the hours of drunken sweat. His cousin's life was in his hands, and his own too. He felt the swirl of the air and the great pull of the sea. It took all his strength to raise Will up close to the level of his chest. Will's feet were still scrabbling for a hold. He looked in Jem's troubled eyes and tried to bring him peace.

"Wasn't true you know," he said, panting cheerily.

"What?"

"What I just told you. Made it all up. You know me. Anything for a laugh. Tell you what, though. Bet I pull her before we reach Vancouver."

Jem looked at his cousin and his charming twinkling eyes.

"Bet you would." He lifted him up level and kissed him on the lips.

"No hard feelings, Will," he said, and let him go.

There was no sound other than the thrashing of the sea far below and the dull roar of the funnel up above. He ran back to the foaming wake and looked out. He could see nothing. He thought he could hear a cry, but it was just a bird screeching or a whistle of steam far below. He jumped up on the railings and stood on the teetering brink with his hands behind his back and his eyes closed waiting for the trap to open. He wanted to drop into the bottomless dark, to feel the cold world close in on him and never open again. He had his son and his wife waiting. They had been waiting for him all their lives, but he could do nothing for them now. He could feel the ship plunge and rear on the roaming sea. It would only be a matter of time before he lost his balance, one way death, the other life. It would not be his choice. He would cry his son's name as he fell, cry it as all the other men had cried names, but his would be out loud. He would cry it till his mouth filled with water, till the scream of the gulls took its place, till the water closed over him. What was the balance of his life, or the balance of this death he had just caused? He did not believe in revenge. All his life he had done what he could to prevent it, and yet what had he witnessed here? Revenge or justice? The waves came higher now, he could see the prow of the ship meet them head-on. The ship rose up slowly, gently and he began to feel the weight of his body lose its equilibrium. He began to fall. In which direction he could not tell but he fell like all the men he had faced, with his world falling with him, not knowing, not comprehending how he had come to this. The deck knocked the wind out of him.

He sat there, his head bare, waiting for the dawn to come up and the Irish coast and the ferry home.

SHE STOOD IN THE DRIVEWAY, WRITING PRICES ON THE BLACKBOARD BY THE roadside stall. Stanley was in the hall, sleeping in his pram. Jeremiah was due back that afternoon.

"Drive carefully, then," she had said. "And come back soon."

If he had noticed the enormity of the remark he did not show it. He merely smiled and poked his head out, kissing her quickly on the cheek.

Another warm and still day. She would take Stanley out into the garden. As she picked him out of his pram there was a knock on the front door. A woman stood on the steps, bareheaded and perspiring. Her shoes were stout and scuffed, and she carried an old-fashioned handbag in her hand. She looked as if she had walked a good distance.

"Is this Bembo Nursery Gardens?" she asked.

"That's what the sign on the stall says," Judith replied.

The woman stepped back into the drive and looked out over the silent fields.

"It's a big place for a woman to be running on her own," she remarked.

Judith shifted Stanley from one arm to the other. "My husband's away. He'll be back in a day or two."

The baby stirred in her arms.

"There's a fine-looking fellow," the woman said. "What's his name?"

"Stanley."

"Stanley." She seemed pleased by the reply.

"I was wondering," the woman asked, "whether there might be work to do. Fruit picking, weeding. Anything. I'm a good worker."

"You're not local then?"

"Just the other side of the downs. I've been looking for the month now. Outdoor if I can get it. Someone told me that you might be looking for a spare pair of hands."

Judith pointed to the For Sale sign sticking out of the hedge.

"This time last year we would have been. But we're selling up as soon as we can. It wouldn't be fair."

A car drew up.

"There's a customer." She turned to put Stanley back in the pram in the hall.

"Here," the woman said. "I'll hold your baby for you."

Judith looked at her hesitantly.

"I've done it before," she laughed. "And my daughter's just had twins. Go on. He'll be safe with me."

She took the baby out in the garden. Dark hair and dark eyes, a touch of mischief in his mouth. Like her own boy, like Danny's father. Half the girls in the town had been in love with that man. They had all watched him in the dance hall, standing in his checked shirt, a pint of porter in the crook of his arm, little specks of blood on his collar where he had nicked himself shaving, looking them over, singing along with the accordion band and later into the ear of whichever girl he chose to lead across the floor that night.

"Look at this," she said. "Such a pretty toy." She took out the glass eye and held it to the light, so that it twinkled and rolled in the sun. "Pretty, isn't it?" she chanted. "Such a pretty toy for such a pretty baby. Would you like to hold it? Touch it? See its pretty colour?" She dropped it back in her bag. "I've got something else for you, something just as nice."

She took the brooch from her blouse, and bending the pin back straight, held the sharp point of the needle above him. It sparkled and shone in the bright sun as she moved it back and forth, his wide, wondering eyes following the glittering movement. He kicked his legs in delight. Danced with every one of us, he did. Not a girl for ten miles who didn't end up in his arms at least once in her life, before he was off again, working the boats and the ferries out of Cork and beyond. God, how they envied him, for none of them had been further than Skibbereen, and back he would come after a month or so, his cheeks glowing from the salt and the unknown sea. Not that the weather or the work ever seemed to mark him. To touch his skin you'd have thought he'd never left his mother's breast. Eight years, she waited, eight years before he walked over. By that time he could have prised her open with a rose. "What shall we get them to play for our first dance?" he had said, and she was halfway into his bed before she'd even taken one step. Why he chose her for a bride she could never fathom. There were others, prettier, younger girls more suited to his temperament, for she was never a flighty thing, not like some she knew, but what was she to know about that?—and that was why he left her in time, for there were prettier girls, flightier girls and ones that were not pregnant either. If she had never taken with him she would not have had Danny. It would have been another someone else. He would be a different boy, maybe not a boy at all, but she had always thought she was destined to breed boys. And all she had to show for it was one, and he had been taken from her.

She brought the needle closer now. She had done what she could and now she had nothing left. Eileen had left, gone back to Ireland with her brother. Not even grandchildren to dote on. The baby's eyes widened as he tried to focus. Which eye was it? She tried to picture the man standing in the carriage, groping in the dark. The baby clutched at her breast but she pushed his arm aside gently. How Danny had fastened on them when he was this age. The stuff had leaked out of her like a faulty tap. Holding them slippery between her fingers he would lie guzzling before he slept on her patterned dress, the room smelling sweet and warm. She drew the pin back and held the baby firm in the crook of her arm. She would mark his only son. He would look upon him and curse the day of his own birth. She looked back. Maybe she wouldn't do it yet. It was too early. They had not grown to love their son enough yet, and he, little baby that he was, would never know what he had lost. She would bide her time. Let him grow. Let them think the world had turned in their favour.

Judith came out into the garden, wiping her hands.

"Is he all right?"

"He's fine. I've just been showing him this brooch. A pretty thing. He likes the way it sparkles."

"You have children of your own, you say?"

"I did have. He's gone now."

"Look, I'm sorry you've come out here for nothing. Would you like to stay for a bit of tea?"

The woman looked at her. She seemed a good woman, she thought, not unlike herself, brought up hard, the soft lines beaten into strength. She held the baby out. "No. Time to go."

Stanley made a young grab for the brooch. The woman clenched her fist around it, hesitated for a moment, then laid it out in her palm.

"Would you like to keep it then?" she asked him, crooning.

"No," Judith replied. "I couldn't."

"Oh go on," the woman scolded. "It's only a cheap old thing. But wait!"

She opened the clasp and worked the pin back and forth until it snapped off.

"There," she said. "That's better. There was a nasty point to it. He could have hurt himself. Poked his eye out."

"I wouldn't want that," Judith joked, "this family's already one short."

The woman nodded. "I'll be off then. Perhaps I'll find a job the other side of town."

"I hope so. Good luck, then."

"Thanks. And good luck to him, eh?"

Judith looked down. "Yes. Good luck to little Stanley."